# Cuck Storm Horizon

# Cuck Storm Horizon

## David McManus

fannypress
Seattle, WA

fannypress

Fanny Press
PO Box 70515
Seattle, WA 98127

For more information go to: www.fannypress.com

Cover design by Sabrina Sun

ISBN: 978-1-60381-447-8 (Trade Paper)
ISBN: 978-1-60381-448-5 (eBook)

Printed in the United States of America

I opened up my journals
Finally, the other day
I could write about it again
—D.L. Brown

# CHAPTER ONE

"The cabin door is now closed."

That's when reality jolted me hard.

I felt shaky. I was sweating.

*What the hell am I doing?* I thought. *I should be home with my wife. Not flying across the freaking country.*

I looked out at the grounds crew ... envious of the ground they were on. That tarmac was still just a cab ride away to Ashley.

"It's just two days," she said, when she kissed me goodbye in the pre-dawn darkness of our apartment. *But it isn't just two days,* I thought. *It's two 24-hour days when God knows what might happen.* And the thing was, I'd already let so much happen—the last couple months, and the past week especially.

The pretty girl beside me would probably ask to have her seat changed if she knew my situation and story—the things going on in my head. I wouldn't blame her. Three months ago, I was normal myself—more so than most, I thought. I'd felt secure in my marriage. My future had clear direction. I'd have rated myself a ten on both.

But then, last summer, all that unraveled.

And I never saw it coming.

I could've reacted differently. I should've. When I realized the "rumor" about Ashley was true, I could've assertively addressed it—hell, confronted her. But I pretended like I hadn't heard.

I could've told her I knew what happened:

*"At that party, Ashley, I know you and Tamara were in the bathroom with Jim. I know about the mock lesbian show you put on for him. And I know you let him screw you, knowing I was right outside."*

I should've asked for an explanation. Or at least gotten an apology. Instead I acted oblivious, like everything was hunky-dory. I was scared.

When we finally did talk about it, I was the one who was nervous, off-balance, on edge. I broached the subject cautiously, pussyfooting around it, saying things like, "It's okay, I'll understand, you can tell me." I said nothing could change how much I loved her.

And then I listened as she admitted it was true. Ashley had indeed fucked her junior salesman co-worker that night at the party.

That's when a lot of husbands would have exploded or stormed out.

I didn't. I just fumbled my words and wound up thanking her for her honesty. But what really plunged me into the deep-end was when I got erect imagining that night. I don't know if things would be different had I decided not to masturbate that day, or if it was inevitable.

But my thoughts were off to the races after that. In the back of my mind, I wondered if it might be chiseling away at my self-esteem. But I also learned, from talking to guys online, that my reaction wasn't so uncommon. And I learned what a *cuckold* was.

In one of the chat rooms, I opened up to a guy named Mike. Eventually we met over beers and I confided in him some more. He'd say things like "I'm there for you, bro," and seemed to genuinely mean it.

He persuaded me to have Ashley join us for drinks and introduce them. He said he could read women and give me insight, insisting that would reassure me. With all that I'd carelessly told Mike already, reading Ashley was probably pretty easy. The night I introduced them, Mike seduced my wife at the bar right in front of me. I was blindsided.

And back in our apartment, Mike persuaded Ashley to dance in our living room in just her bra and thong. I couldn't process it quickly enough to react. Before I realized it, Mike was with Ashley in my bedroom, and telling me "it's cool" as he basically shut the door in my face. Then he locked it, like a do-not-disturb-sign.

Just like that, I had been relegated to the couch. I couldn't believe what had just happened. I had this crippling realization … I was being cuckolded.

Even Mike must've been surprised at how quickly he'd hit the jackpot. He'd gone from shaking Ashley's hand at the bar to fucking my wife in my bed, a few hours later.

The next morning I knew I'd just been openly cucked. Ashley had now seen me let another man alpha-male me out of my own bedroom and take my wife in my bed. I couldn't explain that away.

I was so dumb. I allowed him to do the same damn thing to me two nights later. Only he didn't bother to lock the bedroom door that time. He probably knew I wouldn't interrupt.

\* \* \*

I looked back at the skyline as we ascended. *Somewhere amid those buildings*, I thought, *Ashley's going off to work.* I pictured her walking into the office. I imagined her bopping around in the hallways, smiling and saying hello to guys who surely still whispered about her. I thought of her answering nonchalantly if asked about her weekend.

But inside, she was probably exhilarated, her time with Mike reverberating. And with me leaving town, she was probably extra-spirited. Maybe she'd already texted Mike that I'd left.

"It's just two days," she'd told me as I was leaving. I

wondered if she was thinking, "It's *just* eight hours."

By evening, Ashley would be entertaining Mike in my apartment. It was a behemoth to process. I felt like I had been sent off to Siberia. A work emergency couldn't have come at a worse time.

I knew Mike would be screwing Ashley while I was away. But all that one-on-one time they'd be having really ratcheted up my apprehension. I worried what Mike might tell her, and all that Ashley might believe. Mike wanted me going cuckold. He wanted Ashley seeing me as one.

I pictured him rattling off all the reasons why she should cuckold me more than she already had. And why this was all so "win-win" for her. He might use things I'd said against me. He might make stuff up. Ashley had seen me accept and acquiesce to everything. There'd be no reason to question Mike. He exuded authority. Of course he would have Ashley's ear.

I also knew there was a larger prize Mike was after. He'd emphasized it to me over drinks the night before. He wanted to fuck my wife in front of me. He'd told me I should ask Ashley if she'd let me watch. Like it was my idea. Like I was that insane. There's no way to even couch or refine a question like that. It would just confirm whatever Mike had said about me. I might as well be asking her to make me a full-blown cuckold.

I was gripped by the brazenness. Mike was now seriously talking about fucking my wife in front of me. And he wouldn't be saying it if he didn't think he could make it happen. I got weak in the knees picturing that reality.

Mike would surely choose my bed. I imagined the look on Ashley's face as she reached orgasm. I wondered how I could ever stare into the sun like that. Or what that would do to our marriage. I wondered how Ashley could remotely respect me if she saw me sitting there watching. I thought of the shame I'd feel standing up afterward.

I didn't want that—I really freaking didn't. *That just couldn't be me*, I told myself. I had to get a grip. I had to get out before the waterfall. And start being present. No more standing around like a piece of furniture. I'd start showing resolve. And flick the switch from inaction to action.

*Get mad, motherfucker*, I thought.

It wasn't like I'd be pretending to be someone I wasn't. I just had to reclaim the old me again—the confident guy I was before the summer. And not the wet blanket I'd recently been.

*Maybe I can't stop things while I'm away*, I thought, but Thursday night when I got home, things would be different. I was going to get candid with Ashley. No blowing it off. We would sit down and talk about this. And I'd clear up some big misconceptions.

I would man up. And show her I had some fight in me, goddammit. That's what I told myself. I'd step up to the plate and start swinging for the fences. Stop squandering chances and start showing up.

It was high time ... and way overdue. I had to slow this juggernaut down.

I imagined the preposterousness of me trying to explain this all to my dad:

"So basically, a few weeks ago, I had drinks with this guy named Mike, who I met online. We'd bonded over marital issues. Well, I introduced Mike to Ashley and they got along, well hit it off, kind of. Anyway, one thing led to another, and for the last week he's been spending nights with Ashley in my bedroom. And now he says he wants me there so I can watch him with her. But starting today, I'm not going to stand back and let things just happen."

My dad would look bewildered, befuddled. Not processing.

I thought of my older brother interjecting then:

"Dad, it means that Dave met some random guy on the fucking Internet. And he let this stranger into his life, allowed him to seduce his wife, and fuck Ashley in his own bedroom. You see, Dad, Dave's what you call a cuckold, even if he's still in denial. And unless Dave suddenly grows a pair, he'll be cucked even more when his wife is fucked good and hard—right the fuck in front of him."

I looked out the plane window.

"Grab a mitt, Dave Martens," I said to myself. "Grab a fucking mitt."

# CHAPTER TWO

I saw Mike calling as I got in the cab. And tried to sound matter of fact when I said, "Hey Mike."

"Dave, how you doing, bro? How's Cali?"

"Rainy," I said. "And my flight was delayed, so I'm just leaving the airport."

"You fly first?"

"No way, I was Mr. Coach guy as usual. Twenty-five A."

"Well hey, you got a window, right?" Mike said. "So did it give you some time to settle down from last night?"

"Yeah, and sorry for some of my comments at the end. I was buzzed and still in shock, and it takes time to absorb, right?"

"Right, it's definitely a process. Acceptance takes time. The important thing is we both understand that."

I paused, thinking, *What the fuck is it we both understand and why the fuck is that the 'important thing'?*

"Yeah, well, actually" I said, "I was thinking a lot on the plane about what you talked about."

"Oh yeah? Did you go to the bathroom and rub one out?"

"No," I said. "I was thinking about the importance of Ashley and me doing this together. You told me that was the key to strengthening our marriage."

"Sure, and it is."

"Well, you seeing Ashley while I'm away isn't really the 'husband and wife being together.' It's Ashley and me being apart."

"So you're asking why I'm seeing Ashley when I said you two need to do this together."

"Well, yeah," I said.

"It's a good question, and yes, you both need to be on this journey together. I want you there with her, and believe me, you will be."

"Okay, so that's what I mean. You seeing Ashley now kind of contradicts all that."

"Not really."

"Not really?" I said. "So I guess it's not really raining here. It only looks that way from inside my cab."

"Dave, it's not about always being there with her. Sometimes it's about just being there *for* her. And you're doing that. You're being supportive."

"But why can't things wait until I get back?"

"Relax, man, it's gonna be just fine. Ashley will really benefit from this time alone with me. We'll get to know each other better."

"Well, wasn't that what Sunday night was about? I mean Mike, you need to realize, if there had been any way I could have gotten out of this trip—"

"Sure, I know. You wish you were here. I get that. But business trips won't stop coming up. At least you'll know I'll be taking good care of Ashley for you, and she will appreciate the kind of husband she has."

"But Mike, I'm not being included. I'm being excluded. I mean, can't you see why I feel this way?"

"That's not the way to look at it, bro. I mean, what are you doing wrong? You're making a sacrifice for the woman you love. How awesome is that? You should be proud. She is going to love you for it."

"So you can't even acknowledge that I have a pretty good point?"

"Dave, it's a great point and I'm glad you're thinking about it. But it's not always about you. Right now, it's about

Ashley, isn't it? You want Ashley happy, right?"

"Of course."

"Then appreciate what a special gift you're giving Ashley today. Do you even realize what that gift is?"

I leaned into the phone, not wanting the cab driver to hear, and said, "Letting her fuck you, Mike?"

"No," he said with a laugh. "That's just a symbol. I'm talking about something bigger. You're letting Ashley follow her heart and desires. You're placing her happiness above your own."

"Yeah, okay, whatever. Look, there's something else, Mike."

"What's that?"

"Well, Ashley and I haven't really talked about her seeing you while I'm away. Not even acknowledged it. And I've thought about what you said. She and I really do need to communicate better."

"Cool," he said, "I'm glad you're starting to see that."

"What I mean is, I don't want these next two days to become another elephant in the room, and if we all took a hiatus while I'm away—"

"So talk to her then."

I sighed.

"What?" he said. "You could ask her if she's looking forward to tonight, and if we have plans yet."

"I can't ask her that."

"Why not? It's obvious I'll be seeing her. She knows you know that. Why can't you acknowledge it with her? Do you really think your weird silence is better?"

"No."

"Just say 'Hi, Ashley, I hear you're going out with Mike tonight, and I just want to say have fun.' "

"C'mon, Mike."

"Dave, that's such a normal thing to say. Why is that so tough?"

"Look," I said, "the last thing I want is to be seen as sanctioning this."

"You're looking at it backward, bro. You'd be seen as blessing it. You'd be saying 'Go for it, Ashley.' You'd be saying 'I love you.'"

"Yeah, right."

"Dave, just think of the benefits of being normal with her again. Ashley will feel she can start getting real and open with you again. Think of how good that will make her feel. And you, too."

"Uh-huh."

"I'm telling you, this will strengthen your marriage, bro."

"Okay, man, whatever," I said. "Look, I'm not gonna play fucking dumb. I know I have to acknowledge it."

"Good, man. I bet you'll be surprised how easy it is. Oh shit, I'm late to a meeting, bro."

"Okay, but Mike ...?"

"Yeah?"

"Will you at least consider what I said about all three of us taking a hiatus until I'm back?"

"Sure, Dave."

"Okay, thanks."

"But Dave?"

"Yeah?"

"Now's the time to be supportive, bro."

\* \* \*

I put down the phone and felt sick to my stomach. I asked myself what I'd achieved. I'd shot blanks. When I added it all up, I got a big fat nothing. Then I tried to tell myself it was a long shot anyway. Which was true. Probably nothing I'd said would've stopped him from seeing her.

I filtered out Mike's self-serving spin, but he was right about talking to Ashley. Saying nothing would create another wall. I had planned on having a long, honest talk with Ashley back in New York, but I knew I needed to open up more now.

I went over it in my head. I'd say something like "So you're meeting up with Mike, later," and she'd say, "Yeah," and that's where I'd get stumped. I could say something stupid like "Well, tell him I said hi."

Or I could reply, "Well, I hope you have a good night, Ashley." I thought about it. That seemed down-the-middle enough. I practiced the pause between "good night" and "Ashley." I practiced saying "hello." And then I called her.

"Hey Dave, can I call you back in ten minutes?"

"Sure, Ash."

"Sorry," she said, six minutes later. "I just wanted to talk from outside. What a gorgeous day. How are you? How's San Fran?"

I pictured her at the courtyard across from where she works, sitting at one of the public tables. It's where she goes to relax. I didn't know what it meant—Ashley leaving her office to talk to me—but I wanted to believe it auspicious.

"I'm doing okay," I said. "Not sure what I'll be dealing with here, but I'll find out soon enough."

"I'm sure you'll be fantastic."

"Yeah well," I said, "we'll see."

"Well, they better give you a rock star welcome when you show up at the office today."

"Oh sure, they probably have a big spread of lobster, shrimp, and caviar waiting." Ashley laughed and it made me feel good. "So how was your flight?" she said, "Get any sleep?"

"It was fine," I said, "but I can't ever sleep on planes."

"So what'd you do … work? You practice?"

"Yeah," I said, "but I still have a few hours more before I'll feel even close to ready."

"So, late night prepping?"

"Well, I'm supposed to meet my boy Ryan out for drinks tonight."

"Oh yeah," she said, "tell him I said 'hi.' "

"I will," I said, "so I'm basically looking at an early ass morning for sure."

"At least your body will still be on New York time."

"I guess," I said.

"So how are you doing otherwise?" she asked.

I paused, trying to interpret the question. "Uh, good, how about you?"

"Good" she said. "So you think when you get back we can sit down, lower the volume and have a talk?"

"I'd love that, Ashley."

"Cool."

"You know" I said, "I've been thinking the same thing. I was just going to say that when I got back we should have a talk."

"Well, I wanted to last night, but …."

"I know," I said. "But I came home pretty drunk."

"It's okay. So we'll talk on Thursday."

"Okay, good."

"And also, you know about tonight, right?"

"Uh, I'm not sure exactly."

"Well, you know I'm meeting up with Mike, right?"

"Uh yeah, I guess I thought you might be."

"And you're cool with that?"

"Yeah, I mean, I'm okay. How about you? Are you good?"

"What does 'you're okay' mean?"

"It means I miss you Ashley. And I guess I'm still just processing it all."

"Ditto on that," she said. "It's been a whirlwind for sure. So you're okay with me seeing Mike tonight, right?"

"Uh yeah, I mean, I know that was maybe the plan."

"Okay, cool."

After several seconds of awkward silence, I asked, "So, you going to the gym tonight?"

"I don't think so, actually. I don't think I'll have time."

"Oh right," I said, then paused again. "Well, at least the weather's good there."

"Oh my God, is it ever! I don't want summer to end. I don't see one cloud right now, and tonight's a full moon."

"Oh yeah, that's right," I said. "I'm jealous. It's pouring right now and supposed to rain the whole time I'm here."

"I'm sorry, honey."

"Well, I got an umbrella at the airport, at least," I said. "So, did you do anything for lunch?"

"Not really. Tamara and I just sat outside at a lunch place on ninth."

"Oh, okay. Yeah, I've got to grab some lunch myself."

"You didn't eat on the plane?"

"I'm saving my appetite for the lobster spread," I said with a laugh. "No, I'll probably just pick up a sandwich in the building."

" 'Kay. well, I need to get back inside."

"Sure," I said. "I'm almost at the office."

"Well, stay dry and I'll just text you when I get home tonight. How's that?"

"Yeah, sure. I mean, okay."

"Well, I love you."

"I love you too, Ash."

# CHAPTER THREE

I asked the cabbie to drop me off a block from the office so I could stop in a diner and briefly relax. I knew I wouldn't have to explain myself even if I did run into someone there.

I thought about what Ashley had said as I sat in a booth, looking out at people moving hurriedly in the rain. Tonight was now fully confirmed. Ashley would be seeing Mike while I was away. He'd be in my home. He'd be fucking her in my bed.

All that was out in the open now. I'd given her the green light. I didn't know how else to react. Even if I had asked her not to see Mike, I figured she probably would anyway, which would be worse.

I thought of Ashley telling me she'd be blowing off the gym tonight. I couldn't remember the last time Ashley had done that for me. She couldn't even ask Mike to make it a little later.

*Perhaps,* I thought, she *wants the extra time to look extra hot for him.* I imagined her out of the shower, in front of the mirror, rubbing body lotion over her breasts and ass, an extra twinkle in her vibrant brown eyes.

I wondered how she might dress for the night. I imagined anything from designer jeans to a revealing summer dress. Ashley's not shy in a bikini or fazed by guys checking her out, but she doesn't dress slutty, except for Halloween, when she really shows cleavage.

I knew she'd want to dress sexy for Mike. I wondered

how revealing her outfit might be—if it would be making a statement, if it were newly bought. I pictured Mike taking Ashley back to our apartment and cringed at what my doormen might think.

I thought of the moon, and how Ashley reminded me tonight was a full one. The moon was especially significant for us, sitting up on the roof summer nights. The moon was our jolly old space friend, chilling with us before moving on to visit his party peeps in Hawaii.

Ashley would say things as we went outside. She'd say, "Oh look, he's been waiting for us." And she'd sing it songs like "Fly Me to the Moon." I'd close my eyes and listen, not wanting her to stop. I savored the peacefulness.

She talked to the moon like it was her stuffed animal. And she spoke for it. She'd say, "The moon's saying, 'C'mon guys, it's not even nine—we're all chilling—now open the other bottle.'"

So I had my moon character as well. He wasn't as happy-go-lucky as Ashley's, but he was good-natured and knew he kicked ass. We hung out there a lot, so it seemed natural.

I thought of our first night on that roof, the first weekend we moved in. There was a half-foot of snow and it was still snowing hard. Ashley looked so carefree cute doing snow angels. We made a Statue of Liberty snowman. I shoveled "A&D 4-EVER" by the railing. Ashley took pictures.

But as I looked out at the rain, it all seemed a foregone conclusion. Ashley would be taking Mike to our roof to see the full moon tonight.

I thought of Ashley's lunch earlier with Tamara. Hearing her name had been another punch to the gut. Tamara was with Ashley when all of this started, at the party, getting topless in a bath tub in front of their co-worker. Tamara had asked him, "Which one of us do you want to fuck?" Then she had watched as another man proceeded to fuck my wife.

They were the two stars of the rumor. Of course they talked about it afterward. Ashley probably told her how I reacted when I found out. They were BFFs. But I had to believe she wouldn't tell Tamara about the past week. She wouldn't be telling her she cuckolded me, or that they kicked me out of my room and fucked on my bed. Even Tamara would be speechless. I had to believe that, given the original work rumor, Ashley would keep this secret. But I also thought of Tamara reading Ashley's body language and saying, "I don't know, Ashley. I think there's something you're not telling me."

I looked at my watch and quickly finished my coffee. I had to shake the evening out of my head and one-eighty into business mode. I started thinking of everyone I might see in the office and concentrating on remembering names, especially new people. I thought of safe office humor. Like I could joke about leaving amazing summer weather in New York for this. I went over my boss' talking points again. I use baseball scores from when I was a kid to remember some financial numbers.

I went into the bathroom and redid the knot in my tie. *No one knows you've been cucked*, I reminded myself. Then I practiced smiling. I have a decent smile, but ever since Ashley pointed it out in a photo, I've been self-conscious about it looking fake or forced.

I fixed my hair with my hand, pointed in the mirror, and mouthed, "Game time."

* * *

The receptionist stood up and smiled as I came off the elevator. I put my bags down and gave her a hug. I've known her a while.

I asked her how her Grand Canyon trip was and how her

mother she lived with was doing. I liked her telling me how her mom was writing a recipe book. I liked hearing how her grandmother still danced at ninety-four. I would've stayed to hear more but a sales manager saw me from down the hall. Pretty soon I was doing the tour, saying hello to everyone.

I was in a guest office, looking out at the Golden Gate in the rain, when Joanne knocked and gave me a hug. Joanne was the office manager there. She wanted me to join her for coffee down in the lobby.

We didn't have much business overlap, but had become work friends from office happy hours when I was in town. She was a cute, fun girl to do shots with. She probably liked having someone in the corporate office she could hang out with.

"So, look at you," she said as we sat down, "Mr. rising young CEO of the future, speaking at the Four Seasons tomorrow."

"Oh sure," I said with a laugh. "Well, I'm just the understudy filling in for Brian."

"Well, you and your team put the presentation together, right?"

"Yeah."

"So you probably know it better than he does."

"Brian's really good at thirty thousand feet stuff."

"Well, you're the one on stage tomorrow," she said. "Are you nervous?"

"I'm sure I will be," I said, "but that's normal. I just hope the Exec team's not tuning in from New York."

"Well if they are, it's your chance to show them."

"Yeah, that's the way to look at it, sure."

"Okay, so I have to tell you this. Guess what I did last weekend for the first time in my life?"

"What?" I said.

"Guess."

"Are you serious? Not even multiple choice?"

"It's something I mentioned last spring that I was thinking of doing."

"And that hint's supposed to be helpful?" I said. "All right, I'll say you rode a bull."

"Even better. I went skydiving."

"Wow, okay, so I was sort of in the ballpark. How was it?"

"Amazing," she said. "You and I talked about it once when I was still undecided. At Brad's going-away, I think."

"Oh yeah, okay."

"I remember you telling me your wife had gone skydiving and loved it, and then she wanted you to go, but I think you said you chickened out."

"Oh, c'mon, I didn't chicken out. I told her I'd go. I just wasn't that bummed when she didn't bring it up again."

"Well then," she said, "you really ought to bring it up to her."

"Were you scared?" I said.

"Oh hell, yeah! I was terrified going up in the plane. But once I was falling, my fear turned to exhilaration. The cliché is true. I never felt more alive. I was in awe of how beautiful life is. I know it's crazy, but I started crying."

"Wow, sounds kind of spiritual."

"Oh, absolutely," she said, "You have to experience it."

"Yeah, I'd be game. Maybe for my two-year wedding anniversary, I'll take Ashley to Hawaii and go skydiving."

"You should," she said, smiling. "What did Ashley say about it? Was she scared beforehand?"

"Oh, sure. The night before, she talked of backing out, but the next morning she said she couldn't live with herself if she didn't do it."

"Yeah, you're confronting your fear."

"Sure," I said, "and she had a big fear of heights as a kid. It's something she's proud of. She said it was amazing, too."

"You see? I'm telling you, don't put it on a bucket list. Just do it."

"I think I will," I said, trying to sound convincing.

One of her friends walked up to me and said, "They're looking for you upstairs." I was relieved when she then told me who. I had a meeting with the tech team.

\* \* \*

My boss had begun using a teleprompter and I learned they'd have one set up for me in the morning. I'd never presented that way, but I knew it made things a lot easier. As long as nothing malfunctioned, which happened to my boss his first time.

I had a solid rapport with the tech team, and would hang out just to hang out when I had time. Most of them were still in their twenties—a few geeks, a few hipsters, all very bright.

They had my script on the teleprompter in the conference room when I walked in. As they scrolled the words, I tested the remote and practiced. It was easy to talk like I wasn't reading. I'd still have the Q&A afterwards, but it sure eased the pressure.

Then we all met around the table and I tried to focus as they talked IT details. It was mostly foreign language to me. All I could add was stuff like "sounds good," "mission critical," and "can't have surprises."

"Don't worry, Dave," the manager said at the end. "We'll be there an hour before, and on that one percent chance anything happens, we'll have another one ready to go."

"Awesome," I said, smiling, making eye contact around the room "I really appreciate all your guys' help."

As I walked out into the hall, I saw a text message from Mike. He was already out to dinner with Ashley. He was asking if I wanted him to forward a photo of her he'd just taken.

\* \* \*

I started walking like I was in a hurry. I bypassed the crowded cubicle area and slipped into the men's room. No one was in there and I stood in a stall and re-read Mike's text. I'm six feet tall, so I bent my head, so it wouldn't be obvious I was there if someone walked in.

Any reply had disadvantages. And he'd probably show her my response. A "no thanks" could be read as not wanting to see my wife. "Not necessary" might suggest weird detachment. Not responding at all would be to ignore a message I'd obviously received.

And then there was saying "yes." I might as well be saying, "Please show me my wife right before she gets fucked." Yet it was the best of all bad options; at least I'd be part of it. I was on an island as it was. And beyond that, I just wanted to see her. I was dying to see her.

I debated typing back "sure" or "okay." I thought of Mike replying, "Sure what?" to make me really ask for the picture.

Then I heard the men's room door open, and someone walk toward me. There were three vacant stalls, but the guy chose the one right next to mine. I muttered, "Un-fucking believable" as I flushed the toilet with my foot. I stepped out, washed my hands, and texted back: "sure, send."

I started down the hall and saw the corporate assistant coming toward me, carrying boxes of office supplies. I grabbed most of them from her as I said hello. "Both mail guys are out today," she said, as we walked back to her desk.

I knew Mia mostly from talking on the phone, trying to get a message to her boss. She was a couple years out of school and always seemed upbeat. She was an attractive, hundred-pound Korean girl.

We turned down corporate row and I looked in at the empty offices.

"No one's back yet?" I said.

"Their meeting went way over," Mia replied, as she pointed at where I should put things.

"Yeah, I heard that, but Jack told me they were catching a two-thirty."

"Well, Jack was being delusional," she said, with a smile. "They'll be lucky to get the four-thirty now."

"They're still in LA?"

"Yeah, Jack's about to call."

"Wow," I said, sitting down in the empty cubicle beside her.

"Wow, what?"

"Oh, nothing. It's just that I had a five o'clock with Jack. But I should look on the bright side, right? Like now I've got time to review."

"Maybe more time than you think," she said. "If they miss this one, Jack won't be coming back to the office today."

"Really? How do you know?"

"He's got an hour commute, and with this rain, no way."

"Hmm" I said, "and he's gonna call either way?"

"Yup, any minute."

"Interesting. Mind if I wait with you?"

"Make yourself comfortable," she said as she pulled a bag from her desk. "Care for some pretzels?"

"Yeah, actually. I'd love some pretzels, thank you."

"So," she said, surprising me, "should I feel bad that part of me sort of wants them to miss this flight?"

I laughed and said, "More like, should *we both* feel bad?"

"Well, think about it. What would be so bad about Jack having to take a later flight? I'd be home early for once. Jack would be relaxing with a martini at the Admirals Club. And you … you wouldn't be stuck waiting around for him."

"I like it," I said. "It's very win-win."

"It's not just win-win," she said. "All three of us benefit. It's win-win win."

She pointed at me and I smiled. Then I noticed her eyebrows rise as she stared at the bag in my lap, and at my hand as I took out more pretzels.

"I'm sorry," I said, handing her the bag, "I didn't realize how much I've been chowing."

"Please, eat away," she said, laughing. "Do me a favor and finish the bag."

"Really? Well thank you. I don't know if it's just 'cause I haven't eaten today, but these are the best damn pretzels I've ever had in my whole life."

She smiled and then reached for her phone. "It's him," she said, turning stone-faced. I watched for clues as she said, "Hi, Jack, how are you? Uh-huh, okay."

On her third "okay," she looked at me, smiled and gave me the thumbs up. I just whispered, "Wow."

I gave her a celebratory hug when she got off the phone, and she started packing up to leave. I realized I had no reason to stay. I'd done what I'd needed to do. I figured I should go before I got roped into something unimportant. I grabbed my bags and went straight for the elevators.

I didn't care that it was raining. I didn't care how hard it would be to catch a cab. As I stood on the street, in front of the revolving doors, I was just glad to be outside.

22

# CHAPTER FOUR

I stared at the green light through the windshield wipers. Cars ahead weren't moving and I watched the light turn red for the third time. Mike still hadn't sent the photo.

I assumed that was deliberate. Perhaps he said to Ashley, "Let's make him wait for it." I wondered if he would include her like that. When he took her picture, he might say, "Smile, we're sending this one to Dave."

Whatever she knew or didn't know, I had to assume they'd be even closer after this. Mike was only two years older than Ashley. That also had to bond them. Even on little things, like new music where I had nothing to add.

People said I looked young for thirty-four, but Mike looked really young for thirty-two. I wouldn't say he looked boyish, but very youthful, with a commanding smile. His appearance was always sharp when he met up with us. Like something out of a men's magazine. Like he was THE MAN.

It had been different when Mike and I met for beers, before all this started. Then he was a bit unkempt and wore sneakers, and a t-shirt, and a Yankees cap, and called me his friend. I thought he was. I felt like I finally had someone to talk to. I was insane to trust him. Now I knew. I was being played right from the start. Fucking my wife was his plan all along. And I made it easy for him. They'd only met because of me.

But what I really regretted was playing along with Mike's story. He convinced me to introduce him to Ashley as a childhood friend—from summer camp. He said she'd be more herself and relaxed that way. He was supposed to be my wingman. Instead, I became his.

I even gave him a few minutes alone with her, the first night I introduced them. He'd sprung that one on me as Ashley and I were rushing to get ready. I was supposed to pretend I'd gotten a work call and briefly excuse myself. I didn't realize what that really meant until I was outside on the street looking through the window. That's when unease shot to panic. People were passing me on the sidewalk, so I couldn't flat-out stare. But I saw Ashley laughing and looking attentive as Mike rambled on.

He probably told her a lot in those twenty minutes they were alone. I cringed, imagining what he might have said: *that I'd confided in him ... that he knew about the party ... that I told him I masturbated regularly thinking about that night when she fucked a co-worker, knowing I was nearby.*

I wondered if he'd told her in that first conversation what a 'cuckold' was. Whatever he said, he must've blown Ashley away for her to let him pursue her so brazenly.

I thought what my friends would think, if they knew what was going on. They'd say I brought it all on myself. They wouldn't care it was Mike who encouraged me to talk online. They'd want to know how he came to talk to me in the first place. Or why I met him at a bar.

They'd want to know why I lied to Ashley about who Mike was. They'd ask why I did nothing as he repeatedly fucked my wife in my marital bed. Blaming Mike's manipulation and the alcohol wouldn't spare me. I'd be regarded as a fool and a sucker and a big fucking pussy.

I heard my phone, straightened up and answered, "Hey, Jack."

"Dave, helluva day to travel, eh? You get in okay?"

"Delayed but no problem," I said. "How about you? Are you still at LAX?"

"Yeah, long story, but check this out. All the decision-

24

makers were there today. They asked all the right questions and they might even go in for higher. We'll know next week."

"Wow, that's great," I said.

"Yeah, listen, we're waiting it out, regrouping here. I don't think we'll have a chance to huddle tonight."

"Hey, I understand," I said.

"How about breakfast tomorrow, seven-thirty at Luce? It's a block from the Four Seasons."

I was about to say "sure." But then I thought, even though he's a VP, I was giving the presentation, and it wasn't me who missed our meeting. "Jack, I need to be getting ready, prepping Q&A in the morning. How about afterward?"

"You don't want to go over it with me beforehand?"

"Well I'd like to, but it's too late for changes anyway. Final draft is done. I ran through it with IT today."

"And you're feeling good about it?"

"Yeah," I said.

"Great. Do you need anything from me or the team?"

"Not right now," I said. "Maybe throw some curveball questions at me beforehand. I'll be in a conference room at the back of the lobby."

"Sure, I'll bring Crawford. He's great at coming up with dick-head questions. And more importantly, ways to answer them."

"That'd be awesome," I said. "I could use that."

I was surprised how painless it was. Not just the phone call, but not having to walk Jack through the presentation. It was front-loaded with regression models and detail on assumptions anyway. Jack found that stuff dry and boring. It wasn't even his sector. I'm sure he was glad I didn't ask for help.

I texted my friend, Ryan—said I could meet up earlier, if he wanted.

\* \* \*

I was in line for check-in when Mike finally replied. There was no way not to look. I had to see if he'd sent the picture. I took a deep breath and looked at my phone.

It was there.

I didn't want to wait until I was up in my room. Or wait twenty seconds. I just really wanted to see it. I swallowed hard and there she was—Ashley, smiling, in a sexy pink dress. I looked away an instant later. The woman at the front desk had been trying to get my attention. I walked up and said hello. I explained I was taking my boss' reservation.

It was just nice to get up to my room. It was spacious compared to what I typically stayed in. There was room to pace, which is what I did to ready myself. I sat down on the bed with my laptop and whispered, "One, two, three." And there she was, my wife, on a date ... full screen.

"Oh my God," I whispered. Ashley was dressed to go out. But more like dressed to get fucked. I'd never seen that pink, body-hugging dress before. I would have remembered the plunging V-neck and the cleavage she was showing. I couldn't keep my eyes off her tits in that Little Miss Fuck Me dress. She was Mike's fucking date on the town. Like people would probably guess they were fucking.

I saw why she had no time for the gym. She'd gotten her eyebrows waxed, had her long hair curled. And who knows how much her new dress cost?

I zoomed in on Ashley's face, the confidence in her eyes, the invitation in her smile. She looked carefree and enchanted—like a girl at a country fair.

As if it was all so innocent. And going on a date with another man was normal. And who cares who happens to see us? Just a fun summer night on the Upper West Side.

I looked back at Ashley's tits and how they really popped in that dress. It's what guys notice first. Like at the beach, especially. They're not huge—34C—but for a small-framed girl, they really stand out and get comments. I thought of what my brother once said to me … "perfect tits for titty-fucking."

I looked back up and noticed her earrings. She was wearing the gold ones from Tiffany's that I'd given her last Christmas. I wondered if she realized that when she put them on.

I looked at the restaurant décor behind her and understood why it looked familiar—we'd been there before. It was an Italian place, seven blocks from where we lived. I didn't like how insanely public it was … or picturing them, holding hands, walking back from there.

I started thinking about why Mike would want to send the photo. I thought maybe he saw it as a way to deepen the mental cucking—making me look at my wife out on a date. Before she got fucked. Or maybe he was just showing me what was *his* this evening. The girl I'd been with for five years and loved so deeply—infinity deep—he'd be fucking her in my bed.

When I first started talking to Mike, I blabbed away about the party and my insecurities. And shared intimate details of my marriage. Right from the start, he probably saw me as a guy with a hot wife and high cuckold potential.

But he was in no hurry. He probably figured each time we talked, I was becoming mentally more amenable … more cuckable. And that it was only a matter of time before he'd convince me to introduce him to my wife. I held the fucking door open for him. He saw me as ripe for a cucking. And my wife's pussy, there for the taking. That's when Mike pounced. The most precious thing in the world to me—my wife's sweet, luscious pussy—I allowed to be taken from me. I'd let Mike claim my wife's pussy as his fucking own.

Sending the photo, I figured, was Mike's way of saying,

"Take a look at what I'll be fucking tonight, Dave—the lips that'll be around my cock."

I wondered if Ashley knew when she posed, that the photo would be sent to me. If he said something like, "Smile for your cuckold husband." If he told her I'd likely be jerking off to it in my hotel room later.

"How do you like my *before* photo, Dave?" I imagined Ashley saying. "And my new cock-tease dress, and the way I got all dolled up for Mike … to go out in public as his date. Do you really think we're *not* going to get noticed, holding hands?

"Look at my *before* photo, baby, how excited I look, and think about later … how this dress will be off me, how I'll be naked, in our bed, with Mike's cock inside me. Look at me, Dave, and think of Mike sperming inside me. The first of many while you're away. You know that's gonna be happening, Dave. This afternoon I even got you to okay it. You accepted me fucking another man. Just like a real cuckold would.

"Look at my tits, baby, and think about us on the phone tonight. I'll be lying in bed talking to you, and you'll be entirely clueless that Mike has started titty-fucking me.

"It's not like I won't be able to carry on a phone call with you. I'll just get you blabbing about your San Fran speech … while I'm staring at Mike's fat mushroom head, poking through my tits.

"I'll be asking questions, just to keep you talking. Get you droning on about some meeting you had. So I can suck Mike's cock as you talk. So I can give him a blowjob with my oblivious husband on the phone.

"But I'll have to pick up the phone sometime. Like when I hear you say 'Hello, hello, Ashley you there?' That's when Mike will start jerking his cock in my face … as I talk to you.

"Like when we're wrapping up the call, and I tell you I love you … Mike will start shooting his sperm in my face.

Majorly splashing me, sweetie. When you tell me you love me back, I'll be taking a serious facial. It'll be dripping down my neck, and I'll be trying to get it off my wedding ring.

"Wouldn't you like Mike to send you a photo of that, baby? Mike's sperm on my face, my nose, my forehead, dripping off my chin and onto my tits … onto your blue Giants pillowcase ….

"Don't you want to see the way he fucks me, Dave? The way he brings me to multiple orgasms? Don't you want to watch me ride that big cock as you sit in the room, jerking off, in your cuckold chair?

"Keep staring at my photo, Dave, and understand: this is Mike's now. This is what he'll be having tonight. These lips will be around his cock. His cum will be sliding down this throat. These tits will be bouncing. As he fucks my married pussy in our bed.

"You're looking at the girl who's cuckolding you now, Dave. The girl who watched you get bitch-slapped around by another man. Heard you say nothing as he took your wife to bed. How does it feel to be so fucking cucked, baby? To be the third wheel …the husband who sleeps on the couch?

"Look into my eyes and listen to me, Dave. You know you want this … you know it's gonna happen …. I'm gonna get fucked, honey, right in front of your freaked-out eyes, and you're gonna see how a real man fucks me. It's freaking inevitable, baby. What color do you want your chair in, Dave?"

"Oh Ashley," I muttered, and suddenly came.

* * *

I lay there listening to the rain against the window. I didn't like where my thoughts had taken me. Ashley had never said the word "cuckold" around me. I was just projecting. And I knew that kind of mental reinforcement would only fuck with me more.

Mike would probably tell me he was proud of me if he knew my thoughts as I jerked off. The cuckold chair, especially. He'd tell me to keep imagining it, and to picture myself sitting in one. Which was fucked up crazy. I wanted no part in a cuckold chair. It was a symbol of just how far a man had been reduced. That's so far beyond wondering if you can walk things back. There's no sugar-coating that humiliation.

I wasn't getting branded like that. Fuck that, I reminded myself. I said it aloud: "I'm not going to let Mike fuck my wife in front of me."

I grabbed a beer from the minibar and began slowly pacing. It was nice to be by myself in a quiet hotel room. To have privacy.

Between sips of beer, I started talking to myself. "That won't be fucking me," I said aloud. "I'm not getting cucked like that. I ain't no fucking chair sitter."

I walked by the bed and looked at the photo again.

"Ashley," I continued, "watching is all Mike's idea. I never wanted or asked for it. I never planned for any of this to happen. We can start by slowing things down. A break from seeing Mike, maybe. I need it. Our marriage needs it. We need it. Yes, I've been cuckolded, and you cucked me hard, I admit, but let's put all that on ice for now. Please don't listen to Mike. And just hear what I'm telling you. I swear Ashley. I'm really *not* a fucking cuckold."

Then I noticed the time and texted my friend I was on my way.

# CHAPTER FIVE

Ryan waved to me from the end of the bar as I walked inside. "How you doing, buddy?" he asked, getting up and giving me a hug.

"Doing well, Ry, how are you?"

"Good," he said, as he tossed my umbrella beside his on the floor.

"Well, this is a quaint little pub," I said, sitting down. "Is it usually this empty?"

"It's the night after a three day weekend—and it's pouring out. And didn't you say 'a place where we can talk and hear ourselves?' "

"Not complaining. This is great."

The bartender came over—a smiling girl with an Irish accent—and we ordered two pints.

"So" Ryan said, "you got roped into this 'cause your boss is sick?"

"Yeah, he was in the ER yesterday—passing kidney stones."

"Well that's a pretty good excuse."

"Sure, he'd never miss this otherwise."

"Last year I missed work 'cause I had to have my tonsils out."

"Tonsils?" I said, "Really? You went to the hospital?"

"Uh-huh."

"What are you—twelve years old?"

"Yeah, I heard all that shit back at work."

"What shit?"

"It was actually a serious operation, but anyway. My boss couldn't just say I was out sick. Instead, she had to explain to everyone why I wasn't at some big corporate shindig. And having your tonsils out at thirty-three … of course I was mocked for that. Guys would ask me, like two months later, how my fucking tonsils were doing."

"That's funny," I said.

"In hindsight, maybe," he said, with a laugh.

I asked the girl to put on the Yankee game as she put our pints in front of us. "It's great seeing you, Ry," I said, as we clicked glasses.

"You too, man. It's been a while. I think the last time was May."

"Yeah, you weren't around when I was here this summer."

"So four months," he said. "How things been going?"

"Pretty good. But this trip was a big crap surprise."

"How do you mean?"

"Well, it's bad enough working Labor Day, but then to be told you have to be on the first flight to San Fran the next morning—"

"Yeah, that ain't cool."

"Plus, everyone tomorrow is expecting to see my boss. That's why they're showing up. People will be like '*who the fuck's this guy*?' So I have that to overcome."

"How many people?"

"A hundred, one-fifty maybe."

"That's no fucking fun."

"No," I said. "It kind of sucks, actually."

"So how was your summer? How's Ashley?"

"She's good, thanks. How's Karen?"

"Karen? It really *has* been a long time. We broke up July 4th."

"Wow," I said, putting down my beer, "were you okay with it?"

"Yeah, it had stopped being fun, and we were fighting a lot. Plus she had something going on with her boss. I'm seeing a cute Taiwanese girl now."

"Wow, okay."

"Her name's fricking *Chang*," he said, "but she's very hot and super polite—and really attentive. Like she'll give me a BJ and then bring me a beer. Swear to God. She's a flight attendant and did that once in uniform."

"Nice," I said. "But you'd been seeing Karen for like two years, right?"

"Yeah, I brought her to your wedding, remember?"

"That's right," I said. "So, were you okay with breaking up with her?"

"At the time it sucked, but I also knew there was no getting back to where we were."

"I hear you."

"So, what have you and Ashley been up to? Go anywhere cool?"

"Nowhere … just a week in Florida. But going to Hawaii for Christmas and New Year's."

"Oh yeah? If I'm still seeing Chang, maybe we'll join you. She gets free hotel and airfare."

"Well hell, maybe we can get adjoining rooms," I said, joking. "It's also an anniversary present for Ashley, so we're doing mostly solo couple stuff. But hey, if you and Chang just happen to be in Hawaii, we'd certainly kick it with you for a night."

"Well, I'm hoping we'll kick it sooner than that, my friend. Looks like we're going to New York this weekend for the Open. We found out this afternoon. They changed Chang's schedule. You and Ashley around for drinks—like this Friday night?"

"Uh, yeah," I said. "I have to see about Friday, but we'll definitely be around."

"Cool," he said. "Friday night we're wide open. Just let

me know. So, how's married life been treating you?"

I acted like I was focused on the baseball game to give me a moment to think. "It's good," I said. "No fighting and we still get along great. We've been riding bikes a lot in Central Park. There's an animal in the zoo there she wants me to help her steal."

"Aww. You should do an eHarmony commercial."

"Oh well, hey, I'm not saying it's always like that. At the moment we have to work on better communication, which is why now's not the best time for me to be away."

Ryan gave me a deliberate look, and I tried to appear matter-of-fact. "But no big deal," I added. "It's minor. We'll just talk when I see her."

"So," he said, looking away, "is this game still tied?"

"Yeah, top of the seventh, and a lot of people don't realize this, but you know why this game's so important for the Yankees?"

"Explain it to the guy over there," he said, standing up, "maybe he cares. I have to take a piss."

But I did explain it to Ryan when he returned. And rather than change the subject on me, he started watching and getting interested. Soon we were talking about the game, eating chicken wings, and getting a buzz.

It felt nice to be distracted.

But an hour later, when Ryan took a call and stepped outside, I was left to my own thoughts again. I wondered if Ryan saw anything different about me. I thought I was coming across as engaged as usual, but who knows what people pick up on? I wasn't going to get drunk and spill my guts.

I imagined that dreaded next-day phone call: *Ryan, forget what I said. It was just drunken bullshit. I made all that crap up—everything. There was no guy in my bed or my apartment last night.*

"Sorry 'bout that" Ryan said, sitting back down. "Chang thinks she saw a mouse in her kitchen."

"What? Oh—do you have to go?"

"No, she's fine. So what do you say to a shot of Patrón?"

"I should probably stick to beer. I have to be up before five."

"C'mon, just one."

"Okay, here's the deal. I'll do one, but *literally* just one."

"Cool. I have an early day myself."

We watched the Yankees get the last out before doing the shot. Then he showed me a photo of Chang by a pool. She was small-framed and busty like Ashley.

"You're right," I said, "she's pretty fucking hot. And I like the idea of her fetching your beer for you."

"What? Ashley doesn't do that for you?"

"Maybe on my birthday," I said, "if I'm lucky."

"I'm telling you, Chang is all about hospitality. At first I thought she was just applying her airline training to her whole life. But it's just how she is and the culture she grew up in."

"I hear you," I said.

"So, you said you're having some communication issues with Ashley—"

"Oh not *issues*," I said, "More just getting on the same page on little things."

"Little things—like what? What kind of music to play at dinner?"

"No," I said, with a laugh.

"I've probably been there. What kind of things, man?"

"Well, I'll tell you the main one," I said, clearing my throat. "Ashley's really good friends with this girl she works with. And they go out to happy hours together. And she's kind of wild and not the best influence."

"Okay …."

"Well, I don't know her friend that well, or what they

35

talk about. And I just want Ashley to be more forthcoming. Like she tells me about her other friends."

"What's your concern?"

"I just don't want it becoming something we don't talk about. So, I just want to catch it now, before it's a communication … situation."

"You ever join them out?"

"Not really. I don't know if it's some weird jealousy thing, but the girl's never liked me."

"Why's that?"

"Well, she didn't like Ashley getting married to me in the first place. She acted like she was losing her best friend, which so wasn't true. She was one of Ashley's bridesmaids and barely smiled in photos that day."

"She was a bridesmaid at your wedding? What does she look like?"

"Long blonde hair, pretty, a couple inches taller than Ashley, five-five, five-six."

"Big tits?"

"Oh yeah," I nodded.

"I *know* who you're talking about. What's her name?"

"Tamara?"

"Yup, I talked to her. After your reception. At a late-night party up in the suite. I was pretty drunk. But I know what you mean about her vibe. She didn't seem happy to be there."

"Yeah, well, that's the girl."

"And she still faults you for marrying Ashley? That's why she doesn't like you?"

"Well, I'm also not cool, or trendy, or arty, or—"

"Hey, did you order these?" Ryan said, pointing behind me.

I turned back and saw the bartender pouring us each another shot. "Are you joking?" I said. "Like *I'd* order them. Why'd you fucking do this?"

"I didn't do shit," he said, laughing. "See? It's on the house."

The girl smiled at me and said, "Cheers."

I smiled back and said, "Thank you," but inside I was thinking *motherfucker*. If Ryan had suggested another shot, I'd have said "no fucking way." But it was different etiquette, now that shots were right in front of us. They were thanking us for our patronage. Saying no didn't seem an option.

Ryan started talking to the girl about Irish whiskies and I couldn't pretend being interested for long, so I stood up and checked my phone—made sure Ashley hadn't texted.

"She's going to be our observer," Ryan said, as I sat back down.

"Our what?" I said.

"I told her about the time we were all doing shots. And you poured your shot on the floor of the bar, thinking no one would notice."

"Are you kidding?" I said, and then turned to the girl. "My friend's spouting bullshit. That was at my bachelor party, and people were pushing shots on me non-stop. So, on my fifth or sixth shot—in like half an hour—I freaking poured one out. And this guy still brings it up."

"That wasn't the only time you've dumped a shot," Ryan said, "but who cares? She's just here to verify that this isn't another one—"

"Another one what?" I said, putting my hands out in mock exasperation. "Another one of those times I try to secretly dump my fucking shot on the floor?"

Ryan started laughing.

"Fuck you," I said, as we clicked our glasses and did the shots.

"It's good fucking seeing you, bro."

"You too," I said. "It's been too long. I didn't even know about you and Karen. So what were you saying about her earlier?"

"That I've moved on?"

"Yeah and that's fantastic. But earlier, you were talking about before you broke up. You said something was going on between her and her boss?"

"Yeah, that was the final straw."

"What was?"

"She was fucking her boss" he said, matter-of-fact.

"Wow," I said. "How'd you find out?"

"Caught her in lies and a text that wasn't meant for me. It all added up. She's with him now."

"You still think about her much?"

"A little at first, but since I met Chang … not at all, man."

"That's awesome, Ry. Good for you. Did you know her boss?"

"Talked to him once at a Christmas party. He's a tool, but he's rich. I'm just glad to be done with all that bullshit."

"Sure, I hear you. Ever run into them?"

"I haven't yet, which is surprising, but I could give two shits. Fuck 'em, y'know."

"Yeah, I like the attitude."

"Hold on," he said. "Got a text from Chang."

"Uh-huh," I said, and then noticed I had a text from Ashley. I drank from my beer and read it: "*Hey Dave, just got back, nice night. Don't forget to tell Ryan I said hi. Have a great night, stay dry, and I'm rooting for u tomorrow. Love you.*"

I felt my pulse quicken and reached for my beer. If I was going to leave reasonably early, this seemed like the time.

"Hey man," I said, "I have to deal with a work thing. I'm afraid I'm gonna have to cut things short tonight."

"No worries," he said, "I'm cool with splitting. And damn, that mouse is freaking Chang out, big-time."

"Oh, poor Chang," I said. "Right now she's probably standing on a kitchen counter and holding it in."

"That's why I'm going there now to rescue her, like a fireman."

We settled up and walked out in the rain.

"So I take it we're not sharing a cab?"

"Opposite direction," he said, "but don't forget about Friday. See if you can lock it in. Oh, and also, I'm gonna arrange for Chang to have a long one-on-one with Ashley when we're there. How does that sound to you?"

"Um … sounds fucking weird, actually. Like why would I possibly think that's a good idea?"

"Just fucking with you, D," he said, laughing, "but try to swing Friday, okay?"

"I'm on it" I replied, and then grabbed a cab.

# CHAPTER SIX

I thought about Ashley's text on the ride back to my hotel. It was long, for how little it said. The only reason she told me again to say "hi" to Ryan was to make the text longer.

Her message was, "I'm having a wonderful evening, don't call, talk tomorrow." That's how I read her "good night." It wasn't just a token expression. When combined with "rooting for u tomorrow," it was clear there'd be no before-bed phone call. It seemed to me as if she'd set that up earlier—saying she'd text me when she got home.

I should've at least said, "What, no phone call?"

But I assumed the text was only a means of coordinating a time to talk. I hadn't expected just an acknowledgment that she was home.

I re-read it again. "I'm back ... don't call ... good night." That's how it seemed at its most basic. And that's what played back in my head in the lobby, on my way up to my room. "I'm back, good night, and don't fucking call me, Dave."

It reminded me of Mike slamming my bedroom door in my face the week before. Only this had come from Ashley. I doubted that she meant it that way, but there was nothing to hang onto, no invitation. Nothing like, "I'll be up for a half hour if you want to say a quick good night."

We talked every night when I travelled, no exceptions. Since before we were engaged, a thousand days ago. And now I felt like my hands were tied. I was boxed in. Texting back some version of "good night" was my only option. I didn't want to come right out and say "Can we please talk on the phone tonight?" But I did want to show that I'd welcome that. Get across that I was free to talk. So when I got up to my room, I texted her straight back:

*"Glad you're home. Wish I was there w/you. Just back from hanging w/Ryan & will be up for a while. Look forward to seeing you Thursday. Love you & miss you lots."*

I paced around, waiting for her reply. I didn't get one, so I opened a beer and looked out the window. "No moon for me tonight," I mumbled.

Just an hour or two earlier, Ashley would've taken Mike to our roof. She probably explained to him how meaningful the place was for us. Mike would appreciate hearing that. It would probably make fucking her under the full moon that much more special. He'd have gotten Ashley to cross another threshold. It was another way to rub his achievement in my face and encourage her to cuckold me more. He'd naturally want to run up the score while I was away.

And not just with me, but with Ashley. He'd probably already talked to her about having me watch them fuck. By now, he'd referred to me as a "cuckold" a few dozen times to her. He wanted Ashley thinking, "Let's cuck him hard."

I picked up my laptop and looked at the photo and the random people in the background. I thought about how public that was, having dinner at a nice neighborhood restaurant. I wondered if they'd hold hands or kiss, oblivious to people around them, noticing. I imagined Mike grabbing Ashley's ass as they walked inside somewhere. Or them making out at a bar.

I wondered how Ashley would introduce Mike if she ran into someone we knew. It could be some couple we hung out with, just walking down the street. I wondered if it would show in Ashley's body language—if she'd look like she was about to get fucked. We don't typically run into friends of ours walking our neighborhood, but on a summery

September night, everyone would be out. I imagined a bartender we know, saying, "Look at hot little Ashley Martens ... if only her puss-boy husband could see her now."

And then there were my doormen. They'd seen us coming home with Mike. They'd seen him take Ashley out solo. They'd know he was staying over while I was away. It probably looked obvious as they held the door. Mike was going up to fuck my wife. They had to be talking about it.

I was scared and uneasy. A neighbor might easily notice them going into our apartment. One of my doormen might mention it to the guy I get coffee from. Next thing I knew, the pizza guy'd be giving me funny looks ... people saying "That's him," when I passed on the street.

I wondered if Ashley cared. Would she say, "So a few people laugh at you." Or, "Who cares what Jimmy the doorman thinks?" Like I was supposed to just suck it up. I heard my phone and clicked on Ashley's text:

*"I miss you too and looking forward to Thursday also. Please don't stay up too late working—you need your sleep tonight. Love you & have a good night."*

"Are you kidding?" I said, aloud.

Ashley's assumption seemed insincere. She knew we'd been out drinking, and if I was up "working," I would've had said so. Plus, she knew it was still early here. And "looking forward to Thursday" could mean lots of things. For all I knew, I could be going home to a conversational ambush. Or she might've said that simply because I'd said it. The only real positive was that she replied. She took a couple minutes away from Mike to at least do that, even if she had put the "closed" sign up for the night.

For a second, I considered texting back, "Are you free for a one-minute call good night?" But I wasn't desperate enough to risk the likely downside. She would've talked to me, had she wanted to. Now I'd just be bothering her, interrupting. I thought of her getting off the phone with me and rolling her eyes at Mike. She'd say I was being weird, or needy, or homesick, or drunk ... or cuckoldish.

I looked at Ashley's photo.

"Oh, you are, Dave," I imagined her saying. "Wanting me to tuck you in with a good night call, all while knowing I'm busy ... getting fucked in our bed. I'd say that's very cuckoldish."

I pulled my dick from out of my boxers, looked at the photo and pretended Ashley was just talking away. "Most husbands," she'd say, "wouldn't want to hear from their wives at all. Like, a goodnight phone call? While their wife's home getting fucked? That's not how a normal man reacts. That's something a cuckold wants. Kind of confirms what you are though, doesn't it, baby?

"A week ago, Dave, I hadn't even met him. I thought we were just meeting some old friend of yours for a drink. Not some guy you met online who was there to get you cucked."

"How could you not have realized that was his plan? You let yourself get dominated by him. I watched you act like a timid pussy, in our apartment, right in front of me. I watched another man make a pussy of you. I saw you earn your horns.

"He made such a fool of you, Dave. How can I respect you now? What do you think Tamara thinks of you? You know I've told her. She wants to get you a cuckold t-shirt ... and a cap with horns. Says you should wear it out for Halloween. So others can see who you are.

"Tamara wants to be there—just like she was with Jim Murta—only this time, you're right there ... watching and jerking off.

"Don't you want to watch me get fucked, Dave? I think deep down, you really do. You want to see my pussy take a real man's cock. And see the cock that's now fucking your wife. The cock my pussy now craves ... the cock that's made you a cuckold.

"I'll tell you I love you, Dave—with Mike's cock inside

me, pounding deep. You can tell me 'I love you' as you watch me get fucked. It's time to cross the Rubicon, baby … and ejaculate in front of me … as you watch me ride Mike's rock hard cock. And you know Mike's gonna get you to do it. You know you're going bare-ass on that chair. Because deep down, you know you want this. And that Mike and I want it, too.

"Opening up together will be so freeing, when you float down that cuckold stream. Imagine the orgasm you'll have, seeing me take another man's cock. Like holding hands on a roller coaster. You know you want me to cuckold you. Imagine how hard your dick will be, with a front row seat to me getting fucked. Listen to the cuck inside you. Let go of the railing, and just say the words, baby. Say *cuck me Ashley*."

I looked into her eyes and whispered, "Cuck me, Ashley."

"Stare at my tits, my blowjob lips, the earrings you gave me last Christmas … and say it again, Dave."

"Cuck me, Ash."

"I want you jerking off, watching. I want you sitting there with cum in your hand, knowing there's no going back, as Mike continues to fuck me. You'll see Mike thrust extra-hard and hold it there. You'll see him look you in the eye, as his hot, thick, alpha sperm starts filling my pussy."

"Cuck me, Ash."

"You'll be so insecure around me afterward. Knowing I saw you jerk to completion. And I'll have seen just how much of a cuckold you really are. You'll be wearing horns all right. You'll be a fucking chair-sitter, Dave."

I said "Cuck me, Ashley" and came.

* * *

I looked up at the ceiling, sighing, shaking my head. It was hard to blow off the thoughts I'd just had. When coupled with where my mind went while masturbating earlier, it was a new level of being out there.

The past summer had mostly been about imagining that night at the party. Eventually I did masturbate thinking of more tangential things, like what people she worked with would say about me. And last Friday, I'd jerked off listening to an audio I'd secretly made of Mike and Ashley in my bedroom.

But this was different. This was thinking of future, out-there scenarios, and trying to chip away at my resolve right now. Like it was mentally grooming me to keep letting things happen. I knew that kind of thinking was a path to the chair. I didn't need it creeping in when I masturbated.

I didn't need it, period. Focus instead, I thought, on just Ashley having sex. Stay in the present. It still was planting mental cuckold seeds, but at least I'd be walking things back somewhat. It wasn't like I was going to stop masturbating. And picturing Mike fucking Ashley was better than having Ashley rambling on in my head and bitch-slapping me.

I thought of how Ryan ended it when he heard his girlfriend cheated. There was no picturing it in his head for him. No wondering about the details of how the guy fucked her.

He would never allow himself to get cucked like me. He wouldn't have let a guy he met online take his girl out for drinks. And the Online-guy wouldn't be balling his girl in his bed while he was away on business. He'd have pulled over at the next exit. He'd have confronted his wife, pronto.

There'd be no "It's okay, I understand." Ryan would never say that. That was me. I said that. I was the stooge who fell down that cuckold well. I messaged with a guy from a cuckold chat room, and a few weeks later—there I was—cucked in real life. That would never happen to him. It was so far off the grid.

I was tired. I brushed my teeth, set three alarms, and put in for a wake-up call. I looked up at the ceiling in the dark and listened to the rain, still going strong.

I'd crossed a shit-load of Rubicons in the last six days. And a few more tonight. I was more of a cuckold than ever. I was sure Ashley would say I'd given my okay. Like a new door to cuckolding me had been opened.

There was nothing for her to hide or downplay. My bed was Mike's tonight. Ashley knew I knew that. She had to know she was openly cucking me, now. Like that was understood. I didn't even rate a phone call. I'd accepted a blow-off text message.

I had to take my mind off it. I wanted to fall asleep. I put a pillow over my head and thought of old Yankee World Series games. I imagined the path of a river I canoed a lot as a kid and pictured going down it in an inner tube.

I thought of how Ashley used to read me a bedtime story over the phone when I was away. That was when we were engaged. She even had me snoring once. She read with such calmness and serenity, and her southern accent was more pronounced then. It was *Winnie the Pooh*, mostly. She had voices for all the characters.

I closed my eyes and pictured it. I could hear her inflections, the breath she'd take each time she turned the page … the way she did Eeyore.

There was a song in most of the stories, and I thought of how Ashley would make up some sing-songy melody. I tuned out the rain and could hear her voice in my head. And more than just faintly … like the way she laughed as she messed up a line.

# CHAPTER SEVEN

My alarms went off at four the next morning, and I chugged the water bottle I'd left on the nightstand. "Holy fucking crap," I said aloud, as I sat up in bed. It was dark and still storming out. But I tried to be positive. At least I was still on New York time. The meter was running, though. "T minus six hours," I said after I spat out my toothpaste.

I broke out the sections in my head as I showered. My team had put it together; we'd spent all August on it. I knew it well. Part of me would've been okay with the teleprompter screwing up. I'd get credit for not being fazed.

But the Q&A is what had me a little nervous. The few I'd done had been in front of smaller groups—mostly my peers. This was several grades up. A CEO-level audience. One misplaced word could get major scrutiny.

Still in my boxers, I paced around my room and did a dry run. I didn't need to rely too much on cue cards by the fourth or fifth time. I answered questions I imagined people asking. And my boss emailed me things to emphasize from his hospital room.

It was just past six, and I knew I had to get dressed soon. But I paused going into the bathroom. I had a few minutes, and I didn't want to be obsessing at the Four Seasons. So I grabbed my laptop and lay down on the bed.

I pulled up a photo Mike had sent me a few days before. It was from Friday night—the second time we'd all met up. Mike had asked the waitress to take our photo that night. I had no time to react. So there we were, posing—me, Mike and Ashley.

I stared at the photo. It seemed like Mike was rubbing it in. His confident smile and his arm around Ashley, screamed, "I'm fucking cucking you, bro."

I imagined Mike out at a bar, showing the photo to a friend of his.

"That's the couple I was telling you about."

"The cuckold couple?" his friend would ask. "That's her? That's the hot wife you've been fucking? Damn, she's smoking, bro. Nice fucking titties. Hot little slut you got there, Mike. And that's the chump-ass husband you're cucking? He looks good and humbled. How did you get him to agree to be in it?"

"I just told him to get in the picture," Mike would say.

"That's a 'you know you've been cucked when' moment. Posing with the man who's fucking your wife. Looks like he understands the significance. Or what a third wheel he is. He so doesn't want to be there."

"Yeah" Mike would say, "Like he knew it was his cuckold mug-shot. Reality was definitely sinking in. He knew, posing in that picture, that I was going to do it to him again that night. Take his wife from him and ball her in his bed. Knowing he'd do nothing to stop me. It was understood he'd be sleeping on the couch that night."

"And now he awaits the chair," his friend would say with a laugh, "seeing his wife fucked in front of him. Can't wait for you to pull that off. Getting him to jerk off while you ball her. Being pussified in front of his wife. Then he'll really be rubber-stamped. *You're a fucking cuckold, bitch!*"

"I'm gonna drill his wife doggy," Mike would say, "and have her look her husband in the eye as he sits there. Have Ashley tell him she loves him as I sub her out in front of him. She wants to see him dominated. And we're gonna step it the fuck up. We're gonna really cuck this motherfucker."

I looked at Mike in the photo of the three of us, and imagined him talking to me ….

"I'm going to cuck the fuck out of you, Dave. And show Ashley what kind of man you really are. You'll be so desperate to please her, you'll clean the sheets after we fuck. Like a good, cuckold husband. She's going to love cucking you, Dave. I've been telling her that a lot while you're away.

"Your wife wants you humiliated, you know that. She wants you fucking humbled. Eating out of her hand. Asking 'how high?' when she tells you to jump. You'll do whatever she wants, won't you? Even when she tells you she wants you watching … sitting in a cuckold chair. You'll be fumbling, all nervous. But like a good little cuckold, you're gonna say okay. And then it'll happen, bro. Before you realize it, I'll be balling your wife … right … the fuck … in front of you.

"What must Ashley think of you now, Dave? She watched her husband react like a pure pussy this entire week. Saw you accept your bedroom door getting shut in your face. Locked out as your wife got fucked bare in your bed. Ashley's watched as I made a pussy of you. She's seen just how big a fucking cuckold you really are.

"Look at your wife, Dave—the magical glow about her. That picture. It was Night Two of Ashley cucking her husband. Look at the way she's leaning in toward me, like you're already an afterthought. Look at her smile. Out with her new big-cock'd lover. And you—standing awkwardly beside her.

"She knew I'd boot you from your bed again. She knew you'd spend the night on the couch. And Ashley looks like she's having the time of her life, doesn't she? Out with her new alpha man boyfriend … as you stand awkwardly by her side. After just paying for dinner.

"Look at me and look at Ashley … all of us out in public. Who looks like the couple? Who looks like the odd man out? You're gonna get to see me balling your big-titted wife, Dave.

You'll be sitting in the fucking cuck chair, all right."

I stared at Ashley's tits and suddenly came. A lot. Some down my leg, on my hands.

\* \* \*

"Motherfucker" I said as I wiped it off with the sheet.

Now I had to big-time scramble. I put on my suit, threw my notes in my bag, and grabbed my umbrella. I saw a text from Mike just as I got in the cab:

"*Good luck today. I've got a few minutes now if you're free to talk. Then in meetings.*"

Mike was the last person I wanted to talk to. Especially then, having just imagined him verbally bitch-slapping me. I hadn't expected that when I lay down. I wanted the jack-in-the-box back in the box. I didn't want to even think about it. If I talked to Mike now, I'd have to block that out. And I kind of had to. I wanted him to stop being public with Ashley. And I felt I needed him thinking that I still saw him as a friend. So I called him.

"Dave, how you doing, bro? When's show-time?"

"In three hours," I said. "I'm headed there now."

"Are you nervous?"

"Sure, a little, but that's par for the course before I present."

"How 'bout what's going on here? Nervous about Ashley and me?"

I wasn't interested in *getting real* with Mike, but it seemed like a good time to bring it up.

"Well, here's the thing" I said. "What worries me is people gossiping."

"Are people gossiping?"

"I don't know. But if you guys are out in public together, people are gonna start talking. Like that restaurant you were at last night … Ashley could've easily run into someone there. I mean, this is for her sake as much as mine. Can this please just be more discreet?"

50

"Yeah, I understand. Ashley doesn't need any more rumors. Tell you what. We won't go out to dinner tonight. We'll just all go out together when you get back."

"Well, I'm not talking just restaurants. I mean anywhere in public. Just walking down the street together could start a rumor."

"Unlikely, but I get it. We'll be discreet when you're not here."

"Have my doormen said anything to you?"

"Like what?"

"I don't know," I said. "Something indicating they know what's going on?"

"Well, they must know I'm a friend of yours. And they've seen the three of us together. They must know I'm seeing Ashley while you're away."

"Well, they've got to be speculating," I said.

"Another man staying with your wife while you're away … how could they not, right? But don't worry. You've got professional doormen. I talked with two of them last night. They're good guys."

"Jeez, Mike, why do you have to talk to them?"

"I don't *have* to. I'm being friendly. Besides, they'd speculate more if I acted all weird and aloof."

"Can you just keep it to 'hello' and 'nice day' right now—please?' Can you just help me out here?"

Mike didn't reply at first. "Sure, bro, you got it. When I leave in the morning, I'll just act like I'm running late—how's that?"

"That's great," I said. "And I know some interaction's unavoidable. It's just that times like now, I really hate doorman buildings."

"Don't worry. Being discreet is part of their job. They'd get shit-canned for gossiping. I can remind them of that, if you want."

"Don't fucking remind them of anything," I said. "Can you please just keep it to hello?"

" 'Hello' and 'good morning.' How's that? Cool?"

"Yes—thank you."

"So tell me. How was your first night away from Ashley? Knowing I was with her?"

"I'm sorry, Mike, but I'm at the Four Seasons now. I'm really under the gun, with a ton of shit still to do."

"All right, I understand" he said. "Just call me afterwards."

"Okay. And thanks for agreeing to the no-public thing."

"No worries" he said. "We'll just wait till you get back."

\* \* \*

When I walked into the lobby, a hotel greeter grabbed a pot of coffee and took me down the hall. There was a small conference room at the end. It was really Spartan—small table, four chairs, and a whiteboard. A window looked out to the hall, but I was in the back of the hotel. I could pace and gesticulate without being self-conscious. I broke out my cards and started right in. Then I tried it without any. I practiced the places where I had to segue. I checked my laptop for any breaking industry news.

I had just resumed pacing again when Joanne knocked on the door.

"Nice hiding spot," she said, coming inside. "It took me ten minutes to find you." She looked cheery, bright-eyed, and polished in her blue business suit.

"Morning, Joanne," I said. "Yeah, I kind of wanted some faraway cave, so this is perfect."

She smiled and asked, "Are you feeling ready?"

"I'm getting there," I said. "If I had to give it right now, I could."

"Awesome. Do you want to practice on me? I have a few minutes."

"Oh, it's boring."

"Oh, c'mon. I want the backstage version. And you need to practice with a live audience."

"All right," I said, "I'm game. I'll just do a few minutes of the part I've been tripping up on."

I grabbed my cards and stood by the whiteboard. I didn't rely on them too much. Just for the first sentence. I didn't stumble. Did have to clear my throat at one point. But overall, it was pretty smooth. She clapped when I said, "That's it."

"That was great," she said, "but aren't you using a teleprompter? You seem to have a lot memorized."

"It's my first time using one. I just want to be ready—no matter what. And I'll probably have to present this same talk again—to smaller groups in New York."

"Well, you sound like you know it. Just remember to make eye contact. You hardly made any with me just now, and it's not like you were reading."

"Hmm," I said, looking at her, "that's a good observation. Thank you. I guess I was just overly focused on getting the words right. I'm gonna remember that for the mock Q&A with Jack."

"When's he getting here?"

"I'm about to find out," I said, reaching for my phone. "That's him."

"Should I leave?"

"No, it's fine."

I picked up and said, "Hey Jack."

"Dave, how you doing?" he said. "I have to be quick. The exec call's still going on. And I have to brief Miller after."

"Okay—"

"So I'm delayed, but I'll be there. I'll be leaving here in thirty, forty minutes, tops."

"Take your time, Jack," I said. "I know you're crazy busy, and really, I'm fine."

"You sure?"

"Yeah, of course," I said. "I appreciate your feedback … always. But I shouldn't be the priority here. Really, I'm good."

"Well … the way this morning's been going … it's much

appreciated. But I'll see you beforehand, of course. And if you need anything in the meantime, just holler."

"Sure," I said, "and Joanne's here. So I'm good right now."

"Great. See you in a bit."

I put my phone in my pocket and shook my head at Joanne.

"Wow," I said, "Jack just blew me off again."

"Oh please," she said laughing. "I heard you. You wanted him to blow you off. Like you were talking him into *not* having to show."

"Well, I just meant 'don't worry about being late.' I wasn't saying 'don't meet up with me at all.'"

"Why didn't you say that?"

"I don't know, what would be the point? He's got a lot going on and I could tell he wanted to bail. This is just an obligation that got dumped on him. And the thing is, I'm really pretty cool with it. It's too late for feedback now. And as far as getting drilled with deliberately ridiculous, mock questions … I'm fine with a rain check on that."

"You did him a solid," she said, with a laugh, then looked at her phone. "Oh jeez, I have a call in five. I gotta run."

I went to hold the door.

"So, what are you going to do now?" she said. "Is it back to pacing and mumbling?"

"Yeah, probably. It's just how I prepare. And hey, it's better than sweating and throwing up."

"Is that a possibility?"

I smiled and said, "C'mon."

"Just checking. You sounded great. I'll leave you to your pacing."

I was just getting back in a rhythm when I saw Ashley calling.

# CHAPTER EIGHT

When I saw her name, I tensed up and froze. Then I focused on answering. I was nervous, but I figured I could get off the phone any time. Ashley knew how busy I was. If our conversation got awkward, that was my parachute.

On the third ring, I thought, *Just pick the fucking phone up*.

"Hey, Ash."

"Dave, how are you? You crazed right now?"

"Just rehearsing," I said. "Counting down to ten Pacific. How are you doing?"

"Good," she said. "Are you super stressing?"

"Not through the roof, no. Feeling okay."

"Great. How'd you sleep?"

"Five hours, maybe. But going out with Ryan has me chugging lots of coffee this morning."

"I'll bet. How was it? How's he doing?"

"Doing well," I said. "Has a new girlfriend he seemed pretty into."

"What happened to Karen—they broke up?"

"Yeah, a few months ago."

"Why?"

"I don't know," I said.

"He didn't say ... you didn't ask him?"

"No. I mean, they were fighting a lot, not getting along, standard stuff."

"That's too bad. I really liked her. Did you meet his new girlfriend?"

"She wasn't there," I said, "but he's coming to New York with her this weekend. And he wants us to meet her. He invited us to dinner this Friday. What do you think?"

"Sounds great," she said. "Let's do it.""

"Well, they'll probably want to go out afterward. Y'know, the four of us. They'll still be on Cali-time. So, like an all-night kind of thing."

"Yeah, sure," she said, cheerfully. "Sounds fun."

"Great" I said. "Yeah, I'm sure it will be. Ryan will be psyched to hear we're a 'go.' That's great. So how's your day going?"

"Been a little odd, actually ... though nothing bad."

"Okay, odd how?"

"Just random," she said. "We had a fire drill this morning at work ...."

"Yeah?"

"And the fire captain was doing his safety spiel to my whole floor. And he saw me yawning and singled me out. Suddenly he's asking me safety questions in front of everyone. But somehow, I got them all right. So now I'm the official fire warden for the whole floor."

"What does that mean? Do you have to *do* anything?"

"During fire drills," she said, "I have to make sure everyone gets out of their offices and cubicles and go to the elevators."

"Elevators?" I said. "That's the last place you want to go."

"Yeah, I know. That's where the stairs are. Hey, I didn't get appointed warden for nothing. I just came back from training, actually."

"Fire warden training?"

"Yeah, it's a real thing. He's a real fireman. He reviewed the exits with me, including two I didn't know about. Had me test the call box. And gave me a whistle to blow."

"Wow," I said, stumbling a little. "Well, congratulations."

"Thanks. Something new for my résumé, right?"

"Oh sure," I said, with a laugh.

Which turned into a long pause.

"So," I said, "so … things are good? Last night was good?"

"Yeah, we went to Trattora's on Amsterdam."

"Sure, we've been there."

"Well yeah, we have. But we went before they changed owners. The food there now is oh-my-God amazing. This is the owner's third restaurant. He has two others downtown."

"How do you know that?"

"He came over and sat down … introduced himself. He was really cool and down to earth. Mike knows him. They're friends from college, I think."

"Oh," I said, scrambling for something to say. "So dinner was good?"

"*So* good."

Then I paused for a moment too long.

"Well, I know you're busy," she said. "I'll let you get back to practicing, but I just wanted to say good luck today."

"Yeah, okay, but …."

She waited for me to continue, then said, "But what?"

"But nothing," I said. "I mean, yeah … I have to really crank on this."

"Is there something you want to ask me?"

"What?"

"If there is, you can tell me."

My brain was racing. I dragged out an "uh …." and then started in: "I don't even know what I was gonna say. I think I was gonna ask you about your dinner … what you had that was so amazing. But you're right. Time's not my friend right now. Can I give you a call after this?"

"Sure," she said, "and good luck again. I'm sure you'll knock 'em dead."

"Thanks Ash, I'll let you know how it goes."

" 'Kay, well … I love you."

"I love you, Ash."

\* \* \*

I thought of what Ashley said and had to sit down. *Is there something you want to ask me?*

While not totally out of character, it wasn't something she'd typically say. I hadn't even started a question. Why leap to that assumption? Could she possibly think I wanted to ask her *Mike's* question? That I wanted to see her get fucked in front of me? Or that I was gonna say it now … and here of all places? *Yeah, Ash, now that you mention it, there is something I want to ask you.* Like I would possibly say that.

Maybe Mike said something. Told her I wanted to ask her a question. *Who the fuck knows?* I thought. She may well have meant nothing by it. Just like her being chosen the new fire warden at work. That should be a major nothing. A cute little story to tell her friends. Like she just happened to get picked. But the fireman was not gonna be picking someone like me. Not when there was a hot young big-titted brunette in the front row. I wondered if he was thinking, *Maybe I can fuck her.* Or if he cared she was married. Picking my wife for his personal instruction.

I was grateful though, that Friday night was locked in. That part couldn't have gone any better. Ashley had committed to it, and she didn't bail on things. I thought about it. That meant there'd be no Mike the first two nights. We'd have some normalcy. I'd sleep in my bed with my wife. We'd have time to catch our breath. Talk.

But I knew that back home I'd be facing the public side of all of this. Mike would be pushing for the three of us to go out. I didn't want to be running into people I knew. Like being out to dinner and having to say, "And this is our friend,

Mike." I didn't want to be seen as accepting it. Like to my doormen, who already had to be talking.

I knew I had to confront him. And talk to Ashley. Explain the risk of people gossiping. She couldn't want that. That's when I realized, Mike would probably say he understands. And then propose his friend's restaurant. Say how private it was.

I wondered how close Mike was with the owner ... if they hung out much ... if he'd already told him about me.

Mike's owner friend might have already known, when he talked to Ashley, that she was currently cucking her husband. He might be saying things to Mike like, "Bring him by. I want to meet this pussy. I want to shake hands with this chump."

I thought about Mike asking me, *How was your first night away from Ashley?* He wanted to hear that I'd been jerking off. That question would've been next, I figured. And had I jerked off to the photo he sent? He'd want that detail. He'd press for more, probably. And tell me it was "all good."

I pictured him talking to me:

*"You're been cucked, bro, accept it. It's who you are now. Keep up the jerk-fests thinking about how royally you've been cucked. By a real fucking man. A man you can't possibly measure up to. A big-dicked alpha motherfucker who played you for the cuckold you are. Manned you down every step of the way. Made you a cuckold in front of your wife. I made it happen, bro. I got you to introduce me to your wife. And got you to leave us alone together. I got you to fucking wait outside like a little boy. That's when I knew I'd be taking your wife's pussy from you."*

"Jesus fucking Christ, c'mon!" I said aloud, standing up. "Fucking seriously!"

I had a boner. I grabbed a pad to cover it, in case anyone walked in. I went back to practicing. At first I was on autopilot. But I focused and got into a rhythm in my second run-through. I was feeling like I knew it. Even the Q&A seemed as good as it could be.

I thought of the men's room a few yards down the hall. And how I was in a somewhat remote part of the hotel. But I couldn't get past the headline in my head:

EXECUTIVE CAUGHT MASTURBATING IN FOUR SEASON'S MEN'S ROOM
One Hour before Delivering Company Speech

So I blocked it out and practiced my opening. Just a few sentences. Who I was, why I was there, and that my boss was feeling better. Brief and direct. Wasn't taking chances.

* * *

I felt like I was coming from backstage, walking down the hotel hallway, using the back entrance to get into the ballroom.

I saw an IT guy waving me over, telling me to take the stage so they could test everything. They gave me a thumbs-up, but they let me keep rehearsing, getting used to the teleprompter.

I didn't want to be practicing as people came in, so I stopped halfway through and looked out at the hugeness of the room. It had me nervous, thinking of the seats filling up. But I did feel prepared. Almost like, *Bring it on.*

I went out the front way and walked into the lobby … and saw maybe twenty-five people, mostly men in suits, talking among themselves, drinking coffee.

The head of our L.A. office spotted me and called me over. He introduced me as the guy who'd be speaking. One of them asked how Brian was doing, and I said he was a lot better. Then they seemed to want details on what had happened. I didn't know if kidney stones were something I should be talking about; I thought of Ryan and his tonsils.

"You'll have to excuse me," I said. "I'm being called."

I shook their hands and said, "And Brian's doing great."

I had just started to walk away when I saw Mia making her way through the revolving door.

"Jack's coming," she said, as she hurried over.

"He's not here?"

"He's on his way," she said. "Five minutes."

I heard Joanne addressing the group. "Could everyone please come in and get seated? We're going to be getting started soon."

I turned back to Mia. "Five minutes? So that means what … he'll make it for Q&A?"

"No, he's right behind me," she said. "They took the cab right after us. He won't be late; he's introducing you."

"He is?"

"Yeah."

"Would've been nice to know," I said. "Is there anything else I should know … or any last-minute instructions?"

"I don't think so," she said, "but let's check with Joanne."

We waited for Joanne to finish her greetings, and I counted the number of people in the room. Twenty-nine.

"Is this normal?" I said as she walked up. "Does it fill up at the last minute?"

"What do you mean?"

"Is this it … or are more people coming?"

"I'm sure there's more coming," she said, "and weather delays."

"Like a lot more?"

"What do you mean by a lot?"

"I thought there'd be at least a hundred people here."

Joanne looked at Mia, as if asking for help.

"Well," Mia said, "Jack's bringing his sales team."

"But they're just paid bodies," I said, "cheerleaders."

"The thing is," Joanne said, "a lot of people just come for the luncheon."

"Really? I wish I knew this yesterday."

"But then," Joanne said, "you wouldn't be as prepared as you are right now."

"Hey look," Mia said patting my shoulder, "at the side door. That's three more walking in, Dave."

"Yeah," Joanne said, "and two women, main door."

Then Jack walked in, spotted us, and came down the side aisle.

"Hey Dave," he said, shaking my hand. "Really thought I'd be earlier. Just getting a cab took forever. How are you? Are you ready to go?"

"Yeah," I said. "So *you're* going to introduce me?"

"Yeah, I'll say few words about Brian. How well he's recovering. Then I'll say a few words about you and your role on the project."

I looked at him puzzled. I didn't think he was sure about what my role actually was.

"Brian sent it to me," he added.

"Oh, okay," I said. "So should I just go straight into it?"

"Yeah … unless you have a joke you want to open with."

I laughed and said, "No."

I saw him looking at the crowd and felt as if I should state the obvious. "Kind of a modest turn-out, huh?"

"I don't know," Jack said, "considering the rain, the short week, and people probably heard that Brian wasn't speaking …."

"Oh," I said, "did people hear that?"

"Nothing against you. Brian's well-connected, so he's gonna draw."

"Of course."

"So last night got washed out, but how 'bout tonight? Are you free for dinner?"

"Yeah," I said. "You bet, Jack, sure."

"Let's say seven o'clock," he said, turning to Mia. "Can

62

you … get us a table at Canyon for seven?" She nodded and pulled out her phone.

"Excuse me," Jack said. "I see someone I need to talk to."

I turned and looked at Joanne.

"I get barely one minute with him," I said. "Can you believe that? What are the odds he's gonna blow me off for dinner?"

"Who cares?" Joanne said. "Don't let it distract you from your objective right now … of kicking butt up there."

I laughed. "You're right."

"You're gonna run circles around them up there today."

"Yeah," I said, "and it's only like thirty people when you don't count our office."

"Meaning it's nothing, right? Like, you can handle that?"

"Yeah, I mean, sure, it's less scary. But I'm not taking it for granted. A small group can throw as many curve balls."

"Mia's calling us," she said. "It's time to go on."

"Yeah, thanks."

"You're going to do great, Dave," she said, giving me a hug, "Just get on up there and kick some ass."

I laughed and said, "Okay."

# CHAPTER NINE

I felt my shoulders tighten as Jack started talking. He was a natural public speaker. And very dynamic—even when he was just reading what Brian had written. I didn't pay attention to what he was saying. I just kind of braced myself, and repeated in my head: *Thank you Jack, and thanks to all of you for coming out this morning.* I didn't want to waste their time, even commenting about the rain.

Jack said my name and I walked out and took the podium. I saw my opening line on the teleprompter all cued up. And I looked briefly out at the audience, the ton of empty chairs, and said my greeting.

Within seconds, I was at ease with the teleprompter. Plus, I knew what I was reading—like inside out. I made sure not to talk too fast, or to utter an "uh." I felt my pace slow and realized I was now feeling comfortable. I emphasized key words as I spoke. Took a pause with charts to let people absorb the information. Felt I was on a roll, got a boost of confidence for Q&A.

As I was getting to the conclusion page, I saw a man standing in the side aisle, talking on his phone. Whenever I paused, I could hear him. I took my eye off to look at him and I stumbled over the word *cannibalization*. So I just focused on the prompter and felt I recovered.

I said I'd be happy to answer questions. The first one, on methodology, I welcomed. It was uncontroversial, I was well versed, and I could go on for a couple minutes like I really knew what I was talking about. The second one on risk factors

I also welcomed; I had just reviewed it. The third was a little trickier. I was murky on what I could disclose and knew I'd have to be a little cautious in my reply.

And that's when I saw the man on the side, back on his phone again. I didn't even think about it; I just turned toward him.

"Excuse me, sir …yes you," I said, nodding. "I'm giving a formal presentation here and you're talking on your cellphone which is—"

"I'm sorry," he said, and put up his hands like he'd put it away.

"I understand if it's important—you can talk on the phone outside—but it's really distracting when …."

I watched him take a seat and pretend to ignore me.

"Sir," I said, "I'd really appreciate if you just …" and I gestured to the door.

He gave me a glare but stood back up and walked out.

When I turned back, a few people even clapped.

Suddenly, I thought, *Who the fuck is he? Is he important?*

"I'm sorry," I said, and tried to smile, "can you repeat the question?"

But the curve balls never came. Not softballs either. Just stuff I was prepared to answer.

I felt relief when no more hands went up. "Well, thank you very much," I said, and walked off the stage.

Mia flashed me two thumbs-up and some guys from IT shook my hand.

I walked onto the floor and Jack waved me over. He was with three guys from his team. He smiled, shook my hand and said, "Terrific job today, Dave, and love what you did to Sabio."

"The guy on the phone," I said. "Was that bad?"

"It was fucking awesome," one of the sales guys said.

"Who is he?" I asked. "Not someone big?"

"He works at Jakston," another said, "and he's a fucking douche. Everyone at Jakston knows he's a douche."

"It was great," Jack said, pulling me aside. "Sabio totally

deserved it. Like who the hell does that? Someone's speaking and you're on your cellphone? Good for you, you didn't let him just sit back down—"

"Yeah," I said, with a nervous laugh, "that wasn't too much?"

"It was perfect, Dave. People will forget your talk tomorrow, but what they won't forget is you showing Sabio the exit door ... hell, they applauded you."

"Wow," I said, "cool."

A few people came up to me and introduced themselves. And one econ-professor type asked if he could ask a follow-up question. Which led to more questions and him blabbing on about some Swedish economist. But I was glad just to be done. And that it went well. It was a big-time relief. I pictured Joanne coming up behind me with a barrel of Gatorade.

* * *

I walked into the atrium and saw my boss calling from New York.

"Brian," I said, picking up.

"Dave, how you doing? Listen, I just wanted to thank you for stepping up today. I just heard you did well."

"Oh, thanks," I said. "Anytime. I was just glad I could help. But how are you doing?"

"Still weak, but a lot better, thanks. This time yesterday, though, I thought I was dying. I can't tell you how insanely painful that was. Thought for sure it was a heart attack. But Nancy was here and she used to be a nurse. She knew right away ... kidney stones."

"Jeez, sounds awful," I said. "I'm just glad you're feeling better. Is there anything you need? Do you know when you're getting out?"

"That's the thing," he said, "They're telling me p.m. tomorrow. And I have a committee meeting in the morning. I'd really like for you to be there. You have anything critical still going on?"

"Not really, no. I have a dinner with Jack tonight. That's it, as far as significant things."

"Can you make it a lunch?"

"He's got a 12:30 in Palo Alto. He may have already left, actually."

"Okay," he said, matter-of-fact. "So you'll have dinner next time. Just find a flight that'll get you back tonight. And no red-eye."

"Sure. Just gotta grab my bags from the hotel. Then it's straight to the airport."

"Great" he said. "I'll forward the materials, so you can review on the plane. We don't have much influence—it's fairly peripheral—but we always want to have a presence. Oh, and abstain on the vote."

"You got it," I said. "I'll be there."

"Cool. Well, I have a bunch of calls to return, but good job today."

"Thanks Brian. And really glad to hear you're feeling better."

I put my phone in my coat pocket and just stood there in the lobby. I was going home. I couldn't believe it. I pulled out my cue cards and was looking for a place to toss them when I saw Joanne.

"We're all set," she said. "Nine o'clock at Pearl. And you're safe. They do have karaoke, but not on Tuesday nights. I double-checked."

"Well—"

"Just come by after your dinner. We have a big group going."

"It sounds awesome, Joanne. But I'm afraid I can't go now. I just got called back to New York."

"What?"

"Brian's in the hospital till at least tomorrow, and he wants me back now."

"*Now* as in, you're jumping on the next flight?"

"Unfortunately, yeah. Brian didn't even want me going back for my bags. I mean, of course I am. But after that, I'm gone."

"God, that sucks. I was really looking forward to hanging out tonight."

"Oh, me too. I'm really bummed. I'm done with my speech finally, and all I wanted was to kick back and have some fun tonight. Y'know, with you and my SF peeps."

"Me too," she said, "and you just got here."

"Well, I'll be back next month, and we'll definitely kick it then."

"We have to," she said. "Let me know when you know your dates."

"I will. Tell everyone hi from me."

"I will," she said, "So, quick question: what are you going to remember to do as soon as you get back to New York?"

I smiled, trying to read her expression. "Enroll in skydiving lessons?"

"Well, that too, sure. But also just Google skydiving in Hawaii, Christmas week. And read up on all the beginner options. I'm telling you, that will make your two-year anniversary unbelievably amazing."

"I'm with you," I said. "I'm gonna look into it right when I get home tonight."

She narrowed her eyes. "You're not really going to look into it, are you?"

"What are you talking about?" I said. "I'm gonna research it. This week. I'm sure it's amazing, and you're right. Ashley would freaking love that."

"Oh hell yeah, she would. She'd be super-stoked. So start planning it now. And no over-thinking ... just do it."

"Yeah, you've got me interested."

"Hey, Jack looks like he's leaving."

"What?" I said, turning around. "I thought he'd left. I have to go. I'm sorry."

"I'll see you in a few weeks," she said, giving me a hug. "And you kicked ass up there today, champ."

"Thanks, Joanne." I hustled across the lobby and stopped him just before the revolving doors.

"Jack," I said loudly, "I know you're in a huge hurry, but I just talked to Brian—"

"Yeah," he said, moving us to the corner, "How's he doing?"

"He's a lot better, but won't be released until late tomorrow. He needs me to fill in on some things there. He wants me to fly back this afternoon."

"Wow," he said, with a wry smile. "So you're out of here?"

"Just grabbing my bags, yeah."

"So much for getting together—"

"I know," I said. "This was so last-minute. And with the storm and Brian in the hospital …."

"Hey, I understand. We'll have dinner next time."

"Definitely."

"Well, great job today," he said, shaking my hand. "Good travels home, man."

* * *

I felt like saying "hallelujah" when I got in the cab. My speech had gone great. I'd filled in for my boss. Come through in a crunch. Represented well. That's what I hoped was the takeaway.

And it was over. No more speech-stressing. I felt so much calmer. I loosened my tie, stretched, and looked out the window. The view was dreary—people rushing in the rain. I was taking solace in going home. Then I started asking myself, *"But going home to fucking what?"*

Ashley seeing Mike this evening, seemed like a done deal. I figured the odds of her canceling were dismally low. Even if I told her I was on my way home, and really tired,

Mike would still be there. I'd be going back to my wife being fucked. I'd end up on the couch again.

Unless I said something. And spoke from the heart, maybe. That I want to be alone with her tonight … that it was my first night back. That I'd barely slept. How it would mean a lot to me.

But she'd want to have the "talk" as soon as I got home. I wasn't ready for that. I wanted just to relax on the plane, not sweat the trip to JFK. So, I'd have to somehow get across I just wanted to chill, drink some wine, save the "talk" for the following night. But that didn't seem very realistic. Especially drinking. The subject would be too big an elephant—she'd have to bring it up.

I thought of not telling Ashley I was flying home and getting a hotel room in the city, but couldn't justify the expense. Then I thought of my parent's house in the suburbs—the house I grew up in. I was pretty sure my parents would still be at their condo in Florida. The house would be empty. I could be by myself. I had clothes for tomorrow. I could expense the cab ride to Westchester. I'd get some quiet time to regroup and prepare. I could sit out on the patio and look up at the stars.

It seemed a great back-pocket, but I had to make sure.

So I crossed my fingers and texted my mom. "Are you back home or still away?"

"Florida thru Friday."

"I'm in SF," I texted back. "Brian's out sick. I had to fill in last-minute. Flying back to NYC now. I may have to fly into Westchester from DC late night."

"Why don't you stay at the house?" she replied.

"That's what I'm thinking. Probably will. Same alarm code?"

"Yes, starts with your grandmother's birthday."

"Got it—thanks. Headed to airport now. If I get home late, I'll stay at the house. Enjoy the ocean & love you, Mom."

# CHAPTER TEN

I hurried into my hotel and hustled down the hallway to my room. I wasn't scheduled to check out until tomorrow. And I didn't have a specific flight to catch—whatever was available.

*I don't need to be rushing*, I told myself as I got out of my suit. I looked at the bed and grabbed my laptop. I pulled up the photo of Ashley from the night before—at the restaurant, smiling. I wondered if the owner had taken it. Or if Mike told him he was sending it to me.

I could hear Mike suggesting we go there. And Ashley telling me how much I was gonna love it, how amazing the food was. Like I gave two craps. I wondered if the owner flirted with her, if he knew she was married. If Mike had told him the situation.

I imagined returning to my apartment from JFK later. I'd have to tell her in advance that I was coming. Which probably would change nothing. Mike would still stay over. I could picture it. I'd get in after midnight. The bedroom door would be closed.

If I yelled "hello," they'd probably acknowledge me. Mike would want to play the good guy buddy. Ashley might bust open champagne. In our kitchen, wearing a sexy new robe. And we'd all talk like it was normal. They'd ask me about my speech and say congratulations. Mike might offer some small talk about the Yankees. But fifteen minutes later, I'd be alone in the kitchen, music playing from my bedroom.

I found myself talking to Ashley in the picture as she

looked happily back at me. "Even if I did show up tonight," I said, "you'd go on with the cucking, wouldn't you, Ash? There'd be no canceling Mike. Forget it. It's his fucking bedroom tonight, no matter what, isn't it?

"Of course that's what you'd do," I continued, staring at her tits. "I'd be on the fucking couch. Don't tell me I wouldn't. There'd be no 'Sorry Mike, Dave's coming home early and really needs to sleep in his own bed tonight.' 'Cause Ashley Martens wants to get good and fucked tonight. Doesn't care if her husband's humiliated. She never has.

"I let this happen, Ash, I know. I got totally played. I let him out-man me in front of you. I let him make me a total chump. I allowed him into my apartment and let him dominate me. You saw it all, Ash. You saw me stripped of my dignity. Belittled and dispensed with.

"And now I can't come home, 'cause Mike will be in our bed, balling you. Owning your pussy for the second night in a row. Establishing himself as a fixture in our bedroom, our marriage. Do you even give a fuck, Ashley?"

"Or do you just love Mike's big fat cock just so fucking much that you can't deprive your pussy of such a fantastic fuck? Is doing it in a way that humbles and humiliates me a fucking bonus? Or is that part of the thrill, Ash? Seeing my manhood freaking eviscerated. Is that part of the fun? Seeing another man boss me around in my own home. Locking me out of my bedroom. So he can fuck what I practically gave him … my wife's precious fucking pussy.

"What the fuck have I done," I said, still talking to myself. "I let myself get cucked so fucking hard. My wife taken from me, fucked hard in my bed … regardless of me coming home. And my bedroom would be his … like standard fucking protocol … my wife now Mike's possession … and cuckolds sleep on fucking couches."

I looked in Ashley's eyes and suddenly came.

* * *

I didn't want to think about it, and besides, I told myself, "I have a plane to catch."

I didn't have to rush, but I wanted to. Whatever time I lingered would have to be made up on the back end. I'd be arriving late in New York as it was.

I was out the door and walking through the lobby five minutes later. Even though the rain was picking up, I lucked into a cab dropping people off.

I felt like I was really coming up for air. The presentation was over and I was going home, even if it was Westchester.

I was about to close my eyes and put on my headphones when I heard my phone. It was my brother calling.

"Hey Sean," I said.

"Hey bro, wow—you picked up."

"Like what, I'm gonna screen you? You always *text* me—you never actually *call* me. So what's the deal, what's going on?"

"Just wanted to see if you're going Saturday."

"To Mom and Dad's?" I said. "You bet."

"Cool. And also, how's your Sunday night looking? If I stay in town, could I stay at your place? Probably won't need to, but would that be cool?"

"Sunday night," I said. "Yeah, sure. You'll let me know?"

"Yeah," he said, "at the cookout Saturday."

"Sounds good," I said.

"And remind me to tell you about Badger."

"Is he okay?"

"Yeah."

"So tell me now," I said. "I'm in the back of a cab. I could use a good Badger story. Was he arrested or something?"

"No, nothing bad. You remember how he and I tag-teamed that bride-to-be in Vegas?"

"The engaged girl … you and Badger … brought back to our hotel room. Of course I remember."

"Well, she's not engaged anymore. She canceled her wedding to be with the Badge."

"Yeah, okay, sure."

"No bullshit. It's true."

"What?"

"I'm telling you," he said, "she broke off her engagement. She's seeing the Badge now."

"I don't get it, man. Badger said he came in her face. He said she was fucking furious at him. Didn't he throw her fucking clothes in the hallway and basically tell her to get the fuck out?"

I could hear Sean laughing.

"And now," I said, "she's breaking off her wedding—an event she's spent all year working on, probably—to be with the fucking Badge?"

"Maybe she was gonna break it off anyway."

"So what if she was, man? The girl went to UCLA, probably from a well-off family, right? Like, what are her friends saying? She leaves her fiancé to be with some scumbag she met in Vegas—"

"Hey, the Badge ain't no scumbag—"

"Everyone in her bachelorette party must know the story. Her friends must think she's out of her mind."

"You never know. Friends tend to like the Badge."

"Yeah, okay, whatever," I said. "So what's the deal now? Is she like, totally in love with him? I just don't get how that happens."

"I know. He's a charmer. The kid's good."

"Hey," I said, "can you hold? I've got Ashley calling."

"No worries man. I'll see you Saturday."

"Just wait. I'll be two seconds."

"Gotta run anyway little bro—go talk to your wife. I'll see you this weekend."

* * *

I had wanted to tell Ashley I was on the phone and I'd call her back. And have time to think. I was about to let it go to voicemail when I picked up.

"Hey, Ash."

"Hey Dave, so how'd it go?"

"Really well, thank you."

"Awesome, baby."

"Yeah," I said, "It was a smaller turn-out than I expected—like seventy-five."

"Well, that's more people than I've ever spoken in front of. Were you nervous?"

"I really wasn't, actually. Once I started talking, it went fine. Didn't get stumped on questions. Oh, and I called someone out in the audience for talking on their cellphone."

"You what? Really? While you were on stage?"

"Yeah, during Q&A, I didn't know who he was, but Jack and a few others here did. And they think the guy's an a-hole. So I got major props for doing that."

"Wow," she said. "Did you know who he was?"

"No," I said, "I only found out when they told me. But he was being so freaking rude, talking on the phone like that…I don't think I over-reacted."

"I think it was badass," she said, "I love it."

"Yeah, thanks," I said. "I think today I showed people … y'know, that I can fill in for Brian in a last minute crisis. That I can be counted on."

"I like that," she said. "It's heroic. That is so awesome, sweetie. Congratulations! So, what's the rest of your day like?"

"Meetings mostly—back at the office. How about you?"

"The same—pretty busy. Hopefully the afternoon will fly. You have dinner plans?"

"Yeah, with Jack."

"Awesome. And fresh off your speech. It's perfect

timing. When you're at dinner tonight, you should be talking with some serious swagger."

"What?"

"I'm sure you were a star up there today. He probably sees you as a total peer now."

"Probably not, but I know what you mean. It was high profile. I can have a little VIP attitude tonight, right?"

"Exactly. And make it clear from the get-go that you expect top-shelf everything. And you're there to do the talking—not him. Whenever he thinks you're about to *stop* talking, just say 'and another thing Jack ....' "

"Yeah," I said, "and I'll say how I'm the 'brains' behind New York corporate. And how even some initiative from another department, originally ... yup, that was my idea, too."

Ashley laughed and we got quiet for a moment.

"So" she said, "I'm not meeting Mike out tonight, by the way."

"No?" I said.

"No, he'll just come by later. I'm meeting Tamara out for drinks and Mexican. And Caroline also—it's her birthday."

"Oh wow," I said, "Sounds fun. Do I know Caroline?"

"You'd know her if you saw her—she works in Tamara's department. You've met her at happy hours. She just turned twenty-nine."

"Okay," I said. "Well tell them I said 'hi' and 'happy birthday.' "

"I will. Still raining there?"

"Yeah, but not pouring—just steady. I have to say Ash, I'm so looking forward to seeing you tomorrow."

"Me too," she said. "Do you know if you want to stay in or go out?"

"Well, maybe stay in. A bottle of wine up on the roof?"

"Yeah," she said. "I like that—should be nice out."

"Yeah, I checked—shorts and t-shirt weather."

"Awesome."

My cab driver turned back and began asking me what terminal my flight was. I didn't want Ashley hearing I was going to the airport—so I put out my hand to get him to stop. Then I said, "Okay" loudly to muffle his question.

"Ashley," I said, "can I call you right back?"

"I'm actually already late to a meeting."

"I got ya—okay. Well, really looking forward to seeing you tomorrow, and love you, Ash."

"Love you too. And congrats again, rock star."

"Thanks" I said, with a laugh. "Bye."

* * *

I looked out the cab window at the traffic and the rain. I tried to temper my what-the-fuck feeling, thinking of tomorrow night, out on the roof, under the moon ... alone with Ashley. I was psyched and relieved that she was up for that. It was one big, bright spot in my current situation.

But other things had me reeling. Like Ashley telling me she was meeting Tamara for Happy Hour drinks. *Why the fuck now?* I thought. Right in the middle of two nights with Mike in my home—Tamara maybe knowing—I'm in the midst of a major freaking cuck-storm. Worked over good. I pictured Ashley smiling as she kicked back with Tamara, laughing and carefree ... knowing what she was making me.

I figured Tamara had to know something. And would get Ashley talking over margaritas. Tamara might well know what happened—that I'd been outmanned, locked out of my bedroom, stripped of my dignity in front of my wife. Tamara maybe knew Ashley was fucking Mike while I was away—with my supposed acceptance.

Tamara would love that. I could hear her laughing at me, saying, "Dave's a bigger pussy than I even thought." I could picture Ashley laughing back and saying, "I know." Tamara could influence her. Like the night it all started. Telling me to take a hike. Sending me upstairs. So she could watch my wife get fucked—bare, in a ratty bathroom, by a junior sales guy. I wondered if she'd marveled at how easily it happened.

Or if she knew the details of the past week—Ashley's weekend shopping spree, new clothes for Mike. How he'd taken her Sunday to the U.S. Open. How they'd made out in front of me beforehand. And had me take their photo. How I was left to sleeping on a fucking couch.

Tamara would eat that up. She'd be Ashley's biggest cheerleader. I imagined overhearing their conversation.

"So," Ashley would say, "I have the talk with Dave tomorrow, and then maybe this weekend, we'll take it to another level."

"Meaning what?" Tamara would say, grinning.

"Well, Mike wants Dave to watch us. Wants him to see me getting fucked. Says I'll really have cucked him then."

"I love it," Tamara would say. "You're gonna fuck another man in front of your husband. When?"

"I'm waiting for Dave to ask me. Mike says he will. He wants it coming from Dave. Says it's a cuckold admission he wants Dave to make."

"Nice! Make him beg for the privilege of seeing you fucked."

"As soon as Dave finally asks me, Mike wants me taking him chair shopping. Something for Dave to sit in when I'm being fucked in front of him."

"Get a photo of him like that—and tell him to suck his thumb."

"Well, I think—even more humiliating—we're gonna have him jerking off. Sitting in his cuckold chair. I swear to God, Tamara, I'm gonna look him right in his eyes as he watches me getting fucked. By a real man. I'll stare him down hard, as he gets dominated and pussified right in front of me."

"Cuck him hard, Ash, no let-up. Show him what kind of a pussy he really is."

*Good God*, I said to myself, as I noticed the terminal signs beginning.

# CHAPTER ELEVEN

The earliest flight I could get was three hours later. But I didn't mind really. I had a seat, so no flying standby. And once I got through security, I could relax, eat a burger, have a beer.

The security line would've freaked me out if I'd been running late. It snaked around pretty good just to get to the actual main line. But I looked at the big picture: I was going home.

The guy in front of me complained to an agent about some people being allowed to cut the line, and others started joining in. But I kind of ignored it all and rolled with the snail's pace. I got all of my work calls out of the way—to my team in New York, mostly. And got back to a few pressing emails.

Pretty soon I was putting my belt back on and tying up my shoes and grabbing my bags. I'd never been in that terminal before, but there was a restaurant right near my gate.

In the back was a long bar, and I found a seat by the end. A lot of people seemed alone, looking at their phones or tablets. I pretended to be preoccupied as well. I felt relaxed. I could chill. And someone striking up small talk seemed pretty unlikely.

I ordered a big beer and a cheeseburger. And had a shot when the bartender said it was only three dollars more.

I thought about how Ashley casually told me, Mike would be *stopping by later*. I figured she meant as opposed to them being out in public. Like Mike had talked to her. And she wanted to ease my concern. But the other meaning was obvious. Like she hadn't finished her sentence. *He'd be stopping by later to fuck her.*

It would be Mike's fourth night in my bed … in a week. He was basically living with Ashley in my home while I'm away. I wondered if he went to work from my place in the morning. After giving Ashley a wake-up fuck. It seemed logical. He probably had one of his suits up in my closet. Had maybe used my razor.

I thought about Ashley being with Tamara by now. I wondered if the birthday girl might be a buffer. 'Cause I didn't think Ashley would talk about me with Caroline there. Especially now, since the rumor.

Caroline was Tamara's friend. They worked in Promotions. She was a cute, short-haired brunette. We'd talked a little at Ashley's work happy hours. I thought she was pretty nice and friendly. Which was kind of surprising, her being friends with Tamara.

She was there the night of the party. I remembered complimenting her on her Yankee cap, and then later, I saw her in the kitchen with Ashley. I figured Caroline had to know the details of how my wife was fucked—if she blew him, if was there was dirty talk, what had been going on when I knocked.

Then I thought of Jim Murta blabbing about it to his friends. He must've savored that fuck. Ashley was higher ranked at work. She was the hot director down the hall. He was nailing the married girl with her husband right outside.

"You're practically newlyweds," I imagined him telling me. "That made taking Ashley's pussy even better. I was fucking your bride, dude, in a run-down little bathroom. While upstairs you took a piss, oblivious, I was going balls deep in your wife's sweet puss. That's when Ashley Martens really got her fuck on. I loved getting her to cheat on you in such a slutty, disrespectful way. Her bra and thong strewn on the floor. And no condom, that was the cherry on top, blasting my sperm inside your girl. Pulled my cock back out only after I was good and done. I love that I balled your wife right under your nose. Everyone at work knows that I slutted out your wife, dude. Ashley Martens … married … company cock whore."

I suddenly realized the bartender was talking to me.

"Sir, can I get you another beer?"

"Huh? Yeah, please."

"And another shot?"

"Sure," I said, "why not?"

* * *

Before boarding, I took a long piss in the men's room, washed my face, and chewed on some mints. I arrived at the gate just as my section was called.

I headed for my seat—a middle one in the back. Two heavy men sat in my row, on the aisle and window. I saw them yapping back and forth as I got close. They both had beards and looked like brothers. As I got to my row, I said, "26E" and the guy by the window took his bag off my seat.

I said, "excuse me" to the guy in the aisle seat next to me, but he barely moved. Then they both hogged my armrests. But on the plus side, I thought, it could have been a hot girl asking to change her seat, because I reeked of alcohol.

*I could give two fucks*, I thought, *what these fat fuck shit-kickers think*. So I ordered a double vodka on the rocks, downed it quickly, put on my headphones, and somehow fell asleep.

I couldn't believe it when I woke up and saw we were over Scranton, Pennsylvania. I'd never slept on a plane like that—and in the middle seat, no less. And I wasn't sore from sleeping at a peculiar angle. My foot wasn't asleep, and I had no drool on me. I actually felt well rested. I heard the pilot say, "We're making our initial descent," and smiled.

I checked my phone as soon as we landed. New text messages started showing up. Joanne sent me a photo of office people out on the town, hoisting beer mugs. Said I was missed.

I had a text from Ashley. "Sorry we couldn't talk earlier. Hope you're having a great night and can't wait to see you tomorrow. Love you."

Then came the text from Mike. "At your apartment now. Do you want to see a picture of how Ashley looks tonight?"

It was from four hours ago. I texted back, "Sorry, big work dinner. Just saw your text, yeah, you can send it."

I waited for a response. I wanted to see the fucking thing, see how she'd dressed for him. And what room in my apartment he took the photo in.

Then I texted Ashley back. "Thanks Ash, love you too. Tomorrow can't come soon enough."

* * *

I rolled down the window as I got in the cab. It felt good to be back. I looked at the signs for Manhattan. To me, they all said "Ashley." If I told the guy to keep going straight, I could be there in thirty minutes. I felt torn as he made the turn for the bridge. But as Westchester got closer, I was glad that's where I was going. It felt like my own Camp David retreat.

I liked looking outside as we drove through downtown. This was where I grew up. It was ghost-town dead at that hour. Even the bar was closed. But it sure looked peaceful.

I showed the cabbie the rest of the way and pointed out my house. It was past midnight—dark, lots of stars, and very quiet. The sound of my suitcase rolling up the driveway seemed too loud.

Once inside, I turned on the lights and yelled out "hello." I just didn't want surprises. So I did a quick check on all the rooms—second floor as well. I came back down, turned the TV on for background, and checked out my parents' liquor closet. They had Hendricks, so I made myself a gin martini and walked out on the deck. The woods out back were obscuring the moon, but it felt nice listening to crickets. It reminded me of being with Ashley.

I went back inside and tried one of my dad's Belgian beers. I walked into the living room and looked around. It felt weird being there alone.

On the fireplace mantle was a new photo of my dad and me, one I hadn't seen before. I picked it up and sat down in the light. It was from last Christmas, and we were posing in front of the tree. My dad had his arm around me and looked relaxed and happy. I did too.

I remembered when Ashley had taken it. We were just back from Christmas Eve mass. My dad and I were still in coat and tie. My brother was skiing in Colorado with his girlfriend, so it was just the four of us, having dinner and hanging out.

Ashley kept filling everyone's wine glass in between her playing piano. My mom took me aside at one point in the kitchen—telling me about starter homes she's seen. My dad talked to me in the car about his timeframe for retiring. Shared business lessons he'd learned. And said that nights like this were, "what it's all about." I remember thinking something I rarely think, that my life was progressing as planned … the way it was supposed to.

That any complaints I might have were petty. My family and friends were doing well. My career was on track. My marriage seemed incredibly strong. Over more wine, I told Ashley a version of that, after my parents went to bed. We toasted our happiness. She gave me a blowjob up in my room later. I was grateful for my life.

I noticed the piano and walked over, sat down. It's a

baby grand in great condition. I hadn't played it in years—not since I started seeing Ashley. Hearing me play once early on, she said I had "no rhythm or feeling." She apologized right after, and I shouldn't have cared—I knew I wasn't any good. I took a few lessons when I was twelve, and no one ever said I had talent.

So it shouldn't have bothered me, but it did. I was reluctant to play after that. Not even carols at Christmas. I avoided being asked. My mom played great and Ashley was a high school virtuoso. I was a rank amateur. I didn't want to wonder if my playing had "feeling." So I just didn't play.

*But damn*, I thought, *it's been a fucking long time.*

So I put my beer down and started in with a Counting Crows song I still remembered how to play. Then I searched in the linen closet down the hall and pulled out a box of old songbooks. I found my brother's guitar music from high school. Armed with The Doors' Greatest Hits, I grabbed another beer and went back to the piano.

I used to play from that book. I knew the songs. I tried the descending keyboard line in the opening of "Riders on the Storm"—a few fumbles at first, but it started coming back. Pretty soon I was working the bass line in and had it in synch, or so I thought.

I turned a few pages more till I came to "L.A. Woman." I took a good swig of my beer and got to work. I practiced the bass line and the lead that comes in at the beginning. I never quite got it, but then I just started singing.

I was subdued at first, singing like my parents were upstairs or like someone might walk through the door until I realized I could be as loud as I wanted. So I came in with swagger on the line about getting into town an hour ago. I was banging on the keys with my foot on the sustain pedal. I was belting it out—oh yeah—so alone. By the time I got to singing 'bout my mojo rising, I was howling it.

\* \* \*

It felt strange being in my old bedroom. I'd stayed with Ashley sometimes for holidays. But it had been a long time since I'd been in the house alone like this.

I looked at the boxes sitting next to my old desk. Things of mine from twenty-plus years ago. Like Mom was getting serious about cleaning the attic. I saw my globe of Mars on top. It was not much bigger than a softball. When I was ten, it was my favorite Christmas present. It had all the geography labeled. Like the names were worth knowing.

They all came back to me when I picked it up. Solis Planum, where I used to imagine my spaceship landing. Or Gale Crater—I'd calculated that to be an afternoon jeep ride. On the backside of Mars was a place called Hellas Basin. That's where the villains lived.

I looked at the name on the globe in the light. "Hellas Basin, Mars," I said quietly to myself, "should be my fucking forwarding address tonight."

I put the globe on a bookshelf and went into bed. I had a hard-on, which I kind of wanted to be able to ignore. Because it was just weird, being in my bed from high school. I thought of what the sixteen-year-old me would say if he could see me there now.

He probably wouldn't know what to say—it would sound too fucked up.

"*You see,*" I would explain to him, "*my wife's getting fucked in my Manhattan apartment, so I'm staying here, tonight, to give them privacy. So now I'm going to think of just how fucked up all this is and masturbate. And who's the guy fucking her? Oh, just some random guy I met online and introduced her to.*"

Mike would love hearing how I'd flown home early and stayed at my parents. He'd use it as another example of how big a pussy I am. He'd say I was too afraid to come home. How I knew better than to disturb him.

"You just didn't have the fucking balls," I imagined him saying.

"You could have come home, but you knew I'd be fucking your wife. And you knew where you'd be sleeping. And sure, you'd have a few minutes with Ashley—she'd feel obligated to hear about your trip. But you knew she'd grow impatient. You'd see it in her face—her eyes. The way she'd say 'uh-huh' without any follow-up questions. You'd know she was anxious to get back into the bedroom with me."

"You couldn't face that cuckold reality. Instead you took refuge in the house you grew up in, in your little boy room, in the bed your mom used to tuck you into.

"I'd have liked you showing up tonight, Dave. You coming home … to me in bed with your wife. The bedroom door shut, but unlocked. 'Cause we all know you don't have the balls to disturb us. Ashley would hand you a blanket and kiss you good night. That would be your welcome home. Doused again in your new identity. Dunked in the cuckold deep-end."

"Like you've escaped it by being there. Too afraid to come home. Jerking off in your childhood bed while I pump more sperm inside Ashley. Makes you even more aware of what a full-fledged cuckold you are. And what you are becoming.

"We're putting the smack-down on your cuckold ass, Dave. Two nights alone with Ashley—you must know we bonded real good. She's going to tell you tomorrow. She wants to cuck you hard.

"I'm gonna have you start thanking me. I took good care of Ashley while you were away. Kept her pussy nice and satisfied. And craving for more. Dreaming of my cock back up inside her. That's what she'll be thinking when she talks to you.

"Your wife's pussy is my possession, now, Dave. Ashley's

my personal fuck doll, my little blowjob bunny, the pussy I plant my seed in. And you're helpless to stop it. You know the road you're being sent down. The big fat horns you're growing into.

"And fuck yeah; you'll be watching. You'll be begging to see your wife get fucked. Knowing you'll be bare-ass on a hardwood chump chair. Knowing your wife will watch you jerk off as I ball her pussy hard.

"Think of Ashley's orgasms, her shuddering ecstasy, the way she'll cry my name … like you're not even there. Knowing she's humiliating you, reducing you as a man as I sperm your girl in your fucking bed."

I pictured Ashley writhing in orgasm, and suddenly came.

# CHAPTER TWELVE

I awoke in a panic when I saw the time. I'd fallen back asleep after shutting off my alarm. Now I was really cutting it close. I called for a cab to be in the driveway in fifteen minutes. Then I checked my phone for a photo from Mike—nothing.

I raced into the shower. Two minutes later, I was drying off and putting in my contacts. Shaving took the longest, because I always cut myself when I rushed. I was buttoning my shirt, looking out the window of my parents' bedroom, when I saw the cab. I'd had one leave on me before. And figured I could do my tie on the train.

I made sure I had everything like my wallet, phone, keys … but then realized I hadn't made my bed. It would be a dumbass reason to miss my train, but I didn't want my mom making it. I pulled the sheet up, crammed one side under the mattress, and reached for the blanket. Tried to even it out, but not really—I just didn't have time.

I barreled out the front door and ran toward the cab, constantly checking the time. I needed the two lights to be green. Even then, it was close. The station entrance was blocked with cars, and I saw the train coming around the bend.

I told the driver to keep the change, made a hundred-yard dash for the platform, and boarded with ten seconds to spare. Took a while to catch my breath. Went to the back of the train and found a seat.

I texted Mike: "Still haven't gotten photo. Did you send?"

I thought of calling Ashley—telling her I took the red-eye. I didn't want to lie and say I was just getting on the plane in San Fran. I wanted to be able to talk about the day honestly, to say that I was in New York, going to a big-shot committee event.

But I couldn't explain a train conductor announcing something in the background, so I held off calling Ashley.

I looked at the commuters getting on at the next station. At that hour it was mostly executive types. I had always expected that someday soon, that would be me.

Getting a house in the suburbs had always seemed like a foregone conclusion. As did having kids. Ashley wasn't in a rush, but a few years down the road had always been the plan. Now it seemed like more of an aspiration. As I watched more commuters get on, I started wondering, *Will I ever be one of them?*

It was another reason we needed to talk. I had to find out where I stood.

I knew some embarrassment was inevitable. Certain things I'd have to say. I'd have to acknowledge what had been going on, and my role in it. How naïve I'd been to trust him. And how lame I was now for not stopping it. That I knew they were having sex, that he was fucking her whenever he slept over. I couldn't pretend it wasn't happening.

What I wanted from Ashley was time. A break from Mike. Several days of just the two of us. I'd explain I wasn't talking forever—Mike would still be there, whenever.

Our relationship needed it, I'd tell her. Real husband and wife time. Togetherness. Like right the fuck now.

\* \* \*

I waited till I was out of Grand Central to give Ashley a call.

"Hey there, early bird," she said.

"Hey Ash," I said, "did I get you at work?"

"No, I'm getting a yogurt downstairs, but let me step outside."

I heard her heels clicking on the lobby floor as she walked out. "It's another beautiful day," she said. "What time's your flight?"

"It was supposed to be an hour from now, but Brian needed me here this morning ... so he called last night and said, 'Can you get your ass on a redeye in two hours?' "

"You're in New York?"

"Yeah, already landed, then a long wait for a cab from JFK. And now on my way to a meeting in midtown."

"Wow. Did you sleep?"

"Yeah, I did, actually—despite the middle seat. And I'm feeling okay. How are you?"

"I'm great," she said, "and really excited to see you tonight."

"Oh Ash, me too."

"I have a class I signed up for last month," she said, "so I'll be back by seven-thirty."

"Yeah, sure," I said. "Sounds good."

"What's your meeting for?"

"It's a policy group," I said, "a pretty high level committee, but I'm just going as Brian's representative."

"Don't minimize it," she said. "You're the face of your company today. It shows they have a lot of confidence in you."

"Oh, I know. I just meant these guys are like very senior, so I probably won't be contributing much, but it's still a good networking opportunity."

"Absolutely. That's great. And Brian owes you for hopping on the red eye."

"Definitely," I said. "Well, I'm at the building. I should probably get inside."

"Okay, see you tonight. Can't wait."

"Me too, Ash. Have a great day. Love you."

\* \* \*

Once inside the Yale Club, I was directed upstairs. I muted my phone and walked into a very grand conference room with huge arched windows and a super-high ceiling. Tables were lined up to form a big square. I took a seat on one of the corners after finding my name on the nameplate. Scanning the faces, I recognized no one. They were mostly older, everyone projecting importance.

They were all there to vote on accreditation for some new accounting methodology. But there was a lot to hash out before they'd declare a vote. I'd expected a heated debate, and there seemed to be, but the minutiae went over my head, and people seemed to drone on and on. I was pretty hungry, so I was glad when they broke for lunch at noon on the dot.

I waited for most of the others to stand before getting up myself and made my way to the buffet spread. Suddenly I saw a familiar face—a guy I used to work with—walking up to me. I was glad to see him.

"What's up, DM?"

"Hey Alan," I said. "What are you doing here?"

"I'm always at these," he said. "Why are you?"

"I'm filling in for my boss."

"That's right. Brian's usually here."

"So you always go to these?" I asked.

"My boss said last year that no fucking way was he sitting through another one of these things. So that's why *I'm* here."

I laughed. "Well, I hope Brian doesn't get any ideas like that. I mean, I like some geeky algebra, but this is way too deep in the weeds for me."

"Oh today's fucking brutal," he said. "It's going to a vote, that's why."

"I thought a vote would make it more interesting."

"Yeah, the last five minutes are, but the rest is just talking to be heard."

"I got you," I said. "So how are things?"

"Good, I've been meaning to email you. My wife and I

moved to your neighborhood this summer. We're by the 79th Street subway—like a block from the station."

"Oh yeah?"

"Yeah, well you know my wife, Megan."

"Yeah, sure," I said.

"Megan thought she saw Ashley out shopping the other weekend. But she hadn't seen her since you guys got married, so she wasn't sure. You play cards?"

"What, like poker?"

"Yeah," he said. "I'm trying to get a group together at my place, a once a month kind of thing."

"I don't think so, man. I barely know how to play."

"So what? You'll learn. It's fun. Drink some beers, shoot the shit—"

"Maybe a guest appearance some night."

"Yeah, okay. Or we can have you and Ashley over for dinner."

"Sure," I said, "anytime. If you just want to watch football, there's some decent bars in the neighborhood."

"Sounds like a plan," he said. "Well, I gotta make some calls before this starts up again."

"Yeah, me too. See you back in there."

\* \* \*

I went outside the building to check my voicemail and found one from Mike, sent an hour earlier. "Hey bro, what's with the radio silence? I want to know how your speech went, man, so hit me back."

I thought it important I keep up the pretence of our relationship. To have a window into how he saw things. I called him back.

"There he is," he responded.

"Hey, Mike, sorry. I've been crazed. I took the fucking red-eye last night."

"You're in New York?"

"Yeah, in a meeting."

"Cool, let's meet for a quick drink after work. Before you see Ash."

"I'm beat. All night in the fucking middle seat."

"I'm buying, bro. I want to hear about your presentation."

"Oh, it was nothing, man. It went well. Small turn-out, I wasn't nervous, it was good."

Mike laughed. "You're talking to Ashley tonight. And I thought you might want my take on things, or if I can help, y'know …. C'mon, one fucking beer."

"Uh, yeah, okay."

"Cool, same place as Monday, five-thirty."

"Yeah, sure," I said. "But Mike, what about that picture?"

"What?"

"From last night. I texted you. You never sent it."

"Oh, that had a short window," he said. "Next time, just get back to me when you say you're gonna."

"Mike, I was fucking crazed."

"I know, bro, no worries, there'll be other photos."

"Yeah, okay, whatever," I said. "I'll see you after work."

* * *

I emailed my boss that the meeting was still going at three o'clock and asked if I should stay. He replied back, "Don't leave before the vote." So I sat back in my chair and listened to more droning about probability histograms and sample deviations. Until quarter to five, when I learned there'd be no vote; it was being rescheduled for the following month.

I stashed a page of notes and five pages of doodling in my bag. Then I looked for Alan as the group went to exit.

"You'll have to tell me how the vote goes," I said to him.

"Yeah," he said. "They pulled the old cliffhanger on you. You going into the office?"

"Oh hell no," I said.

"You walking home? I'm headed the same way right now."

"No," I said. "Getting a cab and heading downtown. I'm meeting an old friend for drinks."

"Oh, okay."

"But let's definitely hang out sometime soon."

"Yeah," he said, "and maybe I'll see you around the neighborhood before then."

"Right," I said, forcing a smile.

# CHAPTER THIRTEEN

I had the cab driver swing by my apartment and wait while I dropped off my bags. My doorman saw I was in a major hurry, so I was able to run my luggage upstairs without any dealing.

I arrived at the bar fifteen minutes early, thinking I could chill briefly, but I saw Mike was already there, sitting on a barstool, already drinking a beer.

He turned and smiled as I walked over. "Good to see you, buddy," he said, rising to give me a hug. I went along with it. I wanted him thinking things were cool with us.

I sat down next to him and he ordered me a beer. Mike had just come from work, and looked sharp and refined in his charcoal suit.

"So how you doing, bro?" he said, smiling and clicking my glass.

"Tired," I said. "Crazy last couple of days. I'm fucking beat."

"I'll bet," he said. "So what was it like being so far away?"

"It sucked," I said, trying to sound matter of fact. "I missed her."

"Sure, that's natural. And now you're back, man."

"Hey Mike, does Ashley still believe we first met at summer camp—or did you tell her otherwise?"

"No, I said we met at camp, period. But it doesn't even come up. It's not like she's pumping me for summer camp stories."

"Okay, good. Does she know we're meeting now?"

"I didn't tell her—did you? Hadn't we agreed not to?"

"Yeah, we did. I was just making sure, man, especially with the camp story, since I'll be talking to her soon."

"Well, I ain't said shit … about that or us ever meeting up."

"Okay."

"Like she told me about you coming home drunk Monday. And I played dumb. I was just like 'oh really?' "

"Can you tell me what she said? About me coming home drunk?"

"Just that she had hoped to talk with you before you left."

"Fuck. Yeah, I know. She told me that, too. So is she upset with me? Is that gonna be a big theme tonight?"

"No, I don't think so, bro. I'd say the theme will be more like communication, openness, understanding. It's really pretty simple. Just be honest. Speak from your heart. I know that sounds corny, but just give Ashley that trust, man."

"Yeah, okay."

"It'll be liberating. And swear to God, you're gonna see. Ashley really loves you, bro."

"Yeah, okay, so Ashley's not upset?"

"No, don't worry. Just be yourself, man. I think that's the biggest thing. But also, think about Ashley's perspective. She's seen how you reacted. She's seen the way I've taken over. The other day, on the phone, she basically told you she was cucking you. Maybe you guys can actually use the word 'cuckold' when you're talking heart-to-heart, tonight."

"Yeah, okay, so that's your Dr. Phil for me?"

"I'm just saying, bro, kill that fat, fucking elephant in your room … and get real with your wife."

"I'm going to."

"You bringing flowers?"

"No way," I said, "not warranted."

"Are you kidding? It's a fucking milestone night—the start of a new and deeper bond with Ashley. Now, more than ever, you should be professing your love. Wouldn't it be a statement *not* to? It's a big occasion. Why blow it off?"

"You're right. I'll pick some up on my way home. I'm serious.

"Are you going to bring up what we discussed the other night?"

"Uh, we discussed a lot of things the other night."

"I think you know what I mean."

"No, I'm not asking her that."

"Asking her what?"

"What you keep telling me to fucking say, like I'm gonna fucking say that."

"I think you'll surprise yourself. The words will just flow out. That'll be a big step forward for you both. Try it out on me. Like how would you ask her?"

"Fuck you, Mike. It's not happening."

"You're gonna find yourself asking her, bro. That's what I see happening."

"Fucking no way. Not bringing it up. And if she brings it up—I'm telling the truth—I'm saying it was your idea."

"Bro, you've listened outside the door. I'm sure you jerk off imagining it. How can you tell me you don't want to watch? If there was a video of me and Ashley, don't tell me you wouldn't be begging me to see it."

"Did you guys make one?" I said.

"Just making a point, bro. You know you would. You'd run home and watch it, first opportunity. You'd be jerking all night to it."

"I would probably watch it—yes—but so what?"

"Just think of seeing it live, 3D, right in front of you. How could you not love that?"

"Mike, does Ashley think I want to ask her that, or that I'm going to?"

"Ask her what?"

"What we're fucking talking about."

"I want to hear you say it," he said, "then I'll answer."

"Are you serious?"

"Yeah. Does Ashley think you're gonna ask her what?"

"If she'll let me watch," I said.

"Spit it out, bro. Let you watch what?"

I looked down at my beer. I could tell he was staring at me.

"If Ashley will let me watch her, like you said, getting fucked in front of me."

"See, that wasn't so hard, right? Doesn't it feel good saying it to someone besides yourself?"

"Not really man, no. Just tell me. Does Ashley think I want to ask her that?"

"Not from anything I've told her. That I guarantee. Besides, I want her hearing it from you. If she hasn't already picked up on it."

" 'Picked up on it,' " I said, "What do you mean?"

"Well, she's watched you get cuckolded. Makes sense you'd want to watch her get fucked. Maybe she thinks you'll have some courage tonight and tell her."

"Yeah, okay, like *that's* courage, asking her something you're telling me to say. Look, as far as what to expect tonight, is there anything more than just 'she'll be understanding?' "

"Well, you have to remember, Ashley being understanding tonight is dependent on you being upfront and honest with her. No more ignoring it, y'know?"

"Is she gonna grill me?"

"No, I don't think so. I don't know what she'll say, but I think this is about reconnecting with you. Like getting real and bonding. Seriously."

"Okay," I said. "Bonding is good."

"Ashley and I really bonded while you were away," he said. "We really talked and got to know each other better. She understands me better now, and vice versa. And of course, I really fucked her puss real good this week."

"Yeah, Mike, okay, I fucking get it."

"I'm just saying, I really got to know Ash on a much deeper level. She's a real firecracker, that girl of yours. A lot of fun to be with, and real easy to talk to. How long you been married, nineteen months, right?"

"Twenty."

"Yeah, so you got cucked in your first two years. I love that Ashley's still really a newlywed. I bet she looked great in her wedding dress. So precious and pure ... and irresistibly fuckable. Am I right?"

"Yeah, well, I know you've seen our wedding pictures at my place. Ashley was beautiful."

"She looked like a real hot fuck, Dave. The bride I'd want to fuck hard, in front of her husband."

"Yeah, okay, Mike."

"Think about when Ashley watched me shut you out of your own bedroom."

"I don't fucking need reminding."

"Yeah, but think about it—"

"And you didn't shut it," I said. "You slammed the door in my face."

"Okay, but however she perceived it .... Did she run out and ask if you were okay? Did she lay into me for doing that to her husband? Or even call out to you—to let you know she loved you?"

"Actually," I said, "she mouthed that to me when you were closing the door."

"Nice. Did she blow you a kiss, too? I mean, think about it, bro. She watched me boot you from your bedroom ... quite unceremoniously. She watched you get humiliated. And the guy who humiliated her husband .... What does Ashley do? She fucks him ... in your bed. What does that say?"

"Mike, I don't know. A lot, I'm sure. That she enjoyed seeing me humbled, maybe. Or was drunker than I thought and half-oblivious."

Mike laughed. "I think seeing you humbled really turned her on. That and a big, fat cock, which by the way, Ashley's pussy has become very attached to. Her pussy now pines for my cock."

"Jeez, Mike, please, can you just freaking chill out for a minute and appreciate how fucked up I'm feeling right now. This whole thing has been a colossal mind fuck. One that I still can't believe is happening."

"It's okay, man," he said. "I'm sorry. It takes time."

"You know," I said, "I was thinking about the way we talked before you met Ashley. I felt like I could talk to you about anything—stresses I was dealing with. You were someone I could turn to, you know, in a crisis. 'Cause I considered you a friend."

"So did I," Mike said, "and I still do. I really mean that."

"Like when I was going to Ashley's happy hour, and having to see Jim Murta, you hooked me up with good advice and a pep talk. And I took it to heart. I was nervous, but I held my own. Against all expectations, I kind of kicked ass that night."

"Bro, I was so fucking pumped and proud for you, when you told me at the bar afterward."

"You were really a friend to me that night."

"Yeah, man, I've missed that. And the new situation shouldn't change that, y'know."

"Yeah, I hope not."

"Well," he said, "how did you feel after your speech yesterday?"

"Very good."

"Meeting people afterward, did you feel more confident?"

"Yeah, for sure."

"So … tap into that feeling when you're with Ash tonight. Like you just came back from a big career

100

achievement. That's reason enough to hold your head high tonight, bro."

"Yeah, and I figured I could talk about that to stall for time, so I can get a read on her."

"Yeah, all right, just don't be stalling too long. Because here's the thing …. Ashley knows this has been one helluva ride for you. She's seen your stunned expressions and cuck angst. She knows you've been knocked around, and cucked around …."

"Okay, Mike, she knows this has been hard on me. I get it."

"She loves you, man. She told me that a lot, which makes this better. You'll get sympathy and understanding. And reassurance. I bet you'll be sleeping better. Just remember, though, all bets are off if she thinks you're obfu… if you obfuscate."

"Was that her word?"

"Yeah, that's how she's described you a couple times. She just wants you to be you, man. And if you're not a hundred percent sure what that means, what being you is right now, hey that's okay, so long as you express that. That's the important thing."

"Yeah, okay."

"And one small thing—just a head's up. Don't get caught staring at Ashley's tits too long—particularly when she's talking. She mentioned you've been doing that lately."

"Good God," I said. "Okay."

"And don't be sweating it. I'm sure it will go great, and end up being a big relief. Because at this point, you can't ignore it. No more kicking the can down the road. That's done. You can't pretend like I didn't spend the last two nights living with your wife, in your home."

"I know."

"I don't mean to taunt, bro, but that's just reality. You're going to have to acknowledge reality to your wife. She's taking my sperm now, regularly. She's getting fucked in your marriage bed. She told you we'd be fucking while you were away. This is what you've come home to. You think you can really avoid talking about it?"

"Mike, I get it. I've got to be open."

"Like you were with me, when we first started talking. You were real open. Be like that with her."

"Well, I didn't even know who the fuck I was talking with, when I opened up to you. Just that you didn't seem like a weirdo or an a-hole. And you seemed to care."

"Oh yeah," Mike said. "I really did care. I had a hunch you were genuine, the way you talked about Ashley and your feelings. I don't know. I just found you very likable and engaging. Any time I was online, I wanted to talk to you."

"Yeah, but it was always about getting with Ashley, right?"

"No, at first I didn't have much expectation. I was just interested in what were you saying, and that you were local. It wasn't till you sent me photos that I started considering the possibility. But once I met you in person, I felt confident. It was just a matter of time until I met with Ashley."

"Yeah, I understand. I was blabbing way too personally."

"You kidding, man? It was great. I loved hearing it. Gave me lots of insight."

"Yeah, that you'd later use against me." *As soon as I said it, I wished I hadn't.*

"What the fuck does that mean? What have you said that I used against you?"

"Mike, who knows what you tell her."

"So you got nothing—not one example? Don't be making shit up, bro, that ain't cool. This is about you, following an inner calling … *your* inner calling."

"So what's my calling, Mike? To be a fucking cuckold?"

"I like that. That would be a good t-shirt for you. You'd

have 'What's my calling?' on the front, and 'To be a fucking cuckold—' "

"All right, Mike, you know what? Fuck you!"

"Oh c'mon, bro, I'm kidding, but you know what I'm saying."

"No, I don't, actually, but that's okay. I have to get going."

"Okay, really quick, just wait a second. Forget what Ashley's thinking, and just remember what Ashley's seen this past week—from you, my friend. She saw me take charge and have my way with you. She saw you sleeping on the cuckold couch."

"Yeah man, I fucking know, okay?"

"I'm not trying to stick your nose in it, but that's what she witnessed. Hell, she has it in photos. Like the one *you* took—of Ashley and me in your kitchen. She'll remember making out with me, right in front of you, in your kitchen. I mean, what do you think it says—that she would humiliate you like that?"

"I just felt like she got so lost in the moment, she forgot I was there."

"You're fucking kidding, right?"

"What?"

"Forgot you were there? You're fucking deluding yourself, man. How could she forget? You were five feet away. She was making a statement. She was choosing me and cucking you. You think she found it a turn-on, making out in front of her husband?"

"I don't know. I guess you're saying she did?"

"Why don't you ask her tonight?"

"Well, maybe I will. Listen, I really do have to go."

"Okay, but with tonight's big question …."

I put out my hand for him to shake, but he continued.

"I'm serious. Maybe start by admitting you'd like to see a video of her—"

"Mike, look, I'm not fucking asking her. That's your fucking question. Why the fuck would I be asking that?"

"Deep down, bro, letting you watch her get fucked is your question, and you know it." He took a big swig from his beer, then turned back to me. "Just be yourself and you'll be fine. Remember the flowers. I want to hear how it goes."

"Okay."

"And good luck, bro." He gave me a hug that I quickly ended.

"Oh, and Dave … remember. I know how tempting it is, but no ogling over Ashley's big titties."

"Yeah. See you."

I had to piss, but I didn't want a second goodbye. So I went straight for the exit and into a cab.

# CHAPTER FOURTEEN

*W*ow, I thought, *I just got really fucking bitch-slapped.* Mike wanted Ashley to see me go full-blown. He wanted me saying, "Ashley, could I maybe watch sometime when you're in our bedroom with Mike? Like even from the closet?"

That would be another cherry on top for Mike. A big, fucking cherry, getting me to ask my wife that question. I thought of the power he'd have then. Pulling me across the threshold. Reducing me in front of my wife. Ashley would be more his than ever.

I thought of Mike talking about Ashley in a wedding dress—how she looked extra fuckable. I wondered if that's the way he wanted me to watch her—dressed as my bride taking a cock-pumping, sperm fuck from Mike and his big, fat cock.

I wondered if he'd said it because that's what he was planning. To fuck my wife in front of me in her wedding dress. What she wore when walking down the aisle, the symbol of our life-long commitment—Mike wanted to fuck her in it.

"Near or far corner?" the cabbie asked.

"Here's good, actually."

I got out two blocks early to pick up some wine, cold cuts ... and flowers. I figured that just because it was Mike's suggestion didn't mean it was a bad idea. If she was angry, it said I was sorry. And if she was in a good mood, it could make it a little better. But mostly I hoped it simply said, "I'm glad to be back home with you, Ash."

I walked down the other side of the street and past my building to see who was working the door. It was the doorman I thought it would be—the one who only talked when I initiated it. I hustled across the street and when I approached him, pretended to be preoccupied.

"Evening Bobby," I said.

"Good evening, Mr. Martens, how are you?"

"Glad to be home," I said and kept on walking. No one was waiting by the elevators, but they were both on upper floors. I heard my neighbor's voice greeting the doorman and the sound of her heels marching my way.

She was a hot, blonde girl—mid-twenties, probably— who had moved to our floor two months ago. I didn't know her beyond saying hello, and Ashley had told me she was a model. I'd have taken an exit door to the street, had there been one.

"Oh hi," I said, pretending to be surprised.

"Hello," she said as the elevator arrived. She went in first and I followed with my bags.

"Coming back from somewhere?" she said, holding the *door open* button.

"Yeah," I said, "I was out in San Francisco. I had to give a very big presentation." I stopped myself, thinking, *I sound like an asshole.*

"You're Ashley's husband?" she said, smiling.

"Yeah, hi. I'm Dave, and you're …?"

"Sophia," she said. "Your wife's in my spin class some weekends."

"Oh really," I said, as we reached our floor and got off. "I didn't know that."

She lived on the same hall as me—three apartments down.

"I still haven't gotten my place together," she said, "but

as I told Ashley, around the holidays I'm throwing a party and I'd like for you guys to come."

"Yeah," I said, "sounds great—thank you." I put my key in the door and said, "Nice meeting you Sophia," as she walked by.

"Welcome home, Dave," she replied, and I watched her ass, in tight jeans, walking down that hall.

I wondered if Sophia had seen anything, like Mike leaving our apartment in the morning or the two of them together in the elevator. I wondered if she was thinking, *You know you've been cucked, right?*

\* \* \*

I walked inside and turned on the lights. My apartment looked clean. Not a glass in the sink, countertops clean, and the bed made great. Ashley's laundry was all put away.

I appreciated it—not having reminders. It went along with the theme of fresh beginnings. I thought of lying down on the bed, but I knew where that would lead. And I'd decided I wouldn't masturbate before seeing her.

I figured I should be virile. And I didn't want to jerk off thinking some fucked up thoughts right before my big talk with Ashley. I didn't want to cum saying something like, "Cuck me, Ash." I didn't want that coloring the way I projected myself.

Plus, there'd be nothing wrong with Ashley noticing my erection as we sat on the roof together later. That would say, "You've got a man right here." It might even lift my confidence.

I wondered if Mike had fucked her in any room beside my bedroom. I walked into the living room and wondered if he'd had her on all fours, on the floor, doing her doggy. Or got a blowjob in my shower.

*Maybe*, I thought, *my fucking blonde neighbor really does suspect.* Girls sense things. She might know Mike was fucking her. And be telling her fellow models, "The guy on my floor is a cuckold."

I started getting a boner, so I went in the kitchen and got things ready. Cubed some cheese, cut a baguette, and made some guacamole. I put tortilla chips on one side of a big tray and the bread on the other.

I'd just opened the wine, when I heard Ashley coming in.

"Hey, Ash," I said, walking to the door.

"Dave," she said, smiling, in her work-out clothes, "I'm so glad you're home."

"So great to be back," I said, giving her a hug. "I missed you so much."

"I missed you, too," she said, holding me tightly.

"Yeah," I said, as we walked into the kitchen. "I knew you'd still be at the gym, so I went and put a little spread together for the roof tonight."

"This looks fantastic," she said. "You made guacamole, and what kind of wine is that?"

"The Chilean one you like."

"Oh, thank you so much, honey." She gave me another hug. "Oh my God," she said, covering her mouth with her hand, "you got me flowers. Thank you! They're beautiful."

"You're welcome, Ash," I said, "and thank you … for cleaning the place. It looks great."

"Well, actually," she said, "the girl down the hall has a cheap maid she told me about who was free today, and our apartment really needed it, anyway."

"Oh," I said.

"So how are you feeling?" she asked. "You must be exhausted, honey."

"You know," I said, "I must be past-tired. Like for how little I've slept, I'm feeling pretty good. Maybe just being home with you gave me a second wind."

"That's sweet," she said. "I'm really glad you're back."

"Me too," I said, moving in to kiss her.

"Oh, I'm gross," she said, putting up her hands. "Let me change out of my work-out clothes and take a quick shower."

"Oh, okay," I said.

"But this looks great and I don't want to hold us up, so I will be super quick."

"Okay," I said. "I'll finish up here and start taking things up."

I changed into shorts and a t-shirt and went upstairs. There were a few people outside. But on the side we usually sat in, there was no one. The two comfy chairs we liked were free. I put our stuff down on the table and opened the wine.

I looked out at the Hudson River and the traffic below … and reminisced about moonlit nights up there with Ashley.

# CHAPTER FIFTEEN

"I love it," Ashley said, walking out in her jeans and tanktop. "And once again, no one's here."

"And we've got our styling seats," I said.

"And another beautiful night," she said.

"Can I get my welcome home kiss now?" I asked, leaning in.

She started to let up but I kept on going, and she went with it, but only for a few seconds. Then it became a hug.

"We should probably talk first," she said. "Get that out of the way, right?"

"Yeah, of course," I said, "and have some wine."

Ashley sat down and I poured us each a glass before sitting down next to her. We were close enough to talk, but I'd have to reach over the wide armrests to touch her.

"Cheers, Ash," I said. "I love you."

"I love you too," she said. "To you being home."

We clicked glasses and sampled the wine.

"It's perfect," she said. "It has a nice, raspberry taste."

"Yeah, it's nice."

Ashley took off her sandals and sat back with her bare feet on the table.

"So," she said, as she played with her hair, "it's sure been a crazy, freaky week, hasn't it?"

"Yeah, most definitely," I said, staring at the polish on her toes and the arch of her small left foot. "I'm just glad to be back home with you, Ash."

"Me too. And you couldn't ask for better weather. It's like summer's on extended time."

"Yeah, and we got the moon chilling with us," I said.

"I think the moon's all sad and blue," she said.

"Why?"

" 'Cause he knows what time of year it is. And that pretty soon, we won't be up here at night like this."

"Well," I said, "he'll be kicking it with his Australian peeps for the winter."

"But it's not the same. He doesn't have as much fun."

"Probably not," I said, "but I'm sure there are girls in Australia who'll serenade him with moon songs."

"Oh, don't say that," she said. "You just made him cry. He says those Australian girls don't have as much heart."

"As American girls, or just compared to you, Ash?"

She laughed and said, "We'll sing him carols at Christmas, right? And howl to him on Halloween."

"Of course," I said. "All the holidays. We're there."

"So," she said, tucking her legs under her, "how was your dinner?"

"What?" I said.

"Last night, your dinner with Jack—how did it go?"

"Oh, well, he had some industry thing. We ended up just meeting for a drink. We'll do dinner next time."

"What did he say about your presentation?"

"He was really complimentary," I said, "especially about me showing that guy the exit."

"That's so awesome, honey."

"Yeah, and he said how it's good to know I can be counted on for something higher level like that."

"That's fantastic," she said. "Like Brian's not there, no problem. Dave will step in and kick ass, probably even better than Brian would."

"Yeah, sure." I laughed.

She smiled and said, "So tell me … what about what's

been happening here? What have you been thinking?"

"Just that it's nice to be back."

"I mean about this past week."

"Well, like you said, it's been crazy. I feel like I'm finally coming up for air, y'know?"

"Yeah, but are you okay with it?"

"I'm feeling better now."

"About what's going on?"

"Just better being up here with you," I said, with a smile.

"Well sure," she said. "you're back home now. Which is awesome. And now we can finally talk … and open up, I hope."

"Yeah, absolutely."

"So, what *are* you thinking? Are you okay with what's happened this week? Or *mostly* okay?"

"Well, I guess, the thing is …."

I realized I was staring down at my shoes and quickly returned to looking her in the eye. "I mean, are you?" As soon as I said that, I saw her frustration. I couldn't think of anything else to say, so I just said, "What?"

Ashley shook her head and smiled. Then she leaned in, put her hand on my thigh, looked me in the eye—and said softly, "Just for tonight. Or just for right now even … can we please stop dancing round the obvious? I know it can be a little uncomfortable, but you can talk to me. Really, I want you to talk to me."

"So do I. But it's not an easy question—what I think about all of this. Like what does 'okay' even mean, really? For me it's like an asteroid hit."

"So what is it then? Like reality's different than you imagined?"

"What? No! It's blindsiding. I wasn't expecting any of this. I didn't even know Mike was going to put moves on you, that first night in the bar."

"I didn't either. Why did you introduce him to me, then?"

"Well, Mike kept suggesting it, and we were out drinking, and I wasn't thinking, and I said okay. I mean, yeah, I did talk to him about us … and he seemed to relate."

"Relate to what?"

"Well, I was naive not to realize his motives. And yeah, I know I did very little to prevent it. But all we really talked about was that night at the party. And how I'd fantasized, picturing it. And he said he could understand, and acted all supportive."

"Supportive? Like how?"

"Well, I talked to him before going to one of your happy hours, actually. I knew your work people knew what had happened. That they might be talking about me. I'd probably have to shake Jim Murta's hand. And deal with Tamara. So yeah, Mike was someone I could talk to."

"So you told Mike all this, but were still *completely* surprised when Mike started flirting with me in the bar? That's what you're saying?"

"I know. I was an idiot."

"Then why did you leave to make a phone call? Right after introducing him, why'd you leave us alone for like, half an hour?"

"I had San Fran calling; I told you that. They needed info from me to get their project started."

Ashley looked at me, incredulous, and said, "Okay."

"Look, maybe subconsciously, I was curious as to how it would go. But I didn't foresee what happened."

"Okay, so you were curious? You wanted to see if I'd be interested in Mike?"

"Well maybe, but not consciously. When I walked out of the men's room that first night and saw you guys making out at the bar, I was frickin' stunned. Never saw that coming."

"You saw us making out?"

"Yeah."

"Why didn't you come over and interrupt?"

"I didn't want to cause a scene or embarrass you."

"Why were you cool with Mike coming back to our place?"

"I said it was late. I wasn't gung-ho'ing it. I was just going along."

"What'd you think would happen? One quick drink and Mike goes home?"

"I suspected something might happen, but I didn't know what to do at that point. I know that's not much of an excuse. I think the real reason was, I wasn't thinking a half-hour into the future."

"Are you serious?"

"Yeah, pretty much, as dumb as that sounds."

"All right. So explain this to me … why were you even telling Mike about Jim and me … that it turned you on, that you fantasized about it? Why tell him all that?"

"I don't know, Ash, it just kind of came up."

"So, you reunite with a childhood friend and you start telling him about me at that party?"

"Yeah, I just made an off-hand comment one night. Then he kept asking questions and wanting to know more. We were out drinking. And it was on my mind a lot. He acted all empathetic. And well, yeah, I told him I'd fantasized about it. I was crazy."

"Can you tell me what you fantasized about?"

"Well … I would think about you with Jim, in that bathroom."

"So thinking about that turned you on?"

"I don't know why—it doesn't make sense—but yeah, sometimes."

"So that's what you talked to Mike about?"

"That. Or how I wondered what was going on in the bathroom when I knocked on the door."

"You mean when Tamara told you to go upstairs?"

"Yeah."

"Hmm, well, I'm afraid the answer might disappoint you."

"Why?"

" 'Cause nothing was going on" she said. "I mean I was naked, yeah, but I was still in the bathtub."

"Oh, okay, gotcha, now I know. It was just one of those weird curiosities you fixate on sometimes."

"So those are the kind of things you talked to Mike about? "

"Yeah."

"So after telling him you'd fantasized about your wife with another man, you didn't consider that he'd want to pursue me?"

"I wasn't connecting simple dots, I know."

"C'mon Dave, you introduced me to him … and promptly walked away. For *whatever* reason."

"I know how it looks. Maybe deep down or subconsciously, some part of me knew."

"Meaning what?"

I shrugged impatiently. "Meaning I'm asking questions of myself, like why did I do this or not do that. I've replayed the whole thing in my head while I was away."

"And?"

"And I don't have great answers. But it's not like I haven't been thinking about it. It's that I'm too close to it."

"How do you feel about Mike now?

"Well, that he can be manipulative … opportunistic."

"You feel manipulated?"

"Well, look," I said, "I know that first night I let him walk all over me, which established a precedent, and I should have done something when he locked me out of my freaking bedroom. I was just blindsided and paralyzed."

"Well, he was making a statement, obviously. But he really does see you as a good friend—scratch that, *great* friend—and I hope you know that."

"Oh c'mon Ash," I said. "The guy shut the door in my face. And I've been kicking myself ever since. I should've fought back."

"I figured you wouldn't by then."

"Why's that?" I said.

"I don't know. Mike had already kind of established, well you know … dominance."

"Look, I'm sure it seemed that way," I said, starting to sweat. "I just wasn't on my game … or prepared for that."

"Then why didn't you say something afterward? The next day you acted like you didn't realize I'd slept with Mike. How could you not know?"

"Ash, I did know. But you have to understand: this was freaking earth-shaking to me. It left me punch-drunk the next day. I needed a little distance. I was too nervous and freaked out to talk about it."

"Did you talk to Mike about it?"

"Yeah, last Thursday. I was like, 'You never told me you were gonna pull that fucking stunt.' "

"So you told him off?"

"Yeah, I really did."

"Did you tell him to stop seeing me?"

After a long pause, I said, "No."

"Then you knew it would just keep going then. Sounds like, deep down, that subconscious of yours kind of likes the adventure we're on."

"Look, I know I let things happen. And I get how it looks. And I can't believe how blind and passive I was, either. But you know, Ash, here's the thing …. This past week, I felt really detached from you, and I didn't like that. Especially being away. That really amplified it."

"I know what you mean. Part of that's the situation. But that's why it's so important we start talking about it. So we both feel connected … reattached."

"Exactly," I said.

"And the more we open up, the better," she said. "I'd say that already tonight, we've taken down some barriers."

"Right," I said.

"I know it might not be easy to talk about," she said, "but isn't it nice to just get real, right now?"

"Yeah," I said. "We've should've done this sooner, for sure."

"This is what'll reattach us, talking like this, y'know. I'm really glad your back, Dave."

"Oh me too, Ash," I said.

I watched Ashley finish her second glass of wine. I'd already finished mine. "I just realized," I said, "I left the other bottle downstairs. I'll just be two minutes."

"Okay," she said. "Give me a kiss first?" I leaned down by her chair and was able to put my arms around her. She gave me a couple seconds of tongue and I didn't push it.

I took the stairs instead of waiting for the elevator. I was trying to be super quick. I was taking a piss when I heard my phone dialing. So I pulled it out of my pocket and saw it was calling Mike. I frantically pressed "end call," but I heard Mike picking up as it shut off.

So I started texting him back: "Sorry, butt-dialed. With Ash, can't talk." And quickly hit send. Then I finished pissing and grabbed the wine.

I was in the elevator when Mike texted me back: "Good luck, bro. So far, so good?"

I wanted to text back, "Go fuck yourself." I'd told Mike I'd dialed by mistake and was busy. I felt like he was asking me a question, just to see if he could get me to reply. Like I'd feel obliged. Not that I did—feel obliged, that is. I didn't at all.

It just seemed so dumb that I'd called him. If my phone had dialed anyone else, it'd have been no problem. But I cut myself some slack. I figured, at least what I could control, I did. I had texted back a 'closed' sign. A small victory, admittedly, but I'd cut it off at the pass.

\* \* \*

Ashley was texting on her phone when I returned. I opened the new bottle and poured. Then we said *cheers* and clicked glasses.

"So how about you, Ash?" I said, sitting down. "What have you thought about this past week?"

"Well, I get what you said—about it being like an asteroid hitting. It was totally of out of nowhere. It kind of reminds me of *The Wizard of Oz*. Like nine days ago, we were still back in Kansas."

"Hmm," I said. "I guess I can sort of see that. Have you ever thought that Mike might be the Wizard?"

"No, why?"

"Since you mentioned the movie, I'm just throwing it out there. Random question, I know. Although, we really *don't* know him that well. You've known him a week. I started talking to him … six weeks ago. Knowing him from summer camp twenty plus years ago doesn't mean much now."

"It means your good friend at twelve became your good friend again at thirty-four … and you introduced him to me."

"What it means is, I don't really know the guy well now. We'd only hung out a few times before this."

"Okay," she said, "but there's nothing Oz-like about Mike?"

"I wasn't saying there was. I don't know. I guess I was really just asking what you thought of him."

"Well, obviously, I enjoy his company."

"Yeah, I know."

"And Mike's a great guy. You know, he's your friend."

I paused a moment before replying, "Ashley, maybe I thought he was my friend before. But right now, I really don't consider Mike some good friend of mine. I know his motives now."

"Which are?"

118

"Well, obviously, he wants you. He wants my wife."

"And he wants you, right?" she said. "Like, to be okay with everything."

"Well," I said, "he's probably talked to you about this thing called cuckolding."

"Yeah," she said, with a brief smile, "talk to me."

"Well ... I just figured he'd bring it up, 'cause that's what Mike's trying to do. He's on this whole cuckolding trip. And he wants me to be this ... well, you know, this cuckold husband."

"And what's your reaction to that?" she said.

"Well," I said, "that's something I've got to be aware of with Mike."

"But what's your reaction? Would you say you've been cuckolded?"

I hesitated. "Well ... I'd say I definitely experienced a form of cuckolding this week. I know he was here with you and the situation."

"And what do you think of that?" she said.

"Well, as I said, I felt really disconnected."

"But were you turned on thinking about it? Like would you fantasize about Mike and me ... like you did me and Jim?"

"Well ... I mean ... what turns me on is you, Ash. So picturing you having sex ... of course I'm going to fantasize about that."

"Yeah," she said, "but it's me having sex with another man, right?"

"Well, when I heard about you in that bathroom, that's when it started. I was imagining you having sex. And sure, as I said, that was something I foolishly told Mike about. Which he's probably blown way out of proportion."

"So when you were out in San Fran, you fantasized about Mike and me having sex?"

"Well, I guess, but the focus was on you."

"Were you imagining us in our bedroom, like were you wondering the details?"

"Sure, I pictured it."

"Meaning you masturbated?" she said.

"What?"

"Thinking of me having sex," she said, "did you?"

"Yeah, Ash," I said, "all right, I did. The first night I was out there. I was missing you and thinking about you."

"And you masturbated thinking about me with Mike?"

"C'mon Ash, really."

"I'd just really like to know," she said. "You can tell me."

"Okay, yeah," I said. "That night I did ... I think."

Ashley smiled and took my hand. "I know that wasn't easy for you to say, but I really appreciate you telling me." She leaned in to kiss me, and I leaned in too, but the armrests were in the way, so the kiss was brief.

"So," she said, "what did you mean when you said you experienced a 'form' of cuckolding?"

"What? Well, I just meant, me being away, you being here."

"Okay ...." she said.

"Okay, look," I said. "I know I allowed this to happen. I fucking stumbled and bumbled my way through the past week."

"Maybe that's what you really wanted. Is it possible that's how you really are?"

"It's not how I am, Ash—not fundamentally. I mean yeah, okay, this week, sure. Sitting in my hotel room in San Fran, yeah I kind of felt cuckolded. I got the cuckold experience."

"Did you feel cuckolded by the whole Jim Murta thing?"

"That's when I first heard what a cuckold was."

"And you identified?"

"Well—"

"Or you identify now?" She shook her head. "I'm sorry. I

don't want to make you feel uncomfortable. I think I understand."

"Ashley, just because I acted like a cuckold this week doesn't mean that's who I am."

"I understand. You just went with it this week. And so did I. I mean, I've given up control too. We've both thrown caution to the wind. And you're right, it's been quite a week, a big thrill ride right now."

"I'm sorry, what was I right about?"

"About how one week's not terribly defining. We're just going with the flow."

"What control did you give up?"

"In the bedroom. But also trusting Mike through this. It wasn't easy. That first night, for instance. I wasn't as sure as Mike was that you wouldn't do anything. And he just kind of understood me. Saw things in me, I didn't see myself. Sounds like he was like that with you as well."

"Oh no, not like that."

"Well, he read you pretty well, didn't he?"

"He saw I was vulnerable, susceptible."

"Yeah," she said, "but he must've gotten a vibe from you. That you'd allow him to take over like he did."

"Look, I wasn't giving off anything other than … I don't know. Confusion."

"I just meant Mike can really read people, or seemed to with us, anyway. That's all."

"Okay," I said.

"Well, Dave," she said, "I really appreciated you opening up to me tonight. I know you just got home, and I've put you on the spot with all the questions, but I think it's really good for us to talk like this."

"Me too," I said.

"You look really tired, baby," she said. "Why don't we go downstairs and change. We can talk in bed. What do you think?"

"That works for me, Ash."

# CHAPTER SIXTEEN

Ashley went into the bathroom and I changed in our bedroom, just taking off my shorts really. I poured us each a new glass of wine and put them on my nightstand. I sat down on the bed, thinking of how we'd be talking on the same bed she'd been getting fucked in.

Ashley came out in a pink t-shirt she wore like a mini dress, showing off her thin, tan legs.

I handed her the glass of wine and she smiled as she sat on the bed … on top of the covers, t-shirt tucked under her ass.

"Cheers," she said, as I got in next to her. "I think tonight is really a great night for us and I want to thank you for opening up and being honest. It's so important. I'm so glad we did this."

"Oh sure, Ash," I said. "I mean, we have to talk about it. Very important, of course."

"But I feel bad, like I've put you on the defensive, and that I haven't given you a chance to talk. I'm sorry, and if you have a question or want to say something—"

"Yeah," I broke in, "I do have something … an idea … I'd like to get across."

"Absolutely. Please, I'm listening."

"Well, it's kind of like how we were talking earlier. How we both felt detached this week. In San Fran that feeling was through the roof."

"I can relate," she said. "I'm with you."

"Well," I said, "I think what we really need … what we'd

really benefit from ... is some time together as a couple, a chance to come up for air. I wanted to see what you thought of ... hitting the pause button for a bit, maybe taking some time off from seeing Mike. We could really reattach."

"Uh, yeah, what were you thinking? Like ... how much time?"

"Oh, I don't know," I said. "Several days, a week maybe ... of just you and me."

"Sounds good, but the only thing is this weekend."

"What?" I said.

"Well, Saturday ... we kind of have plans with Mike."

"But my parent's cook-out—"

"It won't conflict," she said. "We're not seeing Mike till later Saturday night. Like after ten."

"But why?" I said, "Why can't we just *not* see him this weekend?"

"Wait ... you don't know? Saturday's Mike's birthday."

"It's what?" I said, confused. "It is?"

"Yeah."

"The actual day?"

"Uh-huh, pretty big bday. Mike turns thirty three."

"Really? Are you frickin' serious? So what does that mean? Doesn't he have any other friends? Are we taking him out ... or are you?"

"No, nothing like that. He'll just come here. A little champagne, very low key. I'll pick up a cake when we're out at your parents. Is that party store still there by the train station?"

I blinked. "You want to throw Mike a party?"

"No." She laughed. "Just have him over for cake. He's having dinner with his brother and will come by after that. So maybe even later, like eleven, eleven-thirty."

"I don't care whatever freaking time, Ash."

"Well, I really do want to have some good one-on-one time with you. We're just making this exception because it's his birthday, and a big one, y'know?"

"Yeah, it's his birthday, I get it."

"And Mike said he doesn't want presents."

"Okay, that's good, right?"

"But he did have one birthday request, which will probably seem a little strange at first."

"What is it?"

"Well, kind of like what you were saying before … about taking pauses. This pause would be really short, though."

"A short pause on what?"

"Mike wants us to wait until we see him … before you and I are intimate again … as a birthday present to him."

I couldn't believe what I was hearing. "What?"

"Which is only two days, by the way."

"What the fuck are you saying? That we're not going to have sex?" I tried not to raise my voice.

"Well, remember, we did that for a month, right before we were married. This is just till the weekend."

"This is not about how many days. Just think about what it says. I'm finally home with my wife again, and he wants us not having sex. He wants me to be deprived. And *that's* the birthday present you want to give him? That you want *me* to give him?"

"Okay, so remember the time when your dad spent three days at that monastery in Vermont?"

"I'm serious, Ash."

"So am I," she said. "Your dad spent like seventy-two hours with the monks, totally silent, never speaking. And what did your dad say when he got back?"

"I don't know, Ash, c'mon."

"He said the quiet could be quite beautiful, how shutting off the world really opened up his thinking. How he learned so much from not opening his mouth."

"Ashley, please, you're not really drawing parallels between that and this." I realized I was rolling my eyes and stopped.

"But it *is* similar," she insisted. "We're going against our natural instincts. Instead of not talking, it's abstaining from sex. It's like we're fasting—except instead of three days, it's two. We're making a sacrifice for a larger reward."

"What fricking reward?"

"That depends on what we make of it. But we need to at least try and be open-minded. We can lower the volume … and bond and be intimate in other ways. We can let our hair down and be ourselves. We can reconnect."

"But—"

"Just think about it … going PG-13 for two days. Like you and me in the early days. I think we'll really learn from it."

"Oh give me a fricking break, Ash. Fast-forward forty-eight hours, when Mike's in our kitchen and we're singing 'Happy Birthday' and popping champagne. I mean, Jesus Christ, Ash. Then you're going to give him his gift? Tell him we didn't have sex, that you followed his instructions, that I agreed to be deprived? Don't you see how fucking embarrassing that is?"

"Nobody's going to know."

"I'm talking about Mike. Looking all superior and asking me how it went."

"Oh c'mon, it's his birthday. He'll just be really glad to see you. And it's not like we're giving him a formal gift. It's not some letter we signed or something we put in a box, with a ribbon for him to untie."

"What?" I said, getting tenser by the minute. "What is it then?"

"It's whatever we want it to be," she said. "Relax, it's all going to be okay. This will be really good for us … and bring us closer together."

I noticed Ashley leaning in, so I slowly leaned toward her. I tried not to look nervous as I tilted my head, and bang, she was kissing me. It was happening. *Seize the fucking day*, I told myself. I lowered my hands down her back till they were on her ass—and she kissed me harder. It was a photo I'd have wanted.

She had her hands in my hair, just the way I liked it. She grabbed two chunks and tugged, then dug into my hair again. It felt great; I had a big-time erection. Ashley noticed when her hand brushed against it. I started kissing her neck and moving to her earlobe, moving in closer. I was almost on top of her when she said, "I'm sorry" and pulled away. Like that, she got off the bed.

She started to pace. I watched her, silently, having nothing to say. I figured it was her turn to explain. Staring at her legs, I glimpsed her black thong. She wasn't wearing a bra, and I watched her breasts bounce. Then I remembered what Mike said about staring at her tits, and thought what a motherfucker he was.

"Look," she said finally, staring into my eyes. "I'm sorry, that probably seemed like a tease, but that's not how I meant it. I know it's frustrating. It is for me too. I didn't want to stop either."

"So why did you?"

"What we've been talking about … abstaining till Saturday."

"Jeez, Ash, we weren't even close to having sex."

"Not yet, but it was getting sexual."

"I didn't even cop a feel. What are you talking about?"

"About sexual relations in general. We definitely were crossing into that. We want to keep this relatively pure if we want to gain something from it."

"I don't want to gain jack shit from it, Ash. Are you telling me 'no sex till Saturday' means no sexual relations, period?"

"We can kiss and express affection—just not like what just happened."

"What just happened? We made out. That's off-limits now?"

"It was just getting a little sexual," she said. "And that would be a distraction … when we're trying to get to a safe, comfortable place to really communicate."

"So that means I can't even make out with you?"

"It means I can't either," she said. "We're in this together, Dave. It's about opening new avenues of communication. Being open and honest again. Without the distraction of sex to get in the way of a dialogue."

"Look, maybe I get that concept, on some level, sort of," I said. "But look who suggested it? Fucking Mike!"

"Forget Mike right now," she said. "It's the idea that matters. It's a chance for us to bond and appreciate each other more. Tap into new channels and bring us some healing, too. But we have to be open to it. And doing this together—that's what makes it special."

"There's lots of things we could do together," I said. "It could be abstaining from something else. I'd even do food if you wanted."

"But this has a purpose," she said. "We want to grow and communicate better as a couple. Let's just give it a chance, okay? We can sleep on it and talk more in the morning. I just noticed the time."

"Okay, but yeah, I do want to pick this up in the morning."

"Sure, whenever you want. And just consider the positives, okay?"

"Sure," I said, dismissively. "I do want to talk about Mike's friggin' request tomorrow."

"Of course," she said, "but I was just thinking …. This was the best, most honest conversation we've had in a really long time."

"Yeah, it's probably been a while."

"Aren't you glad we talked tonight?"

"Well yeah," I said. "I wasn't acknowledging reality before. I had my head in the sand when the subject came up."

"Well, I'm really glad you told me. I want us to keep

talking openly, going forward. But I think this was a big and important first step. How do you feel? Like a big weight is off your chest?

"Yeah, I'm glad we started the conversation—and I will want to clarify some things later—but yes, we don't have to dance around the obvious anymore."

"Yay! Isn't that an awesome feeling?"

" 'Awesome' is a bit strong, but I'm glad we got rid of a few barriers."

"Me too, Dave," she said with a smile, and then leaned in to kiss me. Her lips were luscious wet—a juicy burst of tongue and passion. Only it was over in seconds—then she pulled away.

"I take it we were crossing into being sexual?" I said.

"Just come closer and hug me right now."

And so I hugged her. And rubbed her back. And ran my hands through her hair. I had a good few minutes to hold her close and feel her warmth.

"I really feel," she said, sitting back up, "that tonight has made us stronger already."

"Well," I said, "certainly it was good we talked up on the roof tonight. But I want to talk tomorrow about this birthday thing."

"Sure," she said, getting out of bed. "I'm gonna brush my teeth."

\* \* \*

"So," she said, "I downloaded some children's books. Would you be up for telling a bedtime story?"

"I'd be up for it," I said, "but I'd love it if you read it."

"Well, you're the one who is short of sleep, so okay …."

"What story?" I asked.

"Well, we should probably save it for closer to Halloween, but I was kind of thinking this Washington Irving story—"

" 'Rip Van Winkle'?" I said, prepared to object.

"The Sleepy Hollow story. It takes place in your parent's hood. I figured since we're going out there on Saturday—"

"Sounds great," I said, as she snuggled up close. "Can I give you a kiss first?"

"Of course," she said, giving me tongue for a few fleeting seconds.

"So," she said, pulling away, "I don't want you trying to stay awake while I read. I want you chilling with Mr. Sandman and dreaming of … headless horsemen. Just kidding."

"Yeah, I don't want nightmares," I said. "Will you skip past the really scary parts?"

"Aww," she said, smiling and kissing me on the cheek.

I lay on my side and listened to her read. There was a rhythm and poetry in the lines, which she brought out, seemed to capture. I just let myself be captured in the spell of Ashley's calm, soothing voice.

I heard her stop a few pages in. "You awake?" She yawned.

"Barely," I said. "Your voice is so serene."

"What do you think of the story so far?"

"It's a little over my head," I said, "but I like how you read it. I thought this was a children's story. It ain't no 'Winnie the Pooh,' I'll tell you that."

"Do you want me to keep reading?"

"Oh, please do. I wanna hear what happens to my boy … Ichabod."

"Okay," she said, "but it's long, so you may not find out tonight. I'm pretty tired myself."

"Sure," I said, "I like 'to-be-continued.' "

"Okay," she said, and picked up the thread.

"And good night, Ash," I interrupted. "On the chance I do fall asleep … I love you."

"I love you too," she said, and resumed reading.

A few minutes later, I heard her pause to yawn.

I pretended to be asleep. I didn't want to keep her up. She kept reading and I just lay there and listened.

"Dave?" she said, a short while later.

I breathed heavily and didn't answer. She waited a few seconds and then turned off the light. I heard her roll over onto her side and kick the sheet down to her feet, just as I had. It was hot with the AC off.

* * *

I listened to her breathing deepen as Ashley fell asleep. It was the only sound in the bedroom. I could relax now, adjust my head on my pillow better. Take some deep breaths. I looked at Ashley in her thong next to me. Her ass and back facing me. I tried to stay motionless for a while. Let sleep really kick in for her.

I pulled my dick out through my boxers. Let my erection breathe. I was careful not to wake Ashley—I wasn't going to stroke it. I tried not to touch it. I just let it throb in the open air.

What I wanted to do was slide quietly out of bed and jerk off in the bathroom. I'd done it plenty of times the past couple months. But I was worried about Ashley waking up. I didn't want her wondering where I was. Coming back a minute later, I could explain that I was just taking a piss. But coming back five minutes later—that was tougher. It's not like I often took dumps in the middle of the night. Ashley would suspect I'd been masturbating. It wasn't inconceivable that she'd ask me what happened to my erection. Or say something that was fucked up—like it was a violation of our pledge.

I considered being really quick. But I imagined her waking up and seeing me walk toward the bathroom. And I wouldn't know she hadn't, after I'd locked the door. I just didn't want a confrontation. Even though the whole scenario was pretty unlikely, I didn't want to spin the roulette wheel.

So I just lay there, my hard-on unrelenting.

It wasn't the best view, but I stared down at Ashley's ass in that thong … the contrast of her tanned legs with her milky, white ass.

I wanted so badly just to reach out and touch her. I wanted to put my arms around her and hold her tight. To squeeze her ass and play with her tits. Finger her pussy, go down on her …. *Goddammit*, I thought, *I so want to fuck you, Ashley*.

I looked up at the ceiling and sighed. I wanted to jerk off, right there. I wanted to shoot on her unblemished ass cheeks. And splash on her black silk thong. The way she was breathing, I wondered if she'd even wake up.

I caught my hand each time it gravitated to my dick and realized how deeply I was being deprived. I couldn't even squeeze her tight, toned ass … off fucking limits—per Mike. Like I'd lost all access … was on the other side of the velvet rope. As if lying next to her now was a privilege.

She had to know the cards she was carrying. That she was calling all the shots. *No wonder*, I thought, *she's sleeping so soundly*.

I felt diminished by the evening. Even before Mike's birthday present, *cuckold* was now a word between us. And she gave off a vibe, like, *This is how things are now*. So I was nervous around her—and kind of in awe. She seemed larger than life. Like never before. Which made me feel smaller. Like I couldn't compete with her aura. She was sexy and gorgeous. I was the chump husband who got himself cucked.

And now she'd doubled down. Like she wanted me blue-balled. She'd showed me who mattered—fucking Mike.

*Mike controls her pussy now*, I thought, *getting her to do this to me*. And after Saturday … then fucking what? But one thing was for certain, Ashley would end our pledge by fucking Mike, all night, in my bedroom. And now, for the third time,

I'd be relegated to the couch for the night. I'd be left out to dry while the two of them fucked.

I wondered if Mike had gotten her to agree to the birthday deal while fucking her the night before. Getting her to say "No pussy for Dave," as he pumped inside her.

I figured Ashley's pussy was probably sleeping quite soundly. Well-satisfied and well-fucked. And dreaming of Mike's birthday. When Mike would sperm it again.

And there I was, lying beside my wife with a raging boner. Wanting to shoot right on her ass. I did a slow, up-and-down stroke but suddenly stopped to think about it.

Two strokes would invariably lead to two more. And with Ashley right next to me, it was a wild card—I might not last at all. By then it'd be too late. I wouldn't be able to stop.

So I tried not to think about it. I went over baseball scores—then football—then numbers from the speech I gave. I knew the years every president was born. Something random from the fourth grade that stuck. I got up to Grover Cleveland and somehow fell asleep.

# CHAPTER SEVENTEEN

I woke up to my alarm and heard Ashley already in the shower. I thought about masturbating but figured I would wait until she left. When I wouldn't be stressing about her opening the door.

I could be a little late ... my boss wasn't coming in till later. So I just lay there, trying to distract myself from the boner I was sporting. Thought of work stuff, mostly.

I heard the towel rack rattle and knew she was about to come out. So I pretended to be asleep. I waited until she was next to her desk before opening my eyes. Wearing nothing but a thong, she grabbed a bra out of her dresser and I squinted at her tits, her nipples. When she got close, bending down by her night table, I closed my eyes again.

Ashley was getting dressed for work. White button-down and a navy blue blazer ... as if she had a big meeting or client lunch. I thought of Ashley getting dressed that first week of the rumor. Knowing she was being seen as a major slut. For fucking a colleague with her husband nearby.

Her sweet and innocent image, shattered. The married slut who got spermed right under her husband's nose. But she didn't lose focus, and she weathered the storm. Her boss supported her. And she stopped caring about people talking.

I watched Ashley putting on lipstick and thought about the people she was getting dressed up for. I imagined Ashley saying "Good morning" to them an hour from now. Guys would be checking out her tits, her ass, thinking of the rumor.

They all knew my wife didn't give a fuck that I was right

outside. Jim had spermed her pussy anyway. In their book, I was a sucker, a fool, a pussy. A husband who got royally played.

And they got to watch me being humiliated at one of their happy hours, having to shake the hand of Jim Murta—the guy who fucked my wife and blabbed about it, the guy who didn't give two fucks I was right outside, who probably smirked when I was sent upstairs.

The young guys where she worked probably saw Jim Murta as a fucking icon. At the happy hour I showed up for, they probably saw the photos Tamara took. Those had to get passed around.

Tamara ambushed me that night. Just when I happened to be near the guy, she was right there with her camera. "Oh hey, Dave, Jim, pose together, quick photo. Ashley, get in there." That must've cracked the sales guys up. Seeing Jim Murta posing with my wife and me. Me—trying to look like I didn't know that Jim Murta had balled my wife.

It had only been eight weeks since Jim fucked her. I figured they must talk about her still. Whenever they saw her, they had to be thinking—as she bopped from one meeting to the next—how their junior salesman buddy uncorked inside her pussy.

Three months ago, things had been way different. She was the sharp, polished, communication director, with an office near corporate row. Big-titted and hot, but newly married. The idea that she'd fuck a co-worker—let alone some junior fucking salesman with other co-workers present—that would have been off-the-charts crazy.

Until it happened. And they learned Jim had balled my wife bare from behind. The sales guys probably knew if he'd talked dirty to her. If he'd called me a chump or a pussy when he was balls deep inside her. If he got her to say, "Fuck my husband" before he blew his load. People probably knew how quickly he managed—from the time Tamara opened the bathroom door and invited him in—to get his cock inside my wife and pumping.

And now they saw an entirely different Ashley—the kind of girl who'd fuck a junior level employee and not care that her husband was there, right outside, fucking knocking.

She'd made a public fool of me. Of course that's how they'd see it. And now they all probably wanted a crack at her. Jim Murta had kicked opened that possibility.

I imagined guys going to happy hour just so they could hit on her. Like Ashley with a margarita was a strong corporate fuck prospect. Thinking maybe they could get a blowjob in the men's room. Or fuck her like a dirty girl, bent over in front of a mirror. Maybe a men's room facial … so she could see what a slut she was.

It happened once, they must figure, so anything was possible. Maybe guys were angling for a tag team—Ashley sucking cocks, plural, wearing her fucking wedding ring, a married cock whore, her clothes tossed and scattered on the men's room floor.

"So Dave, are you getting up or what?"

"What?" I said. "Oh, I was just waiting for you."

"I've been out of the bathroom ten minutes. Aren't you going to be late?"

"No. I mean, yeah."

"Well, do you know what I think?"

"What?"

"That you just wanted to watch me."

"What?"

"Getting dressed. I saw you in the mirror. It's okay. It's a compliment, and a very sweet one."

Ashley bent over and gave me a kiss. Then she gave me tongue for a good five seconds. As she pulled away, she reached down and brushed against my erection. I sat there, motionless, hoping.

"I'm sorry, honey," she said, "I really have to go."

"But—"

"You need to get yourself in the shower, mister. You're gonna be late."

"Yeah, but you don't normally leave this early."

"Early meeting and *I* definitely can't be late."

"Yeah, okay," I said. "Well, I quite liked that, Ash," I said giving her a hug.

"Me too," she said. "I'm going to the gym tonight, but I'll be back to get ready before we go out."

"Yeah, okay, well, you look amazingly gorgeous this morning. Have a great day, Ash."

She gave me a quick peck and I shut the door behind her. And locked it. Then I watched the video of the lobby as she left the building. I waited, keeping my eyes on the mini-TV for a few minutes longer to make sure she hadn't forgotten anything.

\* \* \*

I went into the bathroom and pulled Ashley's black thong from the hamper—the one she'd worn the night before—and put it next to me on the bed.

I thought of Tamara cornering Ashley. "So, how did the talk go?"

Ashley would say she'd tell her at lunch.

"Well," Ashley would say, "he pretended like this was all a surprise to him, but he clearly knows he's being cucked. And he admitted that he jerks off while thinking about Mike and me fucking."

"That's a big step toward watching," I could hear Tamara saying.

"Well, we took another big step last night—a chastity oath. Dave can't touch me sexually. We're giving that to Mike as a birthday present."

"I like that it's a present from both of you," Tamara

136

would say, "a present with Dave's fucking name on the card. A present to the guy who took his wife from him."

"Yeah, it'll probably be a little emasculating for him when he faces Mike."

"I love it," Tamara would say, "and right in his fucking home. Do you know what horns are, Ash?"

"Mike's told me, and yes, Dave's horns are starting to show big."

"Yeah, and now that he can't even get a pity fuck—excuse me, a pity hand job—those cuckold horns are gonna sprout up big, for sure."

"If he keeps doing nothing, before he knows it I'll be giving Dave, a big-ass rack of cuck horns."

"He won't do shit. Too much of a pussy. He's going all the way cuckold. And I want a front row seat for the festivities."

"Well, Dave is still too afraid to ask me."

"Well, leave the door open next time you fuck in your bed. I bet he'll be peering in and jerking off."

"No, I'm making him ask for the privilege of watching another man's bare cock pumping deep inside me. That's when he'll really be wearing some horns."

"I want to watch, Ash. I want to see Dave reduced to that, to see you ride cock in front of your jerk-off boy husband."

I leaned forward and brought her thong closer. Even if simply out of principle, I wanted to cum in it. White sperm on her black thong. It'd be taken in with her laundry. Any stains could be Mike's. In a way, I wanted to contribute a stain, something even still faintly noticeable later. So I laid it close by.

I started thinking what a dumbass stooge people would think I was, if they knew. Ashley's pussy had been balls-out taken from me. And now I'd lost all privileges. I could barely fucking touch my wife at the moment. They'd see me as a big-time pussy for going along with all this. For getting so fucking played.

Mike wanted my wife to see me made a laughingstock. He wanted to show her what kind of a pussy her husband was. He wanted Ashley walking all over me. Treating me like a cuck. Showing off her big tits but not letting me touch them. Stopping a hug if she felt an erection. I couldn't even kiss her neck.

I thought of the orgasms Mike probably had fucking Ashley. Gloating over how he just came into my life and took my fucking wife from me. Showed Ashley who the real man was. And got me fucking cucked.

And now he knew he really had her. She'd see him Saturday and she'd done what he asked her to do … deny me even foreplay. Probably liked me having blue balls. Probably loved getting Ashley to go along with that. A real visceral way to say, "Fuck you, Dave."

Ten days ago he'd never met my wife. Now he was calling the shots in my marriage. And fucking my wife regularly. Like he owned my fucking bedroom. A dozen-plus fucks and counting. A lot of big sperm-loads. She was on the fucking pill, but still.

I brought her thong right up close. I wanted my fat load just sitting there afterward. Like graffiti.

"And now, Ash," I whispered, "you're denying me sex as a gift to him. You're fucking giving him my dignity. Letting him strip it away from me. That's his fucking birthday present from you. And from fucking me as fucking well.

"Don't you think it's a fucked up birthday wish? And you're fucking honoring it. I don't get a hand job, can't even touch your tits. When I want to … so fucking badly. But I can't, because that's forbidden. Because fucking Mike told you so.

"For five years, it's just been me and only me … going inside your pussy. And then you let Jim Murta bathroom-ball you. And leave his load inside you. And now you're openly cucking me. You're fucking cucking me, Ash. Fucking Mike regularly in our bed. Letting him … slut you out. Using you like his personal fuck doll. And making a cuck of me in the process.

"You fucking crave his cock, don't you, Ash? He blows me out of the water, right? You like 'em big and fat with a lot of stamina. And mine just doesn't fucking rate. Can't satisfy that pussy. Especially now. Is that fucking it? Is he a fucking eight-incher? Is that how big he is, Ash? Is that what you fucking slobber all over? Mike's big, fat, fucking penis. Do you suck on his fucking balls, Ash? Do you let them swirl inside your mouth? As his cock throbs against your face? Do you kiss me afterward, right after you've sucked his cock? Is that what you fucking think of me, Ash?"

Suddenly I came … hard. I really exploded. Splattered my leg, spilled over my hands, and then just kept on going … down my shaft, my balls. And still had more to go. I was a mess. I hadn't planned on that.

\* \* \*

My regular doorman had his break at nine. That was one positive about being late. Not having to deal. Just taking a rushed walk through my apartment's lobby.

I was relieved that no one came on as I was heading down. I had a smile ready just in case. But as soon as the door opened to the first floor, I switched to a grimace … as if I was all business and running late.

I sprang out of the elevator, nodded hello to the doorman, and made a beeline for the front door. But the doorman waved for me to stop.

"Mr. Martens, there's a FedEx for you." He was a new guy—probably just out of college. We'd never exchanged a word beyond hello. I was grateful for that. "It's in the office," he said. "I'll just be a second."

"Yeah, okay," I said, as if I was in a hurry.

But then, out of the office, came Tommy. He'd been a doorman there since we moved in. He was my age, and we talked sports. I had to say hello.

"Hey, Dave," he said. "How was your trip?"

"Uh, it was fine … yeah."

"Good."

"Yeah, I just got back last night … from San Francisco."

"You bring your rain gear out there?"

I laughed. "Yeah, how did you know? Did Ashley—"

"Giants were rained out this week."

The young doorman came back out and handed me my FedEx.

Tommy waited for me to put it away before continuing, "But other than the rain, your trip was good?"

"Uh yeah," I said, trying hard to read his expression. Then I wondered if he was trying to read mine. "See the thing is, I have a new, side venture, actually. And part of this trip was for that."

"Okay."

"But it's a lot of work. And I couldn't do it all myself. So now I have a business partner."

Tommy looked at me blankly.

"Well actually, you've may have seen him—the guy I'm working with. He's been coming by the apartment a lot, lately."

"You mean Mike?"

"Yeah, okay, you know him."

"You came in with him last Friday night. Sure, I know Mike."

"That's right, yeah. I mean the thing is, he's a good business idea guy, an entrepreneur type. But, it's still in concept stage. So we're up at my place a lot, brainstorming. Like this weekend, probably, too."

"Okay."

Then the younger doorman interjected, "Do you want us to add Mike to our list?"

"What?"

"Will he be getting deliveries here?"

"Oh God, no." I laughed and shook my head. "It's short term. No need for that."

"Okay."

"Yeah, I gotta run, guys. I'm way frigging late."

"I'll get the door," the young doorman said, hustling.

"Thanks, man. Have a good day."

"You, too," he said. But he said something else. The word got clipped when the door shut behind me. What the kid probably said was, "You too, Dave."

But what it sounded like to me was, "You too, bitch."

As I walked to the subway, I kept thinking, *Why the fuck did Tommy ask me again how my trip was, after I'd already said it was fine?*

* * *

I saw that my boss' door was closed and heaved a sigh of relief as I went into my office. Then I learned he wouldn't be in until one. And there was nothing in email or voicemail that couldn't wait a few minutes more. So I did a brief status meeting and then went down to the street. I just wanted to be outside—and not in my office—when I called Mike.

"Dave, how you doing, bro?"

"How do you think, *bro*, when I come home to Ashley telling me I can't even make out with her?"

"Listen—" he said.

"I mean what the fuck?"

"Dave … listen. I'm late for a meeting—and really jammed today. So let's grab a beer at five-thirty. Same place."

"We're going out with friends tonight. Can you just call me as soon as you're out of the meeting you're going to?"

"Your friends aren't till later—I'm talking right after

work. I'm jammed until then, man. And I really gotta run. So does five-thirty work or what?"

"Yeah, okay."

"I'll see you then. And look man, just chill. The two of you—your relationship—will benefit from this. It already has … the way you bonded last night. And I'll explain more when I see you."

"She told you about last night?"

"We'll talk when I see you, bro."

"Yeah, okay Mike, fine. Five-thirty."

I heard him hang up and muttered, "Go fuck yourself."

I went back upstairs and started cranking—doing a bunch of quick meetings with guys from my team, deciding on what charts we needed for third quarter review. That was followed by a long conference call. Little was relevant to my work, but I had to pay attention, because someone would invariably ask me something. I kept my door shut so I could pace and look out the window.

I was in front of my desk when the call ended and everyone clicked off, so I sat down in one of the guest chairs. I took in the view others saw when sitting in my office, talking to me. I looked at the two photos on my desk.

One was of Ashley and me in Canada, on the porch of a cabin in the woods. If asked, I would explain that my uncle owns land there. Tell them how the island has no electricity.

The other photo on display showed my whole family at Christmas … Ashley and me front and center, my parents and brother behind us. Ashley was wearing a red holiday dress, no cleavage. But anyone who sat in the chair and took a close look could tell my wife had big tits.

People would comment most on her smile. Some old company big shot in my office once told me, "She should do Ivory soap commercials." But I'm sure it was her tits guys in my office noticed first. At least that's what it seemed like at company functions I'd brought Ashley to. Her tits stood out no matter how she dressed, and I saw the way guys stared. I didn't care. She was my wife—let them feel envious. I really didn't think twice. Plus it made me look good. Like I was getting it done.

I heard a knock at the door and then my boss saying my name. I sprang up and let him in. His look said *why did you have the door closed* so I said, "I just got off a conference call."

"Do I want to know?" he said, sitting down.

"Just deliverable dates for Transit. Needs monitoring, but it will happen."

"Well, Dave," Brian said, "I just wanted to stop by—I'm running to lunch—but I wanted to thank you for filling in for me out there this week. I heard you were great in Q&A."

"Thanks Brian, anytime—"

"And I got your meeting notes—thank you. I think I'm gonna have you go to the next committee meeting as well."

I laughed, and said, "Sure."

"Everything under control?"

"Yeah, some mini-fires from IT issues, but still on track for a Wednesday changeover."

"Okay," he said, "and I'll be emailing the profiles I need for Monday."

"Sure. How are you feeling?"

"Physically great, but I've got meetings back to back to back. Do you need me for anything?"

"No, Brian. Right now, we're good—under control."

"Good," he said, pausing. "Say, did I miss the RSVP for the Myers dinner? Was that before Labor Day? You got an invite, right?"

"Yeah, it was, but I'm sure it's no problem. It's still a week away."

"You going?"

"Yeah," I said. "I was there last year. It's a nice spread."

"You bringing Ashley?"

"Y'know, I still have to check her schedule. Why?"

"Because I'm bringing Diane," he said. "I was up with Bob this morning, and he said the top guys from Myers are bringing their wives and it would be nice if I brought Diane."

"Should I bring Ashley?"

"I'm sure Bob would say definitely."

"I'll talk to Ashley this weekend."

"And I'll RSVP," he said. "I'm reachable rest of the day, so any problems ...."

"You bet."

I watched Brian head down the hall and sighed with relief. I had some projects to review with my team, and a development meeting, but I knew it was like a summer Friday. I'd be skating out at five.

# CHAPTER EIGHTEEN

Crosstown traffic was a mess, so I didn't get to the bar early, like I'd hoped. From his barstool Mike saw me walk in and stood up and to give me a hug. I pulled away quickly and took my seat beside him. He was drinking a Stella, so I told the bartender I'd have the same.

"So how you doing, man?" he said. "Where are you guys going for dinner?"

"I don't know. My friend picked the restaurant. Mike, seriously, what the fuck?"

"What?"

"You know fucking what. I can't get fucking intimate with my own wife?"

"Ashley's giving you a real nice cucking, Dave, isn't she?"

"Yeah, because you fucking told her to. And thanks for not giving me any fucking heads-up. You had this planned when I met you yesterday. I fucking asked you what to expect."

"Yeah, I know—"

"Mike, you looked me in the eye and told me you wanted to help me. Not fucking blindside me."

"I get it—I do—just hear me out."

"I don't want to hear bullshit about how I'm fucking benefiting. We hung out for over an hour. Why didn't you fucking tell me?"

"For the same reason I'm not telling Ashley about this meeting. I keep private things private."

"But it was your fucking idea."

Mike gestured for me to lower the volume, and I realized I must have been shouting. "She wants to do this, Dave," he said in a low, emphatic voice. "Ashley is really enjoying seeing you cucked. She loved the way I took over your bedroom. This is just another thing. Only, she's the one in charge now, telling you to put your dick back in your pants, telling you her pussy's not for you."

"Yeah, because you fucking told her to."

"And like a good little sub, she listened to me. Is that what you want to hear? Bet you had a boner waking up today. Knowing I'm fucking your wife regularly now, and you can't even touch her." He took a long sip of his beer.

"I asked for *help*," I said. "You could have told me, Mike."

"She wanted to tell you herself. It was important to her. She understood the significance. I couldn't spoil that. It would be a betrayal to Ash."

"Okay, Mike, so can you help *me* now?"

"I'll sure try buddy, what's up?"

"I just need a break, man. I just really need a fucking break. Okay?"

"That's what this time with Ash is—a break. I'm serious. It's not just relationship building, it's relationship bonding. Without having to worry about the sex. Focus on what's important—building a new relationship with your wife."

"Can we just slow things down—catch our breath? I need some time alone with my wife. I feel like a stranger lately. It's hurting my marriage, I know it."

"What's hurting your marriage, bro, is the way you communicate. And I'm talking about Ashley too. That's what tomorrow night's about. I want us all to hang out. We're gonna build on your talk last night. Only this time, I'm going to get Ash to be more real and forthcoming with you."

"Okay, Mike, let me see your license. Show me your birthday's tomorrow."

"You think I'd make it up? Check it out, bro."

I looked at the date and said, "Un-fucking believable."

"That's how Ash learned, too. They carded us at Trattora's. She was like, 'Oh my God, your birthday's Saturday.' And *you* know, there's no way Ashley's canceling that."

"Probably not, no."

"But it's gonna be good. You'll like it, all of us sitting in your living room, doing nothing but talking. And I don't mean like, talk for fifteen minutes and then off to your bedroom. No, nothing needs to be rushed. I want you guys to really talk."

I couldn't believe what I was hearing. "What?" I asked.

"And fucking your wife, Dave," he said, "is a great way to top off my night. Makes turning thirty-three fucking balls-out awesome."

"Yeah, I get it, Mike, but about this big talk … I don't want to see Ashley getting fucked in front of me. And I don't want you claiming that I want to make that request. You say you're all about the truth. Then be accurate. This was never my idea."

"I'm not bringing it up, bro. As I said, that will come from you. Once you fully realize you are her sub, you'll be saying it, bro."

"Look, I'm just saying, I don't want you bringing it up tomorrow night … and in general. I won't allow you to pin that question on me."

"The question's been pinned inside you, bro. When you're jerking off today, you should answer it. You should say it to yourself as you jerk. That you want to watch Ashley … fucked hard in front of you."

I nearly fell off the barstool as I shook my head no. "Mike, I'm telling you, I fucking don't."

"C'mon bro, it's me. Be like you said—the way we used to be. And talk to me, man. You've pictured Ash getting fucked in the bathroom countless times these last couple months. Of course you want to see her get fucked. So tell me, how do you picture it when you jerk off?"

"C'mon Mike, I'm fucking serious."

"Bro, the old you was not a prude talking about this. You don't have to keep it bottled up. Were you up all night jerking or what?"

"No, actually, I wasn't. I didn't ... but that's not the point."

"I just want to know what you think about when you jerk off, man."

"I don't know," I said. "I think about what happened. Not what might or could happen."

"Like the way I've taken Ashley's pussy? And made it mine? Things like that?"

"No, not like that."

"So tell me what it's like. You've imagined me fucking your wife in your bed, right?"

"Yeah, okay, I have. I thought of her being extra-sexual. Pretty horny. And she's my wife. I love her. She turns me on, so it's not surprising."

"It's very natural, bro ... that your wife getting fucked by me turns you on."

"I wasn't saying that—"

"Dave, no more charades. All summer, you were jerking off picturing Ashley being fucked in that bathroom. You wondered how big his cock was, what he was thinking about when he came. You told me all that. Remember?"

"Yes."

"So I know you jerk off picturing me with your wife, now. It's a very normal reaction to have, and yes, sometimes embarrassing to admit. But can't we just stop the fucking pretense? Let it go, bro, and just be real. Give me some old school, deep thinking, Dave."

"What do you want me to say?"

"Well," he said, "tell me how it feels knowing you've been cucked?"

"Mike, I don't frigging know. I mean, yeah, I was in a cuckold chatroom and all, but I didn't fucking ask for this."

"But it's not like you weren't here, bro, while it all was happening right in front of you."

"I know …."

"You led me to Ashley, Dave. You know you wanted it."

"I didn't—"

"Sure you did. When you gave me your cell number, when you met me for a beer, when you introduced me to her—"

"I met you for a beer because I thought you were my friend."

"Don't tell me you saw none of this happening, bro. You were curious."

"I was never asking to be cuckolded, Mike. Not once when we talked did I say that."

"Then I read between the lines, bro," he said. "And once I met Ashley, your actions did the talking … or rather, your inaction."

"What? Because I didn't stand up to you?"

"Because you couldn't," he said.

"Yeah, because I couldn't process what was happening."

"I knew pretty early on," he said, looking me in the eye, "that Ash was gonna be mine. And that you'd be on a cuck adventure."

"I bet you did," I said, "but I'm stating the truth. I didn't introduce you to Ashley thinking you were gonna fuck her. And that's my story, even if you insist on telling her otherwise."

"Keep saying the truth, bro," he said. "I'm serious … you started to peel the onion last night with Ashley, right? Keep doing that. Like you're doing with me, again."

"You just want me to tell her I'm a fucking cuckold. That's *your* truth."

"Bro," he said, "I just want you to be you."

"Okay, Mike," I said, thinking *what-the-fuck ever.*

"Oh, and I forgot to tell you," he said. "I got us tickets for the Giants game. You said first weekend in October was good, and that's what I got … against the Eagles."

"What? You got us tickets?"

"Yeah, my boss fucking hooked me up today."

"Wow, well let me check that weekend."

"And I'll have my car. We'll just drive down, the two of us. Early. That'll give us a few hours to tailgate."

"Tailgate? Seriously? And what? You got a football in the trunk we're gonna toss around in the parking lot?"

"What … is tailgating just too low-brow for you? Something only white trash does?"

"Give me a fucking break. No, I love a good tailgate as much as freaking anyone. But why are we even doing this, Mike? Pretending we're great friends and buddies. Like what is that proving and who cares?" I realized I was over-gesturing and consciously clasped my hands together. "Do you really want to hang out with me one-on-one, all fucking day?"

"May surprise you, bro, but that sounds like a pretty good day to me. It's the Giants. You're a huge fan … like me. And they're good fucking seats. Lower level. What am I missing?"

"Well, no, it does sound cool, man. And I'm up for the game. But why all gung ho and tailgating?"

"I can't remember going to a game and not tailgating. It's pretty fucking easy, not to mention a fucking party, but whatever, bro, we'll just go to the game."

"Look, Mike, I'm totally cool with it. If you want me to go, I'll go. Just wondering why you'd want to even ask me."

" 'Cause you're my friend, and I like hanging with old-school Dave. I'd like to get back to that, bro."

"But is this for Ashley's sake?"

"What?"

"You and me hanging out … you want to show her we're still buddies?"

"Why?"

"I don't know … to strengthen our fucking camp story about us being friends."

Mike laughed. "Hadn't thought about it. Look, it was just a simple thing—a fucking Giants game. Yes, I thought about taking Ash, but I was like *Fuck that, Dave's a Giants fan; he's gonna fucking love it—I'm taking Dave.*"

"Hey, Mike, I do appreciate it and I want to go. So seriously, do count me in." When he didn't respond immediately, I added, "And hey, I'll supply the pre-game alcohol."

"Right on, bro. All right, cool. Really glad you're on board But explain to me … why would you think I wouldn't want to hang out with you? Or that I was doing this for Ash?"

"I don't know, man. Look, I'm not exactly the most confident person right now. I'm a bit fucking insecure. So yeah, I was like, why would you want spend the day with me?"

"We hung out a lot a few weeks ago."

"Yeah, I know, Mike, but c'mon. Back then, you were trying to get to her. Now you … you have Ashley."

"True," he said, "I do have Ashley, but for me, it's never just been about getting with your wife. Like you said the other day, this is something Ashley and you are doing together, that I want you to be a part of. We're all in this together. And I like hanging out with you. You were the first name that came to mind, actually."

"Okay, well cool, I'm glad."

"Plus it'll give Ash a day without either of us, right?"

"Yeah, I guess. Listen Mike, I gotta get going."

"Oh, have one more," he said. "Ash is at the gym. She won't be home for a while."

"No seriously, I got stuff to do at home—stuff for work I didn't finish."

"You mean you're gonna go home and jerk off?"

"No—"

"Like you did every day over the thought of Ashley in that bathroom."

"Mike, I seriously have shit to do. Couldn't get my own stuff done, filling in for my boss this week."

"Either way, you're still jerking off before she comes home."

"Yeah, Mike, whatever. I gotta go."

"Okay, look, I was just kidding. Good luck with the homework. I'm serious."

"Thanks."

"It was some good honest talking tonight, bro. I like having Dave back."

"Yeah. Talk to you later."

"You bet. Oh, and Dave?"

"Yeah?"

"Take care of my girl tonight."

# CHAPTER NINETEEN

In the cab on the way home, I thought of Saturday night, and how much Mike wanted to embarrass me. Not just with the birthday gift, but also with the "talk"—orchestrating some intimate relationship conversation with Ashley. He'd be asking the questions, of course, as if he was some fucking marriage counselor.

As I walked up to my building I pretended to be on the phone. I waved hello to the doorman and said into my cell, "Right, it needs to be ready for 10K filings." I was glad to be going up in the elevator alone.

Mike was right—Ashley was at the gym. Her class was still going on. I had some time, so I went into our bedroom and locked the door. I paused for a moment, but decided there was no way I could suppress it. I saw where that had gotten me the night before. And the desire—or compulsion—was too strong. I figured jerking off would calm me down for the night ahead. I didn't want some boner in the middle of dinner.

I lay down on the bed and pulled down my pants, thinking, *Mike will be in this bed tomorrow.* "The motherfucker wants me cucked hard," I said in a low voice. "He came into my life with that goal in mind ... to take my wife's pussy away from me right from fucking under me. He got her to deny me sex ... wanted me with fucking blue balls."

Tomorrow night he would really rub it in. And want to show Ashley what a cuck I'd become. He wanted me fucking asking her. He'd have Ashley saying yes. And pretty soon, he would do it. I'd be seeing my wife balled in front of me. Mike would take Ashley's "yes" and make it happen.

Then I thought of Ashley's wedding dress—the passing comments Mike had made. I pictured him adding that condition. Like not only did he want me watching my wife fucked in my own bed, but he wanted to fuck her in her wedding dress. He wanted to sperm my wife dressed as a bride.

I thought of where he'd want me. Sitting in a cuckold chair, one he designated. I thought of the wooden chair in our office/storage room that Ashley's talked about throwing out. I pictured Mike suggesting that for me. Stuff like that wouldn't surprise me now.

He might hand me photos of Ashley and me on our wedding day. And have me look at them as I sat naked in the cuckold chair. He'd probably have Ashley looking me in the eye … as I sat with cum in my hand … as she rode his cock to multiple orgasms … consecrating my new reality … as I watched him fuck my bride as his own.

And all because—I reminded myself—I intro-fucking-duced them. I let Mike meet my wife and have twenty minutes alone with her. He was gunning for me all along. Ashley's pussy and my cuck horns—those were the prizes Mike was after. And now he was punching it hard. And encouraging her to cuck me more.

Probably saying why she should want me to watch her get fucked … why for her it was a good thing … how under her thumb I'd be … especially if I was jerking from a cuckold chair. And the wedding dress scenario didn't seem farfetched. I didn't know how Ashley would take to the idea, but it wouldn't surprise me if she embraced the outrageousness.

The dress she walked down the aisle and married me in. She'd be pulling it out from the back of her closet. Asking me to help her with the zipper in the back. Both of us knowing the scene I'd be witnessing shortly—Ashley bent over, her dress pulled up, and Mike balling the bride doggy in her wedding dress.

I thought of Ashley facing me, staring at me, getting a cock-pumping from behind. "Look at me, Dave ... in my virgin white wedding dress ... that I said 'I do' to you in ... that I became Mrs. Ashley Martens in .... Look at what I'm doing in it now. I'm getting fucked in it. I'm taking cock in my wedding dress, Dave ... as you sit in a chair with your dick in your hand. Look me in the eye and tell me you're not a cuckold now?"

I muttered "Oh Ashley" and suddenly came.

\* \* \*

I hadn't liked where my mind had just gone. It was fucked up; I knew that. But I didn't want to dwell. Kind of blocked it out. In the shower I tried thinking of conversation starters for the evening. But not knowing Chang, I couldn't come up with much. I thought of the looks Ryan would give me if I started reeling off flight attendant jokes.

I was replying to work emails in the kitchen when I heard the door.

"Hey, Ash," I said, standing up.

"Hey, Dave. How are you?"

"Great," I said, giving her a hug and quick kiss. "How was the gym?"

"Rough, boy. She really worked us. How was the rest of your day?"

"Good. Brian's back, so I met up with him."

"Is that how you're going out?"

"Yeah. It works, right?"

"I don't know. You're meeting Ryan's girlfriend for the first time. What about the shirt you got last month at Banana?"

"What's wrong with the shirt I'm wearing?"

"You'd just look better. It's Friday night. We're going downtown."

I laughed. "Okay, and what … should I change my shoes, too? Are my jeans okay?"

"I love those jeans on you. Your new black shoes would go great with them."

"You know, I think I'll just go as I am. Keep it real."

Once she could tell I was joking, Ashley smiled. "So I'm going to shower super-quick. Maybe text Ryan and tell him we're running a few minutes behind?"

"Yeah, okay."

I put on a dark shirt and black shoes and looked in the mirror. She was right. It made me look more downtown and cool. I lay on the bed and grabbed my laptop so I could pretend I was looking at that when she came out.

I heard the shower shut off and waited. Only she didn't come out, as if she was dressing in the bathroom. I heard the door open and put my hands on my keyboard.

Ashley came out in a black bra and thong and started rifling through her dresser drawers and bending over to look in the closet. I got a boner. I wanted to smack her tight ass as she bent over even more. I thought of her taking Mike's cock from behind.

"I'm sorry," she standing back up. "I'll be ten minutes, no more."

"Yeah, sure," I said.

I watched her tits bounce in her black silk bra as she looked through more drawers and then hustled back into the bathroom. I thought of jerking off again in the other bathroom, but I didn't want to chance it.

\* \* \*

We walked past the doorman, said hello, and got into a cab.

"So," Ashley said, "any details on Chang, beyond she's a flight attendant?"

"Just that she made it very easy for Ryan to get over Karen."

"Is she Americanized? Did she grow up here?"

"I don't know."

"What do you know? How they met … anything?"

"Honestly, all I know about Chang is she's afraid of mice."

"What?"

" 'Cause Chang saw a mouse. She called Ryan the night I saw him, and he had to rush over. Which ended our night early. But I had speech stuff anyway. He just really wants us to meet her. He brought it up like three or four times."

"Does she drink?"

"I don't even know that. I'm going in as blind as you."

"Okay," she said. "So how's Ryan's job going?"

"I guess it's good. He didn't complain."

"So what *did* you guys talk about?"

"Well, I don't know. He told me he had to have his tonsils out last year."

Ashley laughed. "Well, I'll make sure to ask him about that."

"He said she's very polite."

"Okay, so she's a little uptight," she said. "When is Sean coming in?"

"I think tomorrow morning," I said, "and I forgot to mention it—he probably won't need to—but he asked if he could stay at our place Sunday night."

"You told him he could, right?"

"Yeah," I said. "He'll let me known soon."

"How many people at your parents' tomorrow?"

"Uh … twenty-five, maybe."

"Is your construction guy neighbor gonna be there?"

"Oh, I don't know. I thought it was just family."

"Well, if he's there," she said, "we'll have to apologize."

"For what?"

"For missing his fiftieth birthday party. I mean, we have to acknowledge it anyway. We said, 'sounds good' to going to his party, and then kind of blew it off."

"Oh, we didn't blow off shit," I said. "Like what, we're gonna train up to Westchester for my skeevy neighbor's fiftieth birthday party where we'd know freaking no one? He'd have to be crazy to think we'd go. We don't owe him shit."

Ashley laughed and said "Okay."

She looked down at her phone and muttered, "Oh my god."

"What?"

"Tamara just sent me her mock-up invite. She's planning her Halloween party."

"Already?" I said.

"She likes to do it right," she said. "I bet even you will be impressed."

"Well," I said, uncertain how to respond, "do you have any costume ideas?"

"She hasn't picked a theme yet."

"It's fucking Halloween," I said. "Isn't that the fucking theme?"

Ashley laughed and leaned in to kiss me—soft and tender. Laying her head on my shoulder, she said, "I love you."

"I love you too, Ash," I said, and watched as the cabbie kept making all the green lights.

* * *

There were a dozen people waiting outside the restaurant when we walked up. I said, "Excuse me" a lot, and we squeezed our way inside. It was a small Italian place, and it was hopping. But I saw Ryan waving from a table in the back.

They stood up as we walked over, but it was a tight space. I put out my hand and Chang gave me a hug instead. Then she hugged Ashley.

"I'm friends with the manager," Ryan said as we all sat down. "That's how we blew past the hour-long waitlist."

"I like it," Ashley said. "Look at you ... connections wherever you go."

"Not really," Ryan said, "just an old buddy from college."

"Well, this is great," I said, "and I really like having this corner."

"Have some wine," Ryan said, reaching for the bottle.

Ashley turned and said, "It's so nice to meet you, Chang."

"You too, Ashley," she said, "and you as well, Dave."

"Thanks for thinking of us, Ryan," Ashley said. "I'm really honored to be here with you guys on your Friday night in town."

"I'm honored as well," Chang said. "Ryan's talked so much about you guys. And I just learned last week that Ryan and Dave go back to the third grade, which I think is so cool."

"Yeah," I said, "but we weren't really friends till high school."

"And Ashley," Chang said, "you were captain of your tennis team?"

"A captain, yeah, in college," she said. "Did you play?"

"Yeah," Chang replied, "for Pepperdine."

"Wow," Ashley said. "Very cool."

"Are you able to play much?"

"No," Ashley said. "I just don't have the chance, plus being in New York …. Have you been to the Open before?"

"First time tomorrow," Chang said, "so I'm ultra-jazzed."

"You're going to love it," Ashley said. "I just went a few nights ago." Ashley looked over at me as if she regretted saying that. I was expecting Ryan to ask me how it was, when Ashley added, "With a friend from work."

The waiter was harried, and Ryan recommended the spaghetti, so we all ordered spaghetti and decided on another bottle of wine.

"So, how are your seats?" I asked.

"Close to mid-court but upper," Ryan said. "Not complaining."

"So" Chang said, "who do you like to win, Ashley?"

I saw it coming and rolled my eyes. It was all U.S. Open talk after that … which I didn't follow or care much about. Ashley was giving her opinion on some 30th seed former Soviet Republic girl, and then Ryan started chiming in.

I zoned a bit and checked out Chang whenever she was talking. She had shoulder-length hair, a really cute face, and a sexy little body. Her tits were smaller than Ashley's, but still very nice. I figured that for Taiwanese, they were probably rather big. She was wearing a tight, scooped neck top, and I was stealing glances. Chang was a sexy girl.

Ryan had gotten lucky, I thought. He'd rebounded strongly. He looked happier than I'd seen him in years. And no wonder. He had a BJ-loving Asian girl.

I pictured her pulling down the oxygen mask in one of her flight demonstrations. I pictured her fetching Ryan a beer. Ryan had a thing for Asian girls. So he had to feel like he'd just won the Lotto.

"Not much of a tennis fan, Dave?"

"No, Chang," I said. "I just never got into it."

"And you grew up with the Open right here."

"Hey, I've never been to Belmont, and that's right here, too."

"Yeah, but you're wife's a big Open fan."

"It's not that we haven't gone," I said. "We went twice last year. Not only that, I'm taking her to Australia someday soon, just to see the Open there."

"Yeah," Ashley said. "Dave just finds tennis boring. But I'll admit, he's a trooper. We sat outside one match last year, and it was a hundred degrees and we were right in the sun. I was the one to say 'Let's leave.' "

"Yeah," Ryan said, "but don't think Dave wasn't *thinking* 'Let's leave.' "

"I wasn't," I said. "Here's what it was. I was thinking, it's the U.S. Open. It's a big event for Ashley. And if she wants to watch till the end, then do your thing, Sun, but I ain't leaving, dammit."

Ashley laughed, put her arm around me, and gave me a quick peck on the lips. It was nice. I was glad Ryan was watching.

"Are we really going to Australia?" she said, cheerfully.

"Hey," I said, "just get them to let you take two weeks off, and I'll hit up Brian."

"You guys heard it," Ashley said, pointing at them.

"Yeah, Ryan," I said. "So what … are you guys gonna fly down and join us?"

"Hey, you may be surprised," he said. "We may actually see you in Hawaii."

"What?" Ashley asked.

"Christmas through New Year's" Ryan said, "we may be in Hawaii—when you guys are there. Chang was supposed to go to Taiwan. But her friend flaked. So now she may be free that week."

"Seriously?" Ashley said.

"We're looking into it," Chang said. "We should know by next week."

"Well," Ashley said, "we'd *have* to coordinate something."

"For sure," Ryan said. "Chang's parents used to take the family to Hawaii every new Year's."

"Not every year," Chang said. "Three times. But still, it makes me nostalgic. I love it there."

They served our spaghetti, and Ryan told the story

behind the recipe. I was starving and started eating while he was still speaking. Apparently, they killed the guy who created the recipe, and the guy's brother contracted a posse; then Ryan suddenly realized he'd forgotten the ending.

"That's so lame," Ashley said, laughing, and turned to Chang. "What do you see in this guy?"

"I don't know," Chang said. "Maybe the waiter can tell us the ending."

"But more fundamentally," Ashley said playfully, "really—what do you see in this guy?"

"Like what do I love about him?" Chang said.

"Yeah," Ashley said, "that works."

"Well, I'd say … Ryan's fun, smart, adventurous, compassionate, and he makes me laugh. How's that?"

"Very nice," Ashley said, "but I'm looking for more."

"Okay, how about … he's the only American guy I've been with, and I love his energy and outlook."

"The only American guy?" Ashley said.

"My past boyfriends were all Taiwanese."

"But you grew up in California, right?"

"Yeah, but I was sheltered. And my last boyfriend, I dated since college. We actually just broke off our engagement … earlier this year."

"Wow," Ashley said. "I'm sorry. Are you okay about it?"

"Yeah, it's a big relief, actually."

"Good," Ashley said, "and now you've got Ryan."

"Yeah," Chang said, "and he's got me—a girl who's always packing up her suitcase, which I think he likes."

"Are you kidding?" Ryan said. "That's the one thing I don't like about our relationship."

"Yeah, right," Chang said, giving him a playful punch. "Ryan likes his Ryan time."

"Where'd you guys meet?" Ashley asked.

"At my friend's party this summer," Chang said. "We just really hit it off—instant chemistry."

"Absolutely," Ryan said. "I'm telling you, I was in love that very first night."

"Oh c'mon," Chang said.

"Okay, lust maybe," he said, "but love quickly followed."

Chang laughed. "Yeah, and now he wants us to live together."

"Oh, really?" Ashley said, turning to Ryan for confirmation.

"Chang lives above a bodega," he said.

"I do not," Chang said, laughing. "It's a market."

I listened to the back and forth, half-attentive. I stared at Chang's tits whenever she was talking. Seemed like 34C—like Ashley. They stood out proudly in her cleavage-revealing black top. I thought about what Chang had said—instant chemistry at a party. I wondered if she'd still been engaged at the time. Or if "instant chemistry" was code for *we fucked that night*.

Chang kept talking, so I kept thinking.

I thought of Chang's fiancé. Dating since college could mean seven-plus years. And then, before the wedding, she dumped him. Kicked him to the fucking curb.

I wondered if he knew the reason. If he knew that Chang—the girl he planned to marry—wasn't as innocent as she looked.

I imagined myself talking to him. "She got fucked, bro, at the party you were at. Made a fucking fool of you? Yes, but not only that. You know how Chang only dates Taiwanese— he was American, bro. She was probably wearing your fucking engagement ring. You know you've been cucked, bro, right? And he probably fucked her bare. That's correct. He spermed her.

"Me? I'm just the guy sitting across the table from Chang and the guy she cucked you with. Watching Chang act like she's Sweet Polly Purebred. And not the slut who fucked her new lover—at the party you were at."

I took a sip of wine and snapped myself out of it. I stopped stealing looks at Chang's tits and tried to pay attention. Chang was talking about playing the violin. She'd studied from age six through high school. Like Ashley with the piano. She talked about being rejected at auditions. Ashley described one of her audition mishaps, which had Chang in hysterics.

I wanted to appreciate the moment. Everything was beautifully normal. Two couples out on the town. My wife beside me, Ashley smiling and having fun. And she'd been reassuring. She'd talked about Hawaii as though she had no second thoughts. She'd confirmed it: we'd be celebrating Christmas together. And that was three months away. She'd even talked about Australia. With zero qualifiers. As if she saw our future, going forward … together.

# CHAPTER TWENTY

We walked outside and tried to get our East Village bearings. Ashley started making suggestions of places we could go, but Ryan insisted he knew just the place. It was only two blocks away, which pretty much sold it.

"I've been there before," Ryan said. "Live bands play on the weekend, but in another room, so you can just chill at the bar, too."

"Are we gonna be able to talk," I said, "or hear ourselves?"

"Nobody's probably even on right now," he said. "The stage is in a room attached to the bar. You can hear music, but it sounds like it's next door. Trust me—it's cool."

Chang moved up behind Ryan and put her arm around his waist. I reached for Ashley and held her hand as we all walked to the bar.

I was surprised when we walked in. The place wasn't too crowded, and there were seats at the bar.

"Check it out," Ryan said. "They have Anchor Steam on tap."

"Why's that noteworthy?" Ashley asked.

"From San Francisco," Ryan said. "We gotta represent."

"Have you ever had it, Ashley?" Chang asked.

"I don't know," Ashley replied, "maybe."

A few minutes later, we each had a pint of Anchor Steam and were toasting San Francisco.

Ashley turned to Chang and said, "So what would you say about Ryan? Is he a real San Franciscan yet?"

"I'd say he's close to full citizenship," Chang said, "but he'll always have the East Coast boy in him."

"Why?" Ryan said. "Because when I just ordered the beer, I also ordered tequila shots?"

"No you didn't," Ashley said, with a smile.

"Sure as hell did," Ryan said, smiling back.

As if on cue, the female bartender walked over with a tray of shots.

"I'm in New York," he said. "I'm with my peeps, and it's fucking Friday night."

"I like it," Ashley said, taking her shot off the tray.

Chang grabbed hers like she was used to doing shots. No salt or lime for her.

"I'd like to make the toast," Ashley said, "if that's cool."

The three of us looked at her expectantly.

"Okay," Ashley said, "I want to thank Ryan for making this happen. And Chang, you rock, my friend. I'm so glad we're hanging out."

"Me too," Chang said.

"Is that the toast?" Ryan asked.

"Not yet," Ashley said. "Okay, so my toast is: to Chang and her first American man."

"I like it," Ryan said. We downed our shots and reached for our beers.

Chang and Ashley took two seats at the bar, and Ryan and I said we'd rather stand.

"So, Ashley," Chang said, "I was only able to play tennis a few times this summer, so I was wondering—next time I'm in town—if you're up for it. I have a club we could play at."

"Really?" Ashley said. "I'd freaking love that."

"Awesome," Chang said. "I'll find out when I'm here next and let you know."

"I'd be totally psyched. We can go for cocktails after."

"Even better," Chang said.

There was an awkward pause. I had a sudden feeling

Chang felt she had to invite me as well, just to be polite.

"Watch out, Chang," I said quickly, "Ashley's really good."

"Well, maybe when we're out in Hawaii," Chang said, "we can all play doubles."

I turned to Ryan as if to say, *You're kidding me, right?*

"Well, Chang," I said, "If my team wins, it will have nothing to do with me."

"Oh, Dave's a good partner," Ashley said, "as good as anyone else who hasn't played much."

"Thanks Ash," I said, "I think—"

"It's a total compliment," she said. "Like I bet if you had played a lot, you'd be pretty good."

"Raw natural talent," Chang said, looking at me with a smile.

"I'll take it," I said.

"So, Ashley," Chang said, "for the Open tomorrow, you have any insider tips? What to do—what not to do?"

Ashley looked up at me and smiled.

"Wow, Chang," I said. "with that one question …. Boy, you just wound up that little knob on Ashley's back."

"What?" Chang said, "Are you gonna chew my ear off now, Ashley?"

Ashley laughed, and said, "I'll topline it for you."

"Oh, please don't." Chang grinned. "I don't want you skipping things."

"Okay," Ashley said with a laugh. "But first off, how are you getting there?"

Knowing the girls would be occupied for a while, I turned to Ryan and said, "What's up, mate?" and clicked his glass. "Chang's a great girl." I leaned in, close to his ear, "I'm really happy for you."

"Oh thanks, bro," he said, taking a step away from the girls. "Yeah, I mean, who knows? This is the first girl I've ever actually *wanted* to move in with, y'know?"

"You weren't psyched when you moved in with Karen?"

"Oh no way, man" he said. "I agreed to that, kicking and screaming. But with Chang, I'm like yeah, bring it on."

"How do you feel about getting married, having kids?"

"Well, let's not get carried away," he said, "but who knows? I just mean, like when she's traveling … normally I'd be psyched to chill alone. But now, most nights I'm like *fuck, I wish Chang was here.*"

"Well, yeah," I said, smiling, "she's not there to fucking blow you."

He laughed. "Yeah, but it really is a lot more than that."

"I know what you mean," I said. "You just really fucking love this girl."

"Yeah, basically," he said.

"And Ashley seems to love her," I said.

"Yeah, I figured they'd hit it off," he said, as we stepped a little farther out of earshot. "I mean, just on tennis and music alone—"

"Well, that made it a fucking slam dunk," I said. "Obviously."

"Yeah, but also their personalities," he said. "I think it's more about that, actually."

We saw the band coming through a side door, and we walked over to have a look. The performing space was larger than I'd expected, with a half dozen tables along the side, but otherwise open.

"Hey, check this out," Ryan said. He was standing by the side door.

"What?" I said, stepping out onto the sidewalk.

Ryan pointed across the street. "They finally opened the cigar bar."

"What … is Chang into cigars?"

"No, but maybe later, you and me. We can check it out."

"If it's cool with them, I guess," I said.

"They're yapping away. They won't give two craps."

"Okay."

"Look at them now," he said, as we walked back in, "You think they even realized we were gone?"

Chang was telling Ashley something—she seemed to be in the middle of the story—and Ashley was nodding intently.

As we came closer, both of them gave us cute waves but then went right on back to talking.

They had barely drunk their beers, so they didn't join us for the next round.

Ryan and I said, "Cheers," and went back to standing beside them.

"So I might be able to score 'Niners tickets," Ryan said, "for Thanksgiving weekend."

"Okay ...." I said.

"I know you've got family to see, but I wanted to throw out the offer. You and Ashley could stay at my place. I'd stay at Chang's, which I do anyway."

"Sounds great," I said, "but could be tricky. I'll need to look into it ... logistically."

"It's a tough weekend, I know, and flying back Sunday's a nightmare."

"So having a work trip that Monday is probably the only way it would happen," I said. "Let me talk to Ashley and see if she could get the day off."

But I could tell Ryan wasn't listening. He was trying to overhear what the girls were saying. I saw him start to smile and lean in like he was about to interrupt.

"I heard my name," he said, and the girls turned to look at him. "What are you guys talking about?"

"Well," Ashley said, "I was getting some Hawaii insider tips."

Chang laughed. "And I was telling Ashley about you."

"Oh yeah," Ryan said. "Did you tell her who came to your rescue the other night? And saved you from an infestation?"

"She did, actually," Ashley offered. "Very heroic, Ryan."

"Yeah," Chang said, "but Ashley's been wanting me to get real and personal."

"Mice stories are nice," Ashley said, "but I figured it's an awesomely fun night, so let's let our hair down a little."

"Which I'm doing, right?" Chang said.

"I love it," Ashley replied.

"Well," Chang said to Ryan, "she asked me to describe sex with you in one word."

I smiled awkwardly, just to be part of it.

"And what word did you go with?" he asked.

"Well, I went with 'amazing,' which I could tell Ashley found boring."

"I did not," Ashley laughed.

"So I packed a swearword in the middle," Chang said, "and changed it to, 'fan-fucking-tastic.'"

Ryan smiled—beamed, more like. "I feel the same way, Chang," he said. "I love hearing that. You just made my night."

Ashley smiled and said, "Aww …."

"So," Ryan said, "did you elaborate beyond just one word?"

"No," Chang said, "we got sidetracked. And then, Ashley wanted comparisons."

"To past guys she's dated," Ashley said.

"In terms of what?" Ryan asked.

"Best lover," Chang said, "and you are. The best I've ever had. We just click."

"Did you think we were talking about size?" Ashley said.

"Thought maybe," Ryan said.

"Well, since we're on the subject," Chang said, "you're not just the best, but also the biggest. Which I told you the first time, but I wasn't sure you believed me."

Ashley looked momentarily stunned, then smiled and said, "Wow, Ryan, I'd never have guessed it."

"Fuck you," he said with a smile.

"It must be nice to hear," Ashley said, cheerfully, "that Chang thinks you have a big cock."

"Well," Ryan said, "that's compared to the Asian guys she's been with."

"Good point," Ashley said.

"Hey, wait a sec," Chang chimed in, "my exes weren't small. I was just saying they aren't Ryan."

"And you found," Ashley said, "that you just prefer bigger ... and American."

"What can I tell you, Ashley?" she said, with frustration in her eyes but a mischievous smile. "I just found I have a preference ... for big American cock."

Ryan looked amazed, and Ashley burst out laughing.

I smiled, as if I found it all funny.

"That was fucking awesome," Ashley said to Chang.

I was just standing there, so I muttered, "Do you know where the bathrooms are? Never mind, I see them."

There was a guy waiting when I walked up.

"A girl's in the guy's bathroom," he said to me, "like for five fucking minutes, now."

But I didn't care. I was just glad to hit the eject button. Even for two minutes.

Ryan was handing out shots when I returned—more tequila. The girls seemed fine with it, so I just took the shot from Ryan.

"Do you want to do the toast?" he said to me.

"Oh, you do it, Ry," I said.

"We're the hosts," Ashley said to me.

"Okay, fine," I said.

I wanted to say, 'Hosts of fucking what? Ryan invited us out. He's no out-of-towner. He grew up here. There's no fucking etiquette rule that would say it's protocol for me to give a toast. And what about letting the other couple say a few fucking words?'

But I knew if I said anymore, it would start seeming

weird. With Ryan saying 'I don't fucking care. I'll do the fucking toast then.'

But I kind of froze on what to say when I held my drink out.

"To the four of us being out," I said, "and as Ashley said, and even Chang said, how it's an honor, which it is … and …."

"Sorry to interrupt," Ryan said, "but c'mon." Then he turned to Chang and said, "Why don't you do it?"

Ashley laughed and said, "Yeah, Chang, do it. Something we wouldn't expect. Surprise us."

"Toasts aren't really meant to be surprising, Ashley," she said, "but let me think. Okay, so … so here goes: to making new friends, to New York being a balls-out bitchin' city, and to … big American cock."

Everyone cracked up. I laughed too, trying hard to look amused.

We all clicked glasses, and I looked down the whole time. I couldn't look at Ashley clinking glasses to that. I aimed to keep my expression unfazed as I did my shot.

"So can I propose," Chang said, "we cool it with shots for now?"

"Absolutely," Ryan said. "That was it."

"She meant like to Dave, too," Ashley said, "in case he's thinking of ordering us more shots."

"Oh yeah, Ash," I said, with more of an edge than I intended, "that's exactly what I was thinking. More tequila shots. I was gonna order up four prairie fires—"

"What?" Ryan said.

"Oh yeah," I said, "like had Chang not said 'no' to shots, five minutes from now I'd be making it happen. They'd be pouring the Tabasco."

Ashley burst out laughing and said, "That's great."

Chang smiled, and said, "So you're with me on this, Dave?"

"Of course," I said. "I wasn't a big fan of the second shot."

"Oh c'mon," Ryan said. "We didn't drink much at dinner. Don't be a puss."

"Fuck you," I said.

"I agree with Dave," Chang said.

"You agree what?" Ryan said, "Fuck me? That's what you agree on?"

"On fighting back against peer pressure," Chang said. "That's where we agree. No name calling."

"Yeah, Ryan," I said. "You see, I'm the fucking hero, here. I'm the one with the noble cause. I got truth and motherfucking justice on my side."

"I think you shut him up," Chang said.

"Yeah," Ryan said, "he kind of did. If it was just truth, that's one thing, but then he goes and adds the motherfucking justice on me."

"Nice job," Chang said to me.

"So what else did you guys talk about?" Ryan asked. "With you getting real and personal."

"General bio stuff," Chang said, "school, tennis … the neighborhoods we're considering."

"How about experimenting?" Ryan said.

"No," Chang said dismissively.

"I guess, 'cause I interrupted your convo," he said, "you hadn't gotten to that yet."

"Exactly," Chang said, rolling her eyes.

"We've been talking about her being with another woman," he said. "Seeing what it's like."

"*We've* been talking?" Chang said. "Oh my God, you are *so* lying. The one doing the talking is you."

"I just told her if she has inclinations for another woman," Ryan said, "she has the green light from me to go for it."

"Well, that's mighty noble," Ashley said, with a smile.

"Okay," Chang said, "so a couple weeks ago, Ryan asked if I'd ever kissed a girl. I told him yeah, once, last year at a New Year's party. And okay, so my mistake, I told him I kind of liked it. But oh my God, the questions he asks me—how much tongue, how many seconds."

"The blow by blow," I said, to act as if I was part of the conversation.

Chang laughed. "Ryan has me tell it to him as a bedtime story."

"What can I say?" Ryan said. "It's a nice story to hear, when I'm cuddled up in my PJs."

"Was she Taiwanese?" Ashley asked.

"The girl I kissed on New Year's?" Chang said. "Yeah, she was."

Ryan leaned in and said, "You've kissed a girl before, right, Ashley?"

"On a few occasions," Ashley said. "And just out of college, there was a New Year's Party where I also kissed a girl."

Ashley held her pint out and Chang gave her cheers.

"Any of these occasions go beyond kissing?" Ryan asked.

"I've copped a feel before," Ashley said, "but not as real foreplay for anything. Just to be daring."

"Have you ever kissed an Asian girl, Ashley?" Ryan asked.

"No," Ashley said, smiling.

"Well," Ryan said, "YOLO moments don't come around every day."

"Meaning what?" Ashley said. "You want me to kiss your girlfriend?"

"Only if you want to," he said.

"Yeah, right," Chang said, with a laugh. "Do you want to humor him, Ashley? And be my first American girl?"

"I would be honored," Ashley said and adjusted her chair.

"Maybe we should stand up," Chang said.

I was two feet away as they put their arms around each other. As soon as Ashley leaned in, Chang leaned in as well. It seemed to happen in slow motion, their kissing beautiful, their movements almost balletic.

I looked to see if anyone was looking, but most seemed oblivious. When I turned back around, it was cranking up. Ashley and Chang were making out, their tongues swirling inside each other's mouths, no coming up for air.

Ryan was looking at me like, *How fucking cool is this*?

And then, as if they'd practiced it, they both pulled away. Each seemed to be dazed and catching her breath.

Mike was applauding, so I clapped my hands as well.

"Wow," Chang said, as she and Ashley sat back down. "You're a fantastic kisser, Ashley."

"You're a fan-fucking-tastic kisser yourself," Ashley said.

Chang laughed and turned to Ryan, "Are you happy now?"

"I am," Ryan said. "That was killer. And you enjoyed it, right?"

"It was exquisite," Chang said, "something for my diary tonight."

I leaned in to Ryan and said, "Chang keeps a diary?"

"She's kidding," he said to me, before turning back to Ashley and adding, "I like this side you bring out in my girl."

"Oh," Ashley said, "like you had nothing to do with it."

"Okay," Ryan said, "but I wasn't pushing my girl to say, 'big American cock.' "

"I'd say you made out like a bandit tonight," Ashley said.

"Yes," he said, leaning down to kiss Chang, "and I loved hearing that she feels the same way as I do."

The band started their mic check in the other room. It wasn't distracting, but I knew what it meant—it would be loud soon.

Ryan leaned in and asked me, "Do you want to go now? To the cigar bar?"

"Sure," I said. "If you want to."

"One sec," he said. "I'll tell them."

I didn't lean in to listen to him sell the girls on us leaving. I figured the way his night was going, he didn't need me. Which he didn't. A half minute later he had the green light. They seemed fine with us leaving. I gave Ashley a kiss and told her, "Twenty minutes."

# CHAPTER TWENTY-ONE

"What do you say to a single malt scotch?" Ryan said, as we crossed the street.

"I say, *Dude, we just did two shots.*"

"That pussy shit don't work here," he said. "You don't have Chang to protect you."

I laughed and said, "Hey, if you're buying."

Ryan had to piss, but the bartender was free, so he ordered us two cigars and scotches, and I took a seat at the empty side of the bar.

"I can't believe they did that," Ryan said, as he sat down beside me. The bartender came over and lit our cigars. I rarely smoked them but listened to Ryan talk to the guy about what kind of scotch to drink with different kinds of cigars.

"Sorry," Ryan said, turning back to me. "So, what the fuck was that back there? I cannot believe they really fucking kissed tonight. Wow. And for a few seconds there, they really fucking had at it …. How you doing man?"

"I'm doing good, man," I said. "Yeah, that was kind of crazy."

"Yeah, Chang has been raising the fucking roof tonight."

"Yeah," I said. "So … you must be psyched to be back in New York."

"What?"

"You're back in your old hood, man."

"I fucking love it, of course. But what's going on? Were you not cool with what just went down?"

"No, I'm cool, man," I said.

"I know I encouraged it, but I wasn't expecting that … I really wasn't."

"Oh hey, Ryan, no worries."

"Chang's buzzing fucking nicely. She's really surprising me tonight."

"Yeah, Ashley likewise."

"You don't seem okay with it. Are you pissed?"

"No, it's all good. I don't know. It's just me being overly sensitive."

"About what?"

"About what we talked about the other night—Ashley partying with Tamara. I wonder if she's like this when they're out together. I'm wondering if Ashley kissed Tamara, too."

"Well, please tell me to shut the fuck up, but … do you think Ashley might be having an affair?"

"What? No, nothing like that. Although who can know for sure, right? I just think she's going through a bit of a party phase. And I don't want us not talking about it, y'know."

"What does she say when you do?"

"She'll tell me she was out with Tamara."

"Yeah, and …."

"Well, here's the thing …. I know the basics, like where they went. But she'll mostly say random stuff, like how Tamara wants to go to Burning Man and create some fucking art installation."

"So what stuff do you want to know?"

"At the most basic, why they're friends. I mean, I know, they work together. But outside of work, she's become Ashley's BFF. So I wonder, what does Ashley like about her? What do they talk about when they're getting real?"

"So you're gonna ask Ashley to tell you their heart-to-hearts? "

"No, I didn't mean that. I just want to know more about Tamara. Get a better sense of their relationship."

"Okay," he said, "so tell Ashley you're joining her and Tamara the next time they go out for drinks."

I laughed. "I don't think so. You know how Tamara feels about me."

"Who cares?"

"Ry, I'm telling you, I'd be *so* unwelcome. Tamara does not fucking dig me."

"So fucking what? At least you'd be there."

"No, you're right. I should make an appearance."

"Just fucking hang out," he said, "and talk about what interests Tamara—her fucking self."

"Yeah, I hear you. And I will. I'm gonna join them next time."

"Okay, cool."

"Ryan, when Karen was seeing her boss, did you know she was with him, like before you broke up?"

"I had suspicions … a few weeks before. Is that what you're having, Dave? Suspicions?"

"What? No … I mean, yeah, like any other guy whose wife is off partying with a girlfriend who really doesn't like him … and is kind of wild … and pretty fucked in the head."

"You ever go to where Ashley said she was, just to see for yourself she was there?"

"No. Did you do that with Karen?"

"Once, at the end—the one time she was telling me the truth. She really had gone fucking apple picking with her friend."

"But you were trying to catch her?"

"I just wanted proof that what I heard was true. So the next day I confronted her."

"And she told you?"

"Yeah. Came clean completely."

"Is that when you broke it off?"

"You bet. Hauled my stuff out the next day. I was prepared. I already suspected the guy. How about with

Ashley? Do you have a specific guy in mind who she might be interested in?"

"No, none whatsoever, and it's not like I'm suspicious of an affair. Just being extra careful. But I know it's probably nothing. So what? So, Ashley likes hanging out with Tamara …."

"You know what I bet?"

"What?"

"That Tamara would be an amazing titty fuck."

"Okay," I said.

"Are you telling me you wouldn't want to titty-fuck Tamara?"

"No, of course I would. Who wouldn't?"

I could tell Ryan was buzzing when he put his arm around me.

"I gotta say, Chang is the very best titty fuck I've ever had. And you know what drives me fucking nuts? Seeing her smile, and her Asian eyes, as she waits for me to blast her."

"You cum on her face?"

"Sometimes … in a playful, fun way. Before she showers."

"Nice. Was that one of the times she fetched you your beer?"

"It was," Ryan said, "and that's what Chang's probably talking to Ashley about."

"What?"

"How to take care of her man better. Chang will chat her up with some *Kama Sutra*. And explain why a post-BJ beer just completes the package."

"You're kidding, man, right?"

"Hey, if I was betting, I'd say they're talking about, I don't know … fucking tennis. But even if Chang *is* giving Ashley some techniques and pointers, how's that a fucking bad thing?"

"It's just a little fucking strange, that's all."

"Chang just wants to share and spread what she's learned. Like the proper way to kneel to give a BJ."

"Are you serious? Chang might really be saying that shit to Ashley?"

Ryan laughed. "Doubtful, but who knows? Chang's pretty uninhibited right now. And so fucking what? Ashley would probably love it. At the very least, she'd find it entertaining."

"It's just fucking weird, man … that Ashley might be getting the Gospel according to Chang on how to be like this … me-so-horny, fuck bunny."

Ryan burst out laughing, then said, " 'Me so horny' … that ain't cool, man."

"Well, that's how you're fucking describing her—blowing you in uniform, fetching your beer, and 'Tip number five, Ashley, remember to smile when awaiting a facial.' "

"Chang's very service-oriented," he said with a laugh.

"You plan on smoking the whole thing?" I said.

"You want to get out of here?"

"Well, that cigar kind of jacked me up," I said. "And I do want to get back to the girls."

"Yeah, okay," he said. "What do you say they're up to? You think they're flashing the crowd like it's Mardi Gras?"

I looked back and shook my head. It felt good, walking out of there. I liked the slight autumn chill.

We stopped before going back into the bar.

"So," Ryan said, "I'd say probably nothing to worry about, but next thing you gotta do is invite yourself out with Ashley and Tamara. That's how you can size it up and put a lid on it, if you have to."

"Sure," I said.

"That didn't sound very convincing, man," he said. "C'mon, I'm fucking serious. So what if you're a fucking buzz-kill? You've got to fucking go out with them."

"I know, Ry," I said. "I'm fucking doing it. I will be joining them, believe me. And fuck what Tamara thinks."

"Exactly, bro," he said. "Shall we?"

\* \* \*

I heard the band playing in the other room when we walked back in. Ryan told the girls about the cigar bar and a story about looking for a cigar bar in San Francisco. Ashley turned to me and said, "So, what do you think?"

"What?"

"They sound pretty good, right?" she said. "They're a cover band."

"Well," I said, "I think I'm waiting it out till we hear some originals."

"Yeah, right," Ashley said with a laugh. "Are you boys ready to go in and check it out?"

"Well," I said, "I'm ready, but Ryan here's been saying he wants us to do one more shot."

Ryan laughed, and looked at Chang. "He's kidding."

We gave up our little nook at the bar and headed to the other room. I didn't realize there was a ten buck cover, and I watched in a panic as Chang threw down forty bucks. I insisted she take my twenty, but she'd have none of it.

Which to me meant we were now committed to check out live music for the night. Or at least see a couple bands.

I thought 'checking the band out' meant listening to a few songs and then going back to the bar. I wondered if Chang said "four tickets" simply because she thought that's what we wanted. We hadn't even discussed it. But there we were.

The band was playing some '80s metal anthem. At least I knew it, and they sounded pretty tight. So we made our way through the small crowd, and I followed the girls up to the front.

It was a band of old guys in their fifties. No look, besides jeans and t-shirts. But the singer was bouncing all over the cramped little stage like a wild man. He really loved being up there. That made it cool, and I really clapped after the song.

The singer talked to the crowd like he actually knew a lot of them. And when I looked back, I realized it was an unusually older crowd. I guessed many were friends with the band or had seen them before.

The band started back in with "You Shook Me All Night Long." The singer nailed the intro, and I felt psyched to be part of the scene. I even felt cool when inevitably Ashley and Chang wanted to dance.

It was music I could dance to—Red Hot Chili Peppers, Tom Petty, Guns N' Roses. Upbeat, high energy songs I could move around to. I could show some enthusiasm … and sort of fit in.

We all were pretty buzzed and pumped up. I thought the band was probably psyched, having Ashley and Chang dancing front and center—a hot brunette with her big tits bouncing and a sexy Asian girl shaking her ass in tight jeans.

I felt very in the moment. We were out on the town with another couple, Ashley was having a blast, and I was dancing with my girl.

They started playing "American Girl," and the crowd cheered. Ashley turned to me with exuberance.

She held my hand, I twirled her around, and we both sang out the lyrics. I gave her a quick hug and the four of us applauded. I liked how Chang yelled "Woo-hoo," at the stage, so I yelled out "Woo-hoo," as well. Ryan laughed and gave me a fist-bump.

Suddenly dancing seemed preferable to talking. No fucking toasting to big American cock … or just having to deal. This was music I knew and could dance to. And I loved seeing Ashley moving her body, watching her tits and ass in her form-fitting dress. I didn't miss our conversation in the bar at all.

We danced to a good dozen songs. Each time we'd go to sit one out, they'd play a song Ashley or Ryan liked.

Which is what happened when the band started playing

"Mony Mony." No one wanted to sit that one out.

I hadn't heard the song since college, but I remembered the audience chant. It seemed too frat boy for a hip Manhattan bar, but I thought of the older crowd, and how into the band they seemed.

The guys behind us started in, yelling "get laid," and girls yelled the "get fucked" response. I had my eyes on the floor, but knew I had to deal with this. On the next chorus I might have to join in just to fit in.

Ashley looked excited and stared at me as they came to the chorus. I saw Ryan turn toward Chang, and I sort of looked at Ashley, then beyond at the crowd, and yelled a tepid, "get laid."

We made eye contact as Ashley yelled, "get fucked."

I didn't know if it meant anything, and we just kept on dancing … till Ashley bumped out Ryan and started dancing with Chang.

Ashley and Chang moved in closer as the chorus came around again. So they were right next to each other when they yelled, "get fucked."

Only they weren't yelling it out at the crowd. Their eyes were locked, like they were saying it to each other. Ashley was telling Chang to get fucked and vice versa.

I thought about it as we danced to more songs. How telling each other to 'get fucked' had been a bonding moment for them. A proclamation of how wild and slutty they could be. I imagined Ryan saying I was being insane. How every girl in the place was chanting "get fucked." How it was no different than singing "YMCA" at a wedding.

It was the up-close and yelling it to each other aspect that was different. They said it with conviction, as if the words had meaning. And it wasn't as if they hadn't just made out an hour ago … or hadn't urged us to toast big American cock.

\* \* \*

We checked out a little of the band that followed, but their sound was generic, and every song was about the people rising up or starting a revolution.

The bar was packed when we went back in. There was barely room to stand. I volunteered to get us drinks. Everyone defaulted to beer, and I told Ryan I'd wave when I needed his help.

But the bartenders were crazy busy and a lot of people were trying to get their attention. After a few minutes of feeling invisible, I felt a tap on my shoulder.

"Hey," Chang said when I turned around. I figured Ryan had sent her to help carry our drinks.

"I haven't even ordered yet," I said.

"Ryan's not feeling well," she said. "Claustrophobic, and he had a lot of mixed drinks while we were dancing."

"Oh," I said. "You sure it's not his tonsils?"

Chang smiled and said, "So I'm afraid I've got to get him home, I mean, back to our hotel."

"Oh right," I said. "Sure, I understand."

"I'm sorry we can't stay out longer," she said. "It's been so much fun and so great to finally meet you, Dave ... and Ashley. I feel like I now have friends in New York."

I smiled and said, "Absolutely, Chang. You certainly do."

I gave her a hug and followed her back to our spot. Ashley and Ryan both looked ready to leave, and we walked outside and up to the avenue.

"You know," I said, as I walked with Ryan, "it's freaking ten o'clock San Fran time, and you're calling it a night?"

"Bro," he said, "I was drinking all afternoon with Crowley, and I slept like shit last night. What can I tell you ... I hit a wall."

"Well," I said, "it makes sense to me now ... why they call you tonsil-boy at work. You know ... like with all your excuses ...."

"Oh fuck you, man," he said with a laugh. "Like this isn't *you* a thousand other times."

"You say that," I said, "but what's the reality? It's ten o'clock your time and you're scampering back to the hotel. It's one a.m. my time, and me, I'm going back inside to watch the rest of them bands."

"Yeah, right," he said with a laugh.

Ashley called out from back down the street, "Guys! We got a cab."

"Fucking sweet," Ryan said.

"Hurry," Ashley said, "the cab behind it is also waiting for us."

We hustled down the street and all gave one-second hugs. Ashley and I jumped into the cab behind them.

"Fucking nicely done, Ash," I said.

"You bet," she said as we pulled away in the cab. "We got lucky."

"Yeah," I said, "and good thing. You're looking mighty tired yourself."

"I'm exhausted," she said, putting her head on my shoulder.

We pulled up to a stoplight on the avenue and I saw Chang waving from their cab. I waved back, but shuddered, picturing them popping up like that in Hawaii. I was glad when their cab turned on 14th.

And I didn't mind Ashley sleeping against my shoulder. It took some pressure off. I wouldn't be subjected to drunkenly blunt comments from Ashley ... which was very possible, if she'd been animated Ashley.

She might try to embarrass me by telling the cab driver our story. And about the oath we were taking. And the guy would be looking back at me, like, *Let me see this fucking pussy*.

Even if she was just calling me a cuckold privately in the back of the cab, I much preferred her asleep on my shoulder.

I didn't need any drunken comments to keep my head spinning.

I imagined her saying, "I'd never have guessed Ryan had a big cock, but when you think about it, it kind of makes sense."

* * *

I was glad she had no second wind as we walked through our lobby. And the elevator was free and empty. As soon as I opened the door, Ashley ran for the bathroom.

I went and took a piss in the other bathroom, then watched a few minutes of baseball highlights on the living room TV.

I walked into the bedroom just as Ashley was coming out … in a pink thong and white t-shirt, her nipples poking out nicely.

"Hey, Ash," I said, sitting on the bed, taking off my jeans.

"Oh yes," Ashley said as she got under the covers.

"Tired, Ash?"

"Like beyond, beyond."

"But you're gonna still read me a story, right?"

"I'll be right on that," she said, her voice muffled in the pillow.

"But what about my boy Ichabod, Ash? You left me hanging last night—"

"We're saving it for this week," she said. "Love you, Dave."

"Love you, too, Ash," I said, and went in to brush my teeth.

I hurried through my ritual and was soon in bed with her. I wanted to lie there until I was sure she was asleep. Then I'd know she'd be asleep till morning.

Then I could sneak off to the hall bathroom and not sweat her waking up. I could think about what little horn-dog twins Ashley and Chang had been tonight. The kiss, the toast, the yelling "get fucked" to each other.

I could think about how far she was going with Mike's direction … slapping fucking handcuffs on me and depriving me of even copping a feel. I could mentally picture her being fucked in front of me.

So I waited, and I heard Ashley's breathing deepen. I was about to gently slide out of my side of our bed. I was giving it five minutes ….

But that's when I conked out completely. I was out cold.

# CHAPTER TWENTY-TWO

I woke up startled, hearing Ashley going through her closet.
"Morning, Ash, going to the gym?"

"I think I'm blowing it off today," she said, standing up in shorts and tank top. "It's gorgeous outside. I just want to be out in it."

"How you feeling?" I said.

"Surprisingly, pretty good. How 'bout you?"

"Just tired," I said.

"Yeah, I don't know why, but I've got energy" she said. "I'm gonna take off shortly, so you can sleep more."

"Where are you going?"

"Just gonna take a walk in the Park and enjoy the weather. Go around the reservoir. Feel like joining me?"

"Yeah, absolutely," I said, getting out of bed.

"Really?" she said. "Cool. We'll just shower when we get back ... before going out to your folks."

"You got it," I said, putting on my shorts.

"And we can get bagels," she said, "on our way back."

"Sounds good to me," I said, grabbing my sunglasses.

A minute later I was locking the door and catching some breaks. No one was waiting for the elevator, and we rode down alone. Even Tommy wasn't working. We blew past the doorman with just a "Good morning."

"What a beautiful day," Ashley said, as we started up Columbus. It wasn't even nine, so the streets were fairly empty—people walking their dogs, opening up stores. I started thinking I wouldn't mind some random encounter.

Someone I worked with or some couple-friend of ours. I liked how it looked. Up and at 'em Dave and Ashley, walking to the Park together.

"Aren't we going in here?" I said, pointing.

"I want to cut in on 96th," she said. "We can swing by The Tennis Center and see if Sarah still works Saturday mornings."

"Huh?" I said.

"I played with her a couple times last spring. She said she wanted a rematch. I want to see if she's up for playing some night or weekend."

"What? Like, to get ready for Chang?"

"No," she said with a laugh. "Just talking about it has me wanting to play. And got me thinking, like, why am I not making time for it? I do miss it—a lot."

"No, I understand—"

"So were Chang and Ryan really serious," Ashley said, "about meeting up with us in Hawaii?"

"I kind of assumed it was just talk," I said. "but I don't think he means the week together—or the four of us really playing doubles. Plus, would we even be on the same island?"

"I don't know," she said. "Chang was like, *Ashley, we gotta make it happen.* She said it again when we were leaving. I know we'd all been drinking, but I wouldn't be surprised if suddenly they're coming with us."

"Well, hey, I made it clear to Ryan that it's to celebrate our anniversary. He ain't gonna be in the hotel room down the hall from us, that's for sure."

"Well, I think Chang is awesome, and I love Ryan, so you know I'm cool with whatever. You could suggest nearby hotels, maybe. We could hang out at their pool and vice versa, but still have some space."

"What kind of space is that? That's the non-stop Chang and Ryan show."

"Well, I was suggesting nearby hotels, if you feel you

can't say no to Ryan. I mean what are you gonna say to Ryan, *I don't want you vacationing on Maui?*"

"I'm gonna say, *Don't come out here to spend the week with us.*"

"Are you serious?" she said.

"Look," I said, "it's our two-year anniversary. I'm going thirteen hours to Hawaii to be with my wife. That's what I'll tell him."

"Well, don't go too hard-line," she said. "It's not like it wouldn't be fun having them around."

"Well, sure," I said, "and maybe some other trip. I don't know, maybe we all rent some friggin' cabin up in the woods. But this one is about us."

"Sure, but you had fun last night, right?"

"Oh sure," I said. "I love seeing Ryan, and it was great to meet Chang."

"Yeah," she said. "She's super-cool and super-sweet. I can't be believe I kissed her."

"Yeah, I can't say I saw that coming," I said.

"Me either," she said with a laugh. "When I first met her, the last thing I'd have imagined happening was her slipping me tongue later."

I laughed. "Do you think she has … uh … a crush on you?"

"No," she said, as if that was ridiculous. "Ryan was pleading and pressuring. She just wanted to go along with his fantasy."

"Did she say that?"

Ashley stopped suddenly and said, "That's her."

"Huh?"

"Sarah's walking off the court," she said, pointing, "Do you mind waiting? I'll be five or ten minutes, tops."

"Yeah, sure" I said. "I'll just wait up by the rez … right up there."

She gave me a kiss and went inside.

I walked up a dirt path and looked out at the reservoir. A bride and groom were nearby, posing for pictures. They had the fountain going off behind them and a blue-sky day in the background.

I walked up like I was just ambling through the park. In sunglasses I could stare without being obvious. They were a young Asian couple and the bride looked adorably pretty. The groom looked like a total dud.

I thought of Chang breaking it off with her fiancé. Maybe this guy had 'cuckold' in his future. Standing up there like he was on top of the world. Probably flying off to honeymoon in Bora Bora tomorrow. Spare no fucking expense, right, pal?

*Who knows what little slut thoughts are stirring in that beautiful bride of yours?* I thought, as I looked at him. She might be like Chang—toasting Big American cock, kissing other girls, cucking the guy she was planning to marry.

*Your wife's going to cuck you, bro. You don't deserve her. Give it a couple years and don't tell me she hasn't taken another man's cock. Because someday, motherfucker, you'll be wearing a full set of cuckold horns.*

Suddenly I heard Ashley's voice a few feet away.

* * *

I turned around and smiled hello. "How'd did it go?"

"Good," she said. "We're gonna play next weekend."

"Wow," I said, "so I guess you *are* going to meet up with Chang … play tennis with her?

"I hope so," she said, "though this really has nothing to do with that. But yeah, I'd love to play at Chang's club. I think she's serious about setting something up when she's in town. And it's just fun to compete with someone who's at the same level."

"Sure," I said, "but if you just want to hit the ball around, you know, I could probably leave work a little early some night, you want to …."

"I'd love to," she said. "We haven't played in a while."

"Yeah," I said, "and I can bust my racket out."

"About time," she said. "You know, that tennis racket was the first real present I gave you."

"Yeah," I said, "that first Christmas we were together."

"The poor thing," she said. "It's been so neglected."

"Oh, come on."

"Come on nothing," she said. "If there was a Toy Story movie about your tennis racket, kids would leave the theater crying."

"Hey, I'm taking it to Florida this fall."

"Big whoop," she said. "You always take it. What your racket really wants is to be taken out of its jacket."

"Which I'm gonna start doing," I said. "Now your movie will have a happy ending. The little racket finally gets some love."

Ashley laughed and said, "We'll see."

I smiled and looked out at the water. I liked that we could just look around and not feel pressure to talk or stress about eye contact.

"When the leaves start turning," Ashley said, "it'd be nice to take a drive upstate, catch some fall foliage. We've never done that together."

"Sounds awesome," I said. "We could even stay over Saturday night somewhere."

"Well," she said, "I'm not thinking, like, a drive to Vermont or anything. I'm picturing just going along the Hudson on a sunny, fall afternoon."

"Sounds nice," I said, struggling for something to add. "Who knows? Maybe we'll run into some place that rents canoes."

"Yeah, right," she said. "Can you imagine that disaster?"

"What?"

"The Hudson's big," she said, "like the freaking Mississippi. So what, you and me are gonna launch our canoe and start paddling around the river?"

"Hey, I know how to paddle, and I'd keep us close to shore."

"I don't know," Ashley said. "I see the current being surprisingly strong, me losing my paddle. And before you know it, some big ass freight ship's coming our way."

"I would steer us around it, though," I said. "The captain of the freighter would blow his horn and give me a big thumbs-up as he passed—like, 'Well done, sailor.' "

Ashley laughed. "You look into it then."

"Well, even if we don't canoe, taking a drive up north sounds perfect. Maybe bring food, I don't know."

"Yeah, we could picnic. Just somewhere nice. We'd need to research it. And rent a cool car for the day."

"I'll find some foliage maps," I said, "and make sure we hit the best weekend for it."

"Awesome," Ashley said. "Hopefully it's not the second weekend of October. Or the first, 'cause don't you have a Giants game?"

"Uh maybe," I said. "Mike told you?"

"He said he was gonna ask you."

"Well, it's not definite, and I need to follow up, but yeah, maybe."

"What's the issue?"

"Well, I needed to check my schedule. My mom mentioned something about if I'm around that weekend."

"To do what?"

"Not sure," I said. "I could be wrong. Just want to check and make sure."

"Is there another issue, Dave?" she said, her pace slowing down.

"What do you mean?"

"If you don't want to talk about it," she said, "I understand."

"No, I don't mind," I said. "It's just that Mike was talking big production, tail gating—"

"Which you like."

194

"Totally—and we will. I had this impression, at first, of him picking me up at like eight in the morning."

"So you *are* going?" she said. "Unless your mom needs you."

"I mean, I guess, probably."

"Are you looking forward to it?"

"Well, yeah. It's the Giants."

"Yeah," Ashley said, "and I know I've monopolized Mike lately. It's a good chance for you guys to hang out one-on-one again."

"Did you tell him to invite me?"

"Of course not," she said. "It was all him. And he really worked to get those tickets."

"They sound like killer seats," I said.

"I'm sure. The seats Mike got us for the Open were awesome."

"Right," I said, watching some runners pass by.

"Well, you guys were friends first," she said. "I think it's cool you two are going to the game."

"Well" I said, "I'm there to see the Giants."

"Of course," she said, "but you'll be driving down together and drinking beers in the parking lot."

"Yeah, I know."

"And you're okay with that?" Ashley said. "Or does it make you uncomfortable?"

"What?"

"Being alone with Mike," she said. "Is that why you wanted to dodge saying yes?"

"Well it is different, now—obviously—between us. So will it feel weird hanging out for ten hours? Yeah, it probably will. But I don't understand why that sounds so odd."

"It doesn't," she said. "I get it. It's awkward. But I think you'll be glad you went. It can be like before. You'll reconnect. Just the two of you."

"Oh c'mon, Ash."

"What?"

"Well," I said, "it's not like we need fucking time alone together. Like we're gonna bond as friends. After what he's done—"

"Maybe you're just too close to it right now," she said. "What did Mike do that you have a problem with?"

"Oh c'mon Ash," I said. "This whole no sex thing, and how he made that his fucking birthday present. No, I'm not like, 'Oh gee, great, time alone with my good buddy, Mike.' "

"I understand," she said, "you're angry with him. Over the oath, which is normal. And you've probably wondered if Mike is really trying to help us or if he is being self-serving."

"I haven't wondered, Ashley, I *know*. It's all about Mike. Seeing what he can get us to do."

"Well," Ashley said, "just because Mike's exerting his power doesn't mean we still don't benefit."

"What?"

"For us, the oath is about freer communication. Commitment to each other … rejuvenation."

"No sex with my wife," I said. "That's how most people would see the oath."

"Okay," she said, "so they wouldn't understand it. So what?"

"That's how it feels to me, Ash."

She held my hand and we walked out of the Park, onto the street.

"It's so much more than that," she said, "but it takes time to see that—to take that perspective. I understand."

"You understand what?" I said as we crossed Central Park West.

"That it's hard to realize the benefits when you're frustrated and you're being told 'no.' And I'm not trying to dismiss your feelings." She suddenly came to a full stop.

"What's wrong?"

"Oh my God," Ashley said. "What time's our train—eleven-thirty?"

"Yeah."

"I just remembered," she said. "I have to pick up Mike's cake. The bakery will be closed by the time we get home."

"What? Where is it?"

"By my gym. I thought I'd be working out today and could pick it up afterward."

"Oh."

"I'm just gonna walk up to Broadway and subway down."

"Okay," I said. "I'll pick up bagels. You don't need me to help, right?"

"I'm good," she said. "This is good. You'll get breakfast."

"Right … exactly."

"When I first woke up," she said, "I was like, *Get your ass to the gym, Ash*. But it was so beautiful outside. Thank you for being Mister Rise and Shine Boy today."

"I'm glad you suggested it," I said, giving her a kiss and a hug.

"Me too," she said. "Oh … an everything bagel and a nonfat latte. That would be perfect."

"You got it," I said, with a laugh. "And you're cool going solo? I mean, how big is the cake?"

"Not big," she said. "I'll take a cab home from there."

"Okay."

"See you in a bit," she said, giving me a kiss. "And remember, nonfat milk."

"Got it," I said, walking away.

"And Dave," she called back, "it's a beautiful day. Enjoy the sunshine."

\* \* \*

I walked away, wondering what to make of our conversation. But no matter what she said, or how she smiled, it didn't change what I was facing later this evening—Mike's birthday victory lap around my apartment.

My wife was going out of her way to make the night

special for him. She was probably counting down the hours. T-minus something till Ashley's sucking his cock. She was probably horny thinking about it. Like her pussy longed for Mike's cock. As she was carrying his cake home.

I'd have preferred just Ashley going out with him than having to be there when she gave him our fucking "present." I pictured her telling Mike it was from the both of us. And Mike emasculating me with, "Thank you, Dave." The way I'd been steamrolled, he probably figured he could really have his way with me now, get me to ask the big question.

He wanted to sperm the love of my life in front of me … and reduce me in her eyes. And I was supposed to ask for the privilege.

I realized I had a hard-on walking into the bagel place. So I grabbed a tray as cover and got in line. I had to wait a long while for Ashley's latte, which had me quietly cursing. I really wanted out the door, to beat Ashley back to our place.

I started talking to the cashier girl. Stuff like, "I don't mean to be a pain in the ass, but …." And pretty soon, I had my latte and was speed walking down Amsterdam.

I thought objectively about how it looked. I'd let another man I'd met online come into my life and take my wife's pussy from me. Let him manipulate me into taking a pledge of no marital sex. Like he fucking owned us.

I just wanted to get home and masturbate. A block from my place I started slowing down, but I didn't see my doorman outside. So I opened the door and walked in like I was in a hurry.

"Good morning, Mr. Martens."

I couldn't just blow him off. Jimmy was the head doorman—worked my building for years. We talked Yankees a lot.

"Hey, Jimmy," I said. "Beautiful weather for the game today, huh?"

"Yeah," he said, "and there's a good north wind blowing."

"I'm gonna try and catch it up at my parents," I said, "which is why I'm in a rush. We have a train to catch. Ashley will be here soon—she's about twenty minutes behind me."

"No, she's here," he said.

"What?"

"She just came in, two minutes before you."

"Are you serious?" I said, surprised. I smiled. "Wow, she's quick. Thanks, Jimmy."

*It's okay*, I told myself, *I can jerk off when she's in the shower*. If I'd gotten home earlier, I might have been just starting to jerk off when she walked in. T*his way*, I thought, *my timing is perfect. I'm showing up with breakfast delivery*.

No one was on the elevator or in my hallway when I got out, so I practiced looking happily surprised. I appreciated Jimmy's heads-up.

# CHAPTER TWENTY-THREE

Ashley was in the kitchen when I opened the door.

"Wow," I said, "You beat me."

"The subway was right there," Ashley said, "and my cab ride was nothing. Took five minutes, less even. It was just waiting at the bakery that took time."

"Same here," I said. "I was waiting forever for your darn latte."

"Why?"

"They forgot it on the order, then got it wrong. Finally, I was like, *Hey, I want to speak to the manager*."

"No, you didn't."

"No, but I was close to. I did complain. Just five seconds after I said something, out came your latte."

"Well, it's really good, thank you."

"Oh, you're welcome Ash," I said, and then I saw the cake on the table. I saw the, *Happy Birthday Mike*.

"Yeah, I have to put that in the fridge," she said.

"That ain't no small cake, Ash. It could serve a dozen people."

"I know," she said, with a laugh. "I didn't realize a 'medium' would be this big. Do you mind if I move some of your beer to the top?"

"What?"

"On the bottom shelf—in the fridge—I want to make room for Mike's cake."

"Oh, I'll do it," I said, walking over. "So you want me to move all the beer at the bottom?"

"Yeah, maybe use your office fridge for some," she said. "I'm sorry."

"It's okay. Now I have a new private reserve stock," I said, trying to make light of it.

"Yeah," she said. "You think you're out of beer but no, you've got the reserve stash in hideaway."

I felt foolish for helping her spin it into a positive. Also embarrassed as I held open the fridge door while she put Mike's cake inside.

"Excellent," she said, giving me a kiss. "Well, I guess I should get my ass in the shower."

"No bagel?"

"I'll have it after."

"Okay."

"You sound disappointed," she said. "You wanted us to have a proper breakfast together, is that it?"

"I know we have a train to catch," I said, "but yeah, I thought it'd be nice."

"Well," she said, "my shoulders are still sore from my class last night and I'm feeling very lazy. So in case you have any interest in helping me shower …."

"Helping you shower?"

"Understanding the boundaries, of course."

"But we can shower together?"

"Not 'together' so much as you washing me, with some soap and a washcloth."

"But I'm in there naked with you?"

"Yeah," she said, and smiled. "You don't have to wear a swimsuit or anything."

"Then let's do it," I said.

"Unless you want to eat your bagel," she said.

I laughed and followed her into the bedroom.

"I'm just gonna change into my bathrobe," she said, "if you want to undress here."

"Yeah, okay," I said, disappointed when she shut the

bathroom door. I wanted to see her strip out of her clothes, slip out of her jeans, un-hook her bra.

After quickly taking off my clothes, I looked in the mirror and made a resolution to start going to the gym. I was never gonna be Mike or my brother, but I needed some muscle.

I pulled down my boxers and looked at my hard dick. I was grateful I hadn't masturbated. Seeing Ashley naked would surely have gotten me erect again, but she might have noticed my dick lacking virility and suspected I'd jerked off.

This way, I was rock hard and felt game for anything.

"You want to come in?" she said, opening the door.

"You bet," I said, walking in.

Ashley was in her bathrobe, and I had a towel around my waist. I shut the bathroom door.

"You ready?" I said.

"Yeah," she replied. "Do you want to get the water started?"

"You bet," I said, walking over to the shower.

"Yeah," she said, "Let me know when the water's hot, and I'll come over and feel it."

"It's actually good already," I said.

"Really?" she said, walking over. "Oh yeah, that is good, but three degrees hotter would be even better.

"I don't think I can be that precise," I said, "but okay."

"Would you mind helping me off with my robe?" she said, turning her back to me.

"Of course," I said, pulling it off her shoulders and letting her pull her arms out of the sleeves. I was left holding her bathrobe, with Ashley naked in front of me. I stared at her cute little ass and her tits when she turned around … mesmerized.

"So, are you gonna take your towel off now?" she said.

"Uh yeah," I said, taking it off in a swoop.

"Looks like he's excited," she said, eying my erection.

"You kidding?" I said. "Seeing you naked has him over the moon."

"Well," she said, "just remind him, no funny business. We took an oath to be patient. But let's enjoy it for all that it is ... us naked together."

"Can I give you a kiss?"

"Yeah, but put your towel back on first. That's kind of SR."

"SR?" I said.

"Sexual relations," she said.

"It's just a kiss, Ash."

"Okay," she said and smiled. "Come here, you."

My kiss was slow and tender, and I felt my cock hard up against her. I wanted to grab her ass, but I didn't want to push it, either. I didn't want to lose my invite to the shower.

"Ready?" she said. "You should probably get in first."

"Yeah, sure," I said, opening the shower door.

"And here are some clean washcloths."

"Thanks," I said, walking inside.

We have an oversized shower. There was plenty of room to stand behind her.

I watched Ashley's tits jiggle as she stepped inside. I looked down at her trimmed pubic hair, her triangle. My boner pointed right at Ashley.

"Mighty cozy, isn't it?" she said, with a smile.

"I'm a big fan of cozy," I said, smiling back.

I watched Ashley reach down and feel the water.

"It's good to go," she said, standing back up. "You ready? Do you know which soap to use ... see that bottle on the far right?"

I watched Ashley's bare white ass as she bent down to turn on the shower. It was pretty hot, and we have strong water pressure. I backed away to get out of the spray.

"Too hot?" Ashley said. "Here, I'll lower it. Any better?"

I smiled and gave a thumbs-up.

She smiled back and then turned around and relaxed her body. I just stared at Ashley's ass and what had been mine for the last five years. I wanted to smack it hard and tell her, *I ain't no fucking cuckold. I'm gonna fuck you good and hard, right here in our fucking bathroom.*

She tilted her head back, and said, "Aren't you gonna start on my back?"

I smiled and said, "yeah."

I figured, since she couldn't see me, I'd err on the side of using too much soap. I started lathering her shoulders, going clockwise with the washcloth on her back. I slowly brought it down and hesitated before moving down to her ass. I had my hand on her ass, rubbing the washcloth and copping a feel. Till she looked over her shoulder and said, "That's good."

I crouched down to wash her legs but then sat Indian style. It was a pretty good spot. Ashley's body blocked the spray, and I could look up. I could see her pussy when she had her legs apart. I zoned out just washing her calf, catching glimpses of her pussy lips.

When she turned around, I started washing her feet. She'd lift one foot up and I'd stare at it, admiring its shape, her pretty small toes. But with her looking down at me, there was less chance to ogle, so I didn't linger and moved on to her legs.

She wasn't giving me much inner thigh, and as I crept upward, she said, "I'll take care of that myself."

"You sure?"

"But you can wash my breasts, as long as you're not groping. Let's keep this pure. No copping feels, Mister."

"I won't" I said. "How 'bout I stand behind you closer … so I can wash your stomach better?"

"Okay."

My boner jumped a little as I stared at her ass up close and washed her stomach. It was right up against her, just above her ass. I wasn't grinding her or anything. I used extra lotion for her tits, almost giving them a bubble bath. The washcloth was frustrating. I *so* wanted my bare hands on them.

"It might be easier just to use my hands," I said.

"We're so close," she said. "Let's keep it pure. The washcloth is fine."

"Sure," I said, starting in.

I tried not to be clumsy as I circled her right breast and rubbed the cloth over her nipple. I angled in to get my dick up against her and tended to her left breast.

I was starting on the right one again when Ashley said, "I'm good."

"What?"

"I'm not gonna wash my hair till tonight. I can do the rest."

"Did I just do something wrong?"

"Not at all," she said. "I freaking loved the pampering. Made me feel like some prima donna celebrity."

"Okay," I said.

"Seriously though," she said, "it was really lovely, Dave. And super-sweet. You made me feel like a princess. And you did an awesome job. I'm super clean. I'll just be another couple minutes."

"Yeah, Okay," I said.

"And then you can shower."

"Right," I said, still processing, and stepping out of the shower. I started drying off, but then figured what's the point in getting dressed, so I just waited in the bathroom for her shower to end.

"That was a long couple minutes," I said, as Ashley came out of the shower.

"I'm sorry," she said, as I handed her a towel.

"I'm just kidding, Ash," I said, "I have this other towel. Can I help you dry off?"

"Sure," she said,

I bent down and dried her legs, until she said, "Seriously, I'm completely dried off."

"Sure," I said, standing up again, "but we do have to get moving if we're gonna make this train."

"Do you mind if I just get ready in here while you shower?"

"Go ahead," I said. "I'll be quick."

That's when I knew: I wouldn't be masturbating that morning. Not with Ashley right outside getting ready. I didn't feel comfortable. The glass was fogged up, but she could always open the door to ask me a question. It didn't happen often—a few times a year. But that was enough of a chance for me not to risk it.

So I didn't. Even though my boner sure told me otherwise. I thought of other stuff instead. Like trying to remember the names of my cousin's kids. And I debated if we should take a cab or walk from the station. But mostly I focused on showering quickly. We were already cutting it close. I knew we had to rush.

It didn't matter. Ashley wasn't ready. She didn't like the first outfit she tried on, and the second, and suddenly, making our train looked doubtful. I agreed that one dress showed too much cleavage. But the next was a summery floral one. I said, "Perfect, Ash."

"I'm serious," I said, "that's a dress for frolicking around on the grass on a day like today."

Ashley laughed and said, "I like it. You sold me. I want to frolic."

"Well, save the frolicking till we get there," I said. "We have to high-tail it double time. We might seriously miss our train."

\* \* \*

We caught some breaks, though. No wait for the elevator, and we caught a cab within seconds. I still didn't think we would make it and started giving instructions on how to get there. Ashley usually frowns when I do that, but when I said, "Now cut down 113th ..." Ashley nodded in approval.

"We don't have time for tickets," I said. "We'll buy 'em on the train."

"Sure," she said, fingers crossed.

"I got this, Ash," I said. "Start running. I'll be right behind you."

I told the cabbie to keep the change and bolted into the station. I saw Ashley run up the stairs, urging me to hurry, and heard the roar of the train pulling in.

The station wasn't crowded, and I sprinted past the ticket booths and bounded up the stairs. Ashley was trying to hold the door open with one foot on the platform. They rang the "door closing" bell and Ashley got off the train.

I ran up to her, put my arm around her waist, and pulled her inside with me. The doors closed five seconds later.

"Nicely done," she said, giving me a hug.

"Thanks," I muttered, trying to catch my breath.

"We made it," she said. "Now we can relax, and there are plenty of seats. Do you want the window?"

"Sure," I said, going in first.

The conductor started announcing the stations: Scarsdale, Hartsdale, North White Plains ....

"There's a girl at work," Ashley said, "who sings all the local train stations on the Harlem line—in order. It's a song she wrote when she was twelve."

"The train stops in order are the lyrics?"

"Yeah, but the way she sings it, it seems to rhyme."

"So she sings this at work?" I said. "Like when ... when she's getting ready to leave for the train?"

Ashley laughed. "No, she's not a freak—she grew up in Scarsdale. She sang it to me once at her cubicle."

"Oh, Okay," I said. "So how's it going at work?"

"Good," she said. "We're pacing over budget, so the mood is good."

"How about office politics-wise?"

"Well, my boss is going through the ringer with our CFO. But for me, personally, things are pretty calm. And I'm staying out of things. Tamara has issues with some sales manager, and I'm like, *Tamara, I don't want to know*."

"That's good" I said. "And Jim Murta? No issues dealing with him at work?"

"No," she said. "Ever since he apologized, and I was able to move on, it's been fine. I'm sure people still talk about it, but the more time that passes, the less it defines me."

"You have to deal with him much?"

"No, but it's not like I'll ignore him, either. I mean, he did apologize."

"Yeah" I said, "I understand. I mean, you gotta say hello to him and be normal."

"Oh yeah," she said. "I mean, I don't like talking to him one on one and having people see and speculate that something's going on. So I avoid that. But he stopped by at Caroline's birthday, and it was totally fine and friendly."

"Two nights ago?"

"Yeah," she said. "Jim's good friends with Caroline— from when they interned."

"Oh," I said. "I guess I thought Wednesday was just a girl thing."

"It was," she said. "He just came in for a drink—and to wish her happy birthday."

"You guys talk?" I said. "I mean, you and Jim?"

"Not one-on-one," she said. "Just as a group. The four of us. He had a concert to go to, so he couldn't stay long. And besides, he said he didn't want to interrupt our girl power bonding."

"But it was no big deal being around him?"

"I know it's different for me than it is for you. I see him

at work every day. And it's a couple months now. I thought it was nice he stopped by for Caroline … and nice that he knew not to overstay."

"Well," I said, "I could see Tamara telling him to blow off the concert."

"I could too," Ashley said, "but she didn't. It was just understood that the night was for us girls."

"I got you," I said. "And you had fun, right?"

"Yeah, that's when Tamara brought up her Halloween party," she said. "She texted me this morning, wanted to know what I thought of a Seven Deadly Sins theme."

"Oh good fucking grief. Are you serious?"

"What?" she said.

"It's just so pretentious," I said. "Like what's one of the sins. Gluttony's one, right?"

"That sounds right."

"Okay," I said, "so now you're supposed to come up with a costume that expresses that, right?"

"Yeah."

"So," I said, "now it's a whole scene where everyone's gotta show how creative and artsy and cool they are. Like why does she have to limit what you can wear on Halloween? Why can't you just dress up as fucking Batman if you want to?"

"You can," she said, laughing, "and it won't be like that. Tamara just wants an excuse to dress like a slut."

"How do you mean?"

"She'd dress up as *Lust,*" Ashley said, "which I think is what most people go as. So, no need to worry 'bout how artistic your costume is."

"Yeah, but my point's still true. I can't just say, 'I wanna go as so-and-so.'"

"She won't care how you're dressed," she said. "Seriously, just so long as you're wearing *any* costume, she'll be cool. As I said, it's about her dressing scandalous. And getting her friends to."

"I get it," I said. "Like that cleavage party she had."

"Yeah," she said, "only for this one, guys can dress half naked as well."

"Whatever," I said. "We could also go away, y'know, that weekend. To Florida, maybe."

"Yeah, if the condo's not rented."

"Or a hotel, if it is—just throwing it out there."

"Yeah, okay, and who knows?" Ashley said. "By tomorrow Tamara will probably have a totally new theme."

"Well, I'd like to tell Tamara what she can do with her new freaking theme."

Ashley laughed. "I won't pass that along. I'll just say you're looking forward to it."

"Well, she's gonna know that's a lie," I said.

"No she won't," Ashley said, laughing. "I'll say you're psyched because you're guaranteed to be the only Batman."

"Why say anything?" I said. "And certainly don't commit me yet."

"Well, here's the thing …." Ashley said.

"Yeah," I said, warily.

"I was telling Chang about it last night …."

"You told Chang about Tamara's Halloween party?"

"She told me she might be in town for work that week."

"Oh, so fucking let me guess … Chang's coming, right?"

"First, she has to see if Ryan would fly out for the weekend."

"Oh good God," I said.

"I thought you'd be psyched he'd be there."

"I'd be psyched to go out like we did last night with them, sure. But the four of us going to Tamara's party? How fun is that for them? Why would Ryan want to go to party where he knows no one?"

"He knows Tamara … from our wedding."

"Well okay, "I said, "Okay, okay … well, let's just see if they can swing it."

"But if so, that's cool?"

"Yeah," I said. "If Ryan's in town, great. Maybe we can watch Sunday football out somewhere."

I meant to leave her with the impression that I saw the bright side of Ryan coming to town. So it wouldn't seem like it was my fault when I got Ryan to bail.

I figured Ryan would have to go along with whatever I told him. He knew I couldn't deal with Tamara. *And so what if Chang's pissed?* I thought. *Twenty-plus years of being friends has to trump that.*

I figured I had a much better chance with Ryan than I did with Ashley. So I acted like I'd forgotten about Tamara's party when we got off the train.

# CHAPTER TWENTY-FOUR

"We can do the scenic walk to my parents' place," I said, "if you're down for that. Though it might take about twice as long."

"Sounds awesome," Ashley said. "Let's do it. Have you ever taken me that way before?"

"No, I just thought of it," I said. "I used to bike it as a kid. We do have to cut through someone's backyard, though."

"Danger," Ashley said. "I love it."

I looked up and saw my mom's gray Honda in the parking lot. "Oh, motherfucker," I said.

Ashley saw it too and said, "No way. Did you tell her?"

"Of course not," I said. "If I had talked to her, I'd have said, 'Don't fucking pick us up.' "

"Well, c'mon, we can't just stand here" she said, as I followed her down the stairs.

I could see my mom waving from the car window as we stepped down to the street. Ashley waved back and we walked casually to the car.

"Can't you just tell her," she said under her breath, "thanks, but we'd rather walk?"

"Yeah, you know what?" I said. "I think I will, actually."

"I'm kidding," Ashley said. "You can't say that."

"Why not? My mom will understand."

"She made the effort to pick us up," she said, and smiled at me. "Just be a good son and get in the car."

I returned her smile and told her I'd sit in the backseat.

Ashley gave my mom a hug and a hello.

"How'd you know we'd be on this train?" I asked my mom from the backseat.

"From Sean," she said.

"Is he at the house already?" I said.

"No, your dad's at the airport, picking him up."

"How did that come up?" I said. "Sean giving you my train time, I mean."

"What?" My mom said. Ashley turned and looked back at me.

"Oh nothing," I said. "I'd just forgotten I'd told Sean, that's all."

I slumped back in my seat and let them talk. Mom was telling Ashley about a new movie theater she went to the night before. How the seats were like first class on an airplane, with a wait staff. She was hoping that now my dad would want to see more movies with her.

As we neared our house, I saw the stone wall separating a bunch of backyards. It was part of the scenic route I had planned for us. We could have climbed up on it and walked a good fifty yards. Ashley was wearing sporty sneakers; she'd have been totally game.

I was just pissed at the situation. And at Sean. After years of forgetting to pass along actually important things, he chose today to make sure I had a ride. Still, once I was out of the car and Ashley said, "Yay!" with genuine enthusiasm, I was just happy to be there.

\* \* \*

Mom led us into the kitchen. "I'm making macaroni and cheese," she said, checking the oven.

"Who's doing the cookout?" I said, "Sean and Dad?"

"It's being catered," my mom replied.

"Wow," Ashley said, "look at the Martens getting all fancy."

Mom laughed and said, "Why don't you two sit down.

Let's talk. This dish is almost done. What would you like to drink?"

Ashley held up her bottled water and sat down.

"I'm good," I said. Mom checked the timer and sat down as well.

"The Riley's son started his own catering business," Mom said, "and it's not doing so well. So Dad wanted to hire him for this."

"They take care of everything?" I said.

"Yeah," Mom said. "They bring the food, do the grilling, uh-huh."

"And the best part," Ashley said, "is you don't have to clean up after."

"Yup, for once," Mom said, "someone else is cleaning up."

"Nice," Ashley said.

"Speaking of which ..." Mom said, turning to me—I could tell by how she smiled that something was up—"you really made yourself at home here this week, Dave."

Ashley looked at me, then at my mom, and asked her, "How do you mean?"

My stomach was sinking and I tried to look normal. I knew this was Defcon 1 ... that I had to derail this.

So I turned to Ashley and said, "I stopped by here there this week. My mom's cleaning out the attic. I had some things to sort through."

Ashley and my mom both looked at me quizzically.

"After I came back from San Francisco," I said to Ashley. "I've been meaning to tell you. Do you remember me talking about the Mars globe I had as a kid?"

Ashley looked puzzled, and said, "Yeah."

"Yeah, well, turns out it was up in the attic all this time. It's actually in my bedroom—so I want to show you before we leave."

"Okay," Ashley said. "When were you here, Thursday?"

I knew my mom was looking at me, but I couldn't meet her eyes.

"Yeah, when I went to the committee meeting, I took the train in from here. I meant to explain that before; it's a pretty long Brian emergency story, so it can wait till the train ride back in."

"Okay," Ashley said, then turned to my mom. "So how was Florida? Nice and relaxing, I hope?"

"Very relaxing," she said, "Thank you. A few dinners with friends. We had some great wine. Michael played a lot of golf, and I read on the beach."

"Sounds awesome," Ashley said.

"Yeah, you guys should do a couple long weekends. We won't be down there much this fall."

"But aren't you renting it out?" Ashley said.

"Not till Christmas."

"Wow, Mom," I said, "so when did you learn this? Sean told me a few weeks ago you had someone. I thought it was done deal—that you were renting your condo in the fall."

"With the family reunion in November and Jody being sick, I want the condo to be an option."

"Wow, great," I said, smiling at Ashley. "We will certainly take you up on that."

"Absolutely," Ashley said. "I love it there. Hearing the waves from the balcony. It's so peaceful. We had a great time down there in June."

Ashley started telling my mom which restaurants we went to, and my mom started in on places we should go to.

I thought about that last time in June …. We drank wine on the balcony at sunset. Ashley sang to the moon as we walked along the beach. As we swam in the ocean, we thought we saw a shark—which turned out to be a porpoise. We had sex a few times that week. I had no insecurities, then. In hindsight, it was rather blissful. I couldn't have conceived what would happen when we returned. That she'd even be in that bathroom with her tits out, that she would let Jim Murta fuck her without a condom, let him fucking sperm her pussy … knowing I was there.

Thinking about it now, Florida seemed all about Ashley getting nice and tan and looking extra-fuckable for her return to New York. I pictured Jim Murta saying, "and I'd like to thank Dave for taking Ashley away on vacation, getting her all sun-kissed tan down in Florida. And for being so fucking clueless that night at the party."

"What do you think?" Ashley said, nudging me, "any restaurants stand out for you?"

"The steak place sounded good," I said, "but all of them, really."

"Dave wasn't sure," Ashley said, turning to my mom. "Are any of your neighbors coming today? Like any from the mini-pool party Dave and I threw last month. The Marshmans, the Seevers, Jay …?"

"The Seevers are out of town," my mom said. "But the Marshmans will be here. Jay will be here, too, but not till later."

"Jay's kind of a character," Ashley said. "I met him I guess at our wedding, but only talked to him that day by the pool. How did you become friends?"

It was a question I dreaded. I didn't want Jay being talked about. I didn't want Ashley knowing I'd lied, and finding out he wasn't the crazed domestic abuser I'd portrayed him as.

"Jay built our sun room," my mom said, "twelve years ago now. And when he got married he bought the house at the end of the street. So we were neighbors and got to know his wife. During the blackout he came by and lent us a generator."

"He's divorced, right?" Ashley asked.

"Yeah," she said, "it just was just finalized. We had some champagne with him the other weekend. I think it was a good way to begin his fifties."

"Really?" Ashley asked, sounding skeptical. "I just got divorced and now I'm fifty."

"Well," my mom said, "if being divorced and turning fifty came as a surprise to him, then maybe, but the divorce was liberation for him. Now he's done with all that nonsense. A milestone birthday and he's got his life back. I think for him, especially, life can begin at fifty."

I was sitting there praying for my dad's car to pull up in the driveway

"What kind of nonsense?" Ashley said. "Was it a tough divorce?"

"Well, he wanted to keep the house," he said, "and he bought her out. For a while it seemed smooth. But then she started going after for him for everything. It was very unfortunate."

"Were there altercations between them?"

"Physical?" my mom said. "Oh no, she was already living up in Albany with her new husband or about-to-be husband. And he's a lawyer, so of course he was very involved."

"Yikes," Ashley said. "Did you know his wife?"

"Oh sure," she said, "but not well. She more or less kept to herself. Maybe she was just shy, but she wasn't very warm or friendly."

"Can I ask what happened?" Ashley said. "Why they divorced?"

"She left him for this man," she said, "and I don't think Jay saw that coming. But I thought he handled it well. Though last spring he was put through the ringer."

"Do you mean over legal things?" Ashley said. "I guess I had the impression he had a temper … with his wife. That he had gotten into trouble."

"Trouble?" my mom asked.

"Cops being called or something."

"Oh God, no. Not Jay! I would know if anything like that had happened."

Ashley gave me a stare that said, *So everything you said about Jay that day was total bullshit.*

Then she turned back to my mom and said, "I'm gonna play some tennis again."

Here's the thing: I'd said a lot of shit about Jay. I felt I had no other choice. The guy had met her last time in her bikini, at my parent's pool. I'd watched him hit on her hard. Pushed us hard to go to his fiftieth birthday party. Had her email and cell number when we left.

I felt I had to discourage her on that train ride back to New York. So I insinuated things about Jay and his divorce ... dropped terms like 'restraining order' and 'domestic violence,' and implied the cops had been over there a lot.

And it worked. She ignored his texts when we got back. There was no more Jay. His birthday was forgotten.

But now she was hearing Jay was no villain at all. My mom was freaking vouching for the guy. Ashley would know I was full of shit. I hadn't simply embellished, I'd made the whole thing up—from whole fucking cloth.

Ashley would say it was some big deliberate lie, and I couldn't really argue it wasn't. So I needed to apologize but also explain where my head was.

Not only had Jay had been majorly hitting on her—suggesting she pose at some biker convention at the Javitz Center—and inviting us to his fiftieth birthday party at his house, but he had mocked me because I'd never ridden a motorcycle.

I didn't want her communicating with him. I knew the only reason he wanted me to come to his birthday party was 'cause he wanted to fuck my wife. He was hard-selling it. Even sent us an invite in the mail—he got our address from my mom. He'd handwritten on the card: "Ashley, come by early and I'll let you ride on my pasta rocket."

I knew what the party was about. Making me a chump. Ringing in fifty by fucking my hot, young, big-titted wife.

I figured nothing I'd say could stop Ashley from thinking I'd lied and libeled the guy.

So I decided to default to saying I simply got it wrong—had the wrong guy. How my mom must've been telling me about somebody else. I'd add that it was still no excuse and insist it was an "honest mistake."

She wouldn't buy it—she'd be hurling questions my way. But she couldn't really disprove it. On anything specific, I could always punt.

\* \* \*

We saw my dad's car pull into the driveway, and my mom waved out the window as my brother got out. We all started standing up.

My brother walks with a swagger. He's a tall, athletic guy, and he's loud. We could hear him talking while they were still outside.

"Hey gang," Sean said as he came through the door. He handed my mom a wrapped bottle of wine and gave her a hug.

"What a good son," Ashley said, turning to me. "He was thoughtful and brought a gift."

I rolled my eyes and Ashley gave Sean a hug.

"What's up, little bro?" he said, as we hugged.

Mom asked about his flight and why his girlfriend couldn't make it. And my dad sat down and started asking Ashley about her job. But Sean never joined everyone in sitting around the table. Pretty soon Mom joined Dad in asking Ashley questions, while Sean turned to me and told me he was going to look for a football.

I didn't want to seem rude so I stood tentatively.

"Before all the kids get here," I said, as my mom and Ashley looked up at me, "we're gonna toss the ball around outside. I can get some big bro time."

"Well said," Sean smiled, walking back in.

"I think it's sweet," Ashley said.

* * *

"So," I said, throwing him the ball, "what's the deal with tomorrow night? Do you need to stay over?"

"I really doubt it," he said, throwing the ball back. "But in case Jen's really being a bitch, can you be a back pocket in case of emerge?"

"Yeah, of course," I said.

"So how are you, little bro?"

"Pretty good," I said, making the catch.

"What's been going on?"

"Not much," I said. "I did a big speech in San Fran, filling in for my boss."

"That's cool."

"Yeah, and this morning," I said, "Ashley and I went to Central Park and signed up to play tennis on the courts there after work this week."

"How'd she cajole you into that?"

"Well, years ago she did buy me a racket. She was busting on about how I never use it. But mostly, it kind of does sound fun to me. And a good reason to get out of work on time."

"Is she gonna play left-handed?" he said. "I'm serious; you won't even return her serves."

"Hey," I said, "of course, she can kick my ass. But if she wants to practice her game with me—and she's seen me play—I'm totally down with that."

"Well," he said, "is Ashley going to be wearing a tennis dress?"

I laughed and said, "I don't think so."

"I want to see photos if she does. It's a hot look."

"Well, she's wearing a bikini today, probably," I said.

"Then I will be in the pool," he said, "with my snorkel and mask."

I laughed. "I told you about the O'Brien's kid last summer, right?"

"Ashley caught him jerking off behind a bush, right?"

"Yeah," I said. "She's been paranoid about being out by the pool in a bikini ever since."

"Well, when she's out in her bikini today, I'm gonna have a few possible O'Brien kid sightings. We both should."

"What?" I said. "Just to freak her out?"

"Yeah," he said. "Fuck with her. What's the kid's name again?"

"Tim," I said.

"Okay," he said. "Let's call him Timmy."

"Well, if you want creepier," I said, "let's call him Little Timmy O'Brien."

Sean laughed. "Yeah. Look, Ashley, what's Little Timmy O'Brien doing climbing that tree with his binoculars?"

\* \* \*

I started running routes and Sean was zipping them in. But I was making the catch. And making the effort. I fell down chasing overthrown balls. I kind of hoped Ashley was watching from a window.

Sean tried a punt, but it sliced into the woods and I went in to get it. When I got back, he was talking to Dad on the driveway. Dad was pointing to the garage and the gutter along the roof.

Sean threw me the ball and went into the garage.

I asked Dad, "So how was the drive? Much airport traffic?"

"Not bad, actually," he said. "How did your presentation go this week?"

"Everyone seemed really, genuinely complimentary," I said. "I was comfortable in Q&A and I think it was received really well."

"Well, that's great, Dave", he said. "Sounds like you made the most of the opportunity. So congratulations. But about the other night when you stayed here … did your mom say anything to you about the way you left things?"

"I'm sorry, yeah, she was starting to. I had been going on no sleep, and I just overslept and was running out the door."

"Look, I don't care. It's just that we didn't have it cleaned this week. So your mom sees dishes, your bed thrown together, and a beer can right on her piano—"

"What?"

"You left your beer can on her piano. Right next to a coaster. Couldn't you at least put it on that?"

"Oh wow, Dad, I'm sorry. I'll apologize to Mom. I just had a long day traveling and was nostalgic, I guess ... sentimental. So I started playing the piano."

"It's okay," my dad said with a hint of a smile. "How did you like going into Westchester?"

"Huh?"

"Westchester Airport. Had you flown there before?"

"No, this was my first time," I said. "It's nice."

Sean came out of the garage with a hose, and I helped him unroll it. Then I grabbed the ladder and positioned it against the roof. I wasn't all fired up to unclog the drain, but I figured I'd offer. "I can go up there," I said.

"Just hold the ladder," Sean replied, and started climbing.

"So how's Ashley doing?" Dad said.

"Good," I said. "She went to a fire drill at work the other day, and fifteen minutes later, she was picked to be office fire warden."

"What?"

"It means she's now the go-to person whenever there's a fire drill. Just one of those things that only happens to Ashley."

Sean asked for a tarp to throw the leaves and muck down to, so I went into the garage and Dad went inside.

"Is this cool?" I said, laying it out.

"Yeah, hold on," he said. "Since I'm up here, I'm gonna check the other gutters."

"Yeah, okay," I said, and saw a car pulling up in the driveway. It was two cousins I hadn't seen since my wedding. I walked out on the driveway to meet them and hugged them. They were five years younger and used to look up to me while we were growing up.

One of them had also brought a football—what we had always played as kids—and we started tossing it around. Sean started yelling from the roof, "A little fucking help, please!"

My cousins looked bemused as I walked to the driveway.

# CHAPTER TWENTY-FIVE

My cousin Jen arrived with her kids running up the driveway. Her twin ten-year-old boys were excited to be in a big backyard with a pool. Ashley came out in her floral dress and took Jen's little girls to my mom's garden.

Jen and I had a beer on the deck, and I got the lowdown on my mom's side of the family. She told me all about her husband's dispute with her town's little league.

I watched Ashley playing with the girls. The cartoonish faces she made and whatever she was saying really had them laughing.

I saw the boys playing badminton, and Jen asked if I was up for joining her, playing doubles.

"I'm playing tennis with Ashley this week," I told her. "Hopefully, this will give me some confidence going in."

"Playing against me and two ten-year-old boys?" she said, laughing.

Pretty soon Jen left to greet my uncle, and her boys wanted to play wiffleball. I told them to play each other and I'd be designated pitcher. But by the second inning, my two cousins wanted to play. And by the fourth, my uncle and neighbor were on the teams. Two pitches later, my brother wanted in.

"The score's meaningless now," he said. "We need to start the game over, pick new teams."

"Okay," I said, "but this is last call for new players."

That's when my cousin Jen came out and said, "I'll play." Which made it uneven.

"C'mon, Ashley," Sean yelled. "Big family wiffleball game!" Ashley excused herself from talking to a neighbor and came on over.

We had five on five, which meant the backyard was ridiculously well-covered. But there were a lot of dropped balls, so easy outs soon became in-the-park homeruns. Which is how they won. We were tied with two out, last inning, and I was pitching. Ashley was batting so I eased up on my throw, and she nicked it to third. It was an easy out at first, but my uncle dropped my throw. So I grabbed the ball from the pacasandra as Ashley rounded second. I had her at third, but Jen dropped an easy catch. Ashley pranced home and they won the game. I was pissed. It was just wiffleball, but I didn't like losing to my brother. Especially like that.

"Why did you throw it to Jen?" he said, on the driveway afterward. "Why not throw it at Ashley and get her out? You know Jen can't catch."

"I kind of lofted the ball," I said. "I really thought it was an easy catch. She was yelling for me to throw it, and she's a girl. I was trying to be inclusive."

"Well, you see where that got you, little bro," he said, with a laugh. "Good game."

\* \* \*

My cousins went to their car to get their swimsuits and I went up to my room to change. We were the first ones in the pool, tossing a ball around, and talking about a crazy aunt of ours. The little girls came down in their flotation gear, with Jen and Ashley walking behind them in bathrobes. One of the girls went straight for the pool, and Ashley ran after her.

I saw my cousins' eyes fix on Ashley as she took off her bathrobe. Her tits were on full display in her sky-blue bikini, and they had a great view of her ass as she helped the girls into the pool. But that was okay with me. It made me seem like the man. Ashley reflected well on me.

I hung out with my cousins in a corner of the deep end, drinking beer. Pretty soon my aunt and uncle were in the pool, along with the Marshmans and a neighbor I'd just met.

I was talking with Ashley when Sean swam up to us. "What the fuck," he said, with his eyes on the woods, "is that little Timmy O'Brien hiding up in that tree?" Ashley looked momentarily freaked, and Sean burst out laughing.

Once most of the adults got out, Jen let the boys come into the pool. They started right in doing cannonballs, which immediately changed the scene. Jen was yelling at them for running, and then for splashing, and then for doing more cannonballs. But when one of them deliberately splashed her in the face, it was lights out. She was livid. She ordered the boys out and took the girls up after them.

Which suddenly left the pool to just Ashley and me. I was about to swim over to her, but she went underwater and swam right up to me. We kissed each other tenderly in the deep end. She said, very softly, "I love you," and I held her close.

"Oh, honey," she said, "did you not put on any lotion?"

"What?" I said. "Do I look sunburned?"

"Yes, your nose is very red," she said. "I have some spray in my bag. I'm gonna get you some."

"Well," I said, "I can get shade by the ladder."

"Yeah, but for how long?" she said. "I'll get it."

I checked out her ass as she went up the pool stairs, and then suddenly, Jay was walking up to the gate with a cooler.

\* \* \*

Opening the gate is just lifting a latch. But Ashley felt she should run over and do it for him. She had no second thoughts about greeting Jay in her bikini, her tits upfront and on display. I watched him—he was wearing tight jeans and a form-fitting t-shirt—hug her. Except for two strips of cloth, she was naked. I wondered if Jay had a hard-on.

I watched them talking and my parents walking up to him. Dad shook Jay's hand, and Mom gave him a hug.

"Hey Jay," I said, from the pool, as he walked up.

"What's up, Dave?" he said, and kept on walking.

I heard Ashley ask him if he brought his swimsuit. He held up his bag and said, "I'm changing now."

Ashley grabbed her sun block and came back in the pool.

"So what should we say?" she asked, swimming up to me.

"Huh?"

"If he asks us why we were no-shows for his fiftieth? What do I tell him?"

"Nothing," I said. "We just couldn't make it."

"Well, that's awfully cold," she said. "Why not just flip him the bird?"

"Okay," I said, "we had a wedding to go to—a friend of mine from college."

"I guess," she said.

"Besides," I said, "we never told him yes—that we'd be there."

"And so none of what you told me about Jay was true?"

"Ash, I got my story confused. It was someone else, I guess."

Ashley just looked at me like, *You expect me to believe that?*

"I'll tell you on the train," I said. "Explain, I mean. It'll make sense, I promise."

"Well," she said, "because of what you said, I totally blew him off. Didn't return his texts, didn't even explain why."

"There's nothing to explain, Ash. Your husband asked that you not correspond with other men, and that included him."

"C'mon, that's not what you said."

"I fucking know that, Ash, but jeez, you don't need to be apologizing."

"For treating him like a pariah? I think I do."

"Ashley, please let's talk about this later when it will make a lot more sense."

"Hey, guys," Jay said, walking over and taking off his shirt. I remembered the last time, how Ashley complimented him on his Harley Davidson tattoo and muscles. This time she just said, "Welcome, Jay" in a cheerful voice.

"Jay," I said, "how you been?"

"Good," he said, stepping into the pool and putting his beer down on the side. "You guys missed a good party last month."

"I'm sure," Ashley said. "I'm really sorry. Turned out we were already committed."

"Oh no worries, Ashley. It's more that you missed a good time, you know. It was an event—that's for sure. I knew it was a long shot when I mailed the invite late."

"Mailed or emailed?"

"No, I mailed you a card. Your mom gave me your address."

"Well, we didn't get any card," Ashley said, then turned to me.

"No," I said, trying to look puzzled. "don't remember any invites."

I looked over at Jay and saw his speculative expression. So I said, "No" again, dispassionately, and looked away.

"Well, I definitely sent it," Jay said. "Too bad. It was a lot of fun."

"Yeah," I said, "we had a wedding that weekend in Maine. We realized when we got home."

"Well, maybe next time," he said, smiling, but never taking his eyes off me.

"So … did you get anything good?" Ashley said.

"I got some very good wines and a lot of Rangers' tickets. You like hockey, Ashley?"

"Kind of indifferent," she said. "I've seen a few games, but that was for work."

"Well, let me know when you guys are coming out here sometime. You can stop by my place and do some wine tasting."

Ashley laughed and said, "Thank you."

"I'm serious," he said. "Just let me know."

"Well, we've been out here lately because of the pool. But now it'll be mostly just for holidays."

"Sure," Jay said.

"So," Ashley said, "how did things turn out with that house you were trying to finish by Labor Day?"

That was all it took. Jay took her question and ran with it. All the issues behind the construction delays—some supplier he was suing, his contacts in local government. He showed her before and after photos of the house he had brought with him in his car. I moved next to Ashley to have a look myself—not because I was interested, but just to stay in the conversation. Even if I was hardly listening. He was going non-stop, on and on about himself and his business. Ashley asked follow-up questions, which just fueled his showing off.

I noticed him staring at her tits whenever she replied to something. I figured he probably thought of Ashley as a low-probability, high-reward fuck prospect. Or one that got away. Either way, our no-show at his party wasn't going to stop Jay from flirting with my wife. That was the vibe he was giving off.

I wondered if I was giving off a vibe that could also be picked up on. A subtle "Can't put your finger on it" something I'd acquired after the Jim Murta incident that made Jay conclude I wasn't much of an obstacle.

So I stuck around. Even though I wanted another drink, I didn't want to leave the conversation—especially with Ashley in the pool in her bikini. I tried to get him talking sports, but he turned it into sports he played, and where he skied out west.

Jen came over and said, "They're about to feed us."

Ashley said she wanted to change beforehand. I was just glad to leave the pool. I grabbed a towel and wrapped it around her and she followed me up the stairs. When I pulled my wet bathing suit down in my bedroom, I had a hard-on hanging up my swimsuit. I thought about Ashley changing in my parent's bathroom and imagined Mike going inside as Ashley took off her bikini. Fucking her with my parents and me right downstairs.

There's never been a lock on my bedroom door. Not that someone would likely bust in without knocking. But even though I knew I'd be quick, I told myself, "Not now" and put on my boxers. I thought about baseball and waited till my boner receded before going back down.

\* \* \*

I grabbed myself a burger and a helping of Mom's mac and cheese and sat down on the deck with my cousins. They were talking about a TV show I hadn't seen, and I waved to Ashley when I saw her … sitting with Jen and her kids. I felt I could relax and just appreciate my family.

I sounded off briefly about the Yankees, but mostly I just enjoyed listening. My great uncle came over and told us his story of driving eight hundred miles to be at the Giants-Bears game in 1963 in sub zero temperatures—how his friend got frostbite. I'd heard the story before, but I liked the way he told it and enjoyed seeing him so animated.

People started migrating. My uncle left, and Sean joined us and started talking fantasy football. This sent me in search of a drink, and I wound up sitting down with Jen for a while, getting her kids to yap about baseball. When I didn't see Ashley on the deck, I stood up and spotted her in the yard, talking up the Marshmans.

I grabbed another beer and walked downstairs to the patio. Mom got up from her table when she saw me and walked over. I smiled and said, "Hey, Mom."

"Dave," she said, "I just wanted to apologize."

"For what?" I said.

"I shouldn't have said anything earlier—about you making yourself at home. I should have told you in private."

"Oh," I said, "that's okay, Mom. I should be the one apologizing."

"Well," she said, "I know that trip must have been exhausting. Connecting from DC and not sleeping in your own bed … and the time zones—"

"Well it was all that, but that's no excuse."

"David, I just want to say I understand why you were rushing the next morning and why you had to leave things the way you did. I shouldn't have said anything earlier."

"Well thank you," I said, "but I'm really sorry, Mom—I feel so bad about leaving it like that—especially your piano. Dad told me about the beer bottle—"

"He says you were playing the piano—"

"Yeah," I said, "but I did wash my hands beforehand."

She laughed, and said, "How did it feel?"

"What?"

"The piano. You haven't played in years. How did it feel to play it again?"

"Pretty darn good, actually. I was really jamming on it. I mean, I'm sure it didn't sound very good, but I had a blast."

"That's great, Dave—I'm happy to hear that. You know, you have an open invitation to play it anytime—just no more drinks on top, okay?"

"No drinks, Mom. Never again."

I looked over and saw Ashley playing with the girls again.

"So," my mom said, "Ashley tells me you guys didn't go away for Labor Day?"

"I had to work Monday," I said.

"Well, you should take time off and do a long weekend in Florida."

"Yeah," I said. "I didn't know you weren't renting the condo. But we'll definitely use it. Has Sean locked any weekends in for himself?"

"Just the third weekend in October. But Sean wants to bring Badger, so your dad's still considering it."

"What's Dad considering?"

"Well, he still thinks Badger is the one who broke his toilet, but I'm sure your brother will persuade him."

"That was like ten years ago," I said. Then I thought, *Stay the fuck out of it.* "Well," I said, "I'll talk to Ashley about Florida and I'm sure we'll probably go a few times."

"You should," Mom said, "It's important. You need that time together."

"Absolutely." I said. "Staying home last weekend was just a fluke. We were at the condo in June. We'll be down there, believe me."

"Had you not told Ashley you stayed here this week?" she asked.

"I texted her," I said. "I can show her that. But when I finally got off the plane, it was too late to call. And it was a crazy day back. It hadn't come up."

"Well, it sounds like you were running hard," she said. "Before I forget, if you want that globe not going to the dump, please take it with you today."

"Okay, I will," I said.

"Oh c'mon," she said. "You are not taking that thing back to your apartment?"

"Yeah," I said, "why not?"

"C'mon Dave," she said, "What do you want that thing for? Where you gonna put it?"

"I'll keep it in my closet," I said.

"But why?"

"I don't know," I said, "it's just something cool to have and look at, sometimes."

"Really? That's the reason?"

"All right," I said. "Toss it. Send it to the dump, seriously. I'm good."

"I'll hold onto it for you," she said. "It'll be in your closet. You can look at it whenever you're home."

I laughed and said, "Thank you, but just to be clear, I hadn't seen that Mars globe in twenty years. It's not like it's my Linus blanket."

Mom laughed and I gave her a hug.

\* \* \*

I went up to the deck and didn't see Ashley. She wasn't in the kitchen when I walked inside. I hustled up the stairs, past my bedroom, to the bathroom. No one was using it. I kept the lights off, locked the door, and gazed down at the party below. There was my dad, talking with Sean. And then, out by the pool, I saw Ashley, wearing her floral dress and speaking privately with Jay.

My stomach sank and I focused on just taking a piss. It took a while to get going, but as I was mid-piss, I looked back out at the two of them talking.

I flushed the toilet, and walked into the hall, but no one was waiting or coming upstairs. So I went back inside and re-locked the door. Looking out at Ashley, I pulled my dick from my shorts, took one stroke, and thought, *What the fuck am I doing?*

I didn't want anyone to spot me. That would be too freaky. Besides, I didn't want to be dealing with Jay, having just jerked off to the thought of him manhandling my wife. Plus, I had to hurry and deal. People might notice them off by themselves. I thought of Sean. He picks up on stuff like that.

I got back up close by the bathroom window. "I know what you fucking want," I whispered, looking at Jay, "You want to take Ashley back to your house for some wine tasting, don't you, Jay? You want my wife tasting your cock, and you think you can roll me into letting that happen. Does the fact that I'm the Martens' son mean anything? Trying to seduce my wife at my parents' party. You'd take her and fuck her in our woods if you could, wouldn't you? So what if my parents saw their daughter-in-law getting balled?"

My hand was around my dick and I stopped myself. *Now's not the time*, I thought. I really had to deal. I had to go back outside and walk up to Jay and Ashley. And try and join their conversation … knowing I was imposing on their scene.

I pictured Sean coming up and saying something to me like, "What are you doing, little bro? Don't leave the net so un-fucking protected. The dude's laying the groundwork for fucking your wife."

# CHAPTER TWENTY-SIX

I said hello to people, but I pretty much made a beeline for Jay and Ashley. They were the farthest away, talking by the pool.

"Hey," I said, walking over.

Ashley gave me an enthusiastic, "Hey you."

But Jay didn't smile. He just looked at me and said, "What's up?"

"Just thinking," I said, "I can't believe it's the last summer pool day."

Jay looked at me like, *What the fuck ever*.

"Oh I know," Ashley said, "this is like, official end of summer day."

"Extended a week because of the weather," I said, blandly, but I didn't care. As long as I said something.

"Yeah," Ashley said, "The whole week has been a major bonus."

"Yeah," I said, turning to Jay. "I was in San Francisco this week."

I could tell he didn't give two craps, but I acted like I thought he did. I just wanted a way to plop myself into the conversation. Get a little traction.

"It was like a monsoon," I said, "in San Francisco earlier this week. And I'm talking to Ashley on the phone and she says, 'It's the most beautiful blue sky day here in New York.'"

"Yeah," Jay said, "I saw a great sunset the other night on a ride to Brattleboro."

"Vermont?" Ashley asked. "Is that where you went to see

your friend's band? You rode there and back, same night?"

"Yeah."

"Impressive," Ashley said, "no wonder you didn't get home till dawn. That's like two hundred miles."

"What kind of music is it?" I asked.

"Do you like Warren Haynes or Allman brothers?" he said.

"You like 'Sweet Melissa,'" Ashley said to me. "That's Allman brothers."

"Oh really, Ashley," I said, "is that who sings it? C'mon, I've seen the Allman Brothers live. Saw them twice at the Beacon."

"Yeah, but we live right by there," she said.

"So what?" I said.

"Well," she said, "you're acting like you're a big Allman Brothers' fan. Like we're supposed to think, *wow, the Beacon—two times,* when the Beacon's right down the block from us. Plus, Ryan probably dragged you to see them."

"What I said was a freaking factual statement. I've seen them twice in fucking concert."

Ashley burst out laughing.

"Bottom line," I continued, "I know the A-bros' music pretty well. So that's cool, that's the kind of music your friend's band does?"

"Yeah," Jay said.

"Have they played down here?"

"No."

"And no plans to?"

"No, they live in Brattleboro" Jay said. "That's where the bar was."

"They've been trying," I said, "to get a minor league baseball team in there for years now."

"What?" Jay said.

"In Brattleboro," I said. "The state's one team is in Burlington. That's a good two hundred miles north."

Ashley looked at me like, *Are you fucking serious?* and kind of smiled.

I asked Jay if he'd met all my relatives. That had him looking around as I pointed people out. And anyone who he mentioned meeting, I'd say something about. Like "Yeah, I don't know how Jen does it, with the kids and her husband working those crazy hours."

It kind of worked, actually. 'Cause Ashley would then chime in with something. And I kept doing a lot of talking. I stayed in the conversation.

\* \* \*

All the women were doing a group photo up on the deck, and people started calling out for Ashley to come up.

"I'll be back," she said, with a smile, and hustled upstairs.

"Well," I said, standing there uncomfortably with Jay, "I need another beer."

"Hold up," he said.

"What?" I said, turning back around.

"Have one of mine," he said, opening his mini cooler, and pulling out a can of regular Bud.

"Oh no, man, thanks," I said.

"C'mon," he said, holding it out to me. "It's ice cold."

"I can just grab something inside."

"You can't just drink a Bud with me, man?"

*Jesus fucking Christ*, I thought.

"No, of course I can," I said, taking the beer. "Thank you. Thanks, Jay."

I opened the can and took a big swig. "Yeah," I said, "It's good."

I didn't like the silence and was rattling my brain for something to say. "What kind of aging process is Bud again—Beechwood, right?"

"Dave," he said, "I think you owe me some answers."

"What?"

"What did you say to Ashley about me?"

"What are you talking about?" I said.

"I know you've been saying shit about me," he said.

"No, haven't," I said.

"Dave," he said, "Ashley told me."

"What?"

"That's why she blew me off."

"Jay," I said, "I don't know what you're talking about. I can go up and look for Ashley right now."

"You wanted to make me out to be some kind of asshole?"

"Jay," I said, "like fucking hold up, man. I know fucking nothing about your personal life. I wasn't saying shit."

"What did you tell her about my divorce?"

"Jay, I never said shit—especially about your divorce. You think I'm looped into neighborhood gossip? Fucking zero."

"I don't think you're looped in," he said. "I think you made shit up. How come she didn't get my invitation, Dave? I sent it right to your mailbox. Of course you fucking opened it."

"Jay, I never saw a fucking invitation. For anything."

"Well, next party I throw," he said, edging forward, "I'm gonna make sure your wife gets my invitation."

"Fine," I said, "but it's not like we're even around most weekends."

"Just tell me what you said about me, punk."

"What?" I said. "Jay, I don't talk about you, period. I don't have any fucking reason to."

"Yeah, you do," he said. "You're afraid I'm gonna get with your wife."

"What?"

"Why else would you be intercepting my invite? You're afraid I'm gonna fuck her, aren't you?"

"Jesus man, what the fuck are you doing? Do you really

want to be saying shit like this to me at my parents' end-of-the-year cook-out?"

"You're afraid that's what's gonna happen."

"I'm not afraid, man."

"Well you should be. Little mama's boy is gonna get a little lesson, all right."

"You know what, Jay? You're being fucking crazy inappropriate right now. This is my parents' house. Talk like this is not cool, and it's late and we've all been drinking, and my parents don't need a scene. I think it's time to go."

"What? Are you telling me to leave?"

"Out of respect for my family, my parents, I'm asking you to leave, yes. Please. Let's not have my parents' party ruined."

"I like your parents, Dave, so tonight I'll leave."

"Thank you," I said, "and if you can manage it, leave from the back."

"Yeah, okay, Dave," he said. "You won tonight. But I want to say this right to your face. I want to tell you this, *before* it happens, so you remember it, later. I'm gonna fuck your wife, boy. It's gonna fucking happen. Sleep on that tonight."

I stepped back, a bit stunned. "Jay, just get the fuck out, man. Don't wreck my mom's party. Jesus Christ, now fucking Sean's coming over."

Jay turned to Sean and said, "It's cool, brother. I'm just leaving, like I was told to."

"What?" Sean said.

"Your little brother just kicked me out," he said.

Sean turned to me.

"Look," I said, "he was saying some offensive stuff to me. Maybe he's drunk, but he was threatening me."

"Yeah, okay," Sean said, and turned to Jay. "You gotta go, buddy."

I saw Sean walk with him and I looked away. I prepared

myself for Jay yelling back, "Fuck you," but it never came.

My brother walked back and asked, "You okay?"

"Yeah," I said, "but holy fucking shit, Sean, that was getting scary."

"What did he say?"

"He really attacked me, personally. Made comments about Ashley." I took a couple deep breaths and said, "Wow, that was really fucked up. I don't even want to be here now. I could seriously see Jay coming back all psycho on me."

"Oh c'mon."

"C'mon fucking nothing. I'm serious. That was pretty fucking unnerving. Christ."

"Do you want me to talk to him?" Sean said. "I'll run after him, maybe cool things down."

"Please fucking don't," I said.

"Okay," Sean said. "So what did he say? What was threatening?"

"He was getting up in my face and calling me a fucking mama's boy. All pissed off because we didn't go to his fucking fiftieth birthday party."

"Seriously pissed? Not just busting your balls a little?"

"Wants-to-fucking-kill-me pissed," I said. "He thinks I was the one who decided we wouldn't go to his party. He's fucking insane."

"Why did he care you didn't go?"

" 'Cause he's got a psycho infatuation for Ashley."

"Psycho?"

"Comments he's made. It's why he's psycho on me over the party—because he wanted Ashley there."

"So what's the deal? He mistook Ashley being friendly for being flirtatious?"

"Sean, it's way more than that," I said. "I mean, yes, Ashley was being friendly like she is to all Mom and Dad's guests. He was *so* out of line just now, holy shit."

"Do you want to tell Mom or Dad? Or report this or anything?"

"No," I said, "I'll talk to Mom about it later. I just kind of want to see what time's the next train."

"Bro, don't fucking leave," he said. "No way he's coming back. Let's get you a drink, and just chill out."

* * *

I walked back up to the deck, got a beer, and waited for Ashley to finish talking to my aunt.

"Hey, Ash," I said, "something pretty fucked up just happened after you left."

"What?"

"Jay really wanted to pick a fight with me," I said, "accusing me of making things up about him. It was getting scary. So I asked him to leave."

"What? Are you okay?"

"Yeah, I didn't get punched or anything."

"I'm so sorry, Dave," she said. "I think I'm responsible. I made one really dumb comment which I backtracked from immediately, but Oh God, honey."

"What did you say?"

"He was telling me about his ex," she said, "his side obviously, but it seemed like he was pretty mature about it, philosophical even, which kind of surprised me. So it was dumb, and I was probably being passive aggressive from you making up stories, but I said something like, *Funny, I originally heard differently*."

"Yeah, and …?"

"Well, as soon as I said it, I was like 'Oh wait, I'm thinking of someone else, someone else's divorce,' and then tried to bring up something else, and he kept going back to that comment."

"And what did you say?"

"That I was thinking about a friend of your dad's, but he was like 'So why did you not respond to my texts,' and how we could not have gotten his invite. I said it was a crazy period, late hours at work, and a ton of commitments."

"Well, he's jumped to a thousand conclusions and now he wants to kill me."

"Did he physically threaten you?"

"Basically, and said that I haven't heard the last of him. Look, I really thought he might take a swing at me or more."

"Dave," she said, looking genuinely distressed, "I am *so* sorry."

"Yeah, I'm a bit freaked out still."

She gave me a hug, and said, "It's okay," and held me close for a good, full minute. "I had no idea," she said, "Jay seemed fine when I left you guys. Did it just suddenly hit him?"

"Did *what* hit him?"

"Was he slurring his words? I saw him doing a shot with Mr. Marshman."

"Didn't seem that drunk to me," I said, "and it happened as soon as you left. He said I owed him answers for the lies about him I've been spreading."

"He must've been pretty effed up," she said. "I did not give him that impression. I bet tomorrow he'll feel embarrassed and want to apologize."

"No, Ash, I don't think he will."

"Well, he has my number," she said. "If he does call, that's probably why."

"Ash," I said, "if he fucking calls you, do not fucking answer, please?"

"Okay," she said.

"I have a serious problem with this guy," I said. "I really don't see Jay saying he's sorry tomorrow. Just let me handle this, okay?"

"Okay," she said, and gave me a hug. "I'm sorry I said anything, Dave."

"Thanks, Ash," I said, and hugged her hard.

* * *

"So we're taking the eight, right?" she said.

I looked at my watch and said, "Oh shit."

"What?"

"On weekends, it's 7:42. We've got like fifteen minutes."

I saw my dad walking up from the pool and got his attention.

"Ashley and I have to get back to the city," I said. "We have a dinner to make."

"Okay," he said, "are you leaving now?"

"Yeah," I said. "Sorry, we lost track of time."

"Of course," he said. "How you getting there?"

"Well," I said looking around.

"Sean drank too much," he said. "C'mon, I'll drive you."

Like he'd heard his name, Sean came up from behind us. "What's going on, you leaving?"

"Yeah," I said. "We have a dinner. Ashley just reminded me of the time."

"Well, I don't like seeing you leave, bro," he said, giving me a hug.

"Well, let me know about tomorrow," I said.

"Assume I won't, but let's try and meet up."

"You got it, man," I said, and then leaned into Sean. "And don't worry, I'm going to talk up the Badge to Dad, in the car."

Sean looked at me puzzled.

"So that he lets the Badge stay at his condo," I said. "I mean what's the worst that can happen? Dad has to get a new toilet." Sean started laughing and Ashley hugged him goodbye.

I hugged my cousins and waved to people out on the deck. My dad had pulled the car out, I pried Ashley away from saying goodbye to the Marshmans, and we hurried out to the driveway.

"I'll take the back seat," she said.

"You sure?" I said. "I'll take the back."

"Ashley," my dad said, "c'mon, sit up with me."

Ashley laughed. "Okay." She got in and shut the door. "Thank you so much" she said, "and sorry about being so last minute."

"No trouble at all," Dad said. "How many minutes till your train?"

"Eight," I said, with urgency, "and it's never late."

"Maybe I should drive," Ashley said.

My dad laughed and pulled out onto the main road. "So you're going back for dinner? Meeting friends?"

"Yeah," Ashley said, "it's the birthday of one of our friends."

Ashley gave me a look, *Help me out here.*

"Just a friend," I said, "but we committed weeks ago."

"Is it a surprise?" my dad asked, "a big one—like thirtieth?"

"Um, not that big," Ashley said, looking back at me. "Thirty-three."

"It is a surprise, though," I said from the back.

"When I was first new to email," my dad said, "I ruined a surprise party by accidentally forwarding the invitation to my friend who was being surprised."

With a laugh, Ashley said, "What happened?"

I felt relieved. My dad loves telling stories, and Ashley encourages him. I could sit in the back and not sweat talking around Mike coming over to birthday-fuck my wife.

I didn't like Ashley telling Mike's age to my dad. I thought, *Why the fuck wouldn't you say 'thirty'? You're fucking thirty. All your friends are turning thirty. Thirty is a big deal fucking birthday. It would even make my dad understand better. Why it was important we left his party early.*

244

# CHAPTER TWENTY-SEVEN

"We didn't leave too early, right?" Ashley said, as we sat down on the train.

"I don't think so," I said. "It was gonna start winding down soon. And my dad didn't care."

"When he told me to sit up front," she said, "I knew he'd ask us what we were doing tonight."

"Why?"

"I don't know," she said. "Would your dad remember Mike if you asked him?"

"What?"

"If you told him you'd reconnected from camp days, would he remember him?"

"Oh," I said, surprised, "I doubt it."

"Your dad's Mister Memory. I bet he'd remember if you described him. Was he Mike or Mikey?"

"Ashley, I don't want my dad knowing shit about Mike ... nada ... fucking nothing. I didn't care for him knowing it was a thirty-third birthday."

"He caught me off guard," she said, "but I'm not gonna ask your dad. I was just wondering if he'd remember him."

"Well no," I said. "I really doubt it. I mean, last day of camp your parents show up, and ten minutes later, they're hauling you home. I doubt he ever met him."

"I bet your mom would remember," she said. "She'd probably muster up some old camp letter you wrote home. 'Dear Mom ... and then me and Mike went fishing ... and then me and Mike played baseball.'"

"Ash, I get it. But please, don't fucking ask them."

"I never would, Dave."

"I know, Ash. It's a huge fucking deal to me that you don't mention Mike to my parents. I don't want another thing like with Jay."

"I apologized for Jay, and I'm telling you, I won't mention's Mike name to your parents. No way."

"Thanks," I said, putting my arm around her.

"Speak of the devil," Ashley said, looking at her phone, "Mike just texted."

"Oh," I said, as she leaned in to read it. I thought about the remote possibility of plans falling through, Mike getting sick, car crash, anything.

"He's thinking he'll be at our place by ten-thirty," she said. "How does that sound?"

"Well, I'd rather be spending tonight just with you, Ash, so how can I answer that question?"

"Okay, it's not like you'd prefer it later or anything. So I'm just gonna call him and tell him that works."

"Call him?"

"They're waiting to get seated for his birthday, and he was texting to see if I had a minute."

"Oh."

"He's with his friends, so I won't be long."

"Okay," I said and watched her walk down the aisle.

I thought about Mike's birthday. Tonight he was the man of the hour. Getting a call from the wife he was about to fuck as her husband sat alone on the train.

And after the call, Mike would be sitting down in a high-end steak place. Kicking back with his brother and friends—his boys—who were all-out patting him on the back, celebrating the guy for the night. They'd be stroking his ego, pumping him up.

I imagined how he must feel. Knowing my wife was waiting for him. As his boys drank a shot to him. And he pictured me fucking couched again.

It would be the third time he'd put me there. But this time, he'd see it as a certainty. He'd figure I knew my place and hadn't the balls to stop him. Just another step in pounding in the cucking. Making the couch my norm.

I wondered if guys at his table knew. Maybe they all did. Knew Mike had taken some guy's wife and openly cucked her husband. They might know I gave up my bedroom, my dignity, my wife's pussy—and sex with my wife—as a fucking birthday present to him. They'd be congratulating him on pulling off that fucking stunt.

I saw Ashley walking back and realized I had a hard-on.

"Sorry about that," she said, sitting down. "Ten-thirty's a go. They're just having drinks now."

"Okay," I said.

"So I have time to wash my hair," she said.

"That's good," I said, at a loss for words, "get the chlorine out."

Ashley's phone beeped and she read the text. "Tamara wants me to call her," she said. "Trip advice before she leaves tomorrow."

"What?"

"We have a vendor who's corporate is in Iowa," she said. "I went to this thing she's going to two years ago."

"Oh," I said, "you know, I wanted to mention …. Next time you and Tamara go out, let me know, and if it's cool with you guys, I'll swing by and hang out for a bit."

"Really?" she said, as if I must be joking.

"I mean, if you guys aren't cool with it, or you think it's not my scene—"

"Not at all," she said. "I'm sure Tamara would be cool with that. We're going out this Wednesday, when she's back. I can ask her."

"Well, don't ask her now," I said. "I was talking generally. It doesn't have to be this Wednesday or anything."

"Yeah, but she's leaving tomorrow," she said. "Better to let her know now than last minute."

"Well, yeah, okay, but …. It's no big deal. Another time is totally cool."

"I'll see what she says," she said, standing up.

"Yeah, okay," I said as she walked back down the aisle.

*Thanks a fucking lot, Ryan,* I said to myself, *for your dumbass fucking advice.* Drinks with Tamara was the fucking last thing I wanted to do. Like why the fuck did I listen to him? Or not think it through beforehand.

I'd been all wired from the cookout confrontation and anxious about Mike's birthday, and Ryan acted like it was a no brainer, like it was absolutely the thing to do. Of course he didn't know the whole situation. Maybe it was good advice for the guy I was portraying. If the main thing really was being worried about Tamara, perhaps it made sense. But if Ryan knew everything, he'd say, "It ain't her fucking friend who's the problem. Maybe it's the guy who's marital-bed-fucking your wife."

I realized our train had just crossed the bridge into Manhattan and I signaled to Ashley we were about to get off.

We walked to the subway, and Ashley was asking about my cousin Jen. I was just glad she didn't tell me if Tamara was okay with me joining them. I preferred hearing nothing rather than, "She said it was cool." Maybe she forgot. The later she told me, the easier it'd be for me to back out.

The subway was a madhouse of people waiting, but we were already through the turnstiles and I felt committed. But it took three trains before we got on. Even then, it was tight. We were really squeezed.

We walked down Amsterdam, holding hands, and I thought, to passing strangers, I probably looked like a lucky man.

\* \* \*

*Tommy sometimes works Saturday night.* That's what I thinking as we walked up. Then I recognized his face in the window, and thought, *Motherfucker.*

"Night, Tommy," we said, walking in.

"How are you guys doing this evening?"

"Great," Ashley said. "Are you still working here at ten-thirty?"

"I'm here all night, Mrs. Martens."

"Okay. We're expecting Mike Athens, so when he arrives, just buzz us to let us know he's coming up."

"Yes, ma'am."

"He's the uh," I said, wishing I hadn't started, "the guy I'm working with."

"Yeah," Tommy said, "you told me. Sounds exciting."

Ashley looked at me blankly.

"Yeah," I said, "so who knows? We might be up all night."

"Yeah, well, good luck."

"Thanks," I said, and we walked to the elevators.

"I don't know if I even want to ask what that was about," Ashley said, going up.

"I got a FedEx," I said.

"From?"

"Doesn't matter. But that's why I was talking to Tommy. And somehow us having a visitor a lot came up. So I just said Mike and I were exploring business ventures."

"I like it," she said, "and Tommy's right … it does sound exciting."

I didn't know what to say back. So I just unlocked the door and held it open.

"Yikes," she said, "almost nine-thirty."

"Well, yeah," I said. "The subway screwed us."

"I wish we could just lie in bed for a few minutes."

"Why don't we?" I said.

"I've got to get my butt in the shower and start getting ready."

*Just do it*, I told myself. *Just get your butt into that bathroom. Into that shower. Get one more look at her naked again. Washcloth the soap on her breasts. Stand naked next to your wife, with your dick hard up against her. Just fucking ask her.*

"Maybe I could join you," I said, "like this morning."

"Well, this morning," she said, "gives me really warm feelings. How special it was. I kind of want to preserve that memory. Does that make sense?"

"I don't know. It doesn't sound good."

"It is good. Really good, actually. It means that's how highly I cherish this morning with you."

"So because you cherish it so much, even though you enjoyed it, I can't shower again with you? It's not like I'm gonna be groping you."

Ashley laughed. "I know. I'm only talking about today. Let's talk tomorrow. I need to be pretty quick, anyway."

"Okay."

I heard her hustle into the bedroom, but then I heard her coming back and turned around.

"Yeah, Ash?" I said excitedly. "Need help?"

"No," she said, "but Jimmy told me they fixed the other shower yesterday. The water stream works fine now. It might be easier for you to use that."

"What?" I said. "I don't have any stuff in there."

"There are clean towels in the closet now," she said. "Do you want to get what you need from our bathroom? This way I'm not rushing you."

"Okay," I said, walking to the bathroom. I grabbed my shampoo and shaving kit and walked back into the bedroom.

"Hey," she said, pulling me aside and kissing me. "I know this is a big inconvenience, and I appreciate you being understanding tonight. I feel so much closer to you than I have in a long time."

"Well me too, Ash," I said, "in some ways, anyway."

"In some really *good* ways," she said, blowing me a kiss.

I stood there as she shut the door, holding a bottle of shampoo and my shaving stuff. I felt so empty-handed. And asked myself, *What the fuck do I have to shower for? Because fucking Mike's coming over?*

I sat down in the living room and wondered what had just happened. If she really believed what she'd told me. Or if she just said it so I'd shut the fuck up. Like preserving a memory means you shouldn't do the same thing twice. And then telling me to shower in our bathroom—the barely functional one. Like I was supposed to say, "New towels and the hot water's running again. This is fucking great, Ashley."

I wondered if this was Ashley's way of subtly layering on the cucking, depriving me of being naked with her again. I wouldn't even get to see her tits. Or peer down at her ass as I washed her back. Or have a hard-on, standing next to her, naked.

I heard the shower turn on and muttered, "Goddammit, she's really fucking cucking me, now." And even if she didn't mean it like that, her not letting me shower with her was still an assertive smack-down.

I thought about pulling my pants down and looked around. The front door was locked and I could be quick. But I started thinking of Mike being here an hour later. I could see him asking if I jerked off. And me being paranoid, having to lie and say I didn't. It seemed pretty unlikely, but I didn't want to be burned by some wild card. So I tried not to think about it, turned on the TV, found the Yankee game, and tried to focus on that.

\* \* \*

I heard Ashley coming down the hall, and said, "Hey Ash."

"Hey," she said, walking in. She was wearing a sexy pink robe. "That's what you wore at your parents. You didn't shower yet?"

"No," I said.

"Well then, just use our shower," she said. "I can get my stuff out."

"No, don't bother. I'm fine as is."

"Meaning what? You're not going to shower?"

"I'm serious. We're not going out, so why am I showering? For Mike's birthday?"

"You're showering because you were playing wiffleball and badminton and swimming in the pool, and we just were on a really crowded smelly subway."

I knew I seemed like a five-year-old, resisting taking a shower. "Okay," I said, "because of the subway, I'll shower."

" 'Kay," she said, brushing her hair while she looked in the mirror.

I showered like I was late for work. I didn't daydream, I was efficient. Had an erection but I ignored it. A minute later, I was toweling off.

"Doesn't that feel better?" Ashley said when I came out.

"It does," I said walking over to her. I put my hand on her shoulder and we looked at each other in the mirror.

"Do you want to try your hand at being a stylist?"

"Uh, sure," I said, and she handed me her brush.

"Just comb it out."

"Like this?" I said, as I ran the brush tentatively through her hair.

"Yeah, you're trying to get any kinks out."

"Okay," I said and started in.

"So," Ashley said, "do you have any funny birthday songs to sing tonight?"

"What?" I said.

"Did you write or plan anything?"

"Are you kidding?"

"I don't know, like you did that with Ryan—that song you left on his voicemail."

"That was three years ago," I said, "and it was for Ryan."

"Yeah," she said. "I thought you might do one for Mike, that's all."

"Well no, I didn't write him a fucking personalized birthday song."

Ashley laughed and threw up her hands. "It's okay. I was just asking."

Our intercom buzzed.

"Are you fucking kidding me?" I said, looking at my watch. "He's fucking twenty minutes early."

"We don't know it's him. It could be your brother."

"No, it couldn't," I said and went to the intercom.

"Evening Dave," the doorman said. "Mike just arrived, and we sent him up."

"Thanks, Tommy," I said, hanging up.

"It's Mike?" Ashley asked, as I walked back in.

"Yeah, like who the fuck else would it be? Twenty fucking minutes early."

"We don't know what happened," Ashley said. "He didn't text me. Besides, it's his birthday. You need to remember that tonight."

"Like I could fucking forget it, Ash," I said. "It doesn't excuse him being twenty fucking minutes early. While you're still getting ready."

"I'll be ready in ten," she said. "Why don't you leave me here and congratulate Mike on turning thirty-three. But give me a kiss first."

"Okay," I said

She gave me a quick one—no tongue—and told me she loved me. And to get the door on my way out.

# CHAPTER TWENTY-EIGHT

I really didn't want to get the door. Or have a one-on-one conversation with Mike. But now, because he was ridiculously early, I had to entertain him ... and make him a drink, be cordial like he was a guest, be extra gracious because it was his fucking birthday. There was no way to delay it, so I opened the door.

"Hey Mike," I said.

"Hey, bro," he said, smiling as he walked inside. "How you been?" he said and gave me a hug. It seemed pointless not to reciprocate.

But as I pulled away, I said, "Pretty freaking early dude ... seriously. I mean, Ashley's not ready yet. You said ten-thirty."

"Yeah, I lucked out," Mike said. "Got a cab, not much traffic. I actually thought I'd be late when I left. So how have you been? How was it at your folks'? Good time grilling out?"

"Yeah, it was good," I said. "Saw a lot of cousins I hadn't seen in a while."

"Right on," he said. "So how's your family? Everyone good? See your brother today?"

"Yeah," I said, "everyone's fine and yeah, I saw my brother."

"You ever talk to him about this?"

"What?"

"Your brother. Have you talked to him about being cuckolded? Does he know?"

"Oh God, no."

"You're afraid that if you told him, he'd try and move in on Ashley?"

"Jesus, c'mon," I said. "I'm not fucking telling anyone. Thus, I didn't tell my brother."

"How was Ashley looking?" he said. "She trot around like Miss Bikini Tits out there today?"

"Yeah, I guess kind of. We had a good dozen people in the pool at one point."

"Any drama? Any stories?"

"Oh, happy birthday by the way," I said. "You're thirty-three now, right? How was dinner?"

"Thanks Dave," he said. "Dinner was awesome. I had some killer prime rib, and a few guys from where I grew up surprised me."

"Oh cool," I said. "Do you want anything to drink?"

"One of them beers is cool, thanks. So yeah, it's been a great birthday, but for me, right now is the best part of it. Hanging out with you guys, having a drink, maybe getting Ashley to open up to you more. That would be a good thing, right?"

"I don't know, Mike," I said.

He clicked my bottle and said, "Cheers, bro."

"I really don't want some forced discussion."

"Won't be like that," he said. "It's gonna be very relaxed and easy-going. All I'll be doing is helping you both focus. I know you'll both benefit. I think after Thursday night, this is exactly what your relationship needs."

"Jesus, why?" I said. "Why can't you just *not* lead a discussion about my marriage with my wife?"

"You're the ones leading the discussion," he said. "I'm just getting you to talk. Facilitating communication."

"I'm not asking the fucking 'watching' question," I said, "and you said you wouldn't bring it up, either."

"I won't be the one to bring it up," he said, "trust me. Have you at least practiced for *how* you'll ask her tonight? Like on the chance you have the impulse …."

"Can we just drop it, man," I said, "and honor not

bringing it up? It wasn't my idea. Ashley's about to come out. Can we just please cool it?"

Mike walked to the back of the kitchen and yelled at our bedroom door. "Hey, Ash, how much longer till I get to see you, girl? You about out?"

"Hi, Mike," she called back. "Almost ready. I promise."

Mike walked back to me and we sat down at the kitchen table.

"So," he said, "how was last night with your bud from San Fran?"

"Good," I said. "We met him and his girlfriend for dinner. We saw some music, danced to a cover band, smoked a cigar."

"Cool. You were dancing with Ashley, right? Were you nervous?"

"No, of course not. We had fun, and we're gonna play tennis next week in the Park."

"Sounds nice," Mike said. "I'd like to fuck her in her tennis outfit."

"Yeah, sure."

"C'mon," he said. "Don't you think that'd be hot? Seeing Ashley fucked in her tennis dress?"

"Yeah Mike, I get it, but can we just please chill out, relax right now? It's your birthday. She got you a cake." Mike smiled and I felt compelled to add, "She made me move my beer actually."

"To make room for my cake?"

"Yeah, I said. "We were rushing for the train, and it had to stay refrigerated." I was cursing myself for bringing it up.

"So you moved your beer for my cake," he said. "Well thank you, man. It may seem like a small thing, but I really appreciate it, Dave. It's like we may knock each other around sometimes, but when it really comes down to it, we got each other's back."

I was looking at him a bit incredulously when we heard the bedroom door start to open.

* * *

Ashley strutted into the kitchen wearing a red dress and heels, and unusually obvious lipstick.

"Happy Birthday, baby," she said embracing him. I looked down at the floor as they made out in the kitchen. It was a long half-minute.

"You're looking mighty sensational tonight, Mike," she said. "I really love that sports coat."

"You look freaking ravishing yourself there, baby," he said. "Sorry if I rushed you, tonight. As I told Dave—when I left, I thought I'd be late."

"Oh my God," Ashley said, dismissing it. "We're just glad you're here and spending your birthday night with us."

"I wouldn't want to be anywhere else tonight, Ash."

"Aww," Ashley said.

"Celebrating it with you guys," Mike added, looking at me.

"Thanks," I said, mechanically.

"Well, we need to toast," Ashley said, "and I need a drink. Oh wait, how 'bout champagne?"

"Sounds great," Mike said. Ashley went to get the flutes, but I saw her on tiptoes trying to reach, so I stood and helped her.

"Thanks," she said. "Would you like to pop the bottle?"

"Yeah, okay," I said and she handed it to me. I knew what it meant. After I opened it, there I stood, looking like a fucking waiter, pouring Mike a glass of champagne as he sat at my kitchen table with my wife.

I sat down and we held up our flutes.

"To an evening of balls-out fun," Mike said, "and to learning about ourselves."

I rolled my eyes but clanked my glass with theirs.

"I love your dress, Ash," Mike said. "Sexy with a touch of slutty. I love the cleavage you're showing."

"Well, thank you," she said, smiling.

"Is that the dress you told me about?" he said, "the one you bought to wear for tonight?"

"Yeah," she said, "though I told you I was getting black. But I kind of like this shade of red, so I went with it."

"Well, you look sexy as hell in red," Mike said. "Matches your lipstick. What do you think of her dress, Dave?"

"It's very nice," I said. "Ash, you look amazing."

"Thanks, Dave," she said.

"How would you feel going out in public ... with Ashley dressed this way?"

I forced a laugh and said, "People would stare, for sure."

"Sure they would," Mike said. "They'd wonder 'bout the chances of a wardrobe malfunction, or about the guy she was with—why she was dressed like such a cock tease."

"Yeah," Ashley said, with a laugh. "Never mind Dave being uncomfortable. I surely would be."

"Oh you might be surprised, Ash," he said, "or surprise yourself."

"Oh?" Ashley laughed. "You think so?"

"I think deep down," Mike said, "you like the attention. Like Dave says you were strutting around out there in your bikini today."

Ashley laughed and looked at me.

"I didn't say 'strutting,' " I said. "Mike just asked if you wore a bikini."

"Did you tell him about kicking your neighbor out?"

"No," I said.

"What? Mike said. "So what's the deal? You got off on kicking someone out of your speech, so now you're kicking out your neighbors?"

"Unrelated," I said. "A guy at the cookout was drunk and threatening me. So I told him he had to leave."

"Well," Mike said, "Sounds like you did the right thing. How did he threaten you?"

"He wanted to fight me," I said.

"Big guy?" Mike said.

"He's built like a tank," I said, "and yeah, he'd probably have kicked my ass. So yeah, I was a bit freaked out at the time."

"Sure," Mike said. "Who wouldn't be? So Ash, were you there ... trying to calm it down?"

"No, I wasn't there," she said, "and Dave told me things about Jay before that it turns out he made up. So when he tells me this crazy story, well, I'm sorry, but I can't help but wonder .... When I left them, everything was fine."

"I didn't fucking make that up, Ash," I said. "This guy was so over the top .... If I'd recorded what he said, I could've had him arrested."

"Maybe so," she said, "but you said that about Jay before, how he was arrested for abusing his ex-wife. That turned out to be a total lie."

"They're two different things," I said. "And it wasn't a lie, it was a mistake."

"Oh c'mon, Dave," she said, "like your mom's telling you all this freaking gossip, like you really can't keep track of people's names, and Jay—someone you've known for years, who came to our wedding—like you would really mix him up."

"Well—"

"But I should have known," she said. "Your parents like Jay. He's a genuine friend. And your mom's not gonna be having a borderline criminal over for cook-outs."

"Look, Ash," I said, "I didn't make it up, I mean, I can explain—"

Mike held up his hand for us to pause.

"I don't mean to interrupt," Mike said, "but tell me how you saw it, Dave."

"Look," I said, "this guy today—he wants my wife, okay? And no, he didn't threaten his ex-wife—I got that wrong—

but he was threatening *me,* tonight when he left. So I think my hunch was kind of fucking right."

"Whether you were right," Ashley said, "is not even the point. You still lied to me."

"Hey," Mike said, "you don't know that, Ash. I don't remember half the things my mom tells me. You have to admit, it's possible he just got it wrong."

"Well *possible* leaves it pretty fucking open," she said, "but fine, okay—"

"Hear me out," Mike said. "Even if Dave did say some shit about this guy on purpose, my main question would be why would Dave do this?"

"Okay," Ashley said, turning to me.

"I think it's simple," Mike said, "Dave wanted to protect you."

"From some made-up threat?" she said.

"From a husband's internal instinct," Mike said. "Sounds like Dave got a pretty bad vibe from the guy, and out of love for his wife, he wanted to protect her ... you."

"Look," I said, "this guy was practically ordering us to go to his fiftieth birthday party—"

"He wasn't *ordering,*" Ashley broke in.

"He was pushing his party pretty freaking aggressively," I said, "and he gave me the serious fucking creeps—I don't care that my mom likes him. And now he's got Ashley's cell number and he'll be texting her about his next party."

"Okay," Mike said, "I get it. You were just scared, maybe in a panic, didn't fact-check your story. But c'mon, Ash, sounds like the guy wanted you as the special guest at his fiftieth birthday party. Can you really blame Dave for being worried?"

"Well, then just tell me that," she said. "Just say, 'He gives me the creeps.' "

"Rather than make something up," Mike clarified. "Makes sense. Right, Dave?"

"Yeah, of course," I said, "but I didn't make it up."

"Okay, so then just answer me this," she said. "Why were you at your parents' house this week? Like when were you there? Were you not in San Francisco?"

"What? No, of course I was in San Fran, Ash. I gave the biggest speech of my career there on Tuesday. It's just that Wednesday night wasn't technically the red eye. The flight was a few hours earlier and got me into Westchester at two in the morning."

"Westchester has flights landing at two in the morning?"

"I don't know about regularly, but we'd been delayed. It's a long story. But yeah, I went to my parents'. Got there so late, it's not like I even really slept. And I did want to help my mom ... sort through my crap. She'd carried that all down herself."

"Okay," Mike said, "so Dave didn't want to show up here unannounced. That's considerate. Admirable, I'd say. He respected the situation and found lodging elsewhere for the night."

"Is that it?" Ashley said to me. "You were being considerate and didn't want me thinking I had inconvenienced you?"

"I wasn't going to barge in here at three in the morning," I said, "and there was a flight leaving for Westchester right when I got there. My parents were away, and I had stuff to clear out."

"Yeah," Mike said, "but would you have gone to your parents if I wasn't there? I think that's what Ashley means."

"Not exactly," Ashley said, walking over and giving me a hug. "It's cool," she whispered. "We're both reacting to the experience. But honesty going forward, okay?"

"I should have told you," I said, hugging her back, "when I first found out I was leaving. And honesty ... absolutely."

She gave me a quick kiss and told me she loved me.

"Aww," Mike said with a smile, "I'm a sucker for happy endings."

# CHAPTER TWENTY-NINE

"I love the ambience here tonight," Mike said, as Ashley lit the candles and dimmed the kitchen lights. "Very nice," he said. "This really tops off my birthday."

"We're glad you're celebrating with us," Ashley said, getting up and taking down some party stuff. "Dave," she said, "I'm looking for a lighter. Is your Yankees one handy?"

"Let me look," I said, getting up. I went into our bedroom and found it in my dresser. I figured, *What's the point in saying I couldn't find it?* She would just resort to matches, which would probably seem even more romantic.

"Here you go," I said, joining her in the kitchen.

"Thanks," she said. "Can you grab the cake from the fridge? I'll put in the candles."

It was not as if she couldn't do it herself. I wondered if that was the freaking point.

"Here you go, Ash," I said, putting the cake down on the kitchen counter.

"Thanks," she said. "Do you want to help?"

"What?"

"Putting on birthday candles. Here, take a few."

"Well," I said, nervously, "you're the artist, Ash. I'll just watch you."

" 'Kay," she said.

"That's a boatload of candles," I said as she put more and more on.

Ashley laughed and said, "Good thing it's a bigger cake

262

than I thought. Do you want to grab it? I'll light the candles at the table."

"Sure," I said, picking it up and feeling embarrassed. *What was I doing bringing over his fucking birthday cake?* That's what I thought as I sat down across from him.

"So," Mike said, "I got you a little something, Ash."

"You did?" she said, surprised.

"Well," Mike said, "just something I picked up while roaming the Village this afternoon."

Ashley look puzzled but curious as she opened it. "Oh my God," she said, "did you get me a Marilyn Monroe wig?"

Mike laughed, and said, "Try it on."

I watched, speechless, as she put on the wig.

"You look fucking hot as a blonde, Ash," Mike said.

"Do I?" she said, walking out in the hallway to look at herself in the full-length mirror ... in her blonde wig and conspicuously revealing dress.

"It kind of works, doesn't it?" she said.

"You look fucking delicious, Ash," Mike said.

"Okay," Ashley said, turning to me. "So the other night, we saw a few minutes of some Marilyn Monroe movie. And we were talking about her 'Happy Birthday' song to Kennedy. Mike said he wanted me singing her version to him on his birthday."

"Yeah," Mike said, "and now she'll be singing in costume."

"Oh," I said.

"You've seen the old footage?" he said.

"Yeah," I said.

"Hey, Dave, can you kill the lights completely, bro?" he said.

"Huh?" I said. "Yeah, okay."

"Isn't it too dark now?" Ashley said.

"It's perfect," Mike said, "with just the candles. Why don't you stand in that corner by the fridge ... under the candlelight?"

Ashley walked to the spot and said, "I feel like I'm on stage," as she looked back at us.

"You look perfect like that, baby," Mike said. The straps of her dress were sliding down her shoulders, and she was showing a lot of cleavage. It looked as if her tits might pop out any minute. In her bright red lipstick—which she never wears—and cheap blonde wig, she looked like a total slut.

As she began singing "Happy Birthday," I popped a hard-on. Her voice was soft and sultry, and she drew out every word. Every syllable exuded sexuality. She sang so beautifully, but the song was not for me. Her eyes were locked on Mike. She was calling him "Mister President," fucking serenading him.

"Fucking awesome," Mike said, clapping. "Get on over here."

I just watched from the other side of the table as Mike and Ashley made out in front of me again. I waited till they were done to turn up the lights.

\* \* \*

"Have you thought of your birthday wish?" Ashley said, starting to light his birthday candles.

"I have," he said. "It's for the two of you. What's with the twelve candles?"

"The only multiple of thirty three is eleven," she said. "Plus, it's eleven nights since we first met. Oh, and one for luck."

"Very thoughtful," he said. "Thank you."

"That's a lot of candles," she said. "C'mon and show us them lungs."

Mike blew them all out except for one, and then leaned over and got that one too. I saw Ashley clap and joined in, but then thought, *What the fuck am I clapping for?*

"Thanks so much, guys," Mike said, "that was really lovely."

"You're welcome," she said, giving him another kiss.

I put my hands in my lap to hide my boner.

"Well," Ashley said, pulling away finally, "I guess my song was a hit."

"It was through the roof, baby," he said. "You have a gorgeous voice, and you a make a real sexy blonde. I'm gonna have you wear that wig later."

"Yeah, the wig's growing on me," she said, as she went over to look in the mirror again. "It'd be fun to go out incognito."

"Exactly," Mike said, "wearing that dress, a slutty little blond out at the bar … maybe her husband watching from a table."

"Well," she said with a grin, "I wasn't talking the whole ensemble."

"But I am," he said. "You'll feel less self-conscious in the wig. In fact, it'll probably embolden you. Hell, we can get a much better wig."

"We'll see," she said with a laugh. "Might need a few cocktails, first."

"You're gonna have the whole place looking at you," he said. "You'll fucking own the room."

"Where am I going," she said, laughing, "to a freaking sports bar?"

Mike was also grinning as he replied, "Yeah, for Monday Night football. What do you think, Dave?"

"Yeah, right," I said. "Just the idea of going out like that is …. I mean, it's not Halloween."

"I don't see it happening anytime soon," she said.

"Famous," Mike said, "last—"

"Oh stop," she said. "Besides, we have something we'd like to give to you, now."

"Okay," Mike said.

"Well," Ashley said, "just to back up …. Obviously you came back into Dave's life at a pivotal time, and it's been eleven days since you and I met. And Dave and I are finally becoming more open and honest ... certainly more than we have in a very long time."

"That's great to hear," he said.

"Yeah," she said, "and he and I are getting to understand each other ... *way* better than we have been."

"Beautiful," he said.

"And," she continued, "what really helped us break through was making a statement of trust to you. That was a freedom from distractions, for us."

I observed Ashley in her blonde wig, her blowjob lipstick, with her tits about to bust out, and realized I was agape.

"Ever since Dave got home," she said, "we've voluntarily abstained from sex—for that matter, all sexual relations—in pursuit of higher rewards. We've lived together as a platonic couple. That has given us an openness and understanding we couldn't imagine before."

Mike smiled, and nodded. "Excellent."

"So on your birthday night," she continued, "as you turn thirty-three, we wanted to give you a present of appreciation ... a chastity bond we protected. We're giving it to you—with humility—now."

"Wow, Ash," he said, "that was really lovely. Thank you."

"You're welcome," she said, with a smile.

"So, no sexual relations at all," Mike said, "not even a hand job?"

"Oh no," Ashley said. "He didn't even cop a feel."

"So Dave could look," he said, "but not touch."

"Yeah," she said. "I'm sorry, Dave, did you want to say something?"

"No," I said, "I mean, yes. We all get it. I went deprived."

Mike raised his index finger. "You were enriched at the same time," he said. "Look at what it did for your relationship .... The way you relate to each other now is so much more honest and healthy."

"I get the point," I said, knowing I sounded exasperated. "You can claim it helped us open up more, but c'mon, there were other options, less extreme. I could hardly freaking touch her."

"Making a sacrifice," he said, "ain't easy. I know that. It was a challenge and a commitment you made together. You should be proud, and cherish that bond you shared. I think you'll find that taking the oath will be really grounding."

"Yeah," Ashley said, "it was about doing it together."

"Absolutely," Mike said, "so when did you begin?"

"When Dave got home," she said. "That evening I told him, and it was in effect from then on. And now it's our gift to you." Ashley turned and asked me, "It's *our* gift, right?"

"What?" I said.

"You were my partner in it," she said, "and we met the challenge together."

"Well, it's kind of like driving up Mt. Washington," I said. "It's not like you can really say you *climbed* anything. What did we do? Prove that we could live platonically? I get that in some ways we communicated better, but if sexual anything is a distraction, than I want some distraction."

"With a little time," Mike said, "and distance from it, you'll see the forest from the trees, bro. You'll see the strength of your marital bond grow exponentially. I have no doubt."

"And we just gave Mike our gift," Ashley said, "so we haven't had any time to get perspective."

"Absolutely," Mike said. "I'm really honored to receive this special gift from the two of you. It shows me just how committed you both are to each other ... which makes it extra special."

"Yeah," Ashley said, "when we were at the reservoir this morning, I felt particularly close to Dave. Like all morning, actually. You felt that, right, Dave?"

"Yeah, I definitely felt close to you" I said. "I don't know if the oath thing really had anything to do with that, though."

"Oh, I think it did," she said, "absolutely. You were

looser and cheerier and I had a lot of fun with you this morning—especially in the shower."

"What happened?" Mike asked.

"Dave showered with me," Ashley said. "It was intimate but not sexual … or not overtly sexual, anyway. We were both naked."

"Did he have an erection?"

"Yes, but any grinding into me was prohibited and Dave knew that. He was washing me, so naturally his hands were on me. But he used a washcloth and I told him no fondling—I didn't want us crossing any lines."

"So he washed you in a subservient role?"

"It kind of had to be" Ashley said, "given the sexual limitations."

"Not 'limitations,' " I said, "try 'restrictions.' Did I want to shower with Ash? Yes, of course, sign me up. But because of this whole freeze on all things sexual, how could it be anything more than washing my wife?"

"Sure," Mike said, "naked in a shower with a beautiful woman is pretty good all on its own. Take what you can get, I say. You got to really appreciate Ashley's naked body."

"I did, actually," I said.

"How about her pussy," Mike said, "did you wash that?"

"No," Ashley said, "I did that myself, though he did wash my ass."

"That's still pretty good," he said, "right, Dave?"

"Hey, Mike," I said, "I get the point you're trying to make, but—"

"What point?" he said.

"Rubbing in the limitations put in place by that fucking pledge."

"I didn't realize I was," Mike said. "I'm sorry, bro, I didn't mean to."

I was tempted to challenge him, but I wanted to avoid getting into it.

"All I was saying," I said, "was, sex or no sex, it was still a sweet moment of intimacy."

"Oh, exactly," Ashley said. "It was nice to be pampered, sure, but I just liked the intimacy of Dave beside me. And he's right—it was sweet."

"And that's what the oath's for," Mike said. "Think about it. If you hadn't taken the oath, would there have been any showering together?"

"Right," Ashley said. "The oath had a lot to do with it. Even the park beforehand—would we have bonded like that? And it's not like we shower together often. So yeah, that was a definite benefit."

"Why do you think that was?" Mike asked.

"I think because we reached out in other ways—and wanted to make the effort."

"Yeah," Mike said, "and then communication barriers tend to melt away."

I looked at Mike like, *Shut the fuck up*, but couldn't think of what to say. So I just excused myself and went to the bathroom. I had to piss, anyway.

# CHAPTER THIRTY

As I walked back into the kitchen, I noticed that my bedroom door was closed.

"Ashley went to the bathroom," he said, "and she's gonna change. You want another beer?"

"Sure," I said.

"You got it," he said, handing me one and opening his. "What do you think," he said, "should we go out to the living room, now?"

"Sure," I said, walking in and sitting down on the couch. Mike took my TV watching chair beside me.

"Yeah," Mike said. "So ... Ashley bought some lingerie for tonight. On her lunch hour yesterday."

"Oh," I said, "so that's what Ashley's changing into?"

"Yeah," he said, "some nice fuck-me lingerie. You can really admire her ... before I make love to your wife."

"Okay," I said, looking him back in the eye. "You don't need to rub it in."

"It may seem that way," Mike said, "but it's Ashley opening herself up, too. Dressed in looser clothing, she'll reveal more of her inner self to you. She'll be dressed more comfortably, feel less constricted."

"I don't see a fucking correlation, but whatever, Mike," I said. "I get it, she's changing into 'something more comfortable.' "

"And feel free to strip to your boxers—hell, go naked if you want. Whatever you think will make you most comfortable."

"Dude," I said, "I'm fine as is."

"Well, feel free to change your mind," he said, "like … if you're getting turned on and just want to sit in your boxers with your dick out, that's cool, bro. Just know you can."

"Are you fucking kidding me?" I said. "Like I'm gonna do that!"

"You never know," he said. "I'm just saying it's totally cool if you do."

"Yeah, okay," I said. "Well, thanks for that fucking heads up. Glad to know you'd be cool with that."

"Oh just chill out, bro," he said. "You should be more appreciative. I'm not rushing off with Ash to your bedroom. I want us all making time for this. Your relationship is what is most important. And as I've been telling Ash, it's a two-way street. She's going to open up to you more tonight."

"Mike, you don't have to be like that. Let it be a conversation."

"It will be," he said, "but it's time for Ashley to become more forthcoming herself. I mean, you revealed some embarrassing things the other night, and I think Ash needs to share more with you."

"Okay," I said, "but that's not my idea."

"Are there any specific questions you want me to ask Ash for you?"

"What? No."

"Like what was going on when you knocked on the bathroom door at the party—"

"Mike, I'm not submitting questions to you. Seriously, why can't we just have a conversation?"

"What was the other thing you mentioned a lot … if she blew him? I can ask her that."

"Mike, please, don't drag me into this. If you want to ask questions and she wants to answer them, then hey, okay. But don't be saying, 'This is Dave's question.' I'm fucking serious."

"I won't be," he said. "I just thought this was a chance for you to ask Ashley any question you wanted ... or several questions. I saw it as an opportunity."

"Shh," I said, "she's coming out."

\* \* \*

Ashley walked out in a pastel-pink, see-through baby doll, partially covering her ass. At first she was acting unusually shy.

"That's what I'm talking about, baby," Mike said. "You're looking so fucking fine, girl. Why don't you model it? Yeah right there. Oh, yeah, baby, now show the ass. Bend over, Ash. Yeah, that's it. You got my cock hard, Ash."

Her baby dolls were very sheer, and the pink was so light it seemed almost white. I could see her nipples, the outline of her pink areolas. Her tits were on full display.

"Well, I love it," Mike said. "You look like such a fucking cock-tease, Ash. Doesn't she, Dave?"

"Ash," I said, "you look incredibly sexy right now. Really, just stunning."

"Well, thank you," she said, "I'm glad you guys like it. And sure, being half-naked as I am, maybe it will encourage me ... to be more open and candid."

"Exactly," Mike said. "You look straight out of *Playboy*, Ash. I fucking love it. Dave, slide over."

I saw Ashley coming in and moved to the other side of the couch.

"Now have a seat right here, baby."

"What is this—the hot seat?" she said, as she sat on the couch in her lingerie.

"Nah," Mike said with a smile. "C'mon here, raise your wine glass. Dave, hold out your beer. I just want to say, of all the people in the world I could be spending my birthday night with right now, I pick you guys, Dave and Ashley. That's my toast ... you two guys."

I clicked my beer bottle with them and took a swig.

"So even including celebrities," Ashley said, "you'd still pick us."

"Right," Mike said, "or of any place in the world, I'd choose this apartment, right now."

"Well," Ashley said with a smile, "I think you're just saying that, but we're really glad you're here." My eyes zoomed in on her tits whenever she turned to him.

"Oh no, I'm not 'just saying that,'" he said. "With the candles you put on my cake tonight, you reminded me … eleven nights since you guys invited me into your home."

I watched Ashley lean into him and Mike knelt beside her. I imagined how it would look from a telescope through our living room window. My wife, in tit-showing lingerie, passionately kissing another man, while I sat on the other side of the couch like some obviously cucked husband, quietly waiting for them to finish.

"Okay," Ashley said, sitting back on the couch, "so where do we begin?"

"Well," Mike said, "tell me about your talk on Thursday."

"It was a really good foundation," she said. "We really talked things out, and on critical issues like openness and honesty … I think we're really building on that, now."

"So you guys feel you can talk more freely now?" he said. "Like are certain words okay to say that weren't before?"

"Well, yeah," she said, "like *cuckold* is the big one."

"So you've called Dave a cuckold," he said.

"More like he said he'd been cuckolded," she said. "And it's a word we're both more comfortable saying now."

"Which is big progress," Mike said. "It's something you guys should be proud of. You can start talking candidly again. And I know this sounds cheesy, but it's like fucking watering a plant. And as you said, it's already paying dividends. You both feel much closer already."

"Absolutely," she said, turning to me, as if to second confirm what he'd said.

"Ash, I don't even know what I'd be agreeing to," I said, "certainly not to the watering plant analogy."

"The plant is you and me," she said.

"Yeah, Ash, I freaking get it, but give me a break."

"Okay," she said, "I'm sorry."

"But to go back to the original point," Mike said, "you're both comfortable saying 'cuckold' around each other, which is important. It's part of your … vocabulary now."

"Yeah," she said, "I mean … it's not like we're saying 'cuckold' a lot or anything."

"Right," Mike said, "but when it's appropriate, you can say 'cuckold,' whereas before you couldn't."

Ashley turned to me, so I said, "Right."

"So in a little bit," Mike said, turning to me, "Ashley's promised to tell us about the night at the party."

I nodded. "Uh-huh."

"But right now, I want to hear your perspective, Ash … on how Dave reacted to hearing you got fucked by this work guy."

"The night I told him," she said, "or afterwards?"

"A little of both," he said.

"Okay," she said. "I told him at a bar. And he was nervous—I mean so was I—but he really seemed it. And his one question was if the guy's cock was bigger. And after I told him he was, he wanted to change the subject."

"Because he was nervous?"

"I guess," she said.

"I was dumbstruck," I said.

"I hear you, bro," Mike said to me, "but I want to try and avoid back and forth tangents, and give you a chance to really listen, so let's go with Ashley having the floor right now."

"Yeah, okay," I said.

"Thanks," he said, and turned back to Ashley. "Dave

seemed nervous around you, including afterwards."

"Especially afterwards," she said. "I think he was afraid I was going to leave him or something. 'Cause he started acting differently then."

"How so?"

"For instance," she said, "stuff he'd been talking about doing for months, like cleaning out our office room ... suddenly it's done. Or cleaning the bathroom without me reminding him. Little things ... like deferring to me on what movie to watch, or getting me flowers for no reason ... like for our five hundredth day anniversary. Just kidding—that didn't happen. I'm certainly not being critical. I did really love and appreciate all that."

"He was showing how he much he loved you," Mike said. "How about your sex life. Did that change?"

"Well, I don't feel comfortable talking about it, if Dave prefers I don't."

"Dave," he said, "you don't have a problem with Ashley opening up to us about how she perceived sex then, do you?"

"Look," I said, "we all know I've had performance issues recently. And perhaps thinking about that night with Jim had me overly excited whenever we made love."

"Sure," Mike said. "You were inside a beautiful woman as well as face to face with the cuckold inside you. You got too excited."

"Look," I said, "can you not get into our fucking sex lives?"

"Sure man," he said, "but it kind of coincided with you jerking off to Ash in that bathroom. Which fits the pattern Ash described. You reacted like a cuckold."

"Okay," I said, "what the fuck ever. If you want to say that in hindsight—that looking back at it now, me being stunned, or not reacting quickly enough, is somehow cuckold-type behavior—"

"I kind of thought it then, too, Dave," Ashley said.

"What?" I said, "You thought that at the time—that it was cuckold-type behavior?"

"Yeah," she said, looking back at me.

"Ash," I said, "at the time, you wouldn't have known what cuckoldish behavior even was. Did you even know what a cuckold was before Mike?"

"You think Mike told me what a cuckold was?" she said.

"He didn't?" I said. "Was it Tamara?"

"C'mon, Dave," she said.

"What?" I said.

"Dave," she said, "that Saturday you lent me your laptop last month. I was just looking for restaurant reviews and your history came up—all these links to sites with 'cuckold' in the title. I was not freaking prying, and I never looked at your computer since, but of course I read up on what it was. I wanted to bring the subject up with you, but I figured you'd be embarrassed and probably tell me someone must've been using your laptop."

I didn't know what to say. I knew Mike was going to beat me to the punch.

"Is that when you started seeing Dave in a cuckold way?"

"Well," she said, "I wasn't sure if he identified with cuckolding, but I remember thinking it kind of made sense."

"What do you think of that, Dave?" Mike asked. "That she learned about cuckolding from you."

"I'm ... surprised," I said.

"Well," she said, "I didn't assume you wanted to be a cuckold. I just knew you were at least curious, after I told you the rumor was true."

"Yeah," Mike said, "let's talk about that rumor. Let's talk about that night in the bathroom. What do you think, Ash? Are you ready to throw that weight overboard and get real and open with us?"

"Okay," she said, "but I thought we were going to smoke up before?"

"We are," he said, pulling out two joints from his coat. Ashley asked for my lighter and Mike lit the joint and passed it around.

I didn't really want to, never really cared for pot, but took a hit and passed it to Ashley.

"How 'bout we get on the carpet?" she said.

"What?" Mike said.

"It's just vacuumed and it's comfortable. Even a dog would freaking love it. And it'll be cozier."

"If a dog would love it," Mike said, standing up, "it must be comfy."

"Dave," she said, "can you grab the ashtray?"

We sat down in a triangle and Mike passed the joint around. After two more hits, I started to really feel it. The room felt bigger and Ashley made me nervous, with her tits out like that. I didn't want to be seen as staring, so I was afraid to look at her at all. I wondered why we had to sit like we were around a campfire. Our carpet is fairly plush, but it was still the floor we were sitting on. I started second-guessing sitting Indian style but felt too self-conscious to change my position.

"I think you're going to find this really cathartic," Mike said.

"I think so," she said, "but I want to make sure we're all cool with this."

"You're ready to hear this," he said, "right, Dave?"

"Uh … sure," I said, at complete loss for words.

"Wow," Ashley said, "this is good pot."

"Yeah," Mike said, "and you can ramble as much as you want. Dave's wondered a long time about that night."

"Well," she said, "we started to talk the other night about it."

Mike put the joint out and Ashley put on some classical guitar music. It was an unusual choice for her, but I was glad it was mellow.

# CHAPTER THIRTY-ONE

A shley asked who wanted a pillow.

"All of us," Mike said. "Bring extras."

"Do you need help, Ash?" I said.

"I got it," she said, opening the hall closet.

I didn't want to deal with Mike alone right then, so I asked if he was up for another beer. I poured Ashley a new glass of wine.

We moved the coffee table against the couch and sprawled out in the middle of the floor. It still seemed weird but with two pillows and a cabinet behind me, I was a lot more comfortable. Still feeling very stoned and self-conscious.

Mike positioned his pillow so he faced Ashley, and she said, "Right" and adjusted her pillow to face him back.

I didn't mind being out of the spotlight. I could stare at Ashley's tits a lot more, admire her, without any big risk of being noticed. And I could listen and let her do the talking.

"Okay," Mike said to her, "so I'm gonna lead this along a bit, but mostly I'm going to stay out of the way and let you just talk about that night."

"So are you not asking me questions?" she said.

"No, I will be," he said, "particularly if you're skipping things or going too fast. We just want all the details. Why don't we start with the basics. Who was the guy in the bathroom that night?"

"His name's Jim Murta," Ashley said, briefly glancing my way. "He's in sales where I work."

"He's your age?" he said.

"Two years younger," she said. "Twenty-eight."

"Works on the same floor as you?" he said.

"Same floor," she said, "other side."

"Had you been attracted to this guy for a while before that night?"

"No," she said. "I mean, I thought he was a good looking guy, but I never said more than three words to him, until the month before that night, when he started hanging out at work with Tamara."

"So, a month before he fucked you," Mike said, "you started interacting with him. You started saying more than three words to him. Were you flirting?"

"No," she said. "I considered him Tamara's anyway."

"Tamara fucked him?"

"Yeah," she said. "Twice, after being out drinking."

"But they're not a couple?"

"Not at all," she said. "She did say he fucked like a frigging stallion."

"And that got you curious," he said.

"Not so much at the time," she said, "but I thought about it that night when I saw him."

"Thought of what?" Mike said. "What an amazing fuck Tamara said he was?"

Ashley laughed. "Well, I trust Tamara on things like that. So yeah, when he walked over, I was thinking about what'd she'd told me."

"She said he had a big cock?"

"She did, and that she came three times with him, which is rare for her."

"And you wondered how many times you would come, if that big cock was inside you."

"I was attracted to him," she said, "but I really wasn't expecting to have sex later, not at that point. It just kind of happened. It wasn't really until Jim came inside the bathroom—"

"Back up," he said. "How did you guys all come to be in the bathroom?"

"Well," she said, "we were out on the deck, the three of us talking, and Tamara said she had some pot on her. She asked if we wanted to get high in the bathroom, and Jim was like, *Fuck, yeah*."

"Nice," Mike said. "Where was Dave then?"

"On the deck also, but on the other side, talking to his friend and some IT guys I work with. No one noticed when Tamara and I went inside."

"With Jim?" he asked.

"No, Tamara told him to him to wait a couple minutes … so no one would notice."

"So you went into the bathroom and waited for Jim?"

"Yeah, we checked ourselves in the mirror, and Tamara found her pipe—she thought she forgot it—and started saying how she's gonna ask him to show us his cock."

"What did you think?"

"I thought she might be joking, but I was like, *Hey, if you want to ask him*."

"But you were thinking 'Please fucking ask him, Tamara.'"

Ashley laughed and said, "I was like, *If he's showing it, hey, I'll check it out*."

"I like Tamara wanting to show her married friend another man's cock."

"Yeah, she's an enabler for sure. But she didn't bring it up when he first came inside. I mean, it started kind of innocent, huddled up by the sink, passing a pipe around, blowing smoke out this tiny window."

"Were you guys talking?"

"Yeah. Jim started saying how this was really cool and how he felt like he was in this exclusive club, and how he didn't know I smoked pot. And Tamara was like, *Well, actually Jim, I was telling Ashley about your cock. And I don't think my description did it justice. How about you whip your cock out now and show her."*

"Gotta love Tamara," he said. "So what'd he do?"

"He looked to see my reaction, then he thought she was kidding. But when he realized Tamara was serious, he said, 'How 'bout you both show me your titties, first.' Like so he'd be extra hard when he showed us."

"Nice. Go on."

"Well, soon as the words left his mouth, there went Tamara, taking off her top. So I'm just standing there like, fuck, I guess I'm doing this. Tamara gave me this *what-the-fuck* look when she saw me hesitating."

"How long did you hesitate?"

"Just long enough to think, *What the hell am I doing?* But at the time it seemed more daring than crazy. Plus I had Tamara saying, 'And now your bra, Ashley.' "

"So you gave him a titty show. Who has bigger tits?"

"Tamara. She's a D."

"Whose tits was Jim staring at the most?"

"Well, mine, but he'd seen Tamara's tits before. Mine were new to him."

"Yeah, a hot married girl from corporate, topless. I'm sure he was checking you out real good."

"Well, he asked if we'd 'indulge' him, said he wanted us sitting in the bathtub together. And Tamara was all for humoring him. So we undressed to just our thongs and got in the tub together."

"So he wanted you guys to get his cock hard by sitting naked in the tub?"

"Yeah, basically" she said. "He wanted to see if he could get us to *do* anything. He asked Tamara, 'Don't you want to feel up your friend?' And she looked at me like, *Are you game?* I was up for turning Jim on more. So I just looked at her like, *Hey, do you wanna kiss me?*"

"I bet she made out with you real good."

"Oh, she did, and played with my tits a little, but I turned to Jim like, *Hey now, Mister, time for your end of the bargain.*"

"You wanted to see his cock—that's what you were saying."

"Well, I was saying it on behalf of us both," she said. "Plus, I didn't want Tamara getting carried away."

"Were you thinking this was still nothing but a lark?"

"Yeah, I mean it still seemed innocent till I saw his cock."

"That changed things …."

"It made it real. It made me gulp. That's when I first really thought, *My husband's outside,* or that I was at a party, or this is fucking crazy. I kind of blocked that out and got lost in the moment. *Like wow, Tamara wasn't kidding, he's got a really big and beautiful cock.* Tamara asked me what I thought of his cock, and I'm just like 'uh-huh'… and I told him it was 'very nice.'"

"So you complimented him on his cock," Mike said, "giving him signals, nice. He was standing and you were sitting in the tub. Were you eye-level with his cock?"

"Yeah," she said.

"How close was his 'big and beautiful' cock to your face?"

"Well, he gave Tamara a close-up and then he gave me one, so it was close—a few inches away. But it wasn't for long. Because Tamara told him to step back more to the center. She wanted him to stroke it, and he was totally down for that."

"For what?"

"For jerking off as Tamara and me made out in the tub some more."

"Talk about that."

"Well, I let Tamara suck on my tits and kissed back and everything, but I was also looking back at Jim. It was fascinating in a strange way. Especially when he started zooming in on me."

"Zooming how?"

"Just pointing his cock at me, staring with these lustful eyes and stroking his cock."

"And how did that make you feel?"

"I felt lusted over. I felt naked and objectified and slutty—and liberated and sexy and horny. Like I knew it was crazy, but so what."

"And so what that your husband was outside on the balcony."

"Yeah, kind of," she said. "I was caught up in the moment. And kind of mesmerized."

"Okay, so you were in the tub staring while he stroked …."

"Yeah," she said, "pretty much couldn't take my eyes off it. And that's when … that's when Dave knocked at the door. That's what was going on."

"You were staring at another man's cock when Dave knocked," Mike said, "but you hadn't sucked it. Not yet."

"Right," she said, "and Tamara said, 'Oh just ignore it,' and then we heard Dave's voice asking if anyone was inside."

"How did you feel?"

"I was freaked, like wondering if he knew I was in there. Or if the door was unlocked … if we were busted. But Tamara was like, *piece of cake,* and told him to use the other bathroom. She got him to leave pronto. I couldn't believe it."

"Now that Dave was out of the picture," he said, "Jim must've been happy."

"I'm sure, but he was also looking at me like, *Is she gonna now want to put her clothes back on and leave?* Assuming my husband knocking would be a reality wake-up call."

"But you wanted it even more now, didn't you?"

"Well," she said, "I didn't rush to put my clothes back on."

"How did Dave being sent upstairs make you feel?"

"I don't know," she said. "I mean, it kind of made me hornier. What I was doing was so bold and out there. But I really didn't have time to think. Because right after Dave was sent along, Tamara asked Jim, point blank, 'Which one of us do you want to fuck?' "

"What did you think of her question?"

"I was like, *Wow, that was direct, even for Tamara. And I started thinking, Fuck, I'm entering major slut territory now.*' Because I stayed silent after Tamara said that."

"How do you mean?"

"He'd just been given the choice of fucking me or Tamara, and he'd already fucked Tamara. This was his one chance to fuck the married girl in corporate."

"So you knew he'd pick you?"

"I kind of did," she said, "and by saying nothing, I was saying everything … that I wouldn't stand in the way of it happening, that I was open to being fucked by him. By not reacting to Tamara's question, I was saying that."

"Your silence told him he could fuck you."

"Pretty much."

"Plus, he'd be getting you to cheat on the husband Tamara had just sent away. He'd just heard Dave knock. Of course, he'd want to ball Dave's girl hard now."

"Yeah," Ashley laughed, "probably."

"So he answered Tamara's question, 'Which one do you want to fuck?' "

"Yup," she said, "he just pointed his big cock at me and said, 'Ashley.' "

"And what did you think?"

"That he'd said a lot, just by saying my name."

"How'd you react?"

"Kind of shyly at first," she said. "I smiled and said, 'Okay,' but I had my eyes on the floor. I was a bit freaked."

"Why so?"

"Just the reality of what was happening, that I was about to get fucked with my husband and a roomful of people right outside."

"But that kind of added to the thrill, didn't it?"

"Well yeah," she said. "I was already super horny, so I kind of got off on how utterly slutty it was. But I was also nervous about *anyone* knocking—not just Dave."

"But Jim knew now that you'd just agreed to fuck him."

"Oh yeah," she said, casually. "He just walked over with his big fat boner and helped me out of the tub."

"Okay …."

"Well, he was naked and I still had my thong on, but I was kind of following his lead, so he kissed me and we started making out in the middle of the bathroom."

"Nice. Give us the details, Ash."

"Well, he's sucking my tits and grabbing my ass, and then he yanks my thong down, and his cock's up against my stomach as he gives me tongue."

"Nice. Let Dave picture it."

"Well, Jim starts whispering, 'Touch my cock, Ashley, feel my cock in your hands.' So suddenly I'm making out with him *and* stroking his cock. And he pushes down on my shoulders and says, 'I'd love for you to blow me first, Ashley.' And suddenly Tamara's throwing down some towels, and there I am, tits out, just lost my thong, kneeling in the middle of the bathroom floor."

"So Tamara gave you a towel for your knees?"

"Yeah, she put my bra on top of the towels I knelt on—to make it sluttier, I guess. And Tamara sat down on a towel herself and watched."

"A voyeur," Mike said.

"More like a spectator," she said. "Tamara put down my towel and said, 'I want to watch Ashley suck cock.' I think she was amazed I was doing it."

"So tell us how you took it into your mouth."

"I just took a deep breath, like *I can't believe I'm doing this*, opened my mouth, and he stuck his cock in. No foreplay, licking up his shaft, or anything…"

"You were in a rush," Mike said, "and he wanted a blowjob … from married Ashley Martens."

"Yeah, I'm sure I was making his day."

"Was anyone talking as you sucked his cock?"

Tamara would say things like 'Nice' and 'Good girl' and Jim was mostly saying 'Oh yeah, suck it.' I gagged once, a little, but kept on sucking. And pretty soon, he was like 'I want to fuck you.' "

"Were you thinking, *About fucking time?*"

"No," she said, with a smile, "but hearing that had me wetter."

"So he took his cock out of your mouth …."

"Well, he helped me up and had me sit on the counter, and I was like, *What about condoms?* Jim said he didn't have any and Tamara said she would look in her purse. And Jim asked if I was on the pill, and I said I was, but that he should still wear one. But then Tamara said she didn't have any, and Jim just looked at me, and said, "Don't worry, Ashley. I'm safe and I can pull out and cum on your ass."

286

# CHAPTER THIRTY-TWO

"I was like, *This is crazy, but I've come this far….* I thought about going back on my knees and just finishing the BJ, but I really wanted him to fuck me."

"So you told him it was okay, that he could fuck you bare?"

"Yeah, basically. To pull out when he came. And yeah, I thought that would be safe."

"Sure," Mike said. "Go on, Ash."

"Well, he had me get on the counter—"

"Naked—"

"Yeah, I was bare-ass sitting on the counter, next to the sink. Although I did have a towel under me."

"What were you thinking?" he said.

"That I'm really fucking doing this. That I'm about to take Jim Murta's cock in my pussy."

"And taking it bare," he said, "with Dave walking around, oblivious."

"I know," she said. "I knew how f'd up it was."

"Didn't matter. You wanted him to fuck you."

"It was a thrill ride," she said, "and the stars kind of aligned. And I was like, *I'm not passing this up.* So yeah, what can I say? I wanted his cock that night."

"And he knew it," he said, "Go on."

"So I was naked on the counter with Jim naked and his big cock pointed at me."

"Were your legs spread … showing him your pussy?"

"Yeah. I tried to get him make out again a little, but he

wasn't having any. He was just like, *I want to fuck you, Ashley.*"

"Yeah," Mike said, "and if Dave knocked again he wanted to be already fucking you. Knowing you wouldn't stop if you heard your husband's voice again. You'd let him keep on fucking you … with no thought of stopping … so what happened?"

Ashley closed her eyes. "I tilted back on the counter with my legs spread, and he had his cock on the top of my pussy lips. I could watch his cock slide inside me."

"Did you cry out when you felt it deep inside you?"

"I kept it to a muffled 'Oh my God.'"

"What was Tamara doing?"

"Watching like, I can't believe Ashley's doing this."

"She'd have a good angle to see her good friend getting fucked …."

"Yeah, she was like three feet away. She offered to hold my hand."

"Did you?"

"No," she said. "I wanted my hands free. Plus, it seemed a little weird."

"How did you feel with a big cock inside you, Ash?"

"It felt like too much at first, but pretty soon, as he started to pump inside me, I was like, Oh my god, this is freaking fantastic. I felt super-alive and crazy horny. And like such a slut. The opposite of what people perceived me to be… just wild abandon and filthy lust."

"And fucking loving it, baby, right?"

"It was like being in another world," she said, "on total cloud nine. This sense of utter liberation."

"Did you express yourself as he fucked you?"

"Was I making noise?" she said. "I was suppressing and muffling a few 'Oh Gods,' but mostly I was trying hard to be quiet. Listening to his cock pumping faster inside me. I was close to orgasm, actually, when he stopped and said he had a better position—"

"To fuck in."

"Yeah, he told me to stand and lean over the bathroom sink, in front of a mirror, and I was like *I don't know*, and he was like *Please, you're gonna love it* ... and then he smacked my ass and said, 'C'mon.'"

"Nice."

"Yeah, so I just arched my back and put my ass out, and leaned over the sink, and instantly, he put his hands on my hips and tilted me up more, and thrust it inside me. I was getting fucked from behind."

"So you got quickly into fuck rhythm?"

"Yeah, no slow build-up. And there was this echo in the bathroom, and the party noise was very background, so I just tried to keep quiet and listen to him fucking me. The sound of him slapping his balls up against me .... I tuned out everything else." She was lying on her back on the rug, squirming a little.

"Okay ...."

"So he started pumping faster, and fucking me harder and louder, and I realized I was about to cum. By then I couldn't fully contain myself. I cried out something like, 'Oh God ... oh fuck ... I'm cumming!' and I writhed and felt it throughout my entire body when I orgasmed."

"Did he keep right on pounding you?"

"Oh yeah. There was no let–up. In fact it got even stronger. I was getting fucked pretty fucking hard."

"Was he saying anything?"

"Just 'yeah' and 'fuck yeah.' I heard Tamara say, 'Fuck her, Jim.'"

"I like it," Mike said. "Tamara showing her support."

"Yeah, watching me bent over this freaking sink. I blew her away getting fucked like that."

"I'm sure she fucking loved it ... seeing you slutting out like that. And was he saying anything?"

"Well, yeah, when he was close to cumming, he said,

'You're on the pill, right?' and I'm like 'Yeah, but pull out,' and he's like, 'We gotta do this.' He's pumping me really hard, and I realize I'm about to cum again. He said, 'I'm going inside you, Ashley,' and I kind of screamed, like in the throes of an orgasm. I couldn't control myself." Ashley opened her eyes again and looked around as if trying to reorient herself.

"How did it feel?" he said.

"Surreal," she said, blinking. "Like this rush of warmth and this feeling of being off the ground and in the clouds. I fucked back on his cock and just got lost in another orgasm."

"And Jim?"

"It was building to a crescendo, and I knew he was about to cum. When he did, he thrust and held his cock in my pussy. Not only did he not pull out, he didn't pull out until he came completely … like every last drop."

"He wanted your puss brimming sperm."

She nodded and pulled herself back into a sitting position. "Yeah, it was dripping from me when he finally pulled out and I stood back up."

"You'd just taken another man's sperm with your husband right outside."

"Oh, believe me, that was on my mind when I looked in the mirror."

"Yeah, what did you think?"

"Well, my first thought was, *I'm naked, I'm disheveled, I've got Jim Murta's sperm in my pussy. Where the hell are my clothes? I have a freaking party I have to go back to.*"

"And how about Jim?"

"Oh, he didn't care. He was in no rush to get dressed. He was amused."

"And basking in the satisfaction," Mike said, "of just giving you his sperm."

"Yeah, he had a cocky grin and was looking at me like, *I just fucked you good.*"

"How'd that make you feel?"

She shrugged. "Even more like a slut. And that's how I

felt afterwards, looking for my skirt, picking my bra off the floor. With him watching me frantically getting dressed. Only I couldn't find my thong. I thought it was under the towels I'd knelt on, but it wasn't anywhere. Tamara looked too."

"Did Jim help?"

"No, he just watched me on the floor, bare-ass, looking for it. He said he had no clue where it was. So I just got dressed anyway … and fixed my hair and lipstick. And tried to calm down and look normal. Like all I had done was smoke some pot in the bathroom."

"So what happened to your thong?"

"I don't know. I said to Jim, 'It's really not funny if you have it or know where it is,' but he just said, 'Feel my pockets, pat me down.' So I was like, *Fuck, I guess I'm going out there commando.*"

"Yeah, so what if you have sperm dripping out your pussy?"

"Well, I did my best to clean up, that way, but yeah, I didn't want to have this 'I've just been fucked' look on my face. Not walking back into the party."

"Yeah, or look like you were going commando with a pussy full of Jim's sperm."

Ashley laughed, a little too loud and long, like the pot had really kicked in. "So you see why I was freaking out, then? I mean. Jim—and even Tamara—what did they care? I was the one who now had to deal. Go back out to the party like Miss Normal. And I didn't know if people were waiting to see who came out."

"Were you worried about Dave being one of them?"

"Absolutely. I figured it was a real possibility. I just felt if I stuck to 'I was smoking pot with Jim and Tamara in the bathroom,' I could get through it. And the bathroom did smell like pot—so it would sound authentic."

"Okay."

"So Jim came over and gave me a hug."

"Was he still naked?"

"From the waist down he was," she said, "but I was dressed. So he had his cock on my skirt as he's hugging me. And he says 'If you need me to explain anything ...' like if Dave's asking questions, he could talk to him."

"What did you think of that?"

"I was like, *Are you fucking kidding me?* I said, 'You need to ignore me for the rest of the night.' And if anyone asked, to say we all smoked pot, and that was it."

"Did you give him a kiss?"

"For just a second when he hugged me. I wanted out of there."

"So you went out by yourself?"

"Yeah, but fortunately no was one waiting. A friend of ours, Caroline, from Tamara's department ... after Dave knocked, she put up an 'out of service' sign telling people to go upstairs. She told me that when I walked into the kitchen. And a few people seemed to know the three of us were in there—a few of Jim's friends, I think—just by looks they gave me."

"Little did they know you were thong-less now, and why."

"No, but they probably wondered a lot why we were in there for so long. I figured if they did think anything went on, it would be between Jim and Tamara—the ones still in there."

"And not little Ashley Martens—the respectable, married, conservative corporate girl."

"Well, it would be way more logical. People knew they'd hooked up before. It wouldn't surprise people much."

"Whereas Ashley being the one getting fucked would—"

"Well, yeah," she said, "especially with my husband being there."

"Right," he said, "and a bunch of work colleagues. So you went out to the party?"

"Yeah. When I came out, I kind of hoped I smelled like pot ... and that I looked my normal self. When Caroline asked me about it, I just rolled my eyes like, *Yeah, I left them to do whatever.*"

"Where was Dave?"

"I walked onto the outside deck and saw him talking and drinking with the IT guys."

"How did he seem?"

"Like he was buzzed and having a good time. When I first saw him, he was laughing like he hadn't a care in the world."

"Did you go up to him?"

"No. I met up with a few friends out there and got myself in the conversation—just tried to be ultra-normal."

"Did it work?"

"It seemed to," she said. "Everyone acted normal around me."

"Did you see Jim after he came out?"

"Yeah, he stayed mostly inside, which was good. I didn't talk to him or anything. Besides, he was probably busy telling his buddies."

"Is that how the rumor started?"

"Yeah, but I don't want to get into the rumor and dealing at work and all that, tonight."

"Sure," Mike said, "next time perhaps. But that's how the rumor started? He told his friends when he went back to the party?"

"Yeah," she said, "and told them I lost my thong. So I'm sure his friends were checking me out in my skirt."

"They knew Jim's seed was inside you."

"I'm sure," she said. "I know he told him he came inside me. That was included in the rumor on Monday."

"Did any other guys try to hit on you?"

"No, I stayed on the balcony with a group of friends, girls. I just wanted to blend in."

"Sure," he said.

"Which is a good ending point ... for now, right?"

"Absolutely," he said. "That was great, Ash. And I can't wait for us to go back a little in time as well."

"How do you mean?" she said.

"To before you let some junior sales guy fuck you in a

bathroom. I want to hear what precipitated it. We'll start at your honeymoon. You'll talk about your sex life. What led up to things. How you came to embrace your sluttiness."

"Good grief," she said with a laugh, "why stop there? What about old boyfriends from college?"

"No pressure, Ash," he said. "You'll tell Dave when you're ready."

I could tell Mike was staring at me and looked down at the carpet. We'd all been sitting on the floor and it struck me how still Mike had been, propped up against the chair I watched TV in.

"I will," she said. "This is a really great environment to talk in. But hey, I shared a lot tonight."

"Totally," he said, sitting up straighter. "That was awesome. And doesn't it feel good to open up like that?"

"Yeah," she said, sitting up a little straighter herself. "Hopefully that's another thing we can talk about now."

"Absolutely," he said. "And now Dave has his answers, don't you Dave?"

I acted like I thought his question was rhetorical. Not wanting to be the only one left lying on the floor, I pulled myself to a sitting position.

"Aren't you gonna thank her for her openness?"

"Yeah," I said, feeling on the spot. "Thanks for being open, Ash, though it wasn't like I had all these questions." I was sweating. "My main one, I told you, was what was going on when I knocked. You answered that."

"Right," Mike said. "You hadn't sucked cock yet, right?"

"I had not," she said, "I was still in the bathtub."

* * *

"So Dave," he said, "What did you like best about what Ashley told you?"

"I'm just glad that she can be more open," I said, "that we both can."

"But what part of her Jim Murta fuck story did you like best?" he persisted.

Before I could answer, Ashley started in. "Dave's talking

higher level," she said, "and I'm there with him. It feels great to have maybe gotten it off my chest and rid ourselves of this thing we don't talk about. I really want it to be a two-way street."

"Yeah, right," I said, with a hint of sarcasm.

"And that's what the last couple of days were about," she continued, "getting to a place where we can be ourselves. And now, hearing about Jim, you don't have to wonder anymore."

"Yeah, I appreciated all that, thank you."

"You're welcome," she said and gave me a kiss. But it was quick and no tongue, and felt almost like a pat on the back.

I couldn't really say anything when she pulled away, with Mike there. I didn't want to look disappointed. I felt stoned and socially awkward.

"Well, I think that was a really great start," Mike said. "I'm really glad we did this."

"Yeah, me too," Ashley said, smiling … beaming.

"Dave," he said, "what do you think of the way Ashley looks tonight?"

"Um, amazingly gorgeous," I said.

"And extremely fuckable?" he added.

"Well," I said, "she's always super sexy to me, and yeah, it's my wife in lingerie, so of course she looks incredible to me."

"I bet you wish you had a picture," he said. "Ash, what do you say? Can Dave have a picture with you? Is that cool?"

"Sure," she said, "but it goes without saying, no showing anyone."

"You wouldn't do that, Dave," Mike said.

"No," I said, "of course not."

"Where's your phone?" Mike said. "Seize the moment, my friend."

I pulled out my phone and hurried to picture mode. I focused it on Ashley, sitting upright on the rug in her baby dolls. I could see her nipples, the full shape of her breasts.

"How 'bout you give a sexy pout for the camera?" Mike said. "Lips parted, like you're seconds from blowing me. That's it, take it, Dave."

I snapped her picture and saw I'd gotten it—no thumb or poor focus.

"Nice shot of Ashley's tits," Mike said. "What do you say, Dave? That's a serious keeper, huh?"

"Yeah," I said. "It's a sexy shot of her, sure."

"I meant like how 'bout thanking Ashley?" Mike said, "That was a pretty good present, wasn't it?"

"Yeah," I said, "I mean, thanks for posing, Ash."

"Yeah, a nice pre-blowjob look," Mike said, looking at it again. "Like how she probably looked when you knocked on the door, pouting her lips and waiting for cock …."

"It's a sexy photo," I said.

"And her little white thong showing," Mike said. "It looks wet, Ash."

"Let me see," she said, grabbing the phone. "No it doesn't."

"Well," Mike said, "Don't tell me you weren't a little wet, telling your 'getting fucked in the bathroom' story."

"Sure, I got horny talking about it," she said.

"And you haven't had sex in a few days," he said.

"Which makes me what?" she said, "Extra horny?"

"Yeah."

"I'm sure that's part of it," she said. "I was looking forward to tonight, a lot."

"So was I, Ash," he said, "and this is fantastic. I couldn't have asked for a better birthday."

"Well," she said, "we're glad you're spending it with us."

"And now I want to really top off my evening, Ash."

"Yeah?" she said. "The bedroom?"

Mike didn't reply—he simply stood.

"Dave," she said, "I think we're going to retire now, okay?"

"You're going to bed?" I said.

"Yeah, we're going to the bedroom now, okay?"

She looked in my eyes, like *Just fucking say yes, okay?*

And saying no didn't seem like it would stop her. "Uh-huh," I said. "I mean, okay."

She gave me a kiss, a few seconds of tongue, and hugged me.

Not knowing what to do, I watched her get up. Mike had gone to the bathroom, and Ashley started looking through the foyer closet. It was just instinct, but I stood up and walked over to help her.

"I'm just grabbing these little speakers," she said. "Could you find a candle in the kitchen?"

"Yeah, sure, Ash," I said.

"The red candle right above the sink," she said.

"Yup," I said, "got it."

I turned around and saw Ashley pulling a bottle of wine from our closet. "I'm grabbing the Pinot noir," she said as she took out two glasses and the corkscrew.

Now her hands were full and I knew what that meant. I'd be walking into my own bedroom and delivering their candle. Like a fucking bellhop.

I followed behind her down the hall and stepped into my bedroom. Mike was hanging up his shirt in my closet. I pretended like he wasn't in the room and focused on putting the fucking candle on her desk.

"Do you have your Yankees lighter?" Ashley said. "Oh wait, I snagged it. I can light it."

"Wait a sec, Ash," Mike said. "Maybe Dave wants to light the candle for his wife."

Ashley looked at me curiously and held out the lighter. Instinctively I took it. I didn't want Mike piping in about how I should say a few words beforehand. So I lit the thing quickly.

"Another kiss," she said, when I handed her the lighter.

"You bet, Ash," I said, putting my arms around her, following her lead. But it quickly turned into a hug, and I saw Mike next to my closet, hanging up his jeans.

I squeezed Ashley harder. She held me tight and said softly in my ear, "I love you, Dave."

I watched Mike—in tight, white briefs—turn around from the closet, a long bulge in his underwear. Mike was sporting what seemed like a big fucking boner.

I realized he was looking at me. He smiled when I made eye contact, which freaked me out. I closed my eyes and hugged Ashley tighter.

"Well, good night, Dave," she said pulling away, "and thank you."

"Yeah, sure Ash," I said. "Well, I'm gonna check out some baseball in the other room. And I'll be thinking of showering with you and going to the Park today."

"We shared a great day together," she said. "I'll see you in the morning."

"Good night," I said and walked toward the door.

"Hey, Dave," Mike called out, and I turned around.

"Thanks," he said, lounging on my bed and doing nothing to hide the big, fat hard-on in his briefs. "Thanks for helping Ashley make this such a great birthday for me. I think we really kicked some walls down tonight ... and had some much needed honesty. You should feel really good about that."

I saw Ashley standing by our bed in her see-through baby-dolls, staring at me.

"Uh ... well ... you're welcome," I said and turned back toward the door.

"Have a good night, Dave," he said.

I grabbed the handle very mechanically and didn't look back as I shut the door.

# CHAPTER THIRTY-THREE

I was in the hallway, standing by my bedroom and feeling like I was in outer space. I'd just shut the door for him. After dropping off a candle so he and my wife could have just the right fuck ambience.

I knew the message it must have sent to Ashley—that I was desperate not to lose her, that I'd accepted my new role. Like I was some obedient cuckold. Like I'd make them breakfast in bed if she asked.

I hovered outside the door and almost pressed my ear to the door when I heard whispering. Judging from the sound of the springs, they were on the bed. I heard Ashley say "Okay" a few times, then more whispering. I wondered if they were making out.

Then I heard Mike say loudly, "How 'bout you stand by that wall, Ash?"

I heard them getting out of bed, and I tiptoed back down the hall. Suddenly they sounded really close, right on the other side of the wall, talking.

"I want you," I heard him say, "to lean against this wall and show me … how you looked when he had you bent over the sink."

"Okay," she said, "but you don't have to talk so loud."

"I want Dave to hear us," he said.

"I know," she said, "and if he's listening, I'm sure he can hear us fine. But we're not on stage, we don't need to project. If he is in the living room, he shouldn't be able to hear us."

"Yeah," Mike said, "and if he's there watching baseball,

like he said, he won't hear us at all. But if he's right outside the door, then obviously he wants to listen, which is what cuckolds do."

"I know," she said.

"Why don't you say hello to him, on the chance that he is listening?"

"What?"

"Say hello to your husband … and speak up."

"Okay," she said. "Hi, Dave."

"How about 'Hi, Cuckold'?"

"It feels weird," she said, "talking to him, not knowing if he's even there."

"Well, he's probably too afraid to say 'hi' back anyway. But I'm sure he wishes he had the courage—the kind of courage you have."

"Maybe," she said.

"Now put your hands on the wall," he said, "and show me that nice firm ass. I want to see how slutty you looked that night for Jim … knowing your husband was right outside."

I heard what seemed like Ashley's hands on the wall, and I crept back up to the door. I thought of how to fast-exit, if I heard footsteps coming. There was a hall closet I could say I was going to. For blankets.

"The only way Dave hears us," he said, "is he chooses to. Now tilt that ass for me. I want to see your pussy lips from behind. Oh yeah, baby, let me take a photo of you. Show me that puss … perfect."

" 'Kay," she said, "can I stand back up now?"

"Stay there like that," he said.

"It's kind of an awkward position to—"

"To what? Fuck you in? Like in the bathroom?"

"Well," she said, "at least then I was leaning on the sink … more support."

"What makes you think I'm going to fuck you like that?"

"Well what then?" she said. "Did you want more photos?"

"Oh you little cock-teasing bitch," he said. "Now face the wall, and tilt that milky white ass to me. Did you miss me, Ash?" he said and loudly smacked her ass.

"Oh!" she cried out, and in a slightly strained voice, added, "I missed you a lot."

"What did your pussy miss?" He slapped it again.

"It missed your cock, Mike," she almost groaned.

"Say it again."

"I missed your cock, Mike!"

"Did you enjoy telling your husband what a naughty little cock slut you were that night?"

"I'm glad," she said between panting breaths, "that he knows."

"Knows what a horny cock slut you can be?" he said, spanking her extra hard. "You're a naughty little horn dog, aren't you?" *Smack.* "Not caring that Dave was knocking on the door." *Smack.* "You let him fuck you anyway…" *Smack.* "And walked back out to your husband, with your puss full of sperm." *Smack.* "The married office cock whore who got bent over a sink." *Smack.* "And now you're fucking cucking your husband." *Smack.* "Right in your marital bed." *Smack.*

"Ow!" Ashley cried.

"You're humiliating him." *Smack.* "You're making your husband your fucking cuck." *Smack.*

"Ow!" Ashley said again, and added, panic in her voice. "Wait, wait, I'm serious! I think you made your point."

They stopped talking, and I heard the wet, smacking sounds of heavy kissing. Mike said, "Why don't you grab the pillows on the bed?"

I headed down the hall, took off my belt and shoes in the living room, and proceeded back to my bedroom door with caution.

* * *

"Put them right here, Ash," he said, "yeah, so Dave can listen."

I got up pretty close to the door, but was still prepared to bolt.

"So how should we do this?" she said, "I'm assuming I'm on my knees—"

"Yeah, but give me a kiss first," he said. They sounded just a few feet from the door. I could hear them making out. Ashley moaned, like he was kissing her neck.

I heard the drop of weight to the floor and knew Ashley had gone to her knees.

"Pull out your tits," Mike said, "and pose like you did in Dave's picture. Open your mouth, like you're about to suck cock. Yeah … that's it. Is that what you're about to do, Ash?"

"Isn't it obvious?" she said.

"Well," he said, "why don't you tell your husband what's so obvious."

"He might not even be listening."

"Tell him what you're about to do, baby."

"Okay," she said, "I'm about to suck Mike's cock, Dave."

"What's going in your mouth, baby?"

"Your big fucking cock, Mike."

I heard Mike grunt and mutter, "Oh yeah." I could hear the slurping and sucking sounds of Ashley with a cock in her mouth. I unzipped my fly and pulled out my dick through my boxers. I could still cover up quickly if I had to hurry down the hall.

"Happy birthday to me," he said. "Oh fuck yeah! Suck it, Ash. That's it, you naughty girl. On your knees sucking cock, with your husband on the other side of that door … listening. Let him hear how his wife sucks a real man's cock. C'mon, Ash, make some noise, I want a naughty, sloppy blowjob, baby."

Ashley went right along and the slurping got louder, like she was really sucking him off. Like her saliva was all over Mike's cock.

"And my balls, yeah," he said. "Suck on them balls,

302

Ashley. And stroke my cock with your hand. Oh yeah, that's it … fuck, baby, let me see that wedding ring … as you stroke my cock with my balls in your mouth. That's it … now back in your mouth, you little married cock slut."

I heard Ashley catch her breath and say, "Wow."

"Nice, Ash," he said. "You're taking a lot of cock in that gorgeous little mouth of yours tonight."

"I know," she said. "Probably the most yet."

"Yeah," he said, "you're becoming a fucking great little cocksucker."

"Thank you," she said, with a laugh. "I'm trying."

"Well, try some more," he said. "Oh yeah, right back in your mouth … good fucking girl. Let Dave hear what a cocksucking slut you are …. Oh yeah, Ash, fucking cuck your man and suck that cock, girl."

I started stroking my dick, nervously, knowing I was being such a cuckold. But I was in the moment, and felt like, *What choice do I have?*

I heard Ashley stop to catch her breath and say, "Oh my God."

"You ready to get fucked, Ash?" Mike said.

"I want to get fucked, Mike."

"Tell your hubby what I'm about to do," he said.

"Mike's gonna fuck me now, David."

\* \* \*

I thought he might want to fuck her against the wall, or by the door, and I took a few steps down the hall. But then I heard them get onto the bed … and wondered if Mike wanted to make it harder for me to hear, the part where he fucked her … like he wanted it not as close-up or in my face, to force me to ask for that.

I got down on the floor and put my ear to the crack in the door. I figured the bed was far enough away to hear them in time if they came my way.

After a minute of silence, the bed springs started to squeak, and I knew Mike was inside her. I listened as the bed squeak grew louder, and faster, and I heard Ashley moan and mutter, "Oh God." Pretty soon, the sound of balls slapping went from faint to obvious. They were in sync—every ball smack seemed to pop and echo. I was on the floor, stroking, as he pumped his cock inside my girl, making her yell out, "Oh God," over and over again.

The noises weren't as distinct as with the blowjob, but I could still hear it pretty clearly. I heard Mike say, "Fuck yeah!" and "Fuck back on that cock, Ash."

I listened to Ashley moan in way she never did with me.

The "Oh Gods" continued as the headboard started to shake.

"Did you miss my cock, Ash?" I heard him say.

"Oh God, I missed your cock, Mike. My pussy missed your cock."

"You love my cock, Ash?"

"Oh God, I love your big cock, Mike."

"Say 'Fuck me as my husband listens.' "

"Oh God, Mike, fuck me as my husband listens!"

"Whose pussy is it, Ash?"

"It's your pussy, Mike."

"Tell Dave whose pussy it is."

"Oh my God," she cried, "I'm about to cum!"

"Tell him, Ashley," he said, as the fucking intensified.

"It's Mike's pussy, Dave. Oh my God, I'm cumming …. It's Mike's pussy, now!"

"Oh fuck yeah," he said as he pumped away even more furiously. The bedroom seemed full with the sound of hard ball-slapping, the headboard shaking and Ashley crying "oh God" in wild abandon … in explosive orgasm.

It seemed like they stopped to change positions, only this time the bed bouncing started up almost immediately, and he was back to ball-slapping her pretty quickly.

Ashley's whimpering turned back into moans and "Oh Gods."

I realized I was about to cum and pulled my hand off my dick. I wanted to last, so I let it just throb and calm down.

Mike slowed up on his cock pumping as if he was taking his time, savoring his birthday fuck.

"I fucking love it," he muttered, "making a cuck out of your man, fucking you bare in your marital bed as he jerks off outside."

"Oh my God," Ashley cried, "I'm gonna cum again … oh my God."

"Tell him how you've cucked him, Ash."

"Oh God Mike, oh fuck Mike …."

"Tell him!"

"Oh God, Mike, fuck me!"

"Tell him …."

"I'm cuckolding you, Dave … oh my God … I'm cucking you, David … oh Mike … oh Mike … I'm cumming … oh baby, I'm fucking cumming."

I suddenly realized I was about to cum myself, that it was too late to stop it. I listened to the ball-slapping and looked at my blue bedroom door. In some gesture of resistance, I pointed my dick at the door. I wanted to blast all over the fucking thing. An exclamation point to my feelings, like flipping the bird.

I listened to her cry out, "Oh my God, Mike," and another stroke later, my first shot smacked against the bottom of the door. I followed that up with a few more. I couldn't control it. There was cum on the carpet, on my balls, on my hands.

I reached in my pocket for tissues and looked at my sperm dripping down the bedroom door. "Jesus Christ," I mumbled as I wiped it off. I made sure to get the carpet, too. Now it was just my balls that were sticky.

I wanted to wash up in the bathroom, but Mike was full-throttle fucking Ashley, and I had to listen.

"Whose pussy is it, Ash?"

"It's your pussy, Mike."

"It's my pussy now, baby," he muttered, "and I'm about to seed you … sperm your married pussy."

"Sperm my married pussy, Mike!" she cried.

"Oh yeah," he muttered, "ride that cock, Ash. Let Dave hear what a cum slut you are. Beg me to sperm you, girl."

"Sperm my pussy …. Oh my God … oh fuck … Mike … I'm freaking cumming again—"

"Beg, Ash."

"Sperm my pussy, Mike! Oh God, oh yes, oh Mike …. Sperm my pussy, baby."

I heard him grunt and yell "yeah," and the ball-slapping suddenly stopped.

"Oh yeah, Ash!" he yelled. "Right in your married puss. Fucking own it. It's my pussy now. Oh yeah. Take my fucking sperm, oh baby, oh Ashley … oh fuck, yeah."

I listened as Ashley said, "Fan-fucking-tastic. Happy birthday, Mike. Give me a kiss, baby."

I didn't want to take any chances. It was suddenly all too quiet, so I tiptoed down the hall. I looked back, listening for any sound. But there was nothing, so I went into the kitchen and wiped my balls with a wet towel and put my belt back on.

I heard music start up in the bedroom, but not her typical mellow, chill-out mixes, where maybe I could still overhear something. It was a metal rock mix I figured Mike picked. Ashley would be cool with it drowning out whatever was going on in there.

Either way, until it ended, I wouldn't hear anything. Like the Ashley-in-my-bedroom-channel had its signal pulled.

# CHAPTER THIRTY-FOUR

I grabbed a beer in the kitchen and walked aimlessly into our living room. I didn't turn up the dim lighting or switch on the TV. I just lay down on the couch and stared at the ceiling fan swirling above me.

I thought of Ashley lying naked next to Mike ... in my bed, talking privately in the post-fuck afterglow about how openly they'd cucked me tonight. I wondered if they had opened the wine and were toasting. Bonding over how blatantly I'd been cucked.

I imagined Mike looking back on the way it all it went down ... how easily he made it happen. From the day he first met me—stumbling upon me in a cuckold chat room and noting my vulnerability—to befriending me, and reeling me in. I'd quickly become a major cuck prospect.

It was all about fucking my wife. That was his goal, getting that very first night with her in my bed. And he kept freaking ratcheting it up—coaching her while I'm away, getting her to deprive me of sex, treating my wife like his married fuck doll, taking my bed, my bedroom, taking my wife's pussy from me.

He loved the way he'd bulldozed through me, manning me down in front of Ashley, slamming the bedroom door in my face, making us take a chastity oath, and getting me to act like the fucking butler in my own home.

Mike had talked about the satisfaction Jim Murta must've felt sperming my wife, but what Mike was feeling had to be exponentially stronger. Taking my wife's pussy and making me a cuck in less than two fucking weeks. Installing himself in our lives, our marriage—the big-cocked Alpha guy who fucks my wife while I'm relegated to the fucking couch. I'd let myself get bitch-slapped. Ashley would want me full-blown now …. Mike had to be like, "Fuck yeah."

\* \* \*

I stood up, grabbed another beer from the fridge, and tiptoed up to the bedroom door. I still couldn't hear anything over the music.

I dimmed the living room lights and lay back down on the couch. Noticing the half-smoked joint on the coffee table, I lit it up and took a few puffs. Then I put the rest out like, *I don't fucking need this.*

The thing is, I felt like my whole world was swirling around me. Like a major fucking cuck-storm, within me and carouseling all around me. It wasn't just Mike I had to contend with. There would be other guys looking for weaknesses in me and my marriage, guys who wouldn't think twice about fucking my girl.

I thought about my parents' cookout earlier. I thought about what Jay had said to me. He'd told me in advance he'd be fucking my wife, with real conviction, as if it was his personal mission now to show that pussy Martens boy what it's like to have his wife fucked by a fifty-year-old big-dicked Italian guy who wants to rub it in his face.

Screwing the Martens boy's wife would be a big time coup for him—my mom's hot daughter-in-law. He'd looked me straight in the eye and made the vow right to my face, more determined than ever to daddy-fuck my wife.

And now Ashley would question anything I said about him. My credibility was totally compromised. And I couldn't assume nothing would happen between them. Maybe Ashley would decide fucking Jay would humble me even more … and start cucking me with big cocks, plural.

My heart was racing and I resolved to be direct tomorrow. "No texts, no email. I don't want you talking to him, Ash."

I'd make it sound serious. "This guy wants to put me in the fucking hospital, Ash." And I'd tell her straight-out, "Because of what you fucking said to him."

\* \* \*

I tried to take my mind off Jay. I figured that since I had a plan, I could block out the incident for the night. And then I thought of Jim Murta. I was still processing all the bathroom details, but I started thinking, *As more time passes, I don't know for sure that Ashley won't fuck him again.*

Ashley and Jim seemed on decent speaking terms again. Jim could show up for an intimate girl scene, hang out at their table, and Ashley didn't have a problem with that. And come across to me like, *He's already apologized, move on.*

Which was ridiculous, I thought, because no doubt Jim Murta would love to fuck Ashley again. He'd seize the opportunity as he did the first time. All it might take was Jim getting Ashley alone when she was buzzed, some night when she's out with Tamara.

All I could really bank on was that the last thing she would want is another fucking rumor, one featuring Jim Murta again—the guy who blabbed and started the rumor the first time. That would be fucking insane behavior on her part. Way more than before.

So I had to think she wouldn't hook up with him again. She wasn't gonna jeopardize her career, especially for a junior salesman who had acted like a total asshole. Ashley was far too practical, despite how recklessly she'd behaved that night.

Jim Murta sure had balls, I thought, telling my wife to show him her tits, then getting her to make out with her best friend in a bathtub … just so she could see the size of his cock. I thought of it being right up in her face at the same time I'd knocked on the door. Rather than calling it quits when I knocked, twenty seconds later Jim was pointing his cock at my wife and saying, "I'm gonna fuck you, Ash, with your husband right outside."

The motherfucker moved fast. I'd probably still been upstairs pissing when Ashley took his cock in her mouth. And I might not even have been back out on the balcony yet when he started fucking my wife ... bare.

And then of course he had to fucking sperm my wife and hold his cock in her pussy till he was done ejaculating. He probably loved watching Ashley freaked out and frantically hurrying to get dressed. Watching her walk back out with his sperm dripping down her legs as she went off to find her husband.

\* \* \*

I walked down the hall to the other bathroom to take a piss. I couldn't hear anything by the door, just the music. It sounded like Metallica—definitely not Ashley's choice.

I lay back down in the living room and thought of Ryan. Now that he was with Chang, he seemed to act cooler than before—from having our table reserved to getting my wife to kiss his girlfriend. And now Ashley knew, according to Chang at least, that Ryan had a big American cock.

Ryan and Ashley …. It wasn't hard to imagine. Ryan and Chang might meet Ashley for drinks while I was out of town. They'd nightcap back in their hotel, and suddenly Chang and Ash would be naked on the bed together. Ryan would certainly be tempted to get in the middle of an Ashley-Chang sandwich.

Not that our friendship wouldn't be a deterrent—it would. Ryan believed in bonds and loyalty. He might not allow himself to be drawn into that situation. But he'd seemed pretty okay with pushing the envelope at the bar. He'd asked Ashley for her sex history with women. He'd peer-pressured them into kissing. If opportunity knocked, Ryan might not say no, and if Chang seemed cool with it …. One minute the three of them might be fooling around, and the next, Ryan would be sliding his big American cock into Ashley's pussy.

And it's not as if I felt secure with even my brother. If Ashley sent him signals, I didn't see Sean saying, "I can't, Ashley, you're my little brother's girl." Maybe at first, but if she showed obvious interest, he wouldn't say no to fucking Ashley.

I recalled that time in Vegas with his friend, Badger. They'd double-teamed a bride on her bachelorette weekend, and Badger surprised her with a full-on facial. I pictured Sean's fortieth birthday. He'd probably have it in Vegas, and Ashley and I would be there. She'd be wearing a bikini by the pool, or a sexy cocktail dress at a club. Badger might not be blatant, but he'd flirt with her. If she were to show interest, he'd be all over it. And I wouldn't put it past Sean to go along with Badger. It no longer seemed far-fetched, the idea of Sean fucking Ashley from behind while she sucked on Badger's cock.

It did sound insane that she would let herself be maneuvered into that scenario. At least that's what I'd have thought two months ago—about Ashley getting fucked at a party. I had not understood how crazy or daring she could be until now.

Fortunately Sean's fortieth was still a while away, and normally I never dealt with Badger. Ashley had never met him. And it wasn't as if I saw my brother often. The next time would probably be Thanksgiving.

I wasn't stressed about tomorrow. I'd been on standby before, and Sean rarely stayed over. Even if he did, the situation would be the usual—hang out and go to bed.

He'd be sleeping right here, on the couch I was lying on now, and I'd be in my bed, with Ashley beside me.

\* \* \*

I thought of meeting up with Tamara next week. I'd be having drinks with Ashley's total bitch friend. She'd probably throw curveballs and enjoy seeing me squirm or act nervous. So I decided to ask Ashley beforehand what to talk to her about. And maybe learn some jokes about Iowa.

I only aspired to get by. Any passing grade I'd be fine with. I could do a shot or two beforehand. I had to believe that Tamara wanted me to crash and burn so that I would never want to join them again. *Even if Ashley's told her nothing*, I thought, *Tamara still likes to see Ashley humiliate me.* She wanted Ashley to cheat on me—right under my nose, before her eyes. She wanted my wife fucking on another man's cock.

I thought about the way Tamara had banged that drum from the get-go, telling Jim to show Ashley his cock. She'd dispensed with me like an insignificant obstacle and asked him, 'Which one of us do you want to fuck' ….

I asked myself if it was even possible Tamara didn't carry condoms in her purse. *Fuck condoms*, she probably thought, *I want to watch Jim fuck Ashley bare.* She had to love how it all transpired—seeing Ashley fucked by a junior sales-guy with a big cock. Especially because she'd just sent Ashley's dumb-ass, puss-ass husband upstairs. And then to be a fucking cheerleader as he spermed my wife in a ratty bathroom …. Tamara had to be over the fucking moon. Like what a kick-ass, crazy night for them all. I pictured her smiling as Ashley got dressed in the post-fuck panic.

Tamara must've asked Ashley questions about my reaction to learning she fucked Jim Murta. She had to know some things, like that I'd accepted it. How there had been no consequences. How nervous I was around her now.

I didn't know if Ashley would talk about our sex life with Tamara. I know that girls talk, but I wanted to think that my recent issues with cumming prematurely were off the table, between us. But who knew what Ashley might say on her third cocktail?

That was the thing: I didn't know how much my wife had been telling her work BFF. Given what happened, I didn't believe Ashley could really trust her with much ... if anything.

So ... did Tamara know about Mike? If she did, then she'd know I'd been cuckolded. And she'd want the details. She'd love to hear how some guy had just cucked me out of my bedroom, how they'd rubbed it in my face by making out in front of me, how I'd acted like a pussy and done nothing, how Mike was fucking my wife in my bed with my full acquiescence.

I thought of Tamara hearing about this weekend on Monday. The way Ashley sang "Happy Birthday" in a tits-falling-out dress, the present Mike received from the both of us—our no-sexual-relations, chastity oath. Her screaming out about how she'd cucked me as Mike's big cock pumped her hard. Because I was this total, fucking cuckold now.

Even Tamara would have to be thinking, *Are you fucking kidding me?* Yeah, who could believe I'd help her with Mike's fucking birthday cake and get him a drink, knowing full well he'll be balling my wife in my bed soon?

She'd laugh her ass off at me. She'd definitely be telling Ashley she wanted to be there when I watched her getting fucked in front of me. She'd want to take pictures of me jerking off in a cuckold chair.

I pictured Tamara dressed in something sexy, maybe even slutty, showing off her big tits and cleavage. She'd have this air like, *You couldn't dream of fucking me, Dave.* She'd want me bare-ass on wood and watching. She'd want my wife to see me jerking off, no tissue handy. I'd have to just sit there with my cum in my hand as I watched my wife with a big fucking cock, balls deep inside her.

Tamara would love to see me get the full-on cuck

treatment. But I just had to believe Ashley wouldn't tell her about Mike. She'd have to consider that Tamara might blab to Jim, one night when they were out drinking together.

If Ashley did confide in Tamara, and she told Jim Murta, the story would spread like fucking wildfire. Ashley would have to know that.

I imagined Tamara explaining to Jim that because he fucked my wife in that bathroom, I reacted by jerking off and becoming so cuckold-obsessed that I invited a guy with a big cock like his into my home, a guy who now fucked Ashley regularly in my bed while I slept on the living room couch.

He'd be like *What the fuck* when he learned what a cuckold I'd become, what caused and created it. It was all because of that night at the party, when he bent my wife over the sink and balled her with me standing right outside.

He hadn't just fucked *her*. He'd fucked with my head. Balling my wife in that bathroom. It was what led me to this place—lying on the living room couch while Ashley fucked her lover.

Jim would have to appreciate the mental fuck-job his bathroom fuck on Ashley had done to me. Not only had he balled my wife bare after I was sent upstairs, but because of him I'd been in a fucked-up, humiliating cuckold spiral ever since.

I figured if it got to Jim, he'd pass Tamara's gossip on to his friends, and Ashley's end of summer rumor would catch fire again. Only this time, it would be about me—her husband—the guy who played the chump in the original rumor.

"Yeah, that's right," I pictured one of the young salesmen saying, "the same guy who was outside clueless when Murta was in the bathroom, balling her bare. Well, Ashley's openly cuckolding that fucking wimp now. She's got a lover who sleeps in Dave's bed. And forces Dave to sleep on the couch."

Guys at Ashley's work would be laughing scornfully at my cuckold ass. And think it was open season on fucking my wife.

If that happened, there was no way I could go to her Christmas party, and there'd be no more happy hours for me. It would be hell for Ashley, too. Two crazy sex stories in three months. No way could she live it down. She'd be the hot, married office slut who got fucked at a party and was now cucking her husband. At her work, they'd be offering odds for Jim Murta not just fucking Ashley again, but fucking her in front of me. They'd want me watching with tears in my eyes.

She could never redefine herself from that. She'd be trying to talk business, and they'd be staring at her tits, thinking how Ashley cucked her wimp-ass husband.

She had to realize the potential danger of telling Tamara I'd been cucked. Ashley cared too much about her career, and she'd seen how a rumor could blow up from just telling one person. She'd know it was crazy … fucking reckless risky.

I figured the only person she could talk to about this was Mike, the only one she could trust … the guy who was fucking her now. The guy who was grooming my wife to cuck me more.

# CHAPTER THIRTY-FIVE

Mike had upped the ante, wanting me to hear it like that. He wanted it front and center. To hammer home reality. He wanted Ashley calling out to me as he pumped inside her. Addressing me by name while I was right outside.

Any closer and I'd be in the same room, which seemed like Mike's point. So that actually watching would seem like a smaller leap.

I pictured Mike saying. "You heard it, bro, mid-orgasm, Ashley yelling out she was cucking you. Think about it. As your wife was cumming, she was calling you a cuckold. That was huge. Like after that, being in the room watching … it's like a baby-step, now."

I knew I'd face Mike's big question tomorrow. He'd be pushing hard. Telling me it wasn't much different than me being behind the door.

Only I knew it'd be a lot different. I'd be looking into the eyes of Ashley—the girl I was completely in love with—and watching another man's penis going bare inside her. I'd be watching her orgasm.

Mike, I imagined, would want to make an event out of it, some big production. He'd probably want us taking another chastity oath a few days beforehand. We'd have to go shopping for a chair for me. He'd have Ashley telling me, "Get naked, sit on the chair, put your hand on your dick, and smile."

Those are the kind of things that would happen if I asked her Mike's big question. He might fuck her in her wedding dress or have her watch me jerk off as he fucked her doggy. He might tell her to call me her puss husband. He might cum on her fucking wedding ring.

I wasn't gonna ask Mike's question. And I wasn't gonna admit I'd listened to them fuck. But I wasn't gonna play dumb, either. I'd acknowledge what was going on … that for the last eleven nights, I'd been openly cuckolded by a conniving guy I barely knew who now owned my bedroom and my wife's precious pussy.

The music continued blaring in the distance, and I lay there thinking about tomorrow. I knew it was supposed to be sunny so I thought about going to the Park with Ashley again. Only this time, we could hit the zoo, or better yet, have drinks at the Boathouse.

And when I got her laughing, that's when I'd say, "I want to get back to what we were talking about the other night."

She'd be quite receptive, expecting me to talk more about how royally I'd been cucked.

But I'd say, "Thursday night, we talked about taking a break from Mike. And you were game, Ash, except that Mike's birthday was Saturday. So I said okay, and we agreed to delay it, but guess what, Mike's fucking birthday's over now."

I wouldn't say it like that, not unless she really challenged me.

I'd say, "We agreed this would be good for us, right?"

"How long are you talking?" she'd ask, cautiously.

"I don't know," I'd say, "Maybe a week."

The look in her eyes would say, *You have got to be kidding.*

So without her saying anything, I'd add, "or five days … four days. Doesn't matter how long. A decent span of you and me alone-time. Like we're having right now."

But then I thought, *Fuck that. I don't want to be shaving days off. No need to be conceding anything. Don't fucking do*

*it … don't compromise on a full week alone—at least not so
fucking quickly.*

I'd co-opt her themes of honesty and openness and cloak
my reasoning in that. Use it as my rallying call. I could even
brand it, "Our Week of Openness."

And I'd repeat my slogan, "How can this not be good?"

We'd be turning off the noise, like she said she wanted to
do, getting rid of outside distractions, like she talked about.
Being open and honest and getting really close again.

She'd probably say something like, "I totally agree, but
don't you think a week might be a bit excessive?"

Then I could say, "Okay, five days, but this is important.
Let's not be nickel and diming this down."

She might say, "Okay, so till Friday." Which would be
something. Five straight nights alone in my bed with Ashley
would still be pretty good.

But if she was giving me a lot of *yeah, buts*, I'd emphasize
how important it was to our marriage, that it would enrich us,
and "How can we not benefit from spending some quality
alone time together?" How could she be against a week of
openness and togetherness?

"Openness," I'd say, "is what you've been talking about,
Ash. Building our bond as husband and wife, so we can step
back and get perspective. Taking a break from people in our
lives and focusing on just you and me."

"What about Mike?" she'd say.

"I'm not saying no more Mike," I'd tell her, "but because
his birthday interrupted us really having some alone time …."

I figured I had leverage. I'd already agreed to delay the
Mike-hiatus once. Right upon arriving home, no less.

And if she still didn't fucking like that, I'd slam down my
trump card: "Our marriage fucking needs it, Ash, and our
marriage is freaking important to me. You deprived me of sex
last week, so don't deprive me of couple-time now. Especially
when you already agreed to it that first night I came home."

She'd probably say she never agreed to a week.

"So? I'm not even talking a week now, Ash, it's five freaking days. For the goddamn sake of our marriage …. I mean, are you serious? You really can't do this for me, for our marriage?"

Those were heavy guns I didn't want to pull out, but I had to start winning battles, and this one was important. A long stretch of Mike-free, Ashley-time, and I could make real inroads. It would remind of her why we were together, the fun we had before all this happened. And I could clear up a ton of misconceptions. I could show her I wasn't the caricature Mike had set me up to be.

Suddenly I thought of my parents' condo, and how they hadn't said anything about it being occupied next weekend. I made a note to check with my mom in the morning.

That was another potential ace up my sleeve.

"And then on Friday, Ash," I would say, "we keep the summer going and hit the beach in Florida." That might be a carrot to dangle … a way to grease the wheels for a week alone.

A full week alone, I figured, could derail Mike's ambitions in a big way. At the very least, it would slow things down. It would give not just me, but Ashley, time to come up for air and bond as a couple.

I was sure Mike would try to throw some spike strips down. "Yeah um, *no*, that's not fucking happening."

Mike was the bigger barrier. I resolved to prepare myself, to analyze what pitfalls to avoid. I'd treat it like my San Fran speech. And I figured I had strong arguments on my side.

I'd say, "How can you argue this, Mike? You're the one always talking about strengthening my marriage. How could some alone time together possibly not be fucking good for us?"

He'd say something like, "It's good, bro, but too soon. Your roles haven't been fully established." He might say that would be my reward if I asked her to let me watch her get fucked.

I'd tell him, "It's not about rewards. It's about what's good for my marriage, which is what you claim this all is about."

He might say, "Do you really want to make her pussy feel deprived for a whole week? How's that fair to Ashley?"

I had to be ready for that, I told myself, and anticipate the curveballs. I couldn't stray too far from my key themes and points and I needed to prepare a few all-purpose comebacks.

Like, "Don't you understand, Mike? Ashley and I already agreed to do this. We only delayed it for *your* fucking birthday."

I pulled out my phone and looked at the photo I'd taken of Ashley.

"Good God," I whispered and my dick got hard. Just seeing that photo of Ashley posing for me in see-through lingerie—her tits, her nipples, her thong on display—had me staring hypnotically. I blew it up full screen on my laptop and sat down so that I faced the hall, in case they came out.

It was an unusual look for Ashley. She was always smiling in photos, but this she was posed. She looked like a Victoria's Secret model. This wasn't warm and friendly Ashley. This look was ultra-sexy and a bit intimidating.

She was posing the way Mike had instructed her to do, puckering her lips like she was about to suck cock. Even her eyes seemed to say it. As she posed, she'd probably been thinking that I'd be jerking off to it later. Which would've been hard to deny. Before this, the most revealing photo of Ashley I'd had was in her bikini ... and this one showed her tits fucking beautifully.

I thought of Ashley thinking, *Dave will be jerking off to this photo of me just as Mike says ... like a real fucking cuckold.*

"Is that what you think I am, Ash?" I mouthed, staring at

her. "That's what you called me as Mike fucked you. Did you mean it or were you just saying what Mike told you to say?"

"Oh, baby," I imagined her saying, "I totally meant it. Telling you I've cucked you as I came …. And you can't really be that blind … not to realize how much of a cuckold you are now. You're adopting the role, baby—helping me with Mike's birthday cake, brushing my hair for my date, helping me bathe like my personal assistant, bringing the candle into our bedroom, lighting it as Mike lay on your bed. Then you shut the door behind you, all cucked and humbled."

I stared at her tits and the little camel toe in her thong. Her blowjob mouth and penetrating eyes said it all, "I've cucked you, Dave."

*I fucking know, Ash. I get it.*

"There ain't no going back, baby," she'd say. "You crossed that line a while ago. Mike says I should start giving you a list of chores in the morning. He says now's when we should really intensify the cucking.

"Maybe it's time for you to own it," she'd continue, "own who you really are and what you've become. Don't you think it's time to ask the question—the question that's really yours? You can say it. I know you want to. You want to know if I'll let you watch me get fucked by my big-cocked lover."

\* \* \*

My dick didn't like going back into my boxers, but I wanted to hold off on jerking off. I had some thinking to do. I knew Monday would be too late. I had twenty four hours to change this ship's direction.

*Tomorrow*, I thought again, *I'm pulling us away from Mike's orbit*. I'd suggest going back to the Park after Mike left in the morning. We have no plans, or reasons for her not to be game. And drinks at the Boathouse didn't seem like a difficult sell. I might even get a few good kisses as the sun went down and reflected over the lake.

That's when I wanted to propose it.

I'd say, "Isn't this freaking awesome … this whole afternoon hanging out, just you and me, Ash. I mean, you want to talk about bonding; I'd say this is exactly what we've been trying to get to. Which is why I really think now's the time to do what we were saying … you know, take a break from Mike and have some real couple time."

I daydreamed about talking to Ashley after a few days of no-Mike.

"We got a taste of what it's about," I'd tell her, "cuckolding, I mean. Eleven nights of it—that's a long time. And who knows how we'll look back on this period? A temporary correction in our marriage, maybe, which made me appreciate you more. Far in the future we might be surprised we even tried it, looking back. But the focus now should be on us—on us and our marriage, where it should be."

The music stopped. I waited to see if the silence would continue. After chugging the rest of my beer, I stood up. I was moving with extra stealth, almost in slow motion.

I had no second thoughts. I was responding to a gravitational pull. I wasn't going to not listen to my wife getting fucked. I had to table tomorrow's thinking temporarily and get into an 'Ashley's about to get fucked' mode.

But when I reached the hallway, I didn't hear anything. It was *too* quiet.

So I stood in our kitchen with my ears perked, waiting for laughter or whispering, something to make me feel safe, to reassure me that my bedroom door wasn't gonna suddenly fly open.

I imagined Ashley popping out into the hall in her sexy new bathrobe, and there I'd be, busted and branded again in my wife's knowing eyes … a major league cuckold with big-ass cuck horns.

I could easily picture it. I'd pretend I was going to the bathroom … and probably end up tripping all over my words.

Ashley would realize she was showing cleavage—or even have a nipple slip—and pull her robe to cover up. She'd probably smile and say to herself, once again, Mike was fucking right about me.

* * *

David McManus is the author of *Reluctant Cuckold,* and works in finance in New York. While he intends to some day write a book about the economics of baseball, he felt compelled to tell a more immediate story now.